THE PRECIOUS ONE

THE PRECIOUS ONE

MARISA DE LOS SANTOS

WILLIAM MORROW
An Imprint of HarperCollins*Publishers*

THE PRECIOUS ONE. Copyright © 2015 by Marisa de los Santos. All rights reserved. Printed in the United States of America. No part of this book may be used or reproduced in any manner whatsoever without written permission except in the case of brief quotations embodied in critical articles and reviews. For information address HarperCollins Publishers, 195 Broadway, New York, NY 10007.

HarperCollins books may be purchased for educational, business, or sales promotional use. For information please e-mail the Special Markets Department at SPsales@harpercollins.com.

FIRST EDITION

Designed by Jamie Lynn Kerner

Library of Congress Cataloging-in-Publication Data has been applied for.

ISBN 978-0-06-167089-3 (hardcover)
ISBN 978-0-06-239072-1 (international edition)

15 16 17 18 19   OV/RRD   10 9 8 7 6 5 4 3 2 1

For Susan Davis,
ideal reader and treasured friend,
with love

THE PRECIOUS ONE

CHAPTER ONE

Taisy

IF I HADN'T BEEN alone in the house; if it hadn't been early morning, with that specific kind of fuzzy, early morning quiet and a sky the color of moonstones and raspberry jam outside my kitchen window; if I had gotten further than two sips into my bowl-sized mug of coffee; if he himself hadn't called but had sent the message via one of his usual minions; if his voice had been *his* voice and not a dried-up, flimsy paring off the big golden apple of his baritone; if he hadn't said "please," if it had been a different hour in a different day entirely, maybe—just maybe—I would have turned him down.

Fat chance. He caught me at a vulnerable moment; that's true enough. But the fact is that, in all my life, I have loved just three men. One of them was only a boy, so he might not even count. The other was my twin brother, Marcus. The third was Wilson Cleary, professor, inventor, philanderer, self-made but reluctant millionaire, brilliant man, breathtaking jerk, my father.

Two weeks before Wilson called me, he had undergone a massive myocardial infarction and subsequent quadruple bypass. The irony of this turn of events was so obvious that I didn't need Marcus to point it out to me, but of course he did, with a frequency and satisfaction that was in very poor taste, even if Wilson deserved it. Marcus made bad-heart jokes. Lots of them. After we got word that Wilson had emerged from the surgery more or less intact, I made them, too. Even my mother, whose animosity toward her ex-husband had, as far as I could tell, evaporated years ago, lifted one curled corner of her mouth and said, sweetly, "Well, now, at least we know he has one."

At Wilson's request (a request conveyed to my mother in an e-mail through Wilson's lawyer, a woman named Elspeth Bing with whom Marcus swears Wilson had an affair, back when we were ten), we had not visited him, neither in the hospital nor at his home after he was released. I was outwardly relieved but inwardly a little bruised by this. When I said something to this effect to Marcus, whom I was visiting when we got the news, he knocked gently on my head with his fist in a gesture that meant *Is anybody in there?* and said, "Reminder: we haven't visited the dude in over fifteen years. Haven't visited him *at his request*. Not that I'd go anyway." "*Still,*" I'd protested. "He might have been on his deathbed," and then I quickly added, "And don't say, 'No such luck.'" Marcus grinned and, pointedly, said nothing at all.

It was true: seventeen years ago, in a frenzy of disgust and impatience, Wilson had ditched us—my mother, Marcus, and me—kicked us to the curb. With neck-breaking speed, we went from being his family to being a collection of acquaintances, three people he barely knew and almost never saw. Marcus and I had just turned eighteen. Even before this rupture, before he became a spectacularly terrible father, he had been a garden-variety bad one. Before he was absent, he was absent. Cold. Disapproving. Distant. A workaholic. All the usual bad-father garbage. Since the day he told us he was finished with us, the day my mother told him to take his house and shove it, then packed us up and moved us to the North Carolina town in which she'd grown up, determined to be the leaver, rather than the one who was left, we had seen him a handful of times but had visited him exactly once, on his daughter's first birthday. The real, new and improved, clean-slate, second-time's-a-charm daughter: Willow.

Don't go thinking that I wasn't angry about all this. I was. In fact, I would say that I was at least as angry as Marcus, whose anger stayed red-hot for years before it cooled to something hard and shiny and black. It's just that without wanting to or trying to—and for years I was deliberately trying *not* to—I held on to love. Or it held on to me. Not active love; not love, the verb form. It was more just there, a small, unshakable thing, leftover, useless, as vestigial as wisdom teeth or a tailbone, but still potent enough so that when I heard his voice on the phone, my heart gave a tiny jump of hope that made me want to slap it.

It was a Monday in late September, early morning, as I mentioned before, the sky just beginning to paint gold onto the maple tree in my backyard. Normally, I wouldn't have been awake to see this, but Leo had moved out the week before, and, even though we had only lived together for three months, I hadn't gotten used to sleeping alone again, yet. We weren't meant to be a couple, Leo and I, but I missed him, both because he was nice and because he made sure of it. When he moved back into his house a few streets over, he had left bits and pieces behind for me to find: a tube of his favorite cherry lip balm pocketed in the cardboard egg carton, a balled-up pair of socks (clean) in the basement Deepfreeze, one of the river stones from our trip to Maine tucked into the toe of my shearling slipper.

On top of that, he called me five, maybe six times a day just to say hello or to tell me about the unsettling color of the ham on his sandwich ("Brilliant pink, real dog's tongue pink.") or about the awful music that his neighbor was playing ("Barry Manilow. *Live* Barry Manilow. Who knew there even was such a thing?"). In fact, when the phone rang, I figured it was Leo, all set to regale me with tales about the texture of his toast or something.

"Good morning, Leo," I chirped into the phone. "What've you got for me?"

There was a pause and then that frail voice: "Eustacia."

At the age of two, Marcus had decided to call me "Taisy," committing me to a lifetime of saying the slightly nauseating, if useful, phrase, "Like 'daisy' with a T." Only one person in the world called me by my given name, the name that he had given me.

"Oh." It came out as a whisper. The word *Dad* leaped to the tip of my tongue. I swallowed it, trying to ignore the sudden clamorous beating of my heart.

"Wilson," I said in a flat and noncommittal tone. "Well. You're certainly up early."

"I hope I did not wake you."

As far back as I could remember, Wilson had been famously opposed to contractions, "acts of verbal laziness," although I had noticed, with far too much satisfaction, that in moments of stress or if a conversation just went on long enough, he would slip into using them, like anyone else.

"You didn't," I said. "I've been up for quite some time, actually." A lie, of course, which I instantly kicked myself for telling, since why would I possibly care whether or not Wilson Cleary regarded me as an early riser?

"I am glad to hear it," he said. "I have always felt 'the early bird catches the worm' to be one of the truer truisms."

I dropped my chin into my palm and shut my eyes.

"How are you feeling?" I asked.

"Ah," said Wilson. Wilson had always been a person who said "Ah."

I waited.

"I take it you have heard about the recent, ah, troubles," he said.

The troubles. As if Wilson's heart were Northern Ireland.

"I sent you a note," I reminded him. "And a fruit basket."

"So you did," he said. "Thank you."

"You're welcome."

Silence. Then, an immense and ponderous throat clearing.

"Eustacia, I am calling you this morning with a request, a rather important one," he said.

And there I was, shooting bolt upright in my chair, my hands tightening, of their own annoying accord, around my coffee mug. All ears. The very picture of an eager beaver.

"At least, I regard it as such," he continued. "I hope you will, as well. You and your brother both."

"Really?" It came out as a squeak.

"Yes," said Wilson with a touch of irritation. Wilson hated questions like "Really?" "Really."

I attempted to collect myself. "Fine," I said. "What's the request?"

"I would like you and your brother, Marcus, to come here, to my house, for a visit."

Your brother, Marcus. As if I had any other brother, as if he had any other son. My inner eager beaver slid off its log with a splash. It was one of the great things about Wilson: just when you needed a reminder that you disliked him, he gave you one. Then I realized what else he had just said.

"You've got to be kidding me," I said.

"I recently suffered a catastrophic health event," said Wilson, his irritation turning more acidic. "Would I go to the trouble of *phoning* you only to *kid*?"

"'You've got to be kidding me' is an expression of surprise." My tone was chilly. "A fairly common one that I'm sure you've heard before."

He made a sound of disgust.

"Since I can't remember the last time you called me," I went on, "since the last time I was invited anywhere *near* your home was fifteen years ago, I think I should be allowed a few seconds of surprise at your request."

"I do not doubt that my making a request would surprise you," he said, loftily. "Obviously, I am not in the habit of imposing upon you or of asking you for anything."

I sighed. "Once again, you have completely missed the point."

"I would like you to come," he said. "I am requesting that you and Marcus come here."

"For what?" I asked. "For 'a *visit*'? Meaning what? A social call?"

"Of sorts."

"You know where I live, right?"

"More or less."

"So you know we're talking a seven-, eight-hour drive." I didn't mention the fact that Marcus lived just an hour-and-a-half train ride from my father's town because it might as well have been light-years. No way was Marcus going there. "Can't we just discuss whatever it is over the phone? Through e-mail?"

"You misunderstand me," said my father. "I am not talking about a discussion. I am talking about a visit. Preferably one lasting a fortnight, possibly longer. You have not seen this house, but I assure you there is plenty of room."

"Your house. You want us to stay at your *house*? For two weeks? *Really?* Are you serious? You can't possibly be serious."

This time, Wilson's voice wasn't irritated, only weary. "All right, Eustacia. You are incredulous. You are surprised. No doubt you have reason to be. I register that. You have made your point."

I had an enormous urge to hang up on him then, my finger itching to press the button that would make him disappear. Marcus would have done it. Marcus would've hung up on him ten seconds into the conversation. But I needed to know something first.

"Why?"

"Why what?"

"*Why?*"

"Because I am asking you to come."

Unbelievable. I lifted the phone from my ear and stared with longing at the disconnect button. I breathed for a few seconds, then said, with all the quietness I could muster, "Not 'why' as in 'why should we come?' 'Why' as in 'why are you asking us to come?'"

I knew he would loathe the question. Wilson hated—maybe over and above all the many other aspects of social interaction that he hated—to explain himself; he believed it was beneath him.

"I shouldn't think an explanation was necessary."

Shouldn't. A contraction. A paltry and pathetic victory, but a victory nonetheless.

"It is," I said, firmly.

There was a long pause. When he spoke next, his voice was thinner than ever, thin and exhausted and impossibly old. Wilson *was* old, seventy-one, but at that moment, he sounded ancient.

"I very nearly died," he said, simply.

I couldn't help it. I softened. But just a little, not enough to leave it alone.

"And?"

"Such an experience causes one to . . ." He trailed off.

"What? Reevaluate? Reconsider?" I stopped before I added *Regret?*

"It causes one to look at one's life in a way that one has perhaps not looked at it before."

My heart jumped into my throat, but I shook my head. *Not enough.* I waited.

"Eustacia."

I kept waiting.

Then he said it: "Please."

Tears flooded my eyes. I could hear Marcus's voice: *That's it? That's all it takes?* But it didn't matter.

"Marcus will never agree to it," I said, finally.

"If anyone can convince him, it is you." And then: "But you? *You* will come?"

You. Out of the papery, colorless wasteland of his voice, the word leaped up, like a spark out of ashes, one clear, fluting note: *you.*

"Yes," I snapped, wiping my eyes. "Yes. Fine. Whatever. I'll come."

I NEEDED TO CALL Marcus. There was no getting around this fact. I needed to call him, and I needed to do it soon. But the very thought of telling him that (a) I had just agreed to visit the man he reviled most in the world, to visit him *and* his wife and child, soon and for an extended period of time and (b) I had also agreed to attempt to convince Marcus to do the same made me feel squeezed by dread, physically, like I was wearing one of those horrible body-shaping slip-things, the kind my friend Trillium swore by and spent scads of money on, one that was growing tighter by the minute.

But I think I'm making it sound like I was afraid of my brother, when nothing could be further from the truth. For me, Marcus had always been the opposite of scary, the *antidote* for scary. Like all siblings, like all people who take each other seriously and have known each other their whole lives, we argued. We fought, even, sometimes, yelling, stomping around, swearing, slamming doors. But amid all the noise and frustration (and few people could frustrate me more than Marcus), my brother was forever and ever home to me, the safest place I'd ever been.

No, what I dreaded was hurting him, making him think, even for thirty seconds, that I was taking sides against him. He was a pretty thick-skinned guy, overall; not many things actually did damage, but of course, I knew what they all were, and watching his face or hearing his voice go from normal to confused to hurt was one of my least favorite things in the world. This was how it had always been.

So instead of calling my brother, I poured myself some more coffee and took a shower. It was one of my favorite things, drinking coffee in the shower, and I had it down to an art form: setting the mug on the shelf outside the shower curtain, snaking out an arm and picking it up at opportune moments, standing at just the right angle so that the water fell on me but not into the cup. The steam, the heat, the toasty bitterness, the loamy, chocolaty smell of the coffee mingling with the sharp citrus of my shampoo, all this sent me into my own personal version of a state of grace.

In this floating, unencumbered state, I considered how I would tell Marcus that I was visiting Wilson and that he should, too. If I couldn't come up with something in the shower, I couldn't do it anywhere. Calmly, I turned sentence after sentence over in my mind, looking for the words that would work a miracle on Marcus because I knew a miracle is what it would take.

TWENTY MINUTES LATER, FORTIFIED and damp haired, I called him.

"Hey," he said. "What's up?"

"Okay, Mako," I said. Around the time he had begun calling me Taisy, I had begun calling him Mako. While his nickname eventually evolved into something that only I used and only in private conversations, his had, naturally, stuck to me like glue.

"Hear me out. Don't say no right away."

He laughed the laugh of a person who has no idea that he is about to be asked by someone he loves to do something he'll hate.

"That's a promising start," he said.

"Oh, crap." I sighed. "Crap crap *crap*."

"Again with the promising start," said Marcus.

"Promise you won't say no right away."

"Again with the—"

"Seriously."

"Okay," said Marcus, "I promise."

I took a deep breath.

"Wilson—"

"No," said Marcus.

CHAPTER TWO

Willow

To ANYONE OUT THERE who believes, the way I did, that you live your life on a plane above Darwinian adaptation, step foot inside a school classroom for the first time *ever* at the age of sixteen.

Except I guess I didn't actually, in those first sixteen, preclassroom years, ever straight out think the thought *I exist on a plane above Darwinian adaptation*. Even *I* am not that weird. But you can think things that you don't even know you think until the moment it becomes impossible to think them, until reality hits you smack in the face in the form of a high school classroom. Or hallway. Or cafeteria. Or even, sorry to be blunt, bathroom. Good grief, the bathrooms were awful. The bathrooms were like the Labyrinth at Knossos, only harder to figure out.

Here's where my father, if he were listening, would jump in to correct me, to remind me, kindly but firmly, that Darwin's theory of natural selection is not, in fact, applicable to my situation, as it has, for starters, nothing much to do with survival of the individual. And I would counter with a Tennyson quotation about Nature, "So careful of the type she seems; so careless of the single life," both to show him that I already knew that what he said was true and to tease him by quoting someone he has never read (or has forgotten ages ago). And then I would remind him, with the joking grin he can never resist, that while accuracy matters, being relentlessly literal is really kind of boring. I would tell him he knows exactly what I'm talking about: when you are ruthlessly ripped from your natural habitat and thrown into an alien and hostile environment, you change or die—if only of embarrassment. I'd say these things to him because this was the way my father and I always talked to each other.

Silently, in my head—because this was not the way my father and I *ever* talked to each other—I would drop the grin and go on to remind him that since he was the one who had done the ruthless ripping and throwing, maybe, just *maybe* he could back off and give me a break. And then I would feel guilty, would fall down face-first and drown in guilt, for even thinking such a thing.

But anyway, back to what I was saying about adaptation, which was this: it's *hard*. Hard to the point of possibly impossible. Take anything. Take, say, raising your hand in class to answer a question. It sounds simple, but for someone who has never in her lifetime raised her hand in a class to answer a question, it's insanely intimidating, not just a single decision, but a sticky, complex, confidence-smashing web of decision making. When do you raise it? Before everyone else? After? In the middle? Do you stab it into the air, like Joan of Arc with her sword? (You know where that got Joan!) Lift it barely above shoulder level, a president taking the oath of office? Float it upward, with your eyes pointed away, as if your arm were a separate organism, acting without your knowledge or consent? And then there's the wording of the answer to consider, your tone of voice, your facial expression, the entire wretched eye-contact issue.

I know what you're thinking. I know what I would have thought: *damn the torpedoes, girl, just be yourself!* And I did think just exactly that, in general anyway. It was a philosophy I subscribed to one hundred percent, but somehow, in the moment—strangers at every side, the classroom full of eyes and bodies and hairstyles and judgment thick as smoke—I would scatter like a flock of birds when the hawk dives in and forget the whole concept of rising above.

I waited a week to even try it. And it should be noted that my first week of school was not *the* first week of school. Our family emergency had failed to time itself around the Webley School calendar, which means I came in just after the other new eleventh graders had stopped feeling hopelessly lost but were still lost enough to appreciate the distraction of someone loster, there being no shortage of schadenfreude among the Webley School student body. There weren't many of us new juniors, eleventh grade not being, as the school counselor had warned us, a "natural transition year," an assertion I found to be—insert heavy sigh—all too true. It also means that I arrived after the placement tests had been administered. Having been homeschooled since birth or before (my father read Plato's *Republic* to me nightly during the last trimester of my mother's pregnancy), I didn't have any ordinary school records—apart from attendance records, which were required by the state—and also had no test scores, apart from the PSAT, which, forgive the immodesty, I had aced.

What I had instead were folders full of meticulously detailed and recorded evaluations, handwritten by my father, and several thick portfolios of work in every subject, including a disk with a video of me performing various acts, like playing Beethoven's Piano Sonata no. 8; reciting, dramatically, Browning's "My Last Duchess" by heart; and dissecting a fetal pig at our kitchen counter.

What we ended up bringing to the guidance counselor represented only a sampling of my academic history, since lugging all that my parents had compiled would have taken several large hand trucks and an insane amount of hubris. At one point in her frustration at having to consolidate sixteen years of incessant study and achievement into a pile small enough to fit into four tote bags, since she had somehow decided that four tote bags' worth was the appropriate amount, my mother had suggested that we get my old wagon from the storage shed and bring it with us.

"Muddy," I'd said, gently. (Yes, I called her "Muddy" but only at home.) "Stop for a second and picture us tugging my old red Radio Flyer down the hallways of my new high school."

To which she looked surprised and answered, "But it's in very good shape, almost like new. You always took such care of your toys."

We were quite a spectacle anyway, each of us with two of L.L.Bean's extra large (i.e., absurdly oversized) canvas totes, bright white, trimmed in navy blue, and stuffed to the gills, slung over our bony shoulders. The ocean of ogling students parted to let us stagger by, tall, stick-legged, and humpbacked under our burdens.

As it turned out, we shouldn't have bothered. The counselor, Ms. Janine Shay, took one look at the tower of academic prowess teetering on her desk, casting long shadows across her calendar blotter and threatening to topple what appeared to be a plastic desktop figurine of a groundhog in a red shirt, but which I learned later was a Webley Wombat, and recoiled, visibly.

"Whoa," she said, "that's a lot of material."

"We have more at home," said Muddy, hopefully.

"Oh, no," said Ms. Shay, with a short laugh. "This is quite enough. This will do."

If there was a touch of sarcasm in Ms. Shay's voice, my dear mother didn't hear it. Her tense body relaxed with relief. It was all I could do not to hug her.

Ms. Janine Shay picked up the file with my most recent evaluations and lifted her purple reading glasses from the top of her desk to the tip of her nose. She leafed through for maybe a minute, then bent her head and looked at us over the tops of the glasses.

"We could administer tests," she said, "but that would take time, and we've found that homeschoolers are generally very well prepared for Webley, particularly the ones who embrace the sciences."

She raised her eyebrows. Inquiringly? Accusingly?

"I do," I said and then felt instantly moronic because I sounded exactly like a bride at the altar—one getting married to Darwin's *The*

Origin of Species. So I added, "All of us in the family do—embrace them. All of them. The sciences, I mean."

"Her father is a scientist," chimed in Muddy.

"All right," said Ms. Shay. "Why don't we do this? To save time, why don't we forgo the testing, start Willow in the regular honors courses, and then allow her teachers to decide whether to move her down to college prep, which seems unlikely, or up to AP?"

Let me make one thing clear about my mother: she is a brilliant woman, an artist. The most amazing things take shape inside her mind, beautiful things that exist nowhere in the world, and then she *makes them exist.* How many people can you say that about?

But when it came to the mundane, when it came to, say, arguing with a high school guidance counselor, she got a little nervous. Especially when she was on one of her, as she called them, "bad-sleep streaks," which she was on so often that it was hard to tell where one streak ended and the other began. So my father usually dealt with the mundane. He was brilliant, too, of course, but he could move between living inside his head and living outside of it with an ease that my mother could never manage, probably because the interior of my mother's head was such a shining place to be.

Who wouldn't get rattled and even freeze up at the thought of stepping out of that and into an argument with Ms. Janine Shay, she of the purple reading glasses and groundhog/wombat statuette? In any case, Muddy got rattled. Muddy froze. Luckily, I had prepared for exactly this moment. I took a breath.

" 'Far better it is to dare mighty things, to win glorious triumphs, even though checkered by failure, than to take rank with those poor spirits who neither enjoy much nor suffer much, because they live in the gray twilight that knows not victory or defeat.' "

Into the drab silence of the office, the sentence cascaded like a waterfall and sent a shiver over my scalp, like it always did. I didn't add, "Teddy Roosevelt," not wanting to assume that Ms. Shay didn't recognize the quotation, but I did tip up my chin in a way that I hoped conveyed determination. I was betting on Ms. Shay's being a person with a great big soft spot for determination.

To my relief, she laughed. It was a nice laugh. Then, she whisked off her glasses, and in a quick, single-handed motion, she folded them, like a flamenco dancer snapping shut a fan.

"I must say that I've never heard our honors courses called 'the gray twilight' before," she said, smiling.

I smiled back, humbly. "I meant no disrespect."

"I'm sure the courses will get over it," she said, "although I'd probably refrain from calling the students enrolled in them 'poor spirits,' at least to their faces."

I nodded.

"So I take it you would like to jump directly into the AP courses?"

"With your permission," I said. "And if those teachers decide I don't belong in them, well, *of course,* I'll step down."

"And into the 'gray twilight'?" said Ms. Shay, teasingly. "Oh, somehow, I don't think that will happen."

My mother stirred. "I like that idea. Aiming high. I'm sure Dr. Cleary would like it, too."

As soon as she said that, I was mentally transported to my father's office at home, the President Roosevelt quotation in calligraphy hanging on his wall, next to one by Emerson: "Every wall is a door." The office empty, the computer screen black. I pictured my father in the hospital bed, sleeping the slack, sick-person sleep that was so sad to watch. My father frail and gray-faced, his heart stammering, stammering against the bones of his chest. *If only,* I thought, *if only I get into the AP classes and succeed in the AP classes, my father will get well.* Back then, I was always thinking things like that.

I sprang to my feet and offered the good Ms. Shay my hand.

"Thank you," I said, squaring my shoulders. "I won't let you down."

I was brisk and steady. There were times when I liked to pretend I was a WAC officer addressing General MacArthur, and this was one of those times. I could almost feel the brimmed WAC cap on my head, my hair curling smartly out from under it. I could almost feel my father watching me, nodding his approval.

Ms. Shay gave my hand a hearty shake, then let it go.

"I'm sure you won't," she said.

"You bet I won't!"

It took every bit of self-restraint I had not to click my heels together and salute.

ONE WEEK LATER CAME the hair-raising hand-raising episode.

It was English literature. Jane Austen's *Pride and Prejudice*. I had been pleasantly surprised to find that we were studying a book I had already read, since my literary education was, I have to admit, a little spotty. My father was a scientist, a chaired professor of genetic science at an Ivy League university, even though he didn't really teach anymore. He was also a lifelong history and philosophy buff and a fluent speaker of both French and Italian. The man was shockingly educated. The truth is, though, that he had no use for fiction and even less for poetry, never had, not even as a child. He explained this by saying, "One who truly sees, *sees* the intricacies and fascinations of facts can hardly be expected to be quite so intrigued by nonfacts, can one?," which is a pretty convincing argument, I think. But me? I guess I had an inferior grasp of facts. I loved stories.

Early on, my mother taught my English classes, but after I was about eight or nine, she sort of drifted from the picture, gradually pulled back into her world of glass. In what I liked to think of as a giant demonstration of faith in me, my father let me continue on my own, with the single caveat that I read nothing beyond the end of the nineteenth century, since all literature written after that was, by his estimation, trash. I wasn't so sure about this. It seemed to defy the law of probability that in over one hundred years, no one had written a single item worth reading, not even *by accident.*

But I knew the deeper reason for the caveat, the one that was behind every decision he made, and that was that he wanted to keep me safe and uncorrupted forever, keep me from turning out like the Others, the Earlier Ones, because he loved me more than anyone in the world. He never said this, not in so many words, but he didn't have to. I knew. So I honored the caveat, would have even if I'd had the choice not to (I had no way of buying books for myself after all), but sometimes, in the middle of reading John Donne or Shakespeare or the Russians or the Brontës, all that passion, drinking, madness, murder, and generally poor decision making, I would think, *If you only knew, you'd make me stop reading completely!*, and loyal daughter though I was, no way in the world was I telling him.

But getting back to the hand-raising.

My English teacher, Mr. Insley, was restless, a strider, boldly cutting a path around the perimeters of the rectangular room so that focusing on him usually meant swiveling your neck around until it cricked, something that most of the students didn't bother to do. Narrow shouldered and slim in his tweed jacket, with fine, pale brown, backswept hair, he looked like John Keats, only taller and less tubercular and not forever leaning his chin on his hand as though his neck were too flimsy to hold up his head on its own. On the contrary, Mr. Insley seemed to bristle with energy. When he posed a particularly important question to the class, he would wave one long, skinny finger in the air and stare at us with what could only be called fervor.

I would not have thought that someone could get so impassioned about *Pride and Prejudice*. *Wuthering Heights*, yes, *Tess of the d'Urbervilles*, sure, but *Pride and Prejudice*, well, no, not necessarily. I adore Austen. Adore! Who could read *P and P* without wanting to be Elizabeth Bennet, with her fine eyes and sharp wit? Who wouldn't want to take an elegant turn around a drawing room or sit with a straight back at a writing desk, composing a letter? But to cant forward, the way Mr. Insley was doing, flushed and burning eyed, to ask the quaking-voiced question

"In your opinion, did Elizabeth Bennet marry Darcy for his money?," seemed a little much, a little out of place. Out of place but—I admit it— stirring. In spite of itself, my pulse quickened.

But no one answered the question. I glanced around the room to see if any of my fellow students (I was still stunned at the fact that I *had* fellow students) seemed on the verge of answering. No. Nothing. Clock ticking, ticking. Still nothing. To behold Mr. Insley standing in the front of the room, John Brown-like, practically on fire, his chest rising and falling beneath the thin striped cotton of his dress shirt, was like seeing Mark Antony giving his speech over Caesar's body while all the Romans doodled and stared at the ceiling. Unbearable.

Which I guess is why before I truly understood what was happening, it had happened: my hand was up. On the end of my very long arm, my hand seemed high, high in the air, like a motherless bird in a nest, exposed to wind and weather and my classmates' unreadable gazes.

For a moment, Mr. Insley looked startled, and then he smiled at me and said, without so much as a glance at his seating chart, "*Willow*." He made my name sound like music, like a two-syllable poem. Oh my, his voice. His voice was the most heartening thing that had happened to me in a week.

"Yes," I said. *Yes, I was Willow. Yes, yes.*

He kept smiling. I realized my hand was still in the air and brought it down to rest in the palm of my other hand. Mr. Insley's smile turned from just glad to glad and encouraging, and I realized that, in the presence of this smile, in the presence of his whole presence, my nervousness had vanished. My entire body, including my brain, felt deliciously relaxed. It was like one of those moments in a play where the spotlight falls on two characters in the center of the stage, while everything that isn't them freezes, goes black, disappears.

"Yes," I repeated, with assurance. "Elizabeth was a product of her time and in an awkward position, socially. Like most women back then, she didn't have a lot of choices. She was the daughter of a gentleman, so she couldn't very well get a job, but because of the entailment, she could expect almost no income of her own. Her only hope of keeping up or improving her manner of living and social position was to marry a man, a gentleman preferably, not a tradesman, with money. Someone like Fitzwilliam Darcy."

Mr. Insley was nodding, looking more like Keats than ever, and contemplating me for all he was worth, his eyes swimming with thoughts. I sat completely still, feeling like a Grecian urn, a nightingale.

"Excellent answer, Willow," he said. "Very insightful. Beautifully articulated. Thank you."

I swear his approval lifted me right off the ground, desk and all. But then a voice slashed the air like a bullwhip and yanked me back to earth with a crash.

"*God,* that is just so wrong."

Even as I was turning around to see who'd said it, I knew. Bec Lansing. Hair a liquid fall of coffee-colored silk. Huge dark eyes. Mouth like a poppy. A riveting girl, a girl who shot sparks and walked in beauty like the night. I hadn't spent much time with groups of people my own age, but I'd recognized the queen the first second I saw her, and something inside me had instinctively bowed down.

"Bec," said Mr. Insley, sharply, "are you sharing a differing viewpoint?"

She didn't acknowledge that he'd spoken. She had eyes—long lashed, coal black—for no one but me, and the hate I saw in them made me gasp.

"To say that she *married* him for his *money?* That's just so sad. So cold. She *loved* him!"

"No, I know—" I began.

"You *don't* know!" snapped Bec. "Which is just really sad."

Bec looked about as sad as a cobra.

"I-I think she loved him, too. I don't think she married him *only* for his money."

For the record, this was true. Of course, Elizabeth loved Darcy. My heart ached with their love for each other every single time I read the book.

"Sure," said Bec, with a sneer. "Sure, you do. Way to backpedal."

I felt paralyzed, like I really had been bitten by a snake.

"That'll do," said Mr. Insley.

But it wasn't until the boy sitting next to Bec slid his foot a few inches across the floor and tapped it against her puffy, caramel-colored boot that she turned away from me. She looked at the boy, who gave her an almost imperceptible smile and an even less perceptible shrug, as if to say, *It's not worth it*. The entire exchange took no more than three seconds. I turned around and slid down in my seat, my heart simultaneously sinking and pounding.

"Class is dismissed," said Mr. Insley. "First five chapters of *Middlemarch* for Monday."

Amid the cacophony of groans, I slid my books into my new backpack (I had ditched the extra-large tote bag after the first day of school) and got unsteadily to my feet. I wasn't used to people hating me. Oh, God, I wasn't used to people at all. I fiddled with the zipper on my backpack, allowing time for Bec to get out the door and, I hoped, down the hallway and far, far away before I left. On my slumped and defeated way past his desk, Mr. Insley caught my eye and smiled again.

"Chin up," he said, softly. "It will only get easier."

Oh, how he sounded like my father! I lifted my chin.

" 'Keep calm and carry on,' " I said, with a snap in my voice.

"Atta girl!" He winked.

This time, I didn't hold back. I stood up as straight as my heavy backpack would allow and saluted, and without missing a beat, Mr. Insley saluted back.

MY STIFF-UPPER-LIP ATTITUDE STOOD by me out the door, down the hall, and through an entire double period of AP chemistry, and then, just inside the door to the bathroom, it took one look at the band of hair-brushing, lip-glossing girls lined up before the mirror and fled. I stood all alone, feeling like a stork who's crash-landed into a flock of gleaming jays. They preened. They chattered. At least, until they noticed me standing there. Then: deadly silence; brush- and applicator-holding hands frozen midstroke; an exchange of knowing looks. God, those knowing looks. I'd been seeing them all week. What *could it be* that they all knew? There in that restroom, it hit me that I had not a hope in hell of ever finding out.

I eked out a twitch of a smile before I practically fell into the bathroom stall. To my horror, the chattering did not restart, and because I couldn't imagine anything more soul-killing than to fill that void with the sound of my bodily functions, I sat there, in no small mental and physical discomfort, waiting. Eventually, I heard them filing out, but before the door was closed, one of them hissed, "Frigid!"; another barked, "Bitch!"; and another sang out, "Get it, Zany Blainey." I figured I had Bec's outburst in English to thank for the first comment, didn't know what I'd done to deserve the second, and didn't need to have even the faintest idea of what the third meant to know that it spelled my doom.

That afternoon, when my mother picked me up (do I even need to say that I had no driver's license?), I spent the ride home the way I'd spend every one for days and weeks afterward, formulating sentences that I would say to my father the *split second* I got home. Some days, the sentences were a hotheaded jumble, other days cool and even and perfectly shaped, stacked one on top of the other like rows of bricks. On the worst days, they were hardly more than a wail. But they all had at their heart the same idea: *How could you?*

Because my father had to have known that I wasn't made for this. How could he not, when he was the one who had made me? Scratch that. Creepy. Pygmalion-esque. Not what I mean. Look, I was my own person. But my father had shaped the world that shaped me as carefully, as completely—and yes, as lovingly—as my mother shaped her glass frost flowers and seaweed forests and corals and aurorae borealis (if that's, in fact, what any of her sculptures were meant to be). He gave me a world where everything was beautiful, noble, nutritious, and pure, a life from which everything coarse, crass, ugly, or just plain dumb had been strained out and thrown away. No television! No pop music! No magazines! No sleepovers! No high fructose corn syrup! No unsupervised Internet surfing! No—God, no! Are you *kidding*?—social networking!

Only to throw me into high school at the age of sixteen?

Do you know the story of the dodo bird? It lived on the island of Mauritius in the Indian Ocean for who knows how many centuries, happy as a clam. Somewhere along the line, it lost the ability to fly, or to be more accurate, dumped the ability to fly like the extra baggage it was. Why waste energy on wings when there was nothing to fly from? No predators, no mammals at all on Mauritius. It ate windfall fruit. It was big, about three feet high, and by bird standards, quite zaftig, over forty pounds. It nested and laid its eggs on the ground. It was placid and fearless. Why bother having a quick fear response when there was nothing to be afraid of? No need for flight or fight. In short, the dodo was perfectly suited to its world, a tubby, hook-beaked perfect citizen.

And then the universe played a mean joke on the dodo: human beings. First the Portuguese, then the Dutch. They killed the fat, friendly, unsuspecting dodos for food. Their monkeys, pigs, and rat stowaways gobbled dodo eggs like popcorn. Everything that had made the dodos successful inhabitants of Mauritius for so long now made them sitting ducks. In eighty years, they were kaput. Gone. Every last one.

I think you see where I'm going with this. *I* was perfectly suited to my world, too. I *was*. I was flourishing, damn it. And the thing is, no invaders landed on my shores. Worse, the person I trusted most ripped me out of my world and, with nothing even close to a real explanation, plopped me into a new one, where suddenly everything about me was wrong.

My clothes. My hair. The way I talked. My taste in *everything*. The food I brought in my lunch. The bag I brought my lunch in. Wrong,

wrong. I didn't know how to talk to people. I didn't know how to find a seat in the cafeteria. I didn't know how to raise my damn hand. The dodo held out for eighty years. I knew I wouldn't last eight months.

What kind of father makes his daughter a sitting dodo?

I knew exactly what to say to him. He had always told me that, in teaching me, he wasn't preparing me for college (although there was never any doubt that I would go to college). He wasn't paving the way for others to teach me. No, sir. He was teaching me to do what the only real scholars in history had ever done: teach myself. So here was my pitch: I wanted to come home because I wanted to try going it on my own. Until he was well enough to teach me again, I wanted to pull myself up by my bootstraps, summon my pioneer spirit, and teach myself. It was a fool-proof argument because how could my father argue with the pioneer spirit? Or with his own, inarguable wisdom?

But he never got the chance. Every day, on every ride home from school, I planned how I would say these things to my father. And every day, I didn't.

He looked so sick, for one thing, not just pale but dingy, like old glue. And he was whispery. And shrunken. And much, much, much too old. Looking at him, it was easy to forget what I had always known: my father was never going to die. Even so, I might have said it all anyway. I might have planted my feet and looked him squarely in his tired, dull eyes and argued my case with a clear voice and a lot of quotes by people he admired. Except. Oh, except!

Except that what I knew, what I could never escape, what sat like a rock—not just a rock but a molten, seething, blistering rock, if you can imagine such a rock—inside my chest was this: It was all my fault. All. And at my lowest moments, I believed there was no punishment awful enough to balance what I'd done.

CHAPTER THREE

Taisy

THE LAST TIME I'D been to my father's house, it was December, three days after what had been the best Christmas my mom, Marcus, and I had spent in as long as I could remember. It wasn't the first Christmas after "the combustion" as we had taken to calling it, "separation" being far too bland a term for what had befallen our family. Despite all our best efforts, that first Christmas had been grim beyond saving, a kind of nuclear winter: the three of us still so raw and stinging, tripping over one another in a blank-walled, rented apartment; all of us working part-time jobs we detested; my mother edgy from nights spent studying for the North Carolina bar exam instead of sleeping; Marcus and I making our lonely, resentful, anonymous ways toward graduation at our enormous new high school.

But the second Christmas, the one right before we embarked on the first and seemingly final visit to the home of my father and his new family, had been good. Very good. It had been downright merry, a fact that took all three of us by surprise. That fall, we had moved from the dreary apartment to a tidy little Craftsman-style frosted petit four of a house, butter-yellow and white with tall windows, a porch, and trees in the yard. My mom had gotten the kind of tireless-lawyer-with-a-heart-of-gold job she had always wanted, and Marcus and I were in college—mine just down the road, his at a rival school a few hours away in Virginia. It had turned out that college suited us. After a two-week-long mourning period, at least on my end, even being apart from each other for the first time ever seemed to suit us. Unpaired, we were pure potential, free agents. Marcus wasn't the smart but smart-aleck wayward brother; I was not the goody-two-shoes-but-for-one-cataclysmic-error sister. We could feel those four years stretched out before us, wide open, white as linen.

Still, when Christmas break rolled around, we were happy to see each other. In fact, I was giddy about the whole thing, suffused with holiday spirit, and even Marcus, who didn't go in for giddiness, kept committing spontaneous, weirdly unsarcastic acts like buying and then stringing the porch with white twinkle lights. We spent Christmas Day at our house with the large, loud, motley family my mother had acquired in the year or so since she had moved back to her childhood town: her father, our Grampa Pete; her high school best friend, Wiley, and his partner, Jack; the family next door—a surgeon, her stay-at-home-dad husband, and their two kids; the young couple who owned a gelato place in town; Mrs. Wickett, my mother's fourth-grade math teacher and her tiny, guitar-playing husband. We feasted on beef tenderloin and a bewildering array of pies. We told stories and laughed. We—and I am not kidding—*sang carols in front of the fire*. It was corny and Capra-esque and beyond beautiful.

Three days later, we went to my father's house, where the joy came to a screeching halt.

It might not have been so bad if my father's house had not, at that point, been *our* house, the one in which we had lived back when we were a family. The new family in the old house, my wallpaper on Willow's wall, felt just plain cruel. Although in truth, it's hard to imagine that day being any less bad or any more bad than it was because the whole thing felt fated, like it was all meant to be and all meant to be

just exactly—to the loudest insult and the smallest teardrop—as bad
as it was. I know I'm not explaining it very well. It was like that *As
You Like It* quote: my father's house was a stage and we were merely
players, trapped in a play written by someone a whole lot less funny
and bighearted than William Shakespeare. Even as we made our way
up the familiar brick sidewalk to the familiar door, I heard doom in
every step.

We walked single file—my mother, me, Marcus—each of us holding a wrapped gift.

"Like the effing adoration of the effing magi," Marcus mumbled.

Even though I know she knew how much effort it had taken
Marcus to not say the actual f-word, my mother shot him a black look
over her shoulder. But then she began to hum a slow, funereal version
of "We Three Kings." By the time we got to the front door, we were all
humming it. It was a nice moment, but when it ended, there we stood,
staring at the black door, the brass pineapple door knocker.

"You bought that door knocker," I said to my mother.

"Did I?" She lifted her chin and smiled a smile at me that was
meant to be sly but quavered, a smile that made me want to beat the
crap out of Wilson. "I don't remember."

Then, like the visitor she was, she grabbed the pineapple and
knocked.

I braced myself for the sight of my father's face, for the sound of his
voice, but I was in no way ready for either, particularly since, during
our last face-to-face encounter, he had called me a whore. Even as I
stood on that doorstep and thought this, I could hear Wilson's voice
inside my head, correcting me: *I never name-call, Eustacia. I was merely
reflecting upon your behavior.* Which was true enough. His exact words:
*You have managed to behave in a manner simultaneously whorish and in-
fantile. Quite an accomplishment.* When I was eighteen, "whorish" had
felt like the adjective equivalent of being pushed down a flight of stairs.
At thirty-five, it still felt pretty bad.

But I stood on his threshold and reminded myself that he wanted

us there, now. He had invited us. You don't invite a person to your
house if you don't miss her, do you? When I think today about that
eighteen-year-old, deluded-by-hope girl that I was, I'm torn between
wanting to hug her and wanting to slap her silly.

As it turned out, Caroline was the one to answer the door. Caroline-
called-Caro, called Caro by my *father,* who was generally an outspo-
ken eschewer of nicknames. Caro Bloch, now Caro Cleary, mother of
Willow, wife of Wilson.

I had only met her twice before, and then as now, she struck me
as oddly immaterial. Or maybe I mean something more like under-
materialized. Caro just seemed less *there* than most people, as though
she were composed chiefly of air and distractedness. In any case, as
she stood there in the doorway in her emerald-green dress, with her
startled eyes, her painful thinness and thicket of hair, I found her, as I
had in the past, impossible to hate.

No one spoke. Caro just stood gazing at us, and we just gazed back,
except for Marcus, who shoved one hand into his coat pocket and stared
down the road, wary and faintly squinting, like a guy in a cowboy movie
who sees a cloud of dust on the horizon. This all went on for so long that
it began to seem possible that we would never go in at all, that we would
just stand there, shivering and listening to the sound of the cars going by
out on the main road and to the noise of our own breathing until the sky
above us went black and the streetlamps flared.

"So," I blurted out, "do the Russos still live next door?"

With my peripheral vision, I saw Marcus drop his head back as
though he'd been punched unconscious.

"What?" said Caro, eyes widening, voice breathless.

"Joelle and Sam? Their three kids? Or wait, two kids."

"Two?" asked Caro.

"Well, I mean, they still have three. At least, I assume they do. But
Abigail got married the summer after we, um, relocated. At least, I
assume she—" Marcus kicked my heel with the toe of his sneaker, and
I stopped talking.

Caro gave a start of recognition. I would have said that it was not possible for her to open her eyes any wider than they were already open, but then, lemurlike, she did. "Oh! You mean the woman who brought the pink hat and the casserole after Willow was born!"

Marcus snorted. "Yeah, that's the one."

I knew my mother would chastise him for being rude later, but the sarcasm seemed to jar Caro out of her vagueness. Her eyes shrank; she smiled.

"Sorry," she said. "Between my studio and the baby, I guess I haven't spent much time getting to know the neighbors."

"Eggplant," I said, softly, to myself. "Eggplant parmesan."

The thought of it made my chest ache for all that we'd left behind. At that moment, I believed I would have given years of my life for one forkful of sweet Mrs. Russo's eggplant parm.

"Yes!" said Caro, happily. "That's right. I remember being able to eat it. I don't eat meat."

No shit you don't eat meat. You don't eat anything. I could hear the words in my head as clearly as if Marcus had said them out loud, but he just barely lifted his eyebrows at me and kept quiet.

"Caroline," said my mother, "may we come in?"

"Oh my goodness, of course," said Caro. "What am I thinking?"

This time, Marcus grumbled, "You're not," but in such a low voice that Caro didn't hear it. She stepped back, opening the door, and we all filed past.

"May I take your coats?" she asked, holding out her matchstick arms.

It was a moment of truth. We exchanged glances, and when my mother gave a slight nod, we all set down our gifts, took off our coats, and turned them over to Caro—even Marcus, although he made sure to do it with the air of a detainee forced to give up his passport—and were, officially, there.

Instead of taking our coats to the closet there in the front hall, Caro flitted away toward the back of the house, leaving us where we stood.

"Check that out," said Marcus, nodding toward the wall behind us.

My mother and I turned. There, on the wall above the round claw-foot hall table that had always stood there, was a mounted sculpture made of glass: a cluster of roundish shapes in watery shades of blue and green, so delicate you'd think a breath would dissolve them.

"It's beautiful," I admitted. "It must be one of Caro's."

"Yeah," said Marcus. "Remember how it used to be us?"

When we lived there, in that spot had hung a large framed black-and-white photograph that my mother had taken when Marcus and I were about six. The two of us sitting in an armchair, me in profile, speaking to him, Marcus with his head bent, his face not smiling but about to smile, listening.

"Before we all get too indignant," said my mother, "let's remember that I took it with us when we left. It's hanging in the living room at home."

Marcus grinned and shrugged. "Still—symbolic. Symbolic, right?"

My mother smacked him gently on the head, just as Caro reappeared.

"Oh!" Caro gasped.

"Child abuse," said Marcus. "Alert the authorities."

Caro blinked rapidly, her long lashes all aflutter, and then she smiled.

"I will," she said. "But wouldn't you like to see the baby first?"

"Uhh," began Marcus.

I jumped in with, "Of course, we would. Definitely."

"She's in the nursery," said Caro, glancing at her watch. "I believe she's just woken up from her nap. Regular sleep schedules are really incredibly important."

"Great," I said, without any real sense of which one of Caro's statements I was approving of.

"Well, then!" Caro exclaimed, then swiveled around, and walked rapidly toward the staircase.

"Where's Dad?" I whispered to Marcus, as we watched her begin to mount the stairs.

Marcus shrugged and whispered, "I don't know. Hell?"

On the fourth step, Caro turned and said, "Aren't you coming?"

"Coming?" asked my mother. "You mean upstairs?"

"Well, yes," said Caro, surprised. "To the nursery. The nursery is upstairs, of course."

"Of course," said Marcus.

"Maybe it would be better if we waited here for you to bring her down?" said my mother.

Caro shook her head and said, "No, I don't think that would work. Playtime begins right after naptime."

"Oh," said my mother.

"Please come," said Caro. "It's just up the stairs."

She pointed, and, dutifully, we looked in the direction she was pointing, as though we hadn't each climbed those stairs thousands of times. Then, we followed her, right hands on the banister, presents tucked under our free arms.

Before I saw the baby or the crib or my father, I saw the wallpaper, pale green, with a pattern of white apple blossoms. I had chosen it when I was seven years old, had sat with my mother, paging through the thick book of samples. I remember feeling the gorgeous weight of it: the first decision I had ever made that would have palpable, lasting impact. For years, the wallpaper had made me feel safe and special, like a girl in a book sleeping in a cottage. Now, the sight of it hurt, more on behalf of the girl I had been than the girl I was, but it hurt all the same.

I heard his voice before I saw him.

"Willow, my Willow," the voice sang out. "You have visitors!"

The room was ablaze with sun, and because the rug, the wedding-veil gauzy curtains, and every item of furniture in the room was white, for a second, I was snowblind. Even after my eyes adjusted, I didn't see my father immediately because he was sitting on the floor.

My father. Sitting on the *floor*. Sitting on the floor *cross-legged*. *Indian*-style. And I knew in an instant that I had never before seen my father sit on the floor in this or in any other position. Seeing it now felt so strange, so personal that it was almost indecent. I turned my face away and saw Marcus. He was staring at my father with the same cringing bewilderment I felt. My mother wasn't looking at my father at all, but at something on the other side of the room.

"You're sitting on the floor," said Marcus.

"Yes," said my father, with a magisterial nod of his leonine head. "Forgive me for not getting up to greet you. I am playing."

The floor was littered with blond wooden blocks.

"It's floor time," explained Caro, "originally developed for children with autism but highly beneficial for typical learners, as well."

She looked at her husband, who nodded again.

"Or exceptional ones, as the case may be," said Wilson. "In playing on the floor, eye to eye, I follow her lead. I enter her world, instead of towering above it."

I'm sure it goes without saying that our father had never entered my or Marcus's world. If it had ever occurred to him to try, I'll be a monkey's uncle, and even when Marcus had outgrown him by two inches, my father still managed to tower over our lives, looking down on us, when he bothered to look, from a tremendous height. He would not have had it any other way.

I stood and tried to absorb the new floor-sitting Wilson, the Wilson who played, when before my eyes, he turned into yet another Wilson. He softened and grew radiant and smiled a slow-spreading smile that wasn't knowing or show-offy or cruel. That smile was the purest thing I'd ever seen him do.

In unison, Caro, Marcus, and I all swept our attention to the other side of the room where my mother's had been the whole time. Next to a tiny white table and chairs stood a tiny white tent. Pushing back the tiny tent flap was a tiny hand. Next came a flash of auburn curls, flaming against the white, and then the rest emerged, barefooted and with a stride that was steady with just a touch of Frankenstein. Arms out, Willow made her way toward her father.

Sister, I thought, suddenly and with wonderment. After a lifetime of thinking only *brother brother brother,* the word was a revelation.

But Wilson didn't say "sister." I realized he never had. And in the fifteen years to follow, he never would. What he said was, "Behold the birthday girl! Willow Cleary, aged one year!"

And with a shriek of joy, she tumbled into his arms.

SOMEWHERE TOWARD THE END of the demonstration that followed, Marcus disappeared. I couldn't blame him (although later that day, after everything that happened, I did blame him, vehemently and at the top of my lungs) because what unfolded was at best annoying and at worst something close to creepy. We did not play with Willow. We didn't even really watch her play. Instead, it was as though my father were a field biologist newly returned from the wild and unveiling a hitherto undiscovered species to the Royal Society. There was no PowerPoint (I'm not even sure if they had PowerPoints back then). None of us wore white coats. But it was a presentation all the same.

"At a year old, she has seventeen words." One by one, in response to a verbal prompt or to Wilson pointing to a picture in a book, she said them.

"She performs all the motions to 'Wheels on the Bus.'" To Wilson's full-throated rendition of the song, she performed them.

"She can build a tower of three blocks." She built it.

"She has been pointing, for months." She pointed, expertly.

"She can point to her major body parts, when asked to do so." Toes, check. Nose, check. Hair, check. Eyes, check. Elbow, check. Abdomen (yes, abdomen; no tummies or bellies in the Cleary household), check.

"She is in the eightieth percentile for height, weight, and head circumference." She pointed to her perfectly proportioned head.

I could not have walked out of that room if I tried, caught as I was smack-dab between fascination and revulsion. But when Wilson said,

"She has a remarkably high instep," and lifted her foot in the air, even I had to avert my eyes.

Still, it wasn't as clinical, as strange and borderline-dehumanizing as it sounds. For one thing, Caro had the grace to be embarrassed, laughingly embarrassed, but embarrassed all the same. She teased Wilson, and the ease between them was so authentic it startled me. And for another thing, throughout the whole demonstration, what shone through every word Wilson spoke, what illuminated every dramatic hand gesture and grandiose phrase was, unmistakably, love. Love simple and sweet. For the first time ever, I watched Wilson interact with another human being without having anything close to the upper hand. Even as her father displayed her like a cocker spaniel at Westminster, Willow was clearly the one in charge.

I would be jealous later. I would be hit hard by jealousy the second we walked out of the sunlit room that was no longer, in any way, mine. But while I was in it, watching the two of them, I was only awestruck.

IT MIGHT HAVE GONE on that way: my father throwing his new family in our faces, never asking us a single question about our lives, Marcus stonily silent, my mother holding her head high, me feeling more and more humiliated, more and more invisible, until it was time to take our quiet and bitter leave of that place. But Marcus got drunk.

I'd seen him drunk before, of course, stumbling home—to this very house—after a party, stupid and reeking of beer, although I hadn't seen him like that in a long time. After we moved, friendless and also determined not to make my mother's life any harder than it already was, Marcus had behaved himself, and in college, where most kids went wild, he had done the opposite, becoming the serious student, the designated driver. Back in high school before the combustion, though, apart from a few scary episodes (a trip to the hospital to have his stomach pumped, a camping trip in which he'd wandered off and had to be rescued), Marcus had mostly been a fun drunk, goofy and voluble, even charming. He would fall down, slapstick-style, would sing dumb songs, and make jokes so unfunny they were funny.

But that day at Wilson's house, Marcus wasn't charming. He was narrow-eyed, venomous, and loud, a transformation that did not occur right away, although I knew, as soon as we walked downstairs and into the kitchen and I saw him sitting at the table, that it wasn't iced tea inside his large plastic tumbler. I looked to see if my mother had noticed, but her face bore the faintly smiling, tuned-out look of a person who was pretending she was someplace else. I loved my mother with all my heart, but it was hard to forgive: her downshift into a kind of slow, half-awake gear when things around her got tough. She'd done it for years, long before the combustion, especially at moments when Wilson was at his worst. I felt a kind of hollow disappointment at seeing it now, post-combustion, post-mom-taking-charge-of-her-life. How easy it was, here in this house, for her, for all of us to slide back into our old roles.

Caro had laid out lunch, a basket of sliced baguette and dishes of fancy salads like curried chicken, spicy sesame green bean, roasted vegetable, and one made of artichoke hearts, chickpeas, arugula, and feta cheese. I didn't see any bags or plastic containers, but I knew that the salads had all come from the gourmet grocery down the street. The artichoke heart one had always been my favorite. Now, awash in jealousy and homesickness, I couldn't decide what I wanted more, to cradle the bowl to my chest or to throw the damn thing across the room.

I glanced up, saw Marcus watching me, and gave him one of the two-eyed winks we'd been giving each other since we were practically babies, long before we could manage the regular one-eyed kind. I attempted a smile. The last thing any of us needed was Marcus picking up on my unhappiness and getting angrier than he already was. But instead of winking back, he shook his head to show he wasn't fooled.

"Mako," I whispered. "Eat some lunch."

"I'm drinking my dinner, darlin'," he whisper-drawled. For some reason, times of stress always brought out the cowboy in my brother.

"Bad idea, cowpoke."

He made a shooing motion with his hand and said, "Git along, little dogie."

I filled plates for both of us and set his before him with a little more oomph than necessary, trying, as I leaned over, to get a whiff of whatever filled his cup, but he grinned and covered it with his hand.

Eventually, we were all seated around the table watching Willow, who was enthroned in a pristine white high chair at the right hand of her father. She ate whole-wheat crackers, pieces of soft-cooked organic carrot, and cubes of white, unprocessed cheese, bringing her extraordinary pincer grasp and well-beyond-age-level hand/mouth coordination to bear on every task. After a long couple of minutes of this, Marcus picked up a green bean in his own pincer grasp, pointed it at me, and said, loudly, "Taisy, have you told your father about your first-semester grades?"

I stiffened. *Here we go.*

"We won't get our grade reports until after break," I mumbled.

"*Yet,* you know your grades. Remember how you told me and Mom your grades?"

I shrugged and tried, without success, to swallow my sense of foreboding along with a forkful of chicken salad.

Marcus pointed the bean at our mother.

"Mom, you remember Taisy telling you about her first-semester grades, right?"

"Of course, I remember," said my mother, distractedly.

Marcus pointed the bean at Wilson.

"Wilson," he said, loudly. Everything seemed to freeze for a second. It was the first time either of us had ever called him Wilson. "Wilson, I think you should ask your daughter Taisy to tell you her first-semester grades."

Wilson put down his fork, his face expressionless but beginning to flush. It was a tell, that flushing. His eyes and voice stayed perfectly cool almost always, but when he got mad, his face went red, the madder, the redder. Just now, it was champagne pink, but I had a heart-sinking suspicion that, before all was said and done, it would hit burgundy.

"I fail to see how your sister's grades, or yours for that matter, would be any of my concern at this point," he said. He might as well have slapped me.

"Introduction to Literature I, A; Shakespeare, A; Advanced Conversational French, A . . ." Marcus reeled off the rest of my report card, throwing A after A like poisoned darts.

My father didn't react. He didn't even glance in my direction. Marcus took a gulp from his tumbler.

"Taisy!" said Marcus. "Speak French for Wilson."

I shut my eyes. "No."

"Yeah, that what's his name, Baudelaire thing you recited for me and Mom. The thing from the evil flower thing. Wilson, your daughter Taisy here is *way* above the eightieth percentile in both French *and* Baudelaire."

I didn't have to look at Wilson to know that at "eightieth percentile" his face went the color of cranberry sauce.

"And she's back to taking ballet. Did you know that, Wilson? Taize, get up and show Wilson that move you did the other day." Marcus made a twirling motion with the green bean. "That triple pimpernel."

"Pirouette," I said, quietly, to Marcus. "Stop."

Marcus shook his head at me sadly, then a flick of his wrist and the green bean was airborne. Probably in my horror-struck state I only imagined it, but I believed I could see the bean moving in slow motion, arcing end over end until it bopped lightly against Wilson's crimson, rage-trembling cheek and fell to his lap. At that moment, it seemed to me that anything could happen. The sky could crack open. The house could go up in flames. The hand of God could scoop up Marcus and toss him into a bottomless pit.

Instead, what happened was a giggle. A trill of a giggle that turned into a long musical belly laugh, a deep and goldeny burbling brook of laughter. We all stared at Willow, all of us except Wilson, who, in a motion so unthinkingly protective it bruised my heart, reached out his hand and placed it on the top of his baby's head but never took his eyes off Marcus.

"Get out of my house," he said, with icy calm. "Take your drunken insolence out of my house and away from my child."

Marcus stood up, draining his tumbler and raising it as though to throw it at Wilson, too. When Wilson put his arm in front of his face to ward off the blow, Marcus laughed.

"Psych!" he said. He peered into the tumbler and laughed again, a hard sound. "*My child.*" His imitation of Wilson's voice was uncanny. "You are one sociopathic shit, Wilson."

Then, he dropped the tumbler on the table, where it bounced against a pot of tired-looking paperwhites, gave our father the finger, and strode, staggering only slightly, out of the room. I heard the back door slam.

The air in the room felt simultaneously electric and freezing cold. I drew my arms around myself, slipping my hands inside my sweater sleeves, and was seized by a powerful urge to get out, get the *hell* out of that room. Before I could move, however, someone else did. Caro, whom I had almost forgotten was there. With an audible flutter of breath, she stood and, hair billowing like a storm cloud, dashed out of the room. The back door slammed again. It was the most surreal part of that surreal day: Caro, of all people, going after Marcus.

"My God, Wilson." My mother's voice. Angry. Pitying, too.

Wilson smirked and waved ostentatiously in the direction of the backyard. "That out there is your handiwork, Katharine. Congratulate yourself!"

"'Handiwork?'" said my mother. "He's your *son.*"

Wilson grunted out an ugly laugh. "He is a joke. A bad one. And one of your making. I should never have entrusted anything to you."

I wanted her to scream at him, to claw him with her nails until the blood flowed. And at the exact same time, I wanted him to notice me, to say something nice about me, like that he knew I was different from Marcus. My entire body was waiting for it, leaning into the table, straining to hear it.

"Marcus," said my mother, firmly (was that a *smile?*), "will be fine. So will Taisy. I have never doubted that. But you. The state of your soul makes me shudder."

"Ah, well, do not you worry about me. No need to shudder for *me,*" he mocked, pressing his hands to his heart.

"Not for you." My mother bent her gaze to the little girl in the high chair, happily dropping carrots onto the floor and watching them fall. "For her."

Wilson's face turned so dark, I wondered if he might have a heart attack right there. He sputtered with rage, unable, for the first time ever as far as I knew, to put words together.

Finally, he blurted, "Out. All of you."

"Yes." My mother turned, rested her hand against my cheek, and said, "My beautiful child, I believe it's time to go."

WE HARDLY SPOKE ON the way back to the hotel. I stared blindly out the windshield, nauseated by the smell of the rental car, not even noticing the familiar streets and buildings and houses we passed on our way downtown. Marcus sprawled in the backseat, drumming his fingers on the window, humming a song I didn't even try to make out.

The hotel was the fanciest in town, a gold-encrusted, Gilded Age glory full of mosaic floors, coffered ceilings, and famous paintings. Because we had lived so nearby, we had never stayed there, even though I'd always wanted to. Now, it was much too expensive, even for just one night, but our mother had given it to us as a Christmas gift. A treat. Maybe she had also meant it as a *re*treat, post-visit, as though she had expected the worst, as though splendor, if there were enough of it, could counterbalance rage and grief.

It wasn't until we got to our room, a high-ceilinged, draperied lushness of cream, coral, and marigold, that I cut loose on my brother. This part remains mostly a blur, but I do remember this:

Me (howling): "You had to ruin it the way you ruin everything!"
Marcus (yelling): "He acted like you weren't even there!"
Me: "He wanted us there!"
Marcus: "No, he didn't. He hates us!"
Me: "He doesn't hate me! He *invited* me!"

And then the very worst moment of all:

Marcus: "He didn't want to. It was all Caro. Caro *made* him invite us. She *told* me!"
Me (sobbing, hoarse, broken): "Liar."

But I knew he wasn't lying.

Later, after Marcus threw up in the bathroom for an hour, after all of us had showered and lay clean and bone-tired and awake between the opulent bedclothes in the opulent darkness, my mother and I sharing one bed, Marcus in the other, Marcus said, "I'm sorry, Taize."

"Me, too," I said.

"And don't get mad again, but you have to get rid of it."

"What?"

Marcus said, "The idea that he'll ever love us or want us back."

My mother stayed still, silent, but I could feel her listening, waiting to see what I would say next.

"He's our father," I said.

It wasn't a rebuttal. It wasn't anything but a statement of fact. Marcus didn't say he wasn't our father. No one said anything more. We just let the statement hang there in the air, until it was gone, absorbed into the velvet dark.

CHAPTER FOUR

Willow

THE STORY OF HOW I almost killed my father starts like this: I wanted to run. Is that so terrible? If there is one thing I have in abundance, it's legs, and I wanted to use them. They are long, and somehow, they know how to move. My entire body knows. I'm a decent tennis player, and I think I could have been a decent ballet dancer, if I hadn't been made to quit when I was ten, but when I run, my body stops being a grouping of parts and becomes a single thing. A fluidity. A living, breathing verb.

Sports had always been part of my father's plan. He believed in a life of action, in all that "your body is a temple" business. He would quote Thoreau: "We are all sculptors and painters, and our material is our own flesh and blood and bones." Plus, he had a poorly hidden and scathing contempt for fat people.

When I was a young child, I had swim and tennis lessons at the country club, even though we never stayed for lunch afterward, and I played soccer on a team, which I adored, even though I was breathtakingly bad, and I took ballet classes twice a week for years. But by the time I was ten and a half, I was removed from the group lessons (my fellow swimmers and tennis players had no manners), from the soccer team (my teammates had no manners), from ballet class ("a breeding ground for neurotics and exhibitionists"). When we moved to our new house, my father had a tennis court built in the backyard and hired a private coach. He set up a ballet barre and a mirror in the basement. He also built a lap pool. And he started to take me running with him.

I liked the tennis coach, a six-foot-tall Australian woman with an accent thick and salty as Vegemite, but I hated the tournaments, and so after a drawn-out campaign, I was allowed to quit when I was fourteen. After a few lame attempts at giving myself a ballet class (which is a lot harder and more boring than you might think), I quit that, too. I never did laps in the lap pool, since I have always found being underwater scary and isolating (the blood in my ears roaring!), although I never confessed this weakness to my father. But I loved the running.

Don't get me wrong; I wasn't some prodigy. Not bound for stardom. I was good, though, and I guess I knew it, but for me, being good was not the point. The point was cutting through the air, *using* the air, the way I used the ground. The point was joy. Who cared about good when there was joy like that?

I'll tell you who cared, my father. He was thrilled, pleased as Punch that I was good. He bought a fancy stopwatch. He bought a fancy pedometer. He kept charts. I think this was why, in the end, he could not resist allowing me to be on the team—he wanted to see me race.

I found out about the team from a girl in my homeschooling group, Mary Ruth Coe. We weren't exactly friends. She was so quiet that in the first month I knew her, I privately diagnosed her with a host of disorders, including expressive aphasia and stress-induced apraxia—my father was fascinated by neuroscience and taught me a lot about it—but she turned out to just be cripplingly shy. There was the added difficulty of her being of the variety of homeschooler who does not, as Ms. Shay would so eloquently put it a couple of years later, embrace the sciences. But she was the only girl my age in the very small homeschooling group that I began attending, spottily, reluctantly, and always accompanied by my father, when I was thirteen, so we became some makeshift version of friends.

While her parents and my father had nothing else in common, they shared the belief in the body as temple, and because there is a law in our state that lets homeschoolers participate on public high school athletic teams, Mary Ruth's parents insisted that Mary Ruth join the cross-country team at the local high school. It wasn't the Webley School, which was private, but Thomas L. Mann High, named not after the writer but a local nineteenth-century gunpowder manufacturer, whose middle name turned out to be Lionel. In an unusually long and passionate verbal burst, Mary Ruth told me all about it. She raged. She sobbed. It was heartbreaking, actually, and I had to agree that making this poor, scared, pigeon-toed, gawky girl join a high school cross-country team was bordering on cruel and unusual punishment.

She begged me to ask my father to let me join, too, and even though I didn't really care about running competitively, I went ahead and asked just so I could tell her that I had, fully expecting him to refuse me. When he said he would consider it, I almost fell over, and when he came back later and said, "All right, then. Let us see how you fare, my thoroughbred," I spent a full twenty seconds being as speechless as Mary Ruth at her most speechless.

Then lo and behold, I liked it. A lot, in fact. If I only out and out loved it in moments, it was because only in moments did I feel a hundred percent part of the team, a hundred percent *not* like an outsider looking in. But the other kids were much nicer than I had expected; at worst, they were a little indifferent. No one was mean, which is saying something because—let's face it—Mary Ruth and I weren't your typical high school students. We shared virtually no cultural common ground with the other kids, although if I say that I shared more of it than Mary Ruth did and would have fared better socially if I'd been on my own, I'm not being mean, just honest.

All right, I'm being mean *and* honest. Mary Ruth Coe was a thousand-pound, sopping wet social albatross around my neck. If anyone besides me spoke a word to her, she went pop-eyed, beet-red, and mute, at which point I usually jumped in to answer for her, a task I resented, heartily. What made matters worse was that while I'm fairly sure it had never occurred to Mary Ruth to be a racist, she seemed especially nervous around the black kids on the team. Once, when the African-American team captain, a girl named Naomi Patton, asked her what other sports she played, Mary Ruth was so petrified that on top of the usual response, she turned to me, stricken, grabbed my forearm, and hung on like death, until I gazed wearily at Naomi, whose expression was already turning from friendly to cold, and told her that Mary Ruth had been raised on a regimen of mostly calisthenics, mostly in her backyard, from which she had rarely strayed. All of which was true, even though it wasn't particularly nice of me to say it.

Luckily, Mary Ruth was a tragically bad runner, so once practice began, and her groans from the pre-workout stretching—the one time in the afternoon when she had no trouble vocalizing—had stopped echoing through the treetops, I considered my homeschooler solidarity duty done, took off like a rocket, and never looked back.

There were a dozen or so of us at the front of the group, and while we ran, oh gosh, we became something. Maybe we weren't exactly friends, although I'm no expert on friendship. But we were easy with each other. We chatted or rather the others chatted about their lives—boys, parents, tests—and I listened but not in an uncomfortable, fish-out-of-water way, and I tossed in a comment from time to time. Sometimes, I even got a laugh. Most days, we sang songs from something called *Mamma Mia,* which turned out to be Coach Anderson's favorite Broadway musical. I'd never seen it, of course, but when it comes to songs, I'm a quick study, and after a couple of weeks, I was belting out "Take a Chance on Me" with the best of them. As corny as it sounds, running together like that, our differences fell away. Maybe we weren't friends, but we were teammates, which was close enough for me.

And meets were special, too, the "good lucks" at the start, the oranges and watermelon slices we ate afterward, spitting seeds into the grass, the way we cheered each other into the finish, shouting each other's names. At these times, cheering like that, I was not Willow Cleary or anyone in particular, nothing but another yelling voice. It's odd isn't it? How good that felt. I acted casual, at least I think I did, but I wanted to pack away every high five into my duffel and carry them around with me forever.

I ran with the team for two seasons, and then, in late August, just a week before our practices were set to start in what would've been my junior year if I were someone who went to normal school, my father and I were in a bookstore, and we saw Kelsey Banks, one of my team-mates. Actually, I saw her first, in profile, and the second she turned around and saw me, too, in a flash, I also saw the writing on the wall. With Kelsey's big blue eyes looking into mine, a smile already starting on her face, and my father two steps behind me, I was like Cassandra: I could see the future, every awful bit, and could not do a blessed thing to change it.

My first instinct was to run, to wheel around and go flying like a lunatic out of the store, but before I could, Kelsey was hugging me. Or doing her best to hug me, hindered as she was by her pregnant belly, which looked for all the world like a basketball stuffed under her shirt, the rest of her as girl-skinny as ever.

My father met my eyes, briefly, one hard, laser beam glance, before he relaxed into his usual hale-fellow-well-met demeanor, even going so far as to clap Kelsey on the back and cheerily boom, " 'All shall be well, and all shall be well, and all manner of things shall be well!' "

But I knew that all would be anything but. He didn't say a word about Kelsey on the way home in the car, expounding instead on Julian of Norwich, a fourteenth-century Christian mystic after his own heart, being optimistic, practical, and British. I had heard him expound on Julian before and had always pictured her as a nice Englishwoman talking about her encounters with God while pouring tea and wearing sensible shoes. I tried to find an opening to offhandedly mention that

I hardly knew Kelsey, that we had never especially been friends, and that she was not a person in whose footsteps I would *ever* stoop to follow, and to also remind him that she wouldn't even be on the team this year for obvious reasons, but the Dame Julian quotations were flying fast and furious, and I never got the chance.

For the next few days, I did my best to avoid my father, even though I knew that it was useless, that my fate had been sealed the moment Kelsey had turned and seen me, her arms full of breastfeeding books. Then, one morning, as I was walking by his office, he appeared in the doorway, snagged me lightly by the elbow, and said, "A word, my dear?"

The word, in a word, was *no* of course. He went on for several minutes about the sad moral state of America's youth, and ended with, "It is as clear to me as I am sure it is to you, Willow, that the cross-country team is no place for a sensible, self-respecting girl. I suspected as much when you asked to join; I harbored deep reservations, but you were so adamant that I allowed it, which I regret. I take full responsibility for putting you in harm's way, child, and ask that you forgive me." His tone was contrite; ditto his smile.

I would like to pause here in order to state for the record that I'd gotten angry with my father before. I had disagreed with him, even vehemently. He wasn't a dictator, and I wasn't a mindless puppet. Far from it. But if there was a governing rule in our household, it was: civility always. Temper was for toddlers and the great unwashed. Yelling was for drunks and street punks.

But the second my father told me I could not be on the cross-country team, I understood that I wanted to be on that team more than I had ever wanted anything in my life, and I started to get so mad, madder and madder and madder, until I was boiling with rage. And then, *then* my father patted my cheek and said, "There's a good girl."

I screeched. I stormed and spit venom. I called him name after name and accused him of vile things: injustice, cruelty, kidnapping, imprisonment. I shouted that he was ruining my life and that I hated him. If my mother had overheard, if she hadn't been in her studio in the back of our garden, she would have thought an insane stranger had broken into our house because I never screamed at my father like that. When he tried to take me gently by the shoulders, I pushed him away. I pushed my father.

And then I ran out of the room and out of the house, and if I could've run straight out of the world, I swear I would have. No place was far enough. But because I had run out the back door into our big, fenced-in backyard, my options were limited. I ended up at the pool house, threw open the door, and threw myself onto the sofa where I sobbed until the chambray under my face was soaking. It wasn't even noon, but I fell asleep. If only I hadn't. If only I had stopped crying and quickly made my guilty way back to the house, I might have found him before it happened and apologized and made it not happen. But I fell asleep.

I found him in his office, on the floor next to his desk. I thought he was dead. I can't bear to say any more, but I could live a thousand years and never forget it, not the horrible stillness of his face, not a single detail.

ON MY FATHER'S FIRST day home from the hospital after his surgery, when he told me he thought it best that I enroll at the Webley School, I nodded.

Every day, when I ran up to his room ready to beg to leave school and come home, and he asked me if I had had a good day, I smiled and said yes.

And on the day that I got home and he told me that he had called Eustacia Cleary, my sister who had *never* been my sister, the Other Daughter who was *not* his daughter, the disgrace, the bad one, and had invited her, along with my brother who was *not* my brother, to visit us, and that Marcus had refused the invitation but Eustacia had accepted it, I wanted to shout no, that we didn't need her, that he must be crazy to have done such a thing, but all I said was, "Eustacia. Oh. Well. All right, Daddy."

Tell me, what else could I do? I had almost killed the man, my only father. I knew I wouldn't get a second reprieve.

What's funny is that it took that hideous day for me to see it, the thing I could never escape even if I wanted to (and I'm not saying I wanted to), the thing that had always, every day of my life, been true: I, Willow Cleary, was responsible for my father's heart.

CHAPTER FIVE

Taisy

MY FRIEND TRILLIUM'S FIFTH life rule was that every woman must have one friend for whom a lunch-and-shopping trip is always the solution, no matter what the problem might be.

While many of us have life rules, even if they are, as in my own case, so flexible as to hardly count as rules at all—things like "Never, ever lie, unless it's to spare someone's feelings or to weasel out of something you really don't want to do, but *only* if not doing that something will not result in bodily or even psychic harm to another human being, unless that human being is exceptionally mean in which case minor psychic harm is permissible"—my friend Trillium had gone so far as to collect her rules in an actual rulebook and get it published, not just here in the United States but in so many other countries that we eventually stopped keeping track. It was a handy, pocket-sized (or handbag-sized, since Trillium has another rule about never, ever carrying things in your pockets), bright turquoise, spiral-bound volume titled *Trillium Shippey's Life RULES!* The little book had flown off the shelves and onto bestseller lists, helped along by multiple talk-show appearances and NPR interviews, each more drop-dead charming than

the last, as well as by countless starry-eyed and unsolicited celebrity en-
dorsements along the lines of "Trillium, will you be my BFF? #pure-
goddessgenius" @AnneHath on Twitter."

Trillium was my most famous friend, and while you wouldn't have
to be very famous at all to fill that particular niche, she was. Was,
is, and no doubt always will be because Trillium Shippey—from her
name to her laugh to her pinup girl curves—is different from the rest
of us, built for fame the way Michael Phelps was built for swimming. I
would say that I knew her when, except that I doubt very seriously that
there was ever a moment in Trillium's life when she wasn't palpably,
obviously a celebrity; she was just one that had yet to do the thing she
was celebrated for. I lucked into her, although she would say she lucked
into me. She was my best friend. She was also my first ghostee, and I
was her ghost.

We met at an adult ballet class, a true hodgepodge. There were a
couple of former professional dancers, long on limbs, neck, and thoroughbred skittishness; some mothers with varying degrees of experience who were killing time while their little sons and daughters took
class in another studio; a few men, including Dr. Simon, my dentist;
some true beginners; a trio of luminous women in their sixties who had
been dancing more or less consistently for fifty years and who knew
everything about ballet; and a few students like me, women whose
growing up had been steeped in ballet and who had failed to become
true ballerinas for some reason or another, like college or babies or
short legs or injury or—as in my case—a father whose scorn at a
daughter forgoing college and grad school to dance for a living would
have been scorching and whose opinion held sway with said daughter
long, long after it should have. Plus, I probably wasn't good enough to
become a real ballerina. Plus, I really, really liked to eat.

And then there was Trillium. By rights, she was one of the beginners, but somehow it was impossible to group her with the others, just
as it would turn out to be impossible to group her with anyone ever.
On her first day, she sailed into the room like Cleopatra on her golden

barge, chignoned head held aloft, swathed in a royal purple leotard and layers of legwarmers, chandelier earrings flashing. And then she proceeded to move with such focus and authority and natural rhythm that you almost didn't notice that she had no idea what she was doing.

Afterward, in the sedate dressing room, she bestowed hoots, high fives, and bear hugs on us all. Coming from anyone else, this would likely have gone over like a ton of bricks, but because it was Trillium, we felt something akin to blessed. When she turned to me, caught both my hands in hers, and said, "Your ankles and feet are so gorgeous, they make me want to lie down and cry. Will you have coffee?," it didn't occur to me to say anything but, "Yes!"

That coffee led to more coffee, and then drinks, and dinners, and at every get-together, we talked, mostly about Trillium. Not because she was tedious or self-centered, but because at the particular moment I met her, when it came to the story of her life, Trillium was a woman on fire. This hadn't always been so. For most of her adult life, Trillium had never talked much about her past.

"It wasn't because of shame," she was quick to tell me, resting one long-nailed hand on my arm, "but because I was so softhearted about it. It was so much mine, like a child."

But then there came what she refers to as "The Dark Night of the Orange" (which became the title of the introductory chapter of her book), the winter night on which, after decades of devout citrus avoidance, she had come home from a boring date to find a package on her doorstep, a thank-you gift from a student for whom she'd written a letter of recommendation. The box was packed with navel oranges, a dozen, each tucked tenderly inside its individual square cardboard nest of paper grass. They were perfect, softball sized, and so profoundly orange they seemed to give off their own light.

"They were still cold from sitting on my porch all day. And all I can say is that it came over me that I had to eat one. I couldn't not."

One bite, that first brilliant burst on her tongue, and there it was, all of it, in full color and surround sound, beginning with Trillium at three years old in the orange grove, screaming inside a cloud of bees.

Her story filled her; she teemed with it. Two days later, she came to her first ballet class (as a child, she had always wanted to take ballet, had fashioned tutus out of every available material, trash bags, newspapers), and met me, and handed over, in great gleaming swaths, the story of her life. To say we were bonding doesn't cover it; we were bound: she couldn't not tell and I couldn't not hear. It was like "The Rime of the Ancient Mariner," except that no birds were killed, and the telling was nothing but beautiful for the teller and the listener.

I laughed. I cried. Sometimes, hours or days after I'd last seen Trillium, some tiny, jewel-colored piece of story would come winging toward me out of the blue, and I would laugh or cry again.

The story itself was classic Americana, a gritty, sublime, pull-yourself-up-by-your-bootstraps tale, punctuated by moments of terror, of heartbreak, of joy and luck and shining grace. Her mother, Elena, was a migrant fruit picker, sixteen years old when Trillium was born; her father was—if you can believe it—the son of a plantation owner, a college kid named Packham Boyd who got Elena pregnant over fall break and then went back to school without a backward glance.

Through a combination of smarts, looks, audacity, luck, and an ineffable iridescent effervescence that I would come to call Trillium-inosity, Trill had scratched, scrambled, finessed, floated, and earned her way from fruit picker to Ivy Leaguer to bond trader to revered university professor and inspirational speaker to—and here's where I came in—bestselling writer.

Her story was good. Supergood. Much better than most, but one morning, about two days after she'd finished, after all those hours of telling—and the hours stretched over months—I realized, with a jolt, that it wasn't so different, on its face, from others we've all heard. Rags to riches. The triumph of the human spirit. Et cetera. What made the story special, what made it thrilling and irresistible was Trillium herself: the cadence of her throaty voice, her leaping mind, the way she'd throw words out like handfuls of confetti one minute, and select them, one by careful one, the next. Trillium spoke with her whole body; sentences shot out the tips of her long fingers, ran off her like rain.

I told her to write her story down. I was a writer myself, a freelance business writer and editor. I worked for corporations and law firms, mostly, got occasional work from one of the nearby universities or hospitals. It was a far cry from the kind of writing I'd always hoped to do, but, honestly, I liked it. There was something satisfying about taking raw, messy material, no matter how bland it might be, and giving it shape, rhythm, clarity, a dash of razzle-dazzle. On good days, I like to think I even gave it a little poetry. It was something that had always made me happy, putting words on a page in an order that pleased me. Even writing grocery lists was a small, contained joy; sometimes, I'd add items I didn't need—lemons, figs, buttermilk—just because I liked the words, and then I'd buy them because they were on the list and that's what the list was for.

But Trillium, as it turned out, with her gold mine of a story and her gift for bringing it to life, *hated* to write, had only ever done so in school, under duress, and at the last minute.

"There's nobody *there*," she groaned, referring to the writing process. "It's so dull and lifeless and cold, like the *tundra*."

"Actually, there's plenty of life on the tundra, if you look," I told her.

"You! You and your *Planet Earth*. Like what, for example?"

It's true; I was and am an enormous fan of the BBC series, while Trillium was a die-hard speciesist, adored almost everything that involved people, no matter how questionable (theme parks, reality television, jury duty), and almost nothing that did not.

"Shrubs," I offered in my best David Attenborough voice. "And sedge. A veritable ocean of sedge. So much sedge that the sedge can be seen from space."

In the end, she talked; I wrote. When I brought her the first chapter, the one about the bees, she read it, then sat down on the floor and burst into tears.

After a couple of minutes, when she could speak, she said, "It's like living it all over again. It's *sheer and unadulterated perfect gorgeousness*. It's *genius*! It's *me*—it's so *me*!"

She wiped her eyes, caught her breath, and then said, "But the pancakes, the ones at the hospital, they were blueberry, not chocolate chip. Big, fat, purple splotches in the pancakes. I thought I told you that. Purple. And, oh! You need to include how the epinephrine made me shake, my whole body trembling like a leaf. Not like a leaf! When do leaves actually tremble? Like something else. Something trembly. I'm sure you'll think of it."

This would turn out to be our process: she talked, I wrote, she read, cried, gushed, called me a genius, swore my writing was perfection, and then ordered changes. It was exhilarating. I had never loved any job more.

I discovered that I had a gift for capturing people with words. Wait, capturing is wrong. More like channeling. I might have been a ghostwriter, but I was the one who was haunted. When I wrote, I was ten times more Trillium than I was myself. When I got stuck, I exercised more patience than I had maybe ever, waiting for the right question to come to me (What was the best gift you ever got as a kid? Who is your favorite March sister?). When it did, I'd ask Trillium the question and her answer would unstick me, reveal the path I needed to take.

Trillium's book sold like hotcakes, stayed on the *New York Times* bestseller list enough weeks to choke a goat, as Trillium liked to say. After that, I ditched the business writing and became a ghostwriter for real, and the right question became my secret weapon, my ace in the hole. It never stopped amazing me, how the tiniest fact, once discovered, could pop open a window with a vista-sized view of a person's inner world. How you could learn, for example, that a person had had six dogs in his lifetime, all named Boxer, even though none of them was a boxer, and—boom—there you were, standing smack in the middle of at least an acre of the man's soul.

But getting back to rule number five of the follow-up to her memoir: *Trillium Shippey's Life RULES!*

The second after I finished telling Trillium, in one, long manic rush of words, about my impending visit to my father's house and all the accompanying anxieties, layer upon layer of anxiety, an *anxiety trifle,* she said, "Okay, I'll be at your house in five minutes. Meanwhile, here is what you need to do."

Her voice dropped, got soft and rhythmic, like a rocking cradle. "Close your eyes and draw a magic circle in the sand. Inside the circle are clear air, sunlight, birds singing. Nothing bad can enter the circle, not one bad memory, not one fear for the future, not one regret, not one perceived personal shortcoming."

"Thank you for 'perceived,'" I told her.

"You're welcome. Be quiet. Now, step into the circle, really picture yourself doing it. One leg, the other leg. And once you're in the center, simply be. Root yourself. Let the peace soak into you, all the way into the marrow of your bones. Soak and soak and soak. Is it soaking in?"

And, you know, it really sort of was.

The next thing I knew, we were at the mall.

While it may be hard to maintain a sense of bone-marrow-saturated peace at malls, I mostly like them. They suit me, particularly as I am a mission shopper. If it's a black dress I need, I start at one end of the mall and go store to store, methodically trying on one dress after the next, leaving no stone unturned, spurred ever onward by the possibility that the perfect black dress, the oh-my-God-you-are-the-spitting-image-of-Audrey-Hepburn dress (even though Audrey would naturally never spit) might be waiting, a shining sleeve of night sky on a hanger, in the very next shop.

But going shopping with Trillium is something else altogether. "Shopping" is far too prosaic a word. She's more like one of those people who lead expeditions into rain forests, seeking out new kinds of orchids or thumb-sized lacquered tree frogs or cures for cancer. It's amazing, how she'll walk into a store, zero in on, say, a rhinestone headband, lift it to eye level, gingerly, using just her fingertips, and begin to describe its virtues, the individually clasped stones—five prongs!—the woven silver vines of metal, all in such hushed, wonder-filled tones that you forget that the thing costs $11.99, that you are standing in a teenybopper store with a display of *Cat in the Hat* hats to your right and boy band lunch boxes to your left. All you see is a tiny thing of beauty, a delicate, dew-jeweled spiderweb of loveliness.

The mission was to find a father/daughter/stepsister/stepmother (although, as always, Caro felt like an afterthought, someone I had to remind myself was part of the picture) reunion outfit. I wouldn't go so far as to get an entire new wardrobe. Wilson would have to see me in jeans eventually, despite his bone-deep loathing of them. But the initial meeting outfit seemed especially crucial. I needed to look accomplished, pretty, smart, grown-up, offhandedly chic, emotionally independent, and as though I weren't trying at all.

The first thing Trillium found for me was a pair of leather shorts. And while they weren't especially short and weren't especially tight and could indeed be worn with black tights and a silk blouse, and while I do like to wear clothing that shows off my legs, since they seem to be the part of my body that is best hanging in there, the leather shorts were *leather* and *shorts,* and, as I reminded Trillium, my father had once, not so long ago, called me "whorish."

"Seventeen years ago," singsonged Trillium, turning down the waistband. "*Look* at how immaculately they're lined. You don't see a lining like that every day. And the seams!"

"Lining, seams, blah blah blah. No."

"Oh, you!" She gave me a grandma-style cheek pinch. "How about this: you forget about pleasing him? Let your outfit scream, 'Go to hell, ya big bossy galoot!'"

I did a little internal squirming at this because, obviously, Trillium was right. "Go to hell, ya big bossy galoot" had always been the appropriate response to Wilson, and I hadn't given it anywhere close to often enough. When I had, there'd always been a thrill of satisfaction—and a lot of high-fiving from Marcus. But the thought of doing it now, with the anxiety trifle growing more layered by the minute, just made me tired.

"Don't want to give the man another heart attack," I mumbled.

Trillium raised an eyebrow at me.

I sighed. "Okay. For the time being, I'm in path-of-least-resistance mode."

Trillium considered this for a moment, then nodded. "So be it."

We found some narrow, charcoal gray, almost black ("but much wittier than black" according to Trill) pants made of some kind of smooth, non-itchy, stretch wool ("like wool when it dreams it's silk; this puts the 'fab' in fabric!") and a loose ruby-red cashmere sweater with an open neck ("perfect for the dark-haired girl who what she lacks in cup size makes up for in collarbone gorgeousness"). After I swore on my life to wear a certain pair of flat-soled, black, knee-high boots that Trillium had bought for me for my last birthday (she has a habit of giving gifts so extravagant that you must protest, even though they are so perfect that you sort of hate to), I said, "Are we allowed to eat now?" And we were.

Never one to mince words, as soon as we had placed our order, Trillium leaned in and said, "Okay, let's talk about 'whorish.'"

The waiter, a skinny handsome boy with Tin Tin hair, began, with grave nonchalance, to whistle, never taking his eyes off his notebook, before walking away, "Moon River" trailing in the air behind him.

I sighed. "Wilson never name-calls. He just uses hideous adjectives and stabs people with them."

Trillium made a gnat-swatting motion. "Pfft! Who cares about Wilson? What I want to know is: who was *the boy?*"

For a few seconds, I ceased to breathe. Then, I began whistling "Moon River."

"Nooooooo you don't," said Trill. "Where there's a father saying 'whorish,' there's a boy. Spill it, missy."

I opened my mouth. Shut it.

Trillium reached for my hand. "Hold on. The boy wasn't a bad one, was he? He didn't abuse you or something?"

I shook my head. "He was good."

My mouth was dry. My heart was marbles in a tin can that someone was shaking.

"Name?" asked Trillium.

"Ben Ransom." The tin can shook harder. Clatter, clatter, clatter. After all this time, all it took was saying his name.

"Tall or short?"

"Tallish."

"Outstanding facial feature?"

I shut my eyes, and there he was. I made my way down his face. Dark hair; dark brows; black eyes; fair, flushy skin; cheekbones tilting up; nose tilting down; deep, v-shaped divot in his upper lip.

"I don't know." It was almost a whisper.

I opened my eyes to see Trillium smiling.

"So it's like that, is it?" she said.

I shrugged. "It was. Seventeen years ago."

"Uh-huh."

I shrugged again, shrug overkill. "You know what he looked like? He looked like a guy who should wear corduroy trousers, boots, and a fisherman sweater and maybe some kind of brown jacket, and live in Wales. Or something."

"You've been to Wales?" asked Trillium.

"I have not been to Wales."

"Did he wear all those things?"

"Of course not. He was in high school. I just mean he looked sort of, or gave the general impression of being—forget it."

"Windburned? Tousle haired? With those pink lips that look chapped but aren't?"

I stared at her.

She did a victory dance.

"Don't get carried away," I told her. "Sometimes they actually were chapped."

"You. Must. Tell. Me." She signaled the waiter. "We will get wine, and then you will tell me *everything*!"

In the end, I didn't tell her everything. Apart from Marcus and my mom, I trusted no one as much as I trusted Trillium, but there were some parts of the story that had been stowed away in the dimmest, dustiest corner of my mind for so long that just thinking about pulling them out into the light of day hurt. What I ended up giving her was the story of how we met. I told it carefully and hoped for—what's the word I want? Synecdoche. I wanted that small part to stand for something bigger, if not the whole story of me and Ben, then the essence of it.

And because, if you're going to tell the story or even just part of the story of the love of your life, you should begin with solemnity and maybe even a little pomp and circumstance, I began like this: "In all my life, I've loved just three men. One was only a boy, so maybe he doesn't even count, except that he did and does, and he wasn't an 'only' anything, ever. He was Ben Ransom, the love of my life."

IT STARTED THE WAY a lot of things in tenth grade started, with Itzy Wolcraft shrieking across the cafeteria. Marcus and I had attended the same school since prekindergarten, private, paid for by Wilson but chosen by my mother, so it was a good place, tough on academics and community service but easy on things like dress code and cafeteria shrieking. In this instance, Itzy's shrieks were so high-pitched, so nearly hysterical that they sounded first like undifferentiated noise, then, as she got closer, like an insane and vaguely Japanese chant—"Hagai aga nurshi"—before, at long last, resolving themselves into, "Hot guy at the nursery; hot guy at the nursery; hot guy at the nursery."

The afternoon before, Itzy had gotten in trouble for a C- on a math test and, in addition to losing her phone privileges (which happened a lot, hence her frequent episodes of piercing cafeteria gossip mongering), she had been forced to accompany her mother to Ransom's Garden World to buy fall yard decorating supplies, "mums and pumpkins and hay and corn husky thingies and such."

"And I was sitting in one of those big white chairs, the wooden ones with the flat armrests, where you are in no way supposed to sit because there's a sign saying PLEASE DO NOT SIT, when this totally beautiful wavy-haired guy just *materialized* from behind some rubber trees or something, and I swear to God I was paralyzed, like momentarily *frozen in place,* until I saw that he was wearing one of those man-aprons with RANSOM's across the chest part and carrying a humongous pumpkin that was possibly diseased because it was totally covered with barnacles or possibly plant tumors and was completely disgusting, but luckily he had those leathery or cloth or something gloves on, which *anyway* I realized meant that he worked there, and so no doubt knew that I was sitting illegally, so I started to, you know, scramble to my feet, and you'll never guess what he said."

There were five of us, and we all yelped, "What?"

Itzy dropped her voice to a near whisper, "'Don't worry about it. Everyone sits there. That one's really just a sample.'"

Our excuse was pumpkin shopping. Six teenaged girls dressed in their best jeans and new fall boots and sweaters, lip-glossed within an inch of their lives, and eager—avid, breathless, pink cheeked—for gourds. It was a big place, Ransom's, deep and wide, with rows of open-air wooden tables covered with pots of plants and flats of flowers giving way to rows of larger plants and shrubs, and delicate, hopeful little potted trees, and interspersed throughout, pretty objects: birdbaths and garden furniture made by local artisans, and ceramic planters full of artful arrangements, funny things like purple-hearted cabbages and chili pepper plants and trailing vines mixed in with the usual flowers.

There was a shop, too. A cottagey structure full of vases, wind chimes, fancy, seasonal tabletop decorations, blown-glass hummingbird feeders, candles, crystal garden balls, wreaths made of herbs, pomegranates, eucalyptus. My mother rarely shopped there. "Too expensive," she'd say, "but it's a great place to get ideas."

I'd find out later that Mr. Ransom and his wife had opened the center together, years before Ben was born, and that in the beginning, it was Mrs. Ransom who had been in charge of all the arty things. After they divorced, when Ben was three, Mr. Ransom had taken over that part, too, and, to his surprise, found that he had a knack for it, a real eye. Sometimes, the local rich ladies would even pay him to come to their houses and decorate their yards, dining room tables, and mantelpieces, fill their planters and window boxes. Mr. Ransom didn't really need the extra jobs because the center did fine; he did it because he loved it.

Because the six of us had so much ground to cover, we decided to divide and conquer, some of us starting at the perimeter and walking in ever-smaller circles toward the center, a couple of us taking the cottage, and one of us cruising the displays out front.

I took the front displays, and because, even though I was boy crazy, I was also kind of a nerd, I got interested: gripped by gourds, pulled in by pumpkins. There was a mind-boggling variety of them: the usual basketball orange, of course, but also green-striped ones, bone-colored ones, enormous blond ones, flattish princessy ones, the barnacled type that had made such an impression on Itzy, and giant tear-shaped ones whose long, curved handle-tops made you want to grab one and club something. And all along one bench were the gourds that would change my life. I'd never seen anything like them, not gourds so much as creatures: small orange pumpkins with squatty white legs.

I picked up two of them, one in each hand, and made them toddle, jauntily, along the bench. I hummed a little tune. Behind me, someone said, "Hey."

A boy's voice. Slowly, I turned around. His eyes sparkled under his eyebrows. His smile was crooked and genuine. I noticed he had one dimple, just like I did. I also noticed that he was perfect, man-apron and all, and I was making little pumpkins walk. I stood looking at the boy, my hands full of gourd monopod spacemen. And here's the thing: I should've been mortified. Every interaction with the opposite sex I'd had since the age of ten had taught me that, at that moment, I should've wanted to disappear from the face of the earth. But I *didn't*.

"Hey," I said, smiling back at the boy. "You probably thought I was trying to steal your gourds."

"I don't know about that," he said, shrugging in a way that made his hair fall sideways on his forehead. Luckily, my hands were occupied or I might have brushed it back into place. "Most gourd stealers don't make them dance a jig before they take them."

I snorted. *Snorted*. "Well, that's stupid. How else would they know which ones to take?"

"Good point," he said, grin deepening. "You know, I sort of hate to tell you this, but those Turk's Turbans might not actually be gourds. They might be squash."

"That might matter to me if I were a gourd stealer," I snapped, "which I'm obviously not."

Then, that bright star of a boy tipped back his head and laughed, a sound unself-conscious and ringing, so completely uncool, more like the laugh of a little kid or someone's granddad than like a high school guy talking to a girl his age he had just met. If I'd been in another state of mind, my usual state of mind, I might have felt embarrassed for him. But nothing at that moment was usual, and his laugh was like my own private meteor shower.

"I'm Ben Ransom," he said.

He held out his hand for me to shake, and later, I'd kick myself all the way home for not jumping at the chance to touch him, to grab hold and hang on, but at that moment, I would've given everything I owned to hear Ben Ransom laugh again, so I slapped a Turk's Turban into his open palm and said, "Taisy Cleary."

"I KNOW WHAT YOU'RE thinking," I said to Trillium. "Granddad laughs and dancing pumpkins don't make for the most romantic meeting in the world. But they did! We were sixteen. We barely felt comfortable alone in our own rooms, and we cared more about what people thought of us than we cared about anything, world peace, *anything*. Yet there we stood, talking like no one was watching, like we'd known each other all our lives."

Trillium said, "Actually what I was thinking is that you were insane to ever let him go."

As soon as she said that—*boom*—there was Ben's face again, the way it looked the last time I saw him, stunned, betrayed, a world of hurt in his eyes. I blinked the image away.

"I didn't want to. Trust me. But I was a kid! I didn't have a lot of choices."

This must've come out more plaintive than I'd intended because Trill reached out and took my hand.

"Hey, babe, I wasn't judging. No way. Of course, you were a kid! So let me guess. Wilson caught you doing some totally normal people-in-love thing with Ben that he thought no daughter of his should be doing, called you whorish, and—kaput, Ben and Taisy were no more."

"Yeah. Well. Something like that." I cleared my throat. "Anyway, it was a long time ago."

"You think you'll see him? Does he still live in the area?"

I shrugged and looked away. "How would I know?"

"Pfft! Yeah, right. You googled. Don't try to tell me different, lady. Does he still live there?"

I grinned. "Not still. Again. He went away to college and then grad school in Wisconsin and seems to have lived out there for a while. Anyway, he's back. He has an address."

"So you'll see him!"

"Trill. He's probably married with ten kids."

She stuck out her hand. "Bet he's not. Bet you a refrigerator clean-out that he's not."

I considered. "Since you don't even keep food in your refrigerator and since your rock-and-roll cleaning guy cleans it for you every month, it's a deal."

We shook.

"I hope you see him," said Trillium. "I hope, I hope, I hope."

"Oh, I've seen him. He has all those tattoos and smells like Pine-Sol, but he's still kind of cute."

"Hardy har har."

"You know what Ben did, about three weeks after we started dating? He took a couple of ballet classes, just because ballet was so important to me, and he wanted to see what it was like."

"Wow."

I sighed, chased a pea around my plate with a fork. "What if he's different?"

"He will be," said Trillium.

"Oh, God, what if he's the *same*?"

"He'll be that, too, honey," she said. "Just like you. Just like everyone."

TWO DAYS LATER, I drove the seven hours from my house to my father's with an iPod full of fortifying songs, a suitcase full of a week's worth of clothes, and a head full of Ben. Oh, Ben. His laugh; his Yorkies Busby and Jed; the way he and I would study for hours together without speaking; the things he taught me to like (Ovaltine, basketball, chess); the things I taught him to like (sushi, U2, Barbara Kingsolver); the way his eyes were so dark you could only see his pupils in the brightest sunlight; the way he read books, literally, to pieces; the night he called me in tears (the only time I ever heard or saw him cry) and told me that his mother, who had MS but refused to use a walker, had fallen down the garage steps and broken her hip, how she'd had to lie there for two hours on the cement floor until his stepfather got home.

It was complete indulgence, a memory binge, a Ben bender. After so many years of studied denial, of trying to downplay, shrug off, forget, I didn't so much fall off the wagon as plunge off a cliff. I was so lost in Ben, Ben, Ben that I almost forgot that I was headed Wilson-ward. It wasn't until I saw the exit for what I still thought of as my hometown (even though I'd tried to stop) that I remembered to worry about what waited at the end of my journey, and even then, the worry was only an annoyance, like a mosquito buzzing in the car or a bad smell. I didn't panic. I didn't feel like throwing up or turning the car around. Instead, I squared my shoulders, turned up the Decemberists, thought about the first present Ben gave me (a hand-cranked ice cream maker and a bag of rock salt), and exited.

Wilson's house was on a road that had once been quiet and coun-trified, bordered by farms and fields but which was now pretty well trafficked. Still, the house—a long, white stucco number with a red tile roof—was set so far back from the road that it seemed to be in its own little world, bucolic and meadowy, with trees so old they were probably historic landmarks rising majestically from their pools of shadow. Mixed up among the old trees were newer ones, small and delicate. It wasn't until I was driving down the long, gently curving driveway that I realized that all the young trees were willows.

I stopped the car, midway up the drive, shut my eyes, and took some deep breaths. With a shaky imaginary hand, I drew a magic circle in the sand, stepped into it, one foot, the other foot, and waited for the peace to soak in.

You are an adult, I told myself. *You have a life that you love. You are happy and secure and rich in friends and family. Your mother is a jewel. Your brother thinks you're funny. All of your ex-boyfriends still like you, except Peter, but he never liked you much to begin with. You're a home-owner. You have ghostwritten two international bestsellers. You have long eyelashes and good feet and a famous best friend. Jealousy can't touch you because you exist on a plane above jealousy. High above. Miles. Miles and miles and miles.*

"Miles and miles and miles," I whispered as I put the car in drive.

"Miles and miles and miles," I whispered as I put the car in park in front of the house.

"Miles and miles and miles," I whispered as I rang the doorbell.

I heard footsteps inside the house and stopped whispering.

Caro answered the door. Her eyes and hair looked startled, but her smile was unmistakably real.

"Taisy!" she said. "How wonderful that you're here!"

Then, my stepmother and I were hugging, and I'm not sure, but I can't swear that I wasn't the one who started it.

Maybe it will be okay, I thought, *Maybe it will even be good.*

"Hello, Eustacia," said a voice.

The person was so impossibly tall, lithe, cool-eyed, and collected that it took a moment for me to realize three things, in this order: that she wasn't a grown woman but a girl; that she was Wilson's daughter, the precious one, the one deserving of honorary trees; and that we were dressed in almost identical outfits. Cashmere sweater, tall boots, and what I swear were the same wool pants, except that hers were black.

Charcoal gray is much wittier, I thought, triumphantly, and instantly felt like a heel. She who is driven to comparing shades of stretch wool lives not on a plane above jealousy. It was so petty, I had to smile. Maybe because she thought I was smiling at her, Willow took a step backward, bumped into the stair rail, and flushed, poor child, to the roots of her hair.

"Hey there, Willow," I said, and this time my smile was really for her. "It's been a long time."

Instead of smiling back, Willow lifted her chin an inch and said, "Welcome to our home. My father is sleeping just now, and I think it's best if I don't wake him."

Her chin was trembling, but the rest of her was frozen in place. It's what saved me in the end, the sudden understanding that she was so much more afraid than I was.

"It's okay," I told her, but what I really meant was, "It'll be okay, really it will."

For a split second, and I don't think I imagined it, her eyes flashed like a stricken deer's. Then, Willow pressed her lips together, gave a sharp shrug, and said, "Fine, then."

"Willow," said her mother.

But in a swirl of perfect posture and auburn hair, Willow was gone.

CHAPTER SIX

Willow

During that whole first conversation, he didn't call her "daughter." And I would be lying if I said that wasn't a huge relief to me, a relief that later, once I'd stopped clinging to it like a life raft, transformed itself into a victory, the kind that gives you a little, gloating lift for days afterward, every time you think about it. I was not proud of this reaction. I knew it to be childish, and ignoble, and even, possibly, pathetic. For one thing, let's face it, the chances of his calling her "daughter" when he was actually in conversation with her were pretty slim. Not many people, at least in this century, address their offspring as "daughter" even if they're bursting with paternal feeling. Still, he might've used it obliquely, as in "your duty as my daughter" or in an ironic, quote-y way like "Ah, the prodigal daughter returneth!" (this second possibility had popped into my head right before bed the night before and seemed so plausible that it kept me up for hours).

But, all this aside, it simply shouldn't have meant so much to me, that one little word. It shouldn't have meant *anything*. After all, *I* was the true daughter. *I* was not the one my father had tossed aside in disgust and studiously ignored for going on two decades. It's not overstating things to say I resided firmly on the mountaintop of my father's love, while Eustacia had spent her life at its foot, gazing upward, powerless to get so much as a toehold. I knew this, with both my brain and my metaphorical heart, but not, somehow, with my physical heart, which pounded like thunder for the full ten-minute conversation. Nor with my lungs, which seemed to freeze with dread, waiting, waiting for him to call her the word, my word, mine.

And he didn't. But if I am perfectly honest, I will say that the conversation did not go the way I had wanted it to, even though, up until the last two minutes or so, my father was splendid, was just exactly as I would've hoped. Once I'd made sure he was awake and ready—so handsome in his striped pajamas and crimson dressing gown—and he had granted permission for Eustacia to enter, he'd spotted her hovering in the doorway and waved her in.

"Enter and welcome, Eustacia!" he called out. "I trust you had no trouble finding us and that you have had a little time to shake the road dust from your shoes! Please, please, do not loiter in the doorway! Enter and sit! Be at ease!"

He gestured toward the chair near the foot of his bed, a Victorian chair with a carved wooden back, no armrests, and a velvet-covered seat that was hard as a pincushion. It was the right chair for her, just as all his choices were right, his commanding tone of voice, the raja-like sweep of his hand. Oh, he was grand. He was *majestic*.

It was Eustacia who was all wrong. After what she'd done, she should have been humble, grateful, awed. She should've crept into my father's room like a mouse and perched on the edge of that wretched chair as though she didn't fully deserve to sit in it, and she should've begged with her eyes for any small scrap of approval my father might deign to bestow. Truth be told, I didn't know precisely what it was she or her dastardly brother had done, although I'd come to understand that his transgressions had to do with drinking and maybe also drugs. Common degenerate stuff. Hers were kept more shadowy and vague, which is how I knew they had to do with sex. Probably pregnancy. Teen pregnancy! Like some sad-eyed, droopy failure of a girl on a billboard with a 1-800 number printed under her tremulous chin. What could be stupider? More clichéd?

But here was Eustacia, striding with her shoulders back and her eyes amused, not even giving the Victorian chair a glance, but moving without a second thought to stand, her boot soles planted, at my father's bedside. For a hideous instant, I thought she might lean over and kiss his cheek, but she just stood there, looped a loose strand of hair behind her left ear and smiled.

"Hello, Wilson," she said. "My trip was fine. I'm fine. The question is, how are you?"

The *insolence*!

"I?" said my father, turning slightly pink and sitting up straighter against his pillows. "I am very well, very much on the mend."

"Well, that's good," said Eustacia, a bit doubtfully. "I guess I expected . . ."

"What?" asked my father.

She gave a slight shrug. "Not that you don't look great. You do. But, it's been, what, around a month? I supposed you might be out of bed by now."

The low-down, dirty *insolence*!

I wanted to shake her until her pretty white teeth rattled, but I needed to show my father I believed he could handle her on his own, which of course, he could. I bit my tongue, literally, and gazed down at my nails then out of the window in as bored a manner as I could muster.

"Ah, well, if it were up to me, I would be out in the fall sunshine raking leaves at this very moment," said my father, "but my doctors have been quite adamant in advising bed rest and patience, neither of which suits a temperament like mine."

It was all I could do not to shoot my father a look of surprise at this, since, at his last appointment, his doctor had told him that he could resume moderate physical activity whenever he felt strong enough. This probably did not include raking leaves, of course, but if my father had ever once raked leaves under the fall sunshine or any other sunshine, I'd never seen it. The yard service did that. But after a second or two, I recognized the true message behind my father's not quite true statement: his personal health or lack thereof was none of Eustacia's damn business. *Bully for you, Daddy,* I thought. *Way to shut her up!*

Except that she didn't shut up. Eustacia sat down in the armchair next to my father's bed and yammered on about the arrangements she'd had to make in order to be there, the book she'd put on hold, the redirection of her mail to her mother's address, the college student she'd hired to house-sit. As if she were put out! As if she were the one doing the favor! Well, if she expected my father to thank her for going to the trouble of coming, she was very much mistaken.

"If your point is that you have a life, Eustacia," said my father with twinkly-eyed dryness, "consider it taken."

The odd thing is that she didn't get mad at this. She just paused a moment, regarding him, and then *laughed.*

"You know, I suppose that was my point," she said.

"And you are probably next going to ask how long I would like you to stay."

"I may have been leading up to that," she said, smiling.

"I think we should, as the saying goes, play that one by ear," said my father.

Eustacia's face lost a bit of its geniality, but her tone stayed light.

"I'll only play until I'm ready to stop," she said. "But I can be flexible, for the moment."

"Good," said my father. "Now, in terms of your lodgings, there are two options: one of the guest rooms or the pool house."

"Pool house?"

Ha! My father despised questions like "Pool house?"

"It is by the pool," he said.

"Clever place for it," said Eustacia.

Sarcasm. She dared!

"I think you will find that it is rather nicely appointed. There is a full bath and a small but functional kitchen. A daybed, a sofa, a television, a tile-top table with four chairs."

Ooh, he was selling it! Telling her, in so many words, that she was an intruder, an interloper, that she did not belong under the same roof as his family. It took everything I had to mask my satisfaction!

Then, this happened.

Eustacia said, "Not the white, tile-top table from the old sunporch?"

My father said, "Yes, but the chairs are new. You will remember how the old ones were rickety even then."

I could not have been more stunned if he'd hit me.

At this moment, my mother appeared in the doorway. I saw her before the other two did, her startled glance, her lips pressing together in disapproval. She didn't think I should be there. She thought I should've led Eustacia to my father's room and then gone to my own to do homework as I'd told her I would. Maybe I shouldn't have lied. But I knew she wouldn't understand—how could she not understand?—that someone had to stand guard.

"Well, this is nice," she said, brightly.

"Please join us," said Eustacia, standing.

As if the room belonged to her.

"No, no," said my mother. "I was just looking for Willow. Willow, I'd love to have your help with something downstairs."

At this, I froze, panic rising in my chest. Leave? Oh, but I couldn't leave! No, no, no, no. I scrambled around for a way to turn my mother down without seeming rude. I couldn't seem rude to my mother in front of Eustacia. But I would leave her alone with my father over my own dead body.

Eustacia turned her face away from my mother and, even though she gave me no more than a quick glance, I saw something come into her eyes at the sight of me, a softness I didn't understand. It was there and gone so fast I might have imagined it, as she turned back to Muddy and said, "Actually, would you mind showing me to the pool house first? It sounds like the perfect place for me to stay."

"Oh, of course!" said Muddy. She turned to my father and her eyes turned tender, as they always did when she looked at him. "Do you need anything, darling?"

My father smiled and said, "I am content, Caro. Please do show Eustacia to the pool house."

Eustacia knows she doesn't belong, I thought triumphantly. *She knows that all the stupid tile-table, sunporch memories in the world don't make her belong under our roof.*

"Nice to see you, Wilson," said Eustacia, briskly. "I'll talk to you later."

Go, I thought, *be gone!* She almost made it out the door. She was two steps away. But before she was quite gone, my father said, "Eustacia. Once you are settled in, perhaps tomorrow morning after breakfast, I would like to speak with you."

Good God. Tomorrow morning after breakfast, I would be at school.

"Oh," said Eustacia.

Her eyes flickered in my direction.

"Tomorrow morning," she said, shrugging. "Or afternoon. No need to make a formal appointment now that I'm here, right?"

"Morning," said my father, firmly. "I have something rather important to propose."

"You do?" I blurted out.

My father despised questions like "You do?" He ignored me.

"Shall we say nine thirty?" he asked Eustacia.

Say no, say no, say no, say no.

No one ever said no to Wilson Cleary; saying no to him was almost always the wrongheaded thing to do; but I knew that if anyone could, if anyone would, it would be Eustacia.

But Eustacia sighed and—*damn* her—said, "Yes."

WHAT I MISSED MOST about my old life was that there had never been dread, not true, blue, ice-in-your-chest dread. There hadn't even been much worry. Mostly, my old life was smooth as a silk, each hour, day, week slipping easily into the next.

The flip side of the old life was that there had been also almost no eagerness. Wait, I don't mean that. Sure, I'd looked forward to things: new books, field trips with my parents, summer tomatoes, running at dusk, snow. But when everything is pleasant, nothing leaps out of the darkness, flashing silver like the moon, and announces itself as extraordinary. Nothing dazzles you so much that you get short of breath wanting more of it. To employ a cliché, what I learned is that in order to have a silver lining, you need clouds, and my new life had plenty of those, clouds upon clouds upon clouds.

What my new life also had—cue the fireworks and the soaring music!—was lunch with Mr. Insley. The silverest silver lining you would ever wish for.

The story of our lunches began where such stories often begin: at rock bottom—except that, since Eustacia had yet to drop into my world like a ticking bomb, I only *thought* it was rock bottom. Still, it was bleak enough and maybe the bleakest part was the setting: the east wing stairwell of the Webley School.

As I may have mentioned, Webley was a private school, although I found that no one called it that. They called it, and schools like it, "independent," no doubt because "private" sounded too exclusive (which of course Webley was) and also somehow full of secrets (it was that, too), whereas "independent" conjured images of freedom and power. Ha ha ha groan. But despite its independent state, its high-tech, high-ceilinged classrooms, and its noble, oak-paneled, marble-floored foyer, Webley harbored, within its bowels, pockets of pure desolation, and the worst spot of all was the east wing stairwell, stuffed away behind an unmarked door in the darkest corner of the main building. A word to the wise: if you ever want to create a truly grisly, soul-killing place, choose Band-Aid beige with black freckles for its floor, paint its walls smoker's lung gray, and make it smell like cherry mouth rinse at the dentist's office. Such a place is no place to be; certainly, it is no place to sit down and *eat food,* but that is exactly what I was doing when Mr. Insley found me.

Truth: I wasn't just eating, I was shoveling forkfuls of lamb vindaloo and brown rice into my mouth as fast as I could shovel. I couldn't help it, I tell you. I was hungry! It was nearly two in the afternoon, and, as had become my habit, I'd spent lunch period in the library where eating was strictly forbidden. Most days, I could wait until after school to eat. Stick-to-your-bones breakfasts were part of our household religion, but that morning, I'd slept through my alarm clock, and my mother, after a bad night, had slept through hers. Consequently, I'd run out of the house without eating a thing. So, after finishing my history test with time to spare, I asked to go to the bathroom, tucked my lunch bag unobtrusively under my arm, and made a break for the east wing stairwell, praying hard that no one would walk in and find me.

I was nearly finished when: footsteps in the hallway, door creaking, a man saying, "Willow?"

Even though I knew, in an instant, his voice, his scuffed brown wingtips, his very pant cuffs, I didn't raise my head to look at him. How could I ever look at him again? To be caught mid-gobble, hunched like an animal over my sad thermal food container in the ugliest stairwell on the planet? Oh, I wanted to die. Instead, I did something much worse. I swallowed my food, stabbed my fork into my vindaloo, covered my face with my hands, and burst into tears.

I couldn't have blamed him if he'd turned tail and run. I hoped he would, in fact. But he sat down next to me on the step, put a firm hand on my quaking shoulder, gave it a comradely squeeze, and whispered, "Courage, Willow, courage!," which was so kind that I cried even harder. Once the waterworks began to slow, Mr. Insley said, "Skipped lunch, did you?"

I choked out, "The cafeteria—I-I can't face it."

I was right on the edge of telling all: how Bec hated me with a fiery hate and made other people hate me, how one time, when I sat down, an entire lunch table had gotten up in blank-faced unison and walked away, how those who didn't hate me felt sorry for me and how their pity stuck in my throat like a bone. But, as socially hopeless as I was, I knew enough about teenagers to know that there was nothing on God's green earth more despicable than a tattletale.

"No, of course you can't," Mr. Insley said, matter-of-factly. "What could be duller than a high school cafeteria? I find the teacher's lounge equally numbing. Which is why I eat my lunch alone at my desk. The company's better by far, if I do say so myself."

I smiled at this, wiped my face, and finally got up my nerve to look him in the eye. Mr. Insley's face was so close to mine that I could see a place on his chin he'd missed while shaving and the tiny dark blue flecks in his light blue eyes. A little shiver of alarm ran through me. At least, I thought it was alarm right then. Later, I would realize that it couldn't have been. Probably, it was just surprise; in my sheltered life, I had seen so few faces that close up. I just wasn't used to it. Anyway, two seconds later, Mr. Insley was taking his hand from my shoulder and standing up, and everything was normal.

"Listen," he said. "Not that this stairwell isn't a lovely dining spot, but should you ever decide to make a change, I'd be honored to have you eat with me in my classroom. I believe we share the same lunch period."

It was such a nice thing to offer that I almost felt like crying again, but I cleared my throat and said, jokingly, "Careful! I might just take you up on that."

His smile was so convivial that if it didn't exactly beautify that stairwell, it at least sloughed away a couple layers of hideousness, and it fell upon my upturned face like a ray of sun.

"I sincerely hope you do, Willow," he said.

And so it began. The happiness and the looking forward to the happiness and the remembering the happiness. My daily half hour of silver lining; oh, I'd fill my pockets with it, then pull it out later, at home, wind it around myself like Christmas tree lights, and just bask in the glow. We talked. For a total of two and a half hours each week, we floated high above everything petty and tiresome and mean on a magic carpet of conversation.

Mr. Insley told me about his Ph.D., how he didn't have it yet because he refused to rush through his dissertation on the Pre-Raphaelite Brotherhood; the work was just too important. He told me about the childhood summers he'd spent at his grandparents' lake house in New Jersey, how the bullfrogs' croaking was the most peaceful music on earth. He told me how to bake sourdough bread, which was a lot more interesting than you might think. He told me that he regretted never having learned to play piano, but that he felt himself to be a musician nonetheless because of how he experienced, in his very bones, the music other people played. Once, he read aloud to me a long poem called "The Blessed Damozel" about a beautiful dead woman leaning out over the edge of heaven and longing for her lover, who was still alive, to come to her. I didn't understand some of it and I thought the ending of it was too sad, but Mr. Insley's voice was thrilling—husky and low and charged with emotion. I was so moved I couldn't eat even a bite of my curried chicken salad.

I kept it all, stored it up, not just the words we said but the long lines of Mr. Insley's face; his animated eyes; his fingers pushing back his hair; the way he'd twist his wrist to make his watch slide side to side when he got excited about something. These memories fortified me in my hours of need. They took some of the scorch out of Bec's glares, made trips to the school restrooms less harrowing, helped me worry less about my father's heart. And when Eustacia came to try to upset the already shaky applecart of my life, well, they helped me then, too.

Then, the day after Eustacia arrived, something happened. Mr. Insley and I had just sat down at his desk to have lunch, he on one side, I on the other, like always, when a boy opened the door of Mr. Insley's classroom, took three steps into the room, and stopped. I recognized him from English class. Luka Bailey-Song, Bec's friend.

"Ah, Mr. Bailey-Song," said Mr. Insley. "Your revised paper, I presume."

Mr. Insley stood up and held out his hand to take the paper, but Luka didn't walk over to give it to him. He merely stood there, tall and sort of caramel colored, with his hair sticking out in all directions, and looked, not at Mr. Insley, but at me, right at me. And the strangest thing happened, which was that for a few seconds, it was like Mr. Insley wasn't there at all. Luka regarded me with the oddest expression on his face, an expression I couldn't name but that I recognized because it was so much like the one Eustacia had given me in my father's room the day before, a mix of pity and concern, and it was as though he and I were caught, like two burrs, in the fabric of something, although I couldn't say what, and if none of this makes much sense to you, well, it made even less to me.

But all I know is that I suddenly felt ashamed to be sitting there. My cheeks flushed hot, and I stood up so fast I knocked my lunch bag to the floor. That's when Mr. Insley seemed to reappear, strode over to Luka, and snatched the paper, almost violently, from his hand. Luka didn't give so much as a start of surprise at this. All that happened was that his black eyes stopped looking at me and shifted to Mr. Insley instead, and suddenly, they were the ones who were inexplicably linked, snagged like burrs, and I was the one who wasn't there anymore.

"Giving Willow a little extra help, huh?" said Luka.

One corner of Mr. Insley's mouth turned up. His eyes narrowed.

"More like enrichment I'd call it," Mr. Insley said, coolly.

Even though my cheeks still burned, I shivered.

"Would you like to join us?" I don't know why I said it. The words just tumbled out.

Never taking his eyes off Mr. Insley, Luka shrugged and said, "Maybe next time."

And he left, shutting the door behind him.

It should have been nothing. It *was* nothing. But, for no reason I could name, what it felt like was the end of my lunches with Mr. Insley, which meant it was the end of everything, all my happiness, my glittering silver lining ground to dust. Slowly, like an old woman, I bent over, picked my lunch bag up from off the floor, and pressed it hopelessly against my chest, as the world lurched sideways on its axis.

Then, beautifully, effortlessly, Mr. Insley set everything right. So much better than right! He came over, gently took the lunch bag from my hands, and started unpacking it, taking out the pieces of my lunch and setting them on his desk. My thermos, my knife and fork, my paper napkin. When he got to my apple, he rubbed it against his shirt and laughed the best laugh, a long, loose string of musical notes.

"Well played!" he said. "It was brilliant, a truly brilliant move, asking him to join us."

I had no idea why what I'd said was brilliant, and I didn't understand why my apple in his hand, against his chest should have been the most stirring, the most intimate sight I'd ever seen. What I did know was this: at that moment, Mr. Insley and I became an *us*.

He handed me the apple, shook his head, and said, "Oof! Sometimes, this place just feels so *narrow,* like such a small, confining, predictable world, don't you think?"

I didn't really. To me, school felt vast, as dense, wide, wild, and tangled as a jungle. But I said, "Yes."

"Do you ever just want to get away? Just jump in the car and drive and drive?"

"I don't know how," I said. "To drive, I mean."

"Ah," said Mr. Insley. "Well, maybe someone should teach you."

He rapped the desk with his knuckles and grinned, his face full of mischief and adventure. "Maybe even *I*."

I KNEW IT COULDN'T really happen. My father would never in a hundred million years allow it, but just the thought of Mr. Insley teaching me how to drive an actual car, the simple existence of that idea in the world, made me feel stronger, freer, more reckless, like a wild pony on the plains.

That night, full of this recklessness and wide awake, I crept out of bed and down the stairs, used the key I wore on a thin chain around my neck to open the back door's deadbolt, and walked out into the chilly autumn air. For a second, I stared up at the stars scattered like spilled salt, and then I stole across the yard like a thief toward the pool house. Its windows were squares of light; Eustacia was awake. I hadn't spent much time in the yard at night. It was different, more outdoors-like somehow, full of rustling, cold smells, bizarre shapes, and shadows. Exhilarating. Right on the edge of scary. The grass prickled under my bare feet. Something hooted. Against the pool house's pale stucco exterior, the dying sunflowers looked so much like Giacometti sculptures I'd seen at the Met, so jagged and lonesome, that I almost turned around and ran back to the house.

Buck up, old girl, I told myself, *you, even you, can walk across your own damn yard without turning chicken. And you have to see who she is, who she really is when nobody's around. Forewarned is forearmed!*

I inched, my back and palms pressed against the pool-house wall, toward the nearest window, then slowly, slowly, peered inside.

Eustacia sat on the chambray sofa, with her legs stretched out, a plate of salad balanced on her lap, a book in one hand, a fork in the other. I tried to make out what was in the salad, but couldn't quite. Bits of red and yellow. Maybe peppers. And was that goat cheese? Feta? And what about the book? Oh, why hadn't I brought binoculars? Her hair lay neatly on her shoulders, sleek mahogany brown, shiny where the light rested on it. For some reason, that hair was my undoing. I gasped, turned away, leaned hard against the wall with my eyes squeezed shut.

How do I explain? For so long, she had been almost no one, and now she was a person, a real, honest-to-goodness, detailed person, in pale blue pajama pants and a gray cardigan sweater, setting her fork carefully onto her plate, so she could turn a page. She was *right here*, with her hair and her hands doing things and her lungs breathing air and her brain reading words. It was unbearably ordinary and unbearably strange. And it sent a tremor through my entire life.

I turned back and looked again. She was moving, changing position. She put the book facedown, open, on the table, and—even in my awed, befuddled state—I felt a tiny twinge of satisfaction, since putting down a book this way was forbidden in our household (bad for the spine!). She didn't belong! No, she didn't! But then I saw the cover: *Little Women,* a battered copy that we kept in the little, motley collection of books in the pool house. I had never read that particular copy and hadn't thought about how we came to own it, but when I saw Eustacia holding it there in the pool house, I knew, in an instant, that it had been hers, something she'd forgotten when she left all those years ago.

Except now rose the possibility that she'd never really left, that pieces of her had been here all along. Maybe my father even carried some of those pieces around. No, not maybe. Even if he didn't want to, even if I didn't want him to, even if he would never admit it, he did.

I once had a life I knew everything about.

Do you ever just want to get away? Just jump in the car and drive and drive?

"Yes." I said the word out loud, gave it to the dying sunflowers and the huge sky, and then I said it all the way back across the yard: "Yes, yes, yes, yes, yes."

CHAPTER SEVEN

Taisy

JUST TO BE PETTY, I showed up six minutes late to my 9:30 A.M. conversation appointment with Wilson. Afterward, I decided to wander around the grounds of his house, which I had to admit were ravishing, and call Marcus.

He answered the phone by saying, "You're alive," and then added, "For now, I mean."

"You're leaving me three messages an hour. You're obsessed."

"No, I'm not."

"You're not bombarding me with messages or you're not obsessed?"

"Both. Neither."

I sat down on a bench next to a flame-red, breathy pouf of a tree, set my phone on speaker, made sure the coast was clear, said, "In chronological order, beginning at least two hours before I even got here," and began to read aloud Marcus's texts, some of which were spaced minutes apart, some hours, and none of which I'd bothered to reply to.

"Are you there yet?"

"How about now?"

"How about now?"

"Is he dead yet?"

"How about now?"

"How about now?"

"Now?"

"Now?"

"Now?"

"Idea: swap out nitroglycerin capsules for Ritalin."

"The Spawn will definitely have a stockpile of Ritalin."

[Link to *New York Times* article about Ritalin titled "Risky Rise of the
    Good-Grade Pill."]

"No, you're right. Adderall is much hipper!"

"Only the hippest for the nater poster!"

"Idea: Swap out nitroglycerin capsules for Adderall."

"Hold up. Does Adderall come in capsule form? Will ask long-suffering
    Jane to check."

"Long-suffering Jane says YUP!"

"Okay, okay, forget Adderall. Ecstasy?"

"Okay, okay. Viagra?"

"Viagra? No. Jeez. No. God."

"Is he dead yet?"

"Does he keep his heart in a jar on the mantel?"

"Bedside table?"

"I bet he had it bronzed."

"He had it bronzed, right?"

"I bet it's two sizes too small."

"Taize, Taize, are you there?"

"Taize, Taize, are you dead?"

"The Spawn killed you, didn't she? Damn that Spawn!"

"You're dead, right?"

"Right?"

"Don't tell me."

"You are, though. Right?"

I clicked off the speaker and put the phone back against my ear.

"Mako, you're an idiot," I said.

"Wait, I wrote that I was an idiot?" said Marcus.

I waited.

"I'm not," he said. "I'm concerned. You're in the lion's den, the belly of the beast."

"*I'm* concerned. All this texting is going to get you fired."

"Yeah, it might. If I actually had a boss."

"Remember, there's always another glorified two-bit backroom bookie out there waiting to step into your shoes."

"I can't hear you," he said. "I have a cigarette in my ear."

It was an old joke. Once, when Wilson was in Chapel Hill for a speaking engagement, I'd met him for coffee in the lobby of his hotel. Actually, it was a sneak attack. A friend of mine at the university had forwarded me an e-mail announcing his talk, I'd figured out where he was staying, and I had lain in wait until he showed up. Anyway, at some point, I'd lassoed the conversation and yanked it in the direction of Marcus. I knew Wilson would never ask about him, and while there may have been some tiny part of me that believed Wilson really did, deep down, want to know about his only son, mostly I'm afraid I wanted to throw Marcus's success in his face. Because Marcus was living the dream. Actually, it wasn't my dream, and I'm not even completely sure it was Marcus's, but it was a dreamy dream, replete with a fancy Wall Street office, model-quality girlfriends, and a steel and hardwood apartment shimmering high above the city streets.

Marcus was something called a derivatives trader, which did not, to my mild astonishment, have anything to do with calculus. Whatever the job was, he was apparently awfully good at it, and I really wanted Wilson to know that Marcus, whom he'd always deemed a hopeless failure, was awfully good at something. But when I told Wilson about Marcus's job, casually tossing in a few details about his material success, Wilson sneered and said, "Ostentatious trappings aside, do not you be fooled, Eustacia. He may not have a cigarette behind his ear or a ratty mustache, but your brother is nothing but a glorified, two-bit, backroom bookie."

When I told this to Marcus, he'd laughed and said, "Actually, that description's pretty accurate, except for the cigarette, which is always right here behind the old ear, lit."

"It's not you," I'd told Marcus, comfortingly, even though he was clearly not the one in need of comforting. "Well, okay, it is you. But it's not just you that got Wilson so riled up and alliterative. It's the filthy lucre thing. Wilson thinks making lots of money is unseemly."

The irony of this, of course, was that Wilson had made quite a lot of money himself, by inventing a process, something to do with bonding dye to DNA molecules. On the only occasion I had ever seen him acknowledge his financial success—in an interview I'd watched online—he'd talked about it the way you'd talk about a freakish and rather unpleasant accident, as though he'd just been moseying along and suddenly fallen—oh no!—into a hole full of money. According to Marcus, though, it was widely regarded as impossible for scholars affiliated with a university to personally make money from their discoveries. Such a thing could only have been accomplished through the most scrupulous record keeping, foresight, Machiavellian plotting, and legal loophole-slipping imaginable. In short, Wilson had gotten rich on purpose.

"You should see the yard I'm sitting in," I told Marcus. "You should see his house. You should see his *pool house,* for crap's sake."

"Actually, I shouldn't. Neither should you. No one should ever see Wilson or his house or his pool house. So—what does he want?"

I shifted irritably on the bench, yanked a leaf off the little tree, just out of spite. It burned, perfect and reproachful, a cochineal teardrop, on my palm.

"Why would you think he wanted something? Maybe he just wanted to see me after his near-death experience. Maybe he had a change of heart after his, um, change of heart."

"Uh-huh."

"Well, he did have a proposal for me."

"Don't do it."

"You don't even know what it is."

"You already said yes," said Marcus, with extravagant weariness. "Taisy, Taisy, Taisy."

"Wrong."

"Shut up."

"Wrong."

"Hold on. You said no? You refused Wilson Cleary? Don't move. I need to call the *New York Times*. Wait, that's what long-suffering Jane is for. Jane! Call the *New York Times*! Pronto!"

"You're hilarious. It was a business proposition, if you really want to know. I said I'd think about it."

"Oh, jeez. He wants you to write the story of his life."

It was true, or almost. Wilson's exact words had been: "Not an autobiography in the usual mode, but an adventure tale! About my intellectual journey, my scholarship, my teaching. The life story of a *mind,* if you will."

I'd ignored this and told him, "You know, it could take a while. I'd be starting from scratch, since I know exactly two facts about your childhood. Not even your childhood. I know nothing about that. I know exactly two facts about your, uh, youth, I guess."

The two facts were that he had put himself through boarding school and that while he was there, his parents had died in a car crash. I couldn't even remember how I knew; I'm sure Wilson never told me. Yet I carried these facts around with me always, not just carried them, but cherished them, coddled them and watered them like the two, rare, fragile, living things they were: proof—despite all evidence to the contrary—that Wilson was human.

"Childhood!" Wilson scoffed. "Youth! Who cares about such things? I want you to start with graduate school, of course."

"Wasn't your mind extraordinary in childhood, too?" I'd asked.

"No one is truly interesting until he is in graduate school," pronounced Wilson.

Note: I had never gone to graduate school.

After I told all this to Marcus, he said, "So that's why he invited you."

I'd had this same identical thought myself, and still, it hurt to hear Marcus say it, which is probably why I blurted out, "He could've asked anyone! Another writer, some biographer with a way bigger name than mine. But he didn't. He asked *me*."

It had to mean something that he'd asked me.

Quietly, Marcus said, "So is that the idea? A father/daughter venture? A daughter's up-close, daughterly take on her father's extraordinary mind?"

I tossed the red leaf away and pulled my sweater around me.

"He doesn't want your name on it, does he?" said Marcus.

I sighed. Might as well tell all. It had never made any sense to keep things from Marcus.

"He wants to dictate most of it. He said, 'You will be the pen!' And the researcher, too, I guess. He has a long list of former colleagues, students, scientists I need to contact. For quotes. About his *mind*."

"The *pen*? You need to tell him to go to hell. You know that, right?"

To my credit, I did not bleat, "But, still, he asked meeee!," even though I wanted to.

I let the impulse pass and changed the subject. "She's pretty, you know. Intriguing, even. I mean, she's about ten feet tall, has this cloud of cayenne pepper hair, dresses like an adult, talks like Wilson, God help her, and hates my guts. Seriously, she spits venom at me with her eyes, but there's something about her that sort of tugs at my heart. The poor girl is probably getting eaten alive in high school, for one thing."

Marcus didn't say anything for a long time, even though I knew he was still there, so I sat, closed my eyes, and just *smelled* Wilson's yard.

It smelled dark brown and rooty, tangy as the inside of a pumpkin, wistful, just exactly the way fall is supposed to smell.

"Taize. You are . . . ," began Marcus.

"I know what you're going to say," I jumped in. "An idiot. A push-over. A doormat. A sap."

"Nice," said my brother. "I was going to say nice."

I DROVE TO OUR old house. I hadn't wanted to go there. Or, to put it more accurately, I hadn't wanted to want to. The day before I'd left home for Wilson's, I'd sworn up and down to Trillium that wild horses couldn't drag me anywhere near the place.

"Even if you set aside the fact that last time I was there, I prac-tically got run out on a rail," I'd told her, "it just plain wasn't mine anymore. If those walls could've talked, well, they wouldn't have had a thing to say to me."

"Don't be crazy," said Trillium. "Of course, you'll go! That house is your childhood; the inside of your head looks like that house, am I right? Furniture, rugs, light fixtures, even the damn doormat."

"No."

"Okay. I'll say a word, you tell me what you picture."

"You're making a big deal out of this, and it's not one."

"Kitchen."

I didn't answer.

"You flashed to the kitchen in that house, am I right? The white tile backsplash, the little knobs on the cabinets, the yellow curtains in the window, and how the coffeemaker sat in the corner by the toaster."

"Pale green tile and no curtains, just the big casement window over the sink, eight panes of glass in each window," I said, "and a jade plant in a cobalt pot with a matching saucer on the sill. I mean, maybe it wasn't the same jade plant all those years, but it seemed like it."

"See?"

"So?"

"So reclaim it, baby."

"I don't need it," I told her. "I've made other places home since then."

"I know you have, but all of us need all the homes we can get. Trust me on this. Go!"

Yes, all right, I went, but up until I was actually almost there, I was really only driving to drive. It was something I did quite a lot back home, just getting in the car and going. It wasn't mindless driving, exactly. I obeyed the speed limits, more or less, stayed on my side of the yellow line. I even made deliberate choices about where I was going, but they were choices guided by an instinctiveness that possibly verged on paranoid delusion: turning left because of the oak tree that looked like a gnarled human hand, or right because the street was called Candelaria, or keeping to the road I was on because it was bordered for miles by a forsythia hedge so riotously. yellow, so unreasonably dense that I wanted to climb right in and live there.

Five miles west of Wilson's house, the roads shrank and the trees got bigger, fields spread wide and shone like lakes in the sun, and old stone houses cropped up everywhere, each accompanied by a second stone house, a quirky, peaked-roof structure, tiny as a gnome den. That I knew they were springhouses didn't make them any less wonderful. I could have driven for hours more, but it was just after the second covered bridge, boards thundering under my tires, that I began to feel pulled, as though my car weren't driving forward but were simply tethered to the long line of road and were being reeled inexorably into the past.

Even so, I didn't drive straight to our old house. Instead, I took a few turns around our neighborhood. A century ago, the place had been a fairgrounds, and what had been the oval horse racing track was now an oval-shaped loop of street. As the neighborhood grew— because it was the kind of neighborhood that had come into being over time, not the kind that springs up in a single year—the loop became crisscrossed with other, littler streets, including Linvilla Road, the one we used to live on.

I made the loop three times. The first time, I just let myself relax into the rhythm of the place, its colors and quiet and small movements: squirrels, birds, a man painting shutters, a woman walking beside a kid on a tricycle.

By the second loop, the neighborhood's familiar prettiness started to emerge: the stalwart lampposts; the trees lining the streets, their fallen leaves a brilliant litter on the black asphalt; the mishmash of stone and brick houses—Tudor cottages, Georgians with their chimneys sticking up like ears, even a sly touch of Gothic here and there— each house slate-roofed, sturdy, and snug among its thinning stands of autumn flowers on its swatch of lawn.

It was at the beginning of the third loop that the past swept in like a tide. There was my friend Abigail's screen porch where we used to look at magazines and eat chips until we were sick. There was the Baxters' big side yard, site of the World's Greatest Secret Bike Ramp that Marcus and his friend Porter would put up during the day when the Baxters and their neighbors were at work and take down before they got home and that stopped being both secret and a bike ramp after one wild Thursday in July when the casualties included two broken collarbones (one of them Marcus's) and a concussion. There was the tree-swing tree, the lemonade stand corner. There was the cul-de-sac where we'd have the Memorial Day block party, with the entire neighborhood, kids and adults, eventually being together in the dark because everyone had summer zinging through their veins and didn't want to go home.

I remembered the girl who had walked home down these side- walks countless summer evenings, the world, the whole of the world, effervescent with fireflies, raucous with cicada song, threaded through with the clean scent of honeysuckle; porch lights and kitchen lights and streetlights blooming on around her; every house familiar and strange in the deepening blue-gray dark; and I knew that I was still that girl. Nothing here needed reclaiming because it had never stopped being mine. Then, I turned down Linvilla and parked in front of my house.

I got out and walked around. At first, I was amazed at how much the same it looked: same white trim and black shutters, same stacked stone retaining walls around the flowerbeds; same clematis vine, now flowerless of course, over the arbor entrance to the backyard, same brass mailbox fixed to the bricks next to the front door. But after a few minutes, small changes began to jump out at me. Marcus's basketball hoop above the garage door was gone. So were the redwood picnic table and the blue scallop shell birdbath. The pineapple door knocker was still there, but the door was painted red instead of black, and the weeping Japanese maple Marcus and I had planted for our mother one Mother's Day still wept under its freight of crimson laciness, but it had gone from tiny and Bonsai-like, to tall and sculptural. How could that have happened? As I looked at the maple, the finely cut leaves blurred on the black boughs, and I was crying.

Look, I'm not saying I had a perfect childhood. There was Marcus, who started sneaking out of the house when we were thirteen to drive around in cars with older kids or to hang out on the rocky banks of the Brandywine River, leaving me to lie awake, imagining the awful ways he might get hurt or killed, until he sneaked back in just before dawn. There was my mother, funny, creative, demanding in a good way, her love the sky we lived under, but failing again and again to stand up to Wilson nearly enough.

And of course, there was Wilson. My father had haunted the peripheries of my life in this house, never remembering the names of my friends, never attending a single Memorial Day block party. Maybe he'd sat with us at the redwood picnic table in the backyard and eaten buttered corn, thick slabs of salted tomato, and barbecued chicken, but I couldn't remember a single time. On the occasions when his indifference to or his disdain for us pierced through the fabric of our daily lives, it stung me. His bouts of plain meanness broke my heart. But the upside to having a not-very-nice father who mostly wasn't around was that, well, he mostly wasn't around. If there was always a part of me—a hidden, broken part—yearning for him, most of me went about my days like any kid: my life was pure immediacy, was whatever was right there in front of me. And most of what had been in front of me was good.

But good or bad, it had been mine. No, not "had been." Was. Still was. Is.

The color of a door, the shape of a tree, these things mattered. I had carried them around with me for decades. Even now that they were gone, changed beyond recognition, they were still with me—still *were* me—just the way they had always been.

Oh, Wilson, even you must have a door, a tree of your own.

Wilson wanted me to begin his book with his graduate school years, but how could you write the story of a person's life without including his childhood? You couldn't, plain and simple. I got back into my car, sat there, and decided: a good, truly professional ghostwriter seeks out the story her client wants told and tells it, but when it came to Wilson, I would look for the story *I* needed to hear. If Wilson hated me for it, and he probably would, so be it. But maybe—even though I wasn't doing it for this reason and even though I knew it wouldn't make him hate me any less—maybe it would turn out that Wilson needed to hear that story, too.

CHAPTER EIGHT

Willow

THE TIME I GOT lost at the science museum used to be just an ordinary memory, one thing that happened. It wasn't even especially good or even that much of a memory, since I'd hardly thought about the incident since it happened. I wished it could have stayed that way, insignificant, lost in the clutter of everything else, but after my father's second conversation with Eustacia, which was really their third, since their second took place while I was at school, the memory stirred, shook itself loose, and demanded that I take its full measure.

I was six, I think. I suspect that people who grow up going to actual school have a better sense of how old they were when things happened because there are just more markers, the start of middle school, the summer after fifth grade, and so forth. I led mainly a markerless existence, but I'm nearly positive that I had just turned six. It was winter, January maybe; I remember being hot inside my new red duffel coat with the fur-edged hood, hot in that rosy-cheeked, hair-stuck-to-your-forehead, baked bread way that you get in winter when you're six. My father had advised me to leave the coat at the museum's coat check, but I had loved it too much to part with it, so I spent the day wearing the coat open and half off my shoulders, the toggles dangling.

At this museum, they have a giant heart, plastic or metal or something, two stories high, and you can walk through it, if you're willing to wait in line on a crowded day. The day we went, it was very crowded, and my father refused to wait, not just because the line was long, but because he thought the heart wasn't educational enough to make the wait worth it. He said, "It is little more than a playground toy, child," which was possibly true, but all I knew is that I desperately wanted inside it.

I didn't beg or cry. At six, it was already abundantly clear to me that begging and crying, while often successful means of getting my way with Muddy, would get pointedly ignored by my father. I didn't plan to do anything at all except walk away in bitter disappointment, but then my father had me sit on a bench while he went to make a phone call, and the pull of the heart was irresistible. I didn't mean to actually leave. I only thought to slip off the metal bench and go snag a quick look at the thing in all its dark-pink and violet magnificence, and then slip back on before my father even knew I was gone.

But as soon as I saw the heart, I forgot everything else. What were biplanes dangling from the ceiling or stuffed animals glaring from their shadowbox worlds of trees and rocks compared to a great heart beating like the life force it was right there in the center of everything? I got in line.

The boy in front of me yelled, "We're blood! We're disgusting red blood!"

I tugged his sleeve and shook my head. "No, we haven't gone through the lungs yet. We're blue, not red."

"Shut up, stupid," said the boy.

He touched one of my toggles, his eyes widening.

"They look like animal teeth," he whispered.

"They are animal teeth," I told him.

He turned around, chastened. But as soon as we were inside, the boy might as well have become invisible; that's how wondrously alone I felt inside the heart. With the swoosh of blood reverberating around me, I explored the ventricles, the atria, the pumping lungs, climbed stairs to the aorta, running my palms along the heart's mottled walls. When I went back a few years later, I was stunned to discover that the heart didn't actually move. That day, I could've sworn the walls heaved with a muscular clench and release, propelling me onward. The boy was right: we were the blood, and it was *thrilling*.

I allowed myself just four trips through, four because of the four chambers of the heart, because I didn't want to dilute the magic by too much repetition. I should have gone back to the bench, then, but, under the spell of the heart, I forgot. I made my way around the rest of the museum, consulting the map in my pocket, touching what there was to touch, and reading the informative signs, just as my father would've wanted. In the weather room, as I was watching a video about tornadoes, a man approached me and asked if I were alone, and I gave him a superior stare and said, "How could I be here by myself? I'm six. I'm with my father," and the man smiled, said, "Got it!," and went away.

After maybe an hour had gone by, I was standing next to another girl and learning about gravity when a woman, presumably the girl's mother, rushed up and grabbed her by the arm.

"Lucy! Where in the hell have you been? I was just about to get the guards to look for you!" Lucy's mother was red-faced, almost crying, and it suddenly hit me, as I stood there watching that woman, that my father could be worried, too. I had just started getting scared, looking around me, fiddling anxiously with my coat toggles, when he appeared from behind a pillar.

I didn't throw my arms around him, even though I thought about it, just took his hand and said, "I'm sorry I got lost."

"You?" said my father. "Why you were never lost for a second. I have been following you all the while, watching for what you would do, and I must say that, apart from playing in that blasted giant heart, you made excellent use of your time."

"Thank you, Daddy," I said.

"Let us get a refreshment and hear what you have learned in your wanderings, my little adventuress," he said and took me to the snack bar for a chocolate milk.

And that was all. Nothing much. One field trip among many, except for the chocolate milk, which was not a typical beverage for me, and which tasted like true, blue, bona fide heaven.

But some ten years later, when I had the occasion to recall this day, I realized that it was remarkable, even, to use a drastically overused—especially by my schoolmates—word, amazing. Because until I saw that mother take her daughter by the arm, it hadn't occurred to me to be afraid. I didn't even feel a twinge of guilt until later that night and then only because of how much I had enjoyed the giant heart, despite its glaring lack of educational value.

Here's the thing: even though I didn't know he was there all the time, trailing me, I *knew*. I felt *with* him, watched over, safe, not a bit lost, and, moreover, he knew that I would feel that way. Because that's the way things had always been, every day. So there you have it: the trip was a metaphor for my life, although for all those years, I wouldn't have thought to say that or even to think it because when things just are the way they are, you don't see the metaphor, you merely live it.

Until one day, you don't.

He called her "my daughter." And if I thought I'd been feeling alone at school, well, it was nothing compared to what I felt when I heard him say those words. I stood on the vast plain of my loneliness, the wind pouring across it, flattening the grass, chilling me to the bone. Scratch that. Too melodramatic. But it was almost that bad.

They were talking about the book. At first, I was gleeful to know about the book, since it made Eustacia into little more than a means to an end, the hired help, and solved the mystery of why he'd ever invited her into our home in the first place. The wretched woman was even taking notes in a yellow legal pad, for heaven's sake, a delightful sight. My whole family was there to see it, although I suspect that my mother, who was bustling around serving iced tea and arranging fresh flowers on my father's nightstand, was really there to keep an eye on me. Not that she was on Eustacia's side! Perish the thought. But I knew she feared I might slip and be rude, and my mother, when she stops to think about such things as manners, has an acute allergy to rudeness.

"Now, tell me again, where did you go to boarding school? I seem to have forgotten," said Eustacia, looking up from her pad. Her eyebrows gave her a look of mischief because they were dark and slightly jagged, like seagull wings, and so symmetrical that I wondered if she penciled them, though, to be honest, despite her sordid past, she didn't seem like the type.

Her question was a ploy, of course, pure nosiness, since I'm sure he had never shared such information with her in the first place. If I didn't know where he had gone to boarding school, how could she? My father, naturally, wasn't fooled for a second, nor did he seem to be at all beguiled by the brows. He dismissed her question with a flick of his hand.

"I could have learned as much anywhere as I did there, such was my intellect and determination. I do not intend to give the place credit for my achievements with some cheap form of—what do you call it— product placement!"

Eustacia shrugged and said, "Okey-doke," knowing full well, as she did so, that my father hated both shrugging and stupid, baby-talk phrases like "okey-doke." Good God: okey-doke! In my father's room!

"I had my lawyer draw up a document," said my father, and then, to my mother, "Caro, if you would be so kind."

My mother took the manila envelope off the little writing desk near the window, unclasped the metal clasp on the envelope, and handed it to him. Before he could ask, she had retrieved his reading glasses from his bedside table and placed them in his outstretched hand.

"Thank you," he said, slipping on the round, black-rimmed glasses. He looked wonderful in them, like Winston Churchill, but leaner and with more hair. He slid the creamy pages from the envelope and surveyed them.

"This document will vouchsafe your access to whatever documents we may need for our research, Eustacia," he said. "University files and so forth. You will want my teaching schedules, my student rosters, whatever papers of mine that might be on display or in archives. Photographs, possibly. Whatever I should deem necessary as our process unfolds."

He handed her the papers and took out another one. From where I sat at the head of his bed, I could see it was a personal letter, typed, with his signature, a bit shakier looking than usual, but commanding nonetheless, in black ink.

"As for obtaining interviews with my former students and colleagues, or, I daresay anyone at all, I believe this letter will smooth your way, open all doors. In it, I explain our project."

Every "our" felt like a tiny barb to my soul. However, I understood that in order to encourage Eustacia to do her best, my father had to make her at least feel like she was part of it all. What came next, though . . .

He began to read from the page, and, oh, how the man could charm with language! His heartiness, his wit, his *largeness*, all of it was there. Here was a person who should be writing his own book, all by himself. Oh, if only he had the stamina. Damn that heart attack, anyway!

But then he got to this part: " 'I give you absolute leave and, indeed, entreat you to offer up your time and thoughts regarding my intellectual journey to my daughter, Eustacia Cleary, whom I assure you is most trustworthy,' " and—*schwomp*—a mudslide of sadness engulfed me. Reflexively, I grabbed the edge of the bed, and the document and the manila envelope, which had been lying on my father's lap, slid onto the floor, which was ghastly, of course, but worse than that, my father broke off midsentence and pressed a hand to his heart, to his *heart*.

"Willow! You gave me quite a start. I had nearly forgotten you were there. Are you all right?"

Cheeks and eyes burning, I leaned over to pick up the papers, and murmured, "Sorry, Daddy."

"If you are bored, there is no need for you to stay," said my father, coolly.

But I did stay and endured every last word of their conversation, and it was later that night, while I lay awake in bed, that I unpacked the day at the science museum, laid out all the pieces and saw them with new eyes, especially my father's smile when he found me, his Willow, his girl who had always been safe and never been lost, until now.

THE NEXT MORNING, I understood for the first time that the nightmarish thing about school was also the best thing about school: morning came and you had to go. No matter what, no matter how dark your dark night of the soul, there it was before you, inescapable and regular as the tide, pulling you out into the world, bathed, dressed, hair tied up in a knot, backpack strapped on for dear life.

I wore my new Patagonia down jacket, light as a feather and spring-leaf green, even though the weather was a little too warm for it. It was the first significant clothing purchase I had made as a school-going person, and I had bought it specifically because I had seen girls at school wear similar jackets. Bec Lansing had one in winter white, for example, and even her blistering hatred of me could not dim the fact that she looked marvelous in it. Never fear! I had too much dignity to slavishly follow every Webley School trend, but I wasn't stupid either. All societies have their totems, their rituals, their idioms, their costumes. I began to see that, for reasons too complex for me to bother to parse out, some were off-limits to me. I could wear slim dark jeans and scarves but not Ugg boots, Converse sneakers, or dangly earrings. I would sound like an idiot saying "Whassup?" or greeting my friends with a jovial "Hey, bitches" (and not only because I had no friends), but I could say "Hey" instead of "Good morning." And I could wear a damn jacket. Anyway, I liked it, and green was my color. When your father, who has almost died (and that was ever hanging over me, his almost-death) and who has thrown you to the wolves without a second thought, starts calling another person "my daughter," you wear your favorite color to school; you just do.

Thus armored, I made for Mr. Insley's classroom.

School was still awkward, lonely, and bleak, but there was something peculiarly reassuring about this. At least, it was consistent, which is far more than I could say for my home life. And I suppose it wasn't quite as bad as it had been. My friendless state persisted, naturally, both because of the power of Bec but also, if I'm honest, because I just didn't try very hard, but a few people acknowledged me in the hallways, now. A few even said my name. It's astonishing how agreeable that can feel, being in a crowd of people and hearing your name. The first time it happened, I was so touched that I fled to a restroom stall and fought back tears. Being acknowledged, singled out, named, these things made a difference. And of course, thank the high heavens, every day at school, there was Mr. Insley, who made the biggest difference of all.

Today, when I walked into English, he must have sensed my dejection because he gave me a private smile and whispered, "Courage!" There's something about that word; it pulls your shoulders back, makes your blood quicken in your veins! I found my seat, whipped out my notebook, sat tall, pencil in hand, ready. But then Mr. Insley gave us our *Middlemarch* project assignment, and all my bravery fell to ruin.

It wasn't the project itself, which was of the interesting and open-ended variety I liked best. We were asked to choose a scene or scenes from *Middlemarch* that we saw as iconic, as saying something big and overarching about the book, its time period, or some other time period, or as saying something—some universal truth—about our own lives. Then, we were told to rework the scene, twist it, turn it into another form of art: a video, a scene from a play, a collage, an aria, a piece of musical theater, a rap (I knew what a rap was, never you worry), or anything that struck us as the right form for our ideas. As soon as I heard this list, I predicted, silently, that a good third of the class would choose collage because it was so easy. (I could hear my father intone, "No thing is easy if it is done well," which is absolutely true.) And that not a single soul in that room (myself included) would compose and sing an aria. Accompanying or following the piece of art would be an oral presentation, explaining the meaning of the thing to the class, just in case they didn't get it.

No, it was a good assignment. Perhaps it was a testament to my extreme nerdiness, a trait the existence of which I'd only recently become aware both in the world and in myself, that even before Mr. Insley had finished explaining the assignment and passing around the handout, I was mentally shuffling through scenes in the book, my excitement mounting with every new thought. Because what a book it was! So many plots, each spinning like a plate on the tip of a stick. So many characters, breathtakingly complicated and alive, and all so entangled with one another! And then there was the big, outside world—history, politics, social class, gender roles—surrounding it all like a thick troposphere and permeating even the slightest look, gesture, or touch between people, even the briefest conversation.

I was so busy with the mental scene shuffling that I almost missed what Mr. Insley said next, but one word came whizzing toward me like a stone: group. Oh, in the name of all that is holy: *group*! Group work, hell of the blackest, grimmest kind. The arguing, the everlasting shifting of blame and responsibility, the shirking, and false credit taking, and *time wasting*. It's true that my knowledge of group work derived from exactly two experiences: a world religions project with my homeschooling group (I'd done all the research and writing, while Mary Beth Coe had sung hymns; whirled, allegedly, like a dervish; served a bowl of *charoset* minus the nuts because of allergies and minus the wine because alcohol was for sinners, and read an excerpt from *The Tao of Pooh*); and an experiment that involved testing an unknown sample for the presence of bismuth with my two lab partners in AP chemistry.

But even if there were some alternate universe in which it were possible for students to work in harmony, each ably, cheerfully shouldering his or her part of the load, there would still remain the most hellish part of the hell of group work: choosing the groups. Or, more accurately, being chosen. Or, most accurately, *not* being chosen. After living almost my entire life in a state of perpetual chosenness, my knowledge of this derived only from the AP chem class, but it was knowledge, stone-cold, irrefutable, all the same.

By the time I had descended upon the Webley School, lab partners had already been assigned, so I was in the ignominious position of having to play third wheel to an existing group. The teacher, Mrs. Harbottle, stood me up in the front of the room, like a cow at auction, and asked for a group to volunteer to take me on. Suffice it to say, there were no bidders. Finally, when my face felt hot enough to burst into flames, Mrs. Harbottle sighed and said, "Amanda Simon, Joe Cho, make room for a third at your table."

I would have supposed Mr. Insley to be too sensitive to even assign group work, much less to leave the group-making up to the students, but, after explaining the assignment, he made some vague chopping motions with his hand, said, "No more than three to a group. Divide yourselves!," and sat.

Then, a kind of miracle happened. Before my body could go completely rigid, before my face could fully make the shift from hot to blazing, someone sitting behind me was tapping me on the shoulder and saying, "Hey, Willow, want to work with me?"

It couldn't have been who it seemed to be, Luka Bailey-Song, tall, golden-brown, spiky-haired Luka with his long dark eyes, his high, teardrop-shaped cheekbones smooth as sand dunes. Luka who glided, wide shoulders like a sail, down the very center of the hallways, greeted by everyone, his hands slapped, his fists bumped, his name said over and over and over. Luka whom I was sure despised me, especially after he'd caught me—no, not caught, why would I say caught?—*seen* me spending lunch break in Mr. Insley's room. Bec's Luka.

But when I turned around, that's exactly who it was. And maybe he only wanted me because I was smart, although he was obviously really smart himself, despite all his efforts to make it not obvious. Or maybe it would turn out to be a trick, a mean joke between him and Bec, but right then, as I turned to face him and he gave me a friendly half smile, what it felt like was an entirely good, unexpected thing. A boon. A gift.

I said yes. Actually, I eked out a squeaky "Sure," and I didn't regret it. Not even when I saw Bec's face, stunned and disgusted and, as they say, royally pissed, a phrase that made particular sense when applied to Bec, since everything she did was royal. She didn't matter. Nothing else mattered except that I'd been picked. I was not dangling like a broken kite from a branch. I sat in my chair and thanked the gods on their mountaintop, the fish of the sea and the birds of the air, thanked every blessed thing under the sun for Luka Bailey-Song.

It wasn't until I saw Mr. Insley, his look of—what was it? Disappointment? Betrayal?—and remembered the open dislike he'd shown Luka that day at lunch, that I felt a pang of regret. And still when Luka stopped me on my way out of class to get my phone number and give me his, so that we could "you know, make a plan," it didn't even matter that I had to give him my home number, which was my only number, nor that he had to scribble his down on the back of my notebook, since I had no cell phone in which to save it. Chosenness bubbled and fizzed and filled me like a vessel once again. I smiled all the way to my locker and beyond.

At lunchtime, when I arrived at Mr. Insley's door, he didn't get up from his desk. He gave me a fleeting, sideways glance and said, "Sorry, Willow, I'm skipping lunch today, too much grading."

His voice was cold, impersonal. I stood, shocked. When the shock began to be replaced by panic, I stammered out, "Oh, I'm—I'm sorry."

Mr. Insley slowly raised his eyes from the paper he was reading and regarded me as if across an immense distance.

"Why?" he asked, with his eyebrows raised high on his John Keats brow.

"I-I don't know," I said, and I felt so confused, because truly I was sorry and truly I did not know why.

"I see," he said, drily. He went back to his work, leaving me feeling like I'd failed, mightily. I wasn't sure what I had been tested on; but I knew in my bones that I had just gotten a great, big, red "F."

I turned and left, and just as I was closing the door behind me, I suddenly had the thought, *Everything is slipping away from me.* It was like slamming into a wall. Shaken, I rushed back into the classroom.

"Mr. Insley?" I said, my voice quavering.

He raised his head. There was a pink patch on his left cheek from where he'd been leaning it, heavily, against his palm. Somehow, this strengthened my resolve.

"Yes?"

"I have decided that I would like you to teach me how to drive," I said, lifting my chin and trying to look spunky. "If the offer still stands, that is."

His face thawed, all the edges softening; his smile arrived bit by bit, like a sunrise.

"That's my girl!" he said.

THAT NIGHT, I SPIED on Eustacia again. I hardly knew myself, that's how fearless I felt as I made my way stealthily across the lawn. Before I got to the pool house, a sound cut across the night, her laugh, which was no tinkling affair, as I might have expected from such a person, but a rich, bronzy ringing. She was sitting in the rocker on the pool-house porch. I dropped into a crouch behind a bush not ten feet away from where she sat. Slowing my breathing, I tried to become one with the bush, with the night sounds, and the enfolding darkness.

"No, Mom," she said, presumably into her cell phone. "I haven't seen him. Not in the flesh, anyway. Possibly just to torture myself, I brought a shoebox of old photos from high school. Let me tell you, there's been some pretty heavy-duty nostalgia going on here in the pool house."

The laugh again. I felt a twinge of something akin to envy. Just akin, mind you, since I was constitutionally unable to covet anything Eustacia had. But her tone when she spoke to her mother; it was just so easy, so *chummy.* And who, oh who, was this "him"? The teenage pregnancy billboard flashed into my mind. Surely, even the most pathetic person in the world would not carry around a box of pictures of the cad who had brought such shame down upon her.

"Yeah, it's true," Eustacia went on, with a sigh. "He was one beautiful kid. Okay, stop. Stop! It was forever ago. Hey, I have more willpower than you think, lady. How's this: if I should happen to run into him, you'll be the first to know. Yes, even before Mako and Trill. I swear it."

Who were Mako and Trill? Rely on Eustacia to have acquaintances with stupid names. But there was such fondness in her voice for the "beautiful kid" that I got butterflies in my stomach and pressed my hands to the space below my ribs to make the soft wing beats stop.

"Okay, I'll talk to you later. But, hey, one more thing. Do you remember the name of Wilson's boarding school?"

I balled my hands into fists. The nerve! The gall!

"Yeah, I don't think I ever knew it, either. It's a little odd, isn't it? How much we don't know about him? And what's even odder that it never seemed odd to us, did it? I mean, I know everything about you. Oh yes, I do! Ha ha. Anyway, I asked him yesterday, about the school, but he wouldn't tell me. Oh, well. 'Night, Mama. I love you, too."

"You don't know him at all," I whispered, triumphantly, into the bush. "And you never will. Never, ever."

THE NEXT EVENING, AFTER I finished my homework, I told my mother that I was going for a long run.

My beloved Muddy smiled her soft smile and kissed my forehead.

"Well, I think that's a grand idea, darling," she said. "It'll do you good."

I thought about Eustacia on the phone with her mother, and I wondered what it would be like, talking like that, so relaxed and open. Maybe I would try it, one of these days, but not this day.

"I might even miss dinner," I told her.

"No worries. I'll keep something warm for you. Just keep to the lighted paths and the neighborhoods, the way you always do."

"I will."

I ran to the appointed spot, the parking lot of the nearby state park. By the time I got there, it was already growing dark, but I could see Mr. Insley's car. For a second, I stopped in my tracks and cast a single look over my shoulder in the direction of home, balanced between what lay behind and what lay ahead. Then, I filled my lungs with night air and ran toward the car.

CHAPTER NINE

Taisy

ONE MORNING, I WOKE up and walked outside to find a portable ballet barre standing on the patch of grass in front of the pool house, and for a few sleepy seconds, it felt like a miracle, like I'd wished the thing into being. I'd been at Wilson's house for a little more than a week and despite daily moments of prickly, occasionally excruciating, awkwardness, I was settling in. I liked being back in my hometown, and the pool house was tiny, light filled, and sitting smack in the center of autumn gorgeousness and pearly, bird-song-inflected quiet. But I missed ballet. I'd gone on some power walks (I am allergic to running), and had taken a complimentary yoga class at a studio a few miles away, but the fact was that, after so many years of dance, I carried ballet around in my body—arabesques, développés, and pirouettes residing deep and restlessly inside every muscle, bone, and tendon—and I needed to let it loose on a regular basis in order to feel normal.

I set my coffee mug down on the porch and slid my hand along the smooth barre. It was a little low for me, but I could adjust it later. Facing it, I did a few pliés and relevés in first and second position, and even in my pajamas with grass tickling my feet, it felt lovely.

"I bought it for Willow years ago, but she never really used it."

I whirled around, startled. Caro stood there smiling in sage-green pajamas, her hair wrestled into a wild ponytail on top of her head. She cradled her own mug of coffee between her long-fingered hands. I noticed that her bare, moon-pale skin was remarkably unlined, but that her eyes looked exhausted and there was weariness in the slope of her shoulders. She resembled the tall sunflowers that drooped against the pool-house wall behind her, and it occurred to me to wonder if Caro might be unwell. I hoped not. The woman had to stay healthy, if for no other reason than that Willow needed one parent around who wasn't bedridden and wasn't Wilson.

"Thank you, but—you lugged it all the way over here?" I asked, eyeing her thin frame.

Caro laughed. "I'm stronger than I look, but also I took it apart, brought the pieces over, and then reassembled it. It was quite easy, actually."

"And very nice of you," I said.

She waved this off, and said, "I know the pool house is small, but if you move some things around, there's room for barre work, I think. We've got some CDs you can use, too, if you want."

"Thank you. Did you dance?"

She gave a sheepish chuckle.

"My mother signed me up, but I was uncoordinated and much too dreamy. I'm pretty sure I got kicked out, although no one ever actually told me that. All I know is I was six when I started and six when I stopped."

"So it was a short-lived career," I said, smiling. "Obviously, you had other talents."

"I guess," she said.

"Thank you for the barre. I keep thinking I'll look for a class to take, but I never seem to do it. If I don't dance, I get antsy."

"I knew you would be feeling that way," she said.

She said this so simply and assuredly and didn't follow up with any sort of explanation, as though it were just a natural thing to understand something as personal as this about your husband's estranged daughter, a woman you'd barely met and hadn't set eyes on in years. Years ago, my mother had settled on the word *dotty* to describe Caro, mostly in order to displace the myriad, far meaner adjectives Marcus had employed, but I'd been noticing since I got to Wilson's, how there were moments when the fluttery distraction and tremulousness blew away like smoke to reveal charm and an almost uncanny perceptiveness. It was a long leap from "dotty" to a word like *intuitive,* but in Caro's case, it seemed a natural one, although as she reminded me just a few seconds later, if you could leap from one to the other, you could also leap back. Right after her insight about the ballet barre, Caro launched herself, landed, froglike, on "dotty," and sat there, blinking at me with her colossal green eyes.

"You know what, I've got some breakfast stuff over there," she said, gesturing extravagantly with her mug. The coffee sloshed over the side and onto her hand, but she didn't seem to notice, which I hoped meant that it wasn't hot. A woman who could fail to realize she was being scalded was probably not someone who should be employing a glass-blowing torch on a daily basis. She waved her free hand. "Outside the house, on the, um, table."

Even though the house wasn't visible from where I stood, just to be a good sport, I cast a look in its general direction.

"Oh," I said. "Well, don't let me keep you. Thanks for the barre. I really appreciate it."

She blushed and laid a hand against her throat.

"I meant to ask if you would like to join me. Sorry, I forgot to say that part. I get flustered when I invite people to do things they might not want to do."

Maybe because I'm a sucker for candor and self-deprecation or maybe because I was actually starting to like this person who had ignited the combustion of my family all those years ago, I said, "But I do want to."

Caro beamed.

"Good! There's apple coffee cake that, thankfully, I didn't make myself."

As we made our way to the flagstone patio behind the house, I caught a glimpse of a building I hadn't noticed before, tucked into a copse of silver birches in a far corner of the garden, a weathered brown, barnlike structure, the linear birch trunks glowing white against it. I stopped and pointed.

"Is that your studio?" I asked.

"Yes," said Caro. She spun around, her eyes lit with hopefulness, and stood there for a few seconds, breathing. I could see the effort on her face, which I assumed meant she was beating back fluster and dottiness, and it must have worked because when she extended the invitation, her voice was steady. "Would you—like to see it?"

"I'd love to."

Her smile was so openly delighted, and I was touched at how much this place meant to her, how glad she was to share it with someone. She took my hand, and for an alarmed moment, I thought she was going to hold it and lead me through the trees like something out of a fairy tale, but she just gave it a quick squeeze and let it go. I watched her striding, slender, pale, and birchlike, through the birches, anticipation and energy suffusing every step, and it occurred to me that I had no idea what it was like to really be an artist, to have making things sit in the very center of your world. But when we got to the door of the studio, it was locked, and all the energy vanished. Caro leaned her back against the door.

"I guess Willow forgot to unlock it before she went to school," she murmured.

"Don't you have the key?"

She turned her face away.

"No. Wilson used to, but now Willow does."

This wasn't an explanation (what grown woman doesn't have a key to her own studio?), but I said, "I see," and because she was just standing there, looking so wilted and downcast, I gave her a light punch on the shoulder and said, "Race you to the patio!"

Caro gave me a startled glance, said, "Aw, no thanks, Eustacia," in the same defeated voice, dropped her mug into the grass, and took off like a shot. The woman was faster than I ever would've suspected and had the advantage of not being barefoot, but I made a pretty good push there at the end, and we hit the edge of the patio in what I swear was a photo finish.

The coffee cake was thick with apple chunks and so buttery it was damp. There was milk instead of cream for the coffee, which is what I like. The orange juice was fresh and made me think of Trillium the way everything to do with oranges always does. As Caro and I sat eating, sunlight sluiced the yard; the sky went aquamarine; the trees and bushes kindled against it; and there was just no way on earth not to be filled with a sense of expansiveness and well-being.

Which is maybe why when Caro asked me if I'd seen any of my old friends since I'd arrived in town, I said, "No, but I'm thinking of looking up Ben Ransom."

There were a host of excellent, rock-solid reasons for me not to have said this, ever, to Caro. For one thing, the topic of Ben Ransom was my hallowed ground, not to be trod casually with a near stranger. For another, the story of our breakup—and Caro's husband's heartless role in it—was still, after all these years, tender as a new bruise. And for a third, I was sure that Caro had heard some version of the Ben part of my life that was so Wilson-twisted as to be horribly unflattering to me and, what was much more important, to Ben. But somehow right then, none of that mattered. I said his name, released it into the air of the yard, and it felt so lovely to have it there, hovering in the bright sky like something weightless and winged.

As it turned out, Caro knew almost nothing about Ben—let alone the crashing end we'd come to at Wilson's hands—either that or she was awfully good at pretending, but she didn't seem at all like a person who would be. Probably Wilson had not thought the story was important enough or he had not wanted to sully his new family with sordid tales of his first one. But I told her about Ben anyway, not about the breakup, but about him. Frankly, she was the best listener I had ever met, better even than Trillium, who would sometimes catch hold of a random sentence I'd spoken and run with it, tugging the conversation in a wild direction, before I was really finished. Better even than Ben himself, who used to give me so much space to speak that he was almost too quiet at times, too hands off. Caro nudged, prompted, questioned, all with clear-eyed interest and a pliant receptivity. I would've bet that this was the same way she made her art—gently bending and shaping, staying watchful, taking her cues from the glass itself.

"What made him special?" she asked, at one point, so I told her how, for Valentine's Day, instead of candy, he gave me a box of heart-shaped things: stones, shells, leaves he'd collected back in the fall and pressed inside a dictionary. I told her how I'd be studying and find, highlighted on a page of my book, words or parts of words and phrases that together made funny sentences, like "It is the best year for elephant fishing" or "Put a big, blue beetle in your milk." I told her how he worshipped Carl Linnaeus and was crazy for the names of things, and how when we'd go hiking, he would hand them over to me, like weird little gifts. A bumblebee became *Bombus pensylvanicus*. A robin became *Turdus migratorius*. The foamy yellow stuff in the dirt became "dog vomit slime mold."

"Yes," said Caro, with a touch of impatience. "Those things are beautiful, partly because he knew you'd like them before you knew. But they're extras. What was essential?"

No one had ever asked me this question before.

"It wasn't just that I could be myself around him," I said, carefully. "It was that I couldn't *not*. I couldn't tell half-truths or dissemble or tell white lies or overdramatize, all of which pretty well describes how I interacted with other boyfriends. I mean, it was high school. One day, Ben asked me to make a pact with him to never say anything we didn't mean."

I remembered this moment so clearly. We were at Ben's house doing math, sitting at opposite sides of the kitchen table, and his dad was cooking. Bolognese sauce simmered on the stove, and bread was baking, and if there is a heaven, I swear it will smell exactly like that kitchen, and Ben's dad was singing while he cooked, the way he always did, which was loudly, badly, and with unconstrained joy. I'm pretty sure it was "Kodachrome," but it might have been anything off *The Essential Paul Simon*. Anyway, he hit a wrong note, and Ben and I looked at each other, like we always did at the especially bad singing moments, and Ben said, just the way he'd say anything, not especially solemnly, "How about we promise to never, ever say anything to each other that we don't mean? Not even if it seems like a small lie and not even if we think it would make the other person happy to hear it."

I put down my calculator, sat up straight, and considered his proposal.

"What if it's something that we're ninety percent sure we mean but we're not a hundred percent sure?" I said. It seemed important to completely nail down the details.

"Right. We say that. We don't just fudge that last ten percent. Ever. Deal?"

"Deal," I said.

I stretched my hand across the books and papers, and we shook on it.

"It was the easiest promise I ever made," I told Caro.

"You kept it?" she asked. "Both of you?"

"Yes."

"How extraordinary," she said. "No wonder he was the love of your life."

At no time had I ever said to her that Ben was the love of my life. Apart from Trillium, I'd never told anyone that, although I figured my mom and Marcus knew it without being told. It took me aback, frankly, how—just like that, without fanfare, in the same tone she'd used to say the coffee cake had apples in it—Caro had pronounced one of the great truths of my life. I could hear Marcus in my head, mad at her presumptuousness, her overstepping, saying, "Jesus, Taize, she doesn't even know you," and, for a few seconds, I considered getting indignant. But what was the point?

"I know," was all I said, and the two of us sat there with that between us. After a few seconds, though, shyness hit me, and I looked around, searching for something else to say.

"This yard is perfect, you know," I said. "Really beautiful."

Caro smiled. "Thank you, although I don't think I followed any of the rules of garden layout. This place is just the product of my whim."

"Are there rules of garden layout?"

She laughed. "See, that's something I should know, and I have no idea! But all the colors are mixed up, and fancy flowers are cheek-by-jowl with lowbrow ones. Those sunflowers by the pool house, for instance, I think have no business here at all, they're so big and gangly, but I adore sunflowers, the really towering ones. Wilson thinks they're awful."

Thunk. Into the middle of our morning, there plopped Wilson. I stiffened, but Caro didn't seem to notice.

"But I remind him," she went on, "that he left the yard to me. Well, all except the front yard. He oversaw the planting of all those—" She broke off.

"Willows," I finished. "Willows for Willow."

Caro nodded, reddening. "Yes, right after she was born."

There was a silence, during which we both looked into our cups of coffee.

Then, Caro said, "I think he fell in love with willow trees when he was a teenager at Banfield. Apparently, they had some huge, old ones on the campus."

I was so busy trying (and failing) to imagine Wilson, my father, falling in love with trees that it took a moment for me to realize what else she had said. I lifted my eyes from my coffee.

"Banfield?"

"Academy," she said, distractedly, fiddling with her fork.

Banfield Academy.

I stared at Caro with a shock that she didn't register because she was gazing absently at what was left of her cake, and as I watched her, a thought dawned. I considered the patio table set for two. I considered the little porcelain pitcher of milk and recalled that just the day before, I had mentioned to her that I liked milk instead of cream or half-and-half in my coffee. Caro's invitation to breakfast had seemed impromptu, but was it possible that the entire morning, beginning with the ballet barre, had been leading up to this revelation? And if it had, *why?* "Don't be stupid," I could hear Marcus say. "She's Wilson's minion for life. It was just another of her brain-dead episodes." But I wasn't so sure.

Caro took another bite of coffee cake and smiled up at the treetops. Her expression was unreadable, as smooth as glass.

BANFIELD ACADEMY TURNED OUT to be in New Jersey, not far from Princeton, which meant it was only an hour and a half away, and somehow this floored me, not just that Wilson's school was so close, but that it had been there all along, while Marcus and I had been growing up on Linvilla Road, totally oblivious to its existence. *You'd think we would have sensed it,* I thought, which was obviously ridiculous. Still, I couldn't shake the proximity eeriness. It was like discovering that the neighbor who'd lived down the road from you your entire childhood was actually a secret agent. Okay, maybe it wasn't exactly like that, but it was unsettling all the same.

I decided to go, of course. Wilson would have been outraged at the very idea, but for once, his opinion was irrelevant to me. I was interested neither in obeying nor defying him; I just wanted to be in a place that had been Wilson's before he was Wilson. When I told Marcus this, he said, "Wilson was always Wilson. Trust me on this."

"No, no," I told him. "Think about it: Wilson is fundamentally un-young; a fourteen-year-old Wilson is a physical impossibility. Like a giant microbe. Or a tiny blue whale. He had to have been someone else at some point."

"You're wrong. But that's okay. You should definitely check out the school anyway. Take pictures. Get copies of his report cards, especially the bad ones. Come back wearing a Banfield sweatshirt."

"You're evil."

"Hell, buy him his own Banfield sweatshirt. And one for the Spawn. Jeez, don't forget one for the Spawn!"

Even though I knew Wilson would never allow me to put Banfield Academy in the book, I looked forward to visiting it and embarking, for once, on a real quest for information. So far, my research for the book had consisted of two breathtakingly boring phone conversations with other scientists in his field who were happy to use the subject of Wilson's brilliant scientific work as a launching pad for a description of their own; five e-mails to set up phone calls; and one lunch with a former student of Wilson's, a woman in her thirties who called him, with tears in her eyes, "my mentor" and waxed lyrical about his support and kindness in a way that should've warmed my heart but that instead made me feel like crap. How was it that he could be so generous to everyone but me, my mother, and Marcus?

In any case, I was chomping at the bit to uncover something beyond hero worship. So the morning after my breakfast with Caro, I donned my standard grown-up, semiboring, professional, trust-inspiring outfit (camel-colored pants, black suede ballet flats, a black cashmere sweater, and a string of pearls), slid the documents giving me access to Wilson's personal records into my professional, trust-inspiring red leather satchel, programmed my car's GPS with the address of Banfield Academy, and hit the road.

My GPS had a clipped, aristocratic way of giving me instructions that I found nigh impossible to disobey (my old boyfriend Leo had dubbed the voice "Robo Hepburn"), but when it came time to turn right onto the highway, I ignored the voice, kept going straight, then went left, then right until, before I knew it, I was pulling into the gravel parking lot of Ransom's Garden World. As much as I'd considered what I would do when I got there—and that wasn't much at all—I figured I would sit in my car for a few minutes and just soak the place in.

But while I was doing just that, I couldn't help myself. If it were only the beauty that called me—and it was all so sumptuously pretty, so abundant, with heaped brilliance everywhere, every pot running over with an exuberance of saturated golds, velvety greens, dusky magentas and pinks, and every shade of orange—mums, dahlias, succulents, sedum, ornamental peppers and cabbages, gourds tucked here and there, vines cascading over every edge—I might have been able to resist, however regretfully. But the trouble was that I saw Mr. Ransom, Ben's dad, in all of it, in every display, every pot—his sensibility, his eye, his touch, his humor, his kindness, if that makes any sense—and I missed him so sharply that, after a couple of minutes, I was scrambling out of my car to find him.

He was in the back lot, behind the cottage shop, pushing a wheelbarrow full of rich black soil. I remembered that soil, so dark and luscious-looking you wanted to eat it. Because I saw him before he saw me, I had a moment to really take him in, and what I saw hurt. He looked like someone who had been through a hellish time, scarecrow thin inside his plaid shirt and gardening apron and old, so old, more than seventeen years' worth of old, his face under his Ransom's cap not so much lined as crumpled.

When he saw me, confusion crossed his face, vanished, and he went completely still. So did I. I wanted to run right over to him, but I felt suddenly nervous. Without a word, carefully, Mr. Ransom let go of the wheelbarrow handles, took off his gloves, tossed them onto the mound of soil, walked closer to me, and said, his voice tinged with amazement, "Taisy."

"Hi, Mr. Ransom," I said.

He took off his hat and stuffed it in his apron pocket. I wanted to run and hug him, but I wasn't sure if he'd want me to. He had always liked me a lot, made me feel welcome every second I'd been in his life, but I knew he loved nobody like he loved Ben. It had been one of my favorite things about him. And I was the person who'd stomped on Ben's heart and—or so it must have seemed to Mr. Ransom—left without a backward glance.

"Well, it's nice to see you. Are you home or just passing through?"

"Visiting, I guess," I said. I gazed around me and breathed in the smell of the place. "But right this second, it kind of feels like being home."

He smiled. "You always did like this place."

I realized I was right on the edge of crying. More than I didn't want this man to hate me, I didn't want him—I could not bear for him—to think it had been easy for me to walk away from him or his store or his son. I burst out with, "I looked back."

Mr. Ransom said, nodding, "Oh." But he was just being nice. He stopped nodding. "Actually, I'm not sure what you mean."

My face was hot. My eyes stung.

"I know it probably looked like I just walked away and never looked back, but I want you to know I looked back all the time."

His face softened. "I never thought anything else," he said.

"I'm sorry I didn't keep in touch."

Mr. Ransom held up his hand to stop me. "Hey, it was a long time ago. And you sent me that note once you were settled in down south, which meant a lot. I guess I never told you that, though."

He didn't apologize for this, and I didn't expect him to. I knew why he hadn't written back; he was too busy being up to his ears in the mess I'd left behind. I can only imagine how long it had taken him to forgive me for what I'd done—if he'd forgiven me at all. I wondered if he knew about the flood of letters I'd sent Ben. I hoped so, but I wasn't about to tell him.

"So what have you been up to all these years," he said, "and what brings you back?"

And there was a flash of the old Mr. Ransom. He was a quiet man most of the time, but, even so, he managed to say exactly what was on his mind, a quality that would have made many people insufferable. He gestured to a cast-iron garden bench nearby, took out his cap, gave the already clean seat a few swipes with it, and waited for me to sit before settling in beside me. The fact that he cared enough to ask filled me with gratitude. I was so glad about it that I laughed.

"What?"

"You always did cut to the chase."

"All right," he said, "fill me in."

I told him about the writing, which he already knew about ("Saw you on one of those morning shows with your friend Trillium. She's an intriguing person, isn't she?"), about Marcus, and my mom, and, in a Herculean display of self-restraint, I mentioned just once that I was single, but I made sure to say it slowly and clearly. All the same, I wasn't sure if he'd heard me. We talked for a while more, and, after an interval of silence when Mr. Ransom seemed to be deciding whether to say something or not, he told me, "Ben's not married yet, either. As a matter of fact, he just broke off his engagement with a girl in Wisconsin before he moved back here."

"Oh," I said. It was all I could manage what with my heart pogo-sticking under my ribs.

"I can't say I was surprised about the breakup," said Mr. Ransom, but he didn't explain why, and I thought it would be overstepping to ask. Anyway, I wasn't interested in Ben's fiancée, at least not right at that moment. I was only interested in Ben.

"So Ben's back? To stay?"

Mr. Ransom grinned. "Now who's cutting to the chase?"

"I am," I said, grinning back.

"He's renting right now but says he's looking for a house to buy. He came home eight months ago, right after my second wife, Bobbie, got cancer."

"Oh, Mr. Ransom, I'm so sorry," I said and before I knew it, I was taking his hand. It occurred to me that I hadn't held my sick father's hand, or touched him at all, even casually, since I'd been staying at his house. In fact, in the two years Mr. Ransom and I had been in each other's lives, I'd probably touched him more than I'd touched my own father in my entire lifetime.

"Thank you," he said. "We had eight good years. She was sick for just three months and went down fast once she was diagnosed. Ben took over for me here, so I could take care of her. Bobbie got to be at home with her cats and books and things right up until the last few days, and it meant the world. It really did."

He shut his eyes and took a few deep breaths, smiling in a way that meant he was remembering. I waited, and eventually, he opened his eyes and swiped at them with his thumbs. I did the same to mine.

"I'm glad," I said. "I bet Ben didn't think twice about coming."

"No, he didn't. Also, he was glad for some time to think. He'd been teaching botany at the university out there in Wisconsin, but even before I called him about Bobbie, he said he was thinking of trying something new."

"Really?" I said. "Why?"

"He claims he had no gift for teaching. I'm not sure I believe that. But he says he hated university politics, and that I can believe."

"Me, too."

"I'm back running this place, but Ben still helps most days, whenever he can. He enrolled himself in the professional gardener program at the university here. Most of his learning is hands on over at Windward, though. You remember how he loved that place, even as a boy."

Windward, the botanical gardens just over the state line in Pennsylvania, a gorgeous place. Ben and I had walked through the vast glass conservatories and the exquisitely maintained outdoor gardens more times than I could count, and I still had a picture of us, arms around each other, grinning to beat the band, in front of one of the water lily pools. I would get transported by the grandeur—color and lushness rising up on every side, hanging from the ceilings, the foun-

tains and fruit trees—but Ben went for the details, the tiny, speckled
clown face of an orchid, the tight snail-like spirals of a fiddlehead fern,
the odd, oily smell of the silvery plants in the desert room. It made me
happy to think of Ben working there. In fact—Banfield Academy be
damned—I could have spent the day just like that: sitting with Mr.
Ransom on that garden bench in his store and picturing Ben at Windward Gardens. But that's not how it worked out.

I saw the dogs first, impossibly tiny Yorkies, two silky gold and
blue-gray mops springing across the lot, and they looked so much like
Ben's dogs Busby and Jed, the ones he'd brought with him when he
came to live with his dad back in high school, that I turned to Mr.
Ransom in surprise, but he only had eyes for the dogs.

Then they were upon us, bouncing up Mr. Ransom's shins, their
stubby tails wildly tick-tocking. He lifted the bigger one onto his
lap and a kiss-fest ensued. I remembered that this was also how Mr.
Ransom had always been, generally low-key but prone to bursts of free
and easy, slightly goofy joy. I was so happy to see he hadn't lost that.

The smaller dog placed one paw on my shoe and turned his doll
face upward. His nose was a shiny black triangle, and his eyelashes
were an inch long, so I picked him up—he was light as a lunch sack
full of feathers—and set him on my knee, and he gave my chin a single
decorous flick with his tongue.

"Ah! The elusive Pidwit kiss!" said Mr. Ransom with a hoot. "He
doesn't give those away every day."

"Pidwit," I said. "That's what Ben used to call Piglet from Winnie-
the-Pooh. His mom told me that."

"He wasn't even two. Dragged that stuffed pig around everywhere. And this," said Mr. Ransom, planting a kiss on the other dog's
head, "is Roo."

Roo had eyes like Audrey Hepburn, one up ear, one down ear, and
a toothy grin. Really and truly, the dog was smiling.

"No offense, but he doesn't look much like a kangaroo to me," I
said.

Then, a voice from a few feet away said, "It's because of the way he hops through tall grass."

Ben. *Ben.* I knew it was Ben because it couldn't have been anyone else in the world.

A shiver ran down the back of my neck, and Pidwit turned his head to give me a deep brown, doe-eyed look of concern. I touched the tip of my nose to his, mostly because his nose was so tempting, but also to buy myself time, after which I lifted my head and looked straight into the eyes of Ben Ransom.

"He was doing it when I went to pick him up from the breeder," said Ben.

"Hopping?" I said.

"Yeah. Actually, he looked more like a dolphin leaping through waves, but right after I saw him, I met Pidwit, who was obviously a Pidwit."

"Obviously," I said. "So then Roo made more sense than . . ."

"Flipper," supplied Ben.

I wanted to say something witty, but after that first, brief wave of coherence, the only thing inside my head was *you you you you you,* hooting like a crazy owl.

"Well," said Ben, after a short silence. "This is unexpected."

I swallowed hard, tried to smile, but managed only to clench my teeth.

"I'm going to go feed these dogs," said Mr. Ransom, standing and lifting Pidwit from my lap. He tucked him under his left arm like a football. Roo was tucked under his right.

"I fed them earlier," said Ben.

"He calls that food?" Mr. Ransom said to the dogs. "That crunchy guinea pig garbage? You're carnivores, aren't you? You need meat." He nodded at me. "Good to see you, Taisy," he said and started off toward the cottage.

"I don't think they eat poached chicken in the wild, Dad," said Ben.

"Like he knows," said Mr. Ransom to the dogs and then, over his shoulder. "You tell him, Taisy!"

Ben shot his father a look of exasperation that wouldn't have fooled a baby. How moving I'd always found it, the way, even as a teenager, Ben had adored his dad.

"Okay, tell me," said Ben, eyebrows up. "You think they eat poached chicken in the wild?"

I considered this. While I considered it, I considered him, tried to take in as much of him as I could. He was a leaner, starker version of himself, less red-cheeked. Some cute boys age into boyish, faintly silly-looking men, their prettiness gone all to seed. But maybe because Ben had never looked that boyish, even as a boy, he seemed to have grown into a truer version of himself, as though this man had been inside of him all along, biding his time, waiting to emerge. His dark hair was cropped short, and I missed its falling on his forehead, but I liked how now there was less to distract you from his black eyes and all the craftsmanship of his face. And, oh, that sharply cut divot in his lip was the same as ever.

"Do they eat poached chicken in the wild? That's your question. They're Yorkies," I said. "Are they *in* the wild? Not just your Yorkies, but any Yorkies? Ever?"

Then, for the first time in seventeen years, Ben Ransom smiled at me, and his smile was what it always had been, a sudden, reckless, white-light event that took over his entire face. Smiles like that aren't just pleasant, they're inspiring; they make you want to deserve them. Ben's smile sent courage charging through me.

"Listen," I said, fervently. "I have to go somewhere. Will you come with me?"

He should have said yes. I should have held out my hand, and he should have grabbed it, and together we should've run to my car and spent the next several hours intermittently pouring out our hearts and being quiet together, and asking for forgiveness and telling each other there was never anything to forgive, so that by the time we got back

home, our fresh start would have spread out all around us like a field
we stood in. I wanted it so much that I could see it happening. I just
held my breath, waiting for the yes.

But Ben didn't say it. His smile fell away, became so gone that it
was like it had never been there at all.

"Just like that?" he said, with an edge in his voice. "Is that what
you thought would happen?"

"No! I mean, yes." I sighed. "I just thought we could talk."

Ben rubbed his forehead with the heel of his hand in a gesture so
familiar I wanted to cry.

"You can't just show up like this. I haven't seen you in seventeen
years, and you know what? I was pretty sure I'd never see you again."

"Really? But didn't you ever want to? I know I wanted to see you."

It was a risk, but there is a time for naked honesty, and I was
hoping that this was that time. Ben took another step backward and
said, coldly, "So that's why you came back? To see me."

I wanted so badly to shout yes, but we'd sworn to always tell each
other the truth. What would happen to our fresh start if I kicked it off
with a lie? How would I ever deserve it? *Oh, let the dogs come back,* I
thought, miserably, staring down at the ground. *Let things be funny
and easy the way they were before I ruined them.*

"That's what I thought," he said.

When I looked up, he was walking away.

I ALMOST DIDN'T GO to Banfield. What the hell did it matter where
Wilson had gone to school? The man had ruined my life, plain and
simple, and learning who he'd been before he did it wouldn't change
that. But I realized that if I went back to the pool house, all I would
do is play the meeting with Ben over and over inside my head, feeling
more and more sorry for myself, and just the image of my tearstained,
thirty-five-year-old self, lying on Wilson's blue couch in Wilson's pool
house, mourning Ben like a schoolgirl was so humiliating, reeked so

completely of failure that it made me want to scream. So instead I drove, dry-eyed and trying for fierceness, turning up the music until the only voice that could break through the din wasn't Wilson's or Ben's or even my own, but Robo Hepburn's, telling me, without a trace of emotion or uncertainty, her tone as barren as the moon, exactly where to go.

THE SCHOOL WASN'T NEARLY as grand as I thought it would be, no spires or domes casting shadows or declaring their majestic shapes against the sky, but its stone buildings were old enough and weathered enough to be dignified and to offset the samples of '70s architecture that had sprung up among them. The kids wore jeans and fleeces, not uniforms or coats and ties, and they whizzed by on bikes or clacked along the brick walkways on skateboards, both of which they abandoned on the grass outside the entrances to the buildings when they went in to their classes.

I tried to imagine the place as Wilson would have known it, erasing the newer buildings, shrinking the trees, slicking down the hair of the boys who walked by, but the present was too insistent, too young and loud and alive. As I walked around, following the map I'd printed out online, I could imagine being one of those skateboard kids, jostling into the classroom with my friends, sitting down at my desk red-faced and breathless, a little sweaty, yanking the earbuds out of my ears, but I couldn't, for the life of me, imagine Wilson. I went to the library, to the science building, to the oldest dormitory I could find, searching high and low for Wilson's high school ghost, but he was nowhere to be found.

At the main administrative office, I showed the secretary, Edwina Cook, Wilson's letter and the paper from his lawyer and asked if I might see whatever records they still had of his time there, and lo and behold, the documents worked. Edwina Cook was a sturdy, capable-looking woman, with unexpectedly long, red nails. When she finished reading the documents, she clapped her hands.

"A book! How exciting! And what a father you've got!" she said. "We're still in the process of digitizing the old paper files, but I think we've gotten all the way up to sixties."

Her nails clicked, lightning fast, on the computer keys.

"There! I think I've got everything for Wilson Cleary. Isn't much, but you're welcome to it. You want me to print copies?"

"Please," I said.

There was his transcript: difficult-sounding classes, straight As, class rank 1. None of which surprised me. And there was his work/study contract, which surprised me a little. Apparently, Wilson had put himself through school by doing whatever needed doing: serving food in the cafeteria, helping the groundskeeper, shelving books in the library. Wilson in an apron? Ladling mashed potatoes onto his schoolmates' plates? If the past Wilson had been anything like the one I knew, he must have been writhing with ire and humiliation for four straight years.

Wait. *Four straight years?* I looked back at the records and noticed for the first time that they didn't span four years, but two, his junior and senior. There was nothing from his freshman and sophomore years, and, then, I noticed something odder, still: no home address on any of it. The work/study contracts extended through the summer. It was as though Wilson had lived at the school. And where were his parents' names? I leafed carefully through the sheets of paper. Nowhere. I went back to Edwina.

"You know, I'm quite sure that my father was here for all four years, but I'm not finding anything for his first two. Would you mind checking again?"

Looking just a tad annoyed at my questioning her thoroughness, she checked. *Clickety click click click.* Nothing.

"Can you check by social security number?" I asked.

"I don't think the school used them back then," she said. "I don't know if minors even were issued them in the fifties. I suspect not."

"Oh," I said, downcast.

"Now don't you get discouraged," she chirped. "I'm sure we can figure this out. I'm one of those who likes a knotty problem."

I smiled at her. I liked this knotty-problem-liking Edwina Cook, clicks and all.

"I'll bet you are," I said.

She scooped up the sheaf of papers and read them with hawklike attention, narrowing her eyes.

"Aha!" she cried, making me jump.

"What?"

"Looks like they assigned every student an identification number. I'll try searching by that."

Clicks. Fifteen minutes later, the first two years of Wilson's prep school education were sliding out of the printer.

"Voilà!" said Edwina and handed them over. "It was the name change that got me."

"Name change?"

"Looks like he must have done it the summer between his sophomore and junior years. You didn't know?"

I shook my head, spreading the new sheets down on the table, trying to understand what Edwina was telling me, and there it was: Wilson Ravenel. *Well, I'll be damned, Marcus had been wrong; Wilson had been a different person when he was fourteen and fifteen, and presumably for all the years before that.*

"I wonder why," I said.

Edwina shrugged. "Guess you can ask him, right?"

Wrong.

"You know," I said, slowly, "one thing that happened around that time is that his parents died."

"Oh, how awful, honey," said Edwina. She clucked her tongue. "Such a tough age to lose a parent, let alone both."

"I know. There was a car accident. He doesn't really talk about it."

We sat in thoughtful silence, and then, Edwina said, "You never know, do you? How that kind of thing would affect a kid."

"What do you mean?"

"Well, a bereaved child, dropping his parents' last name like that. You wouldn't think it, would you?"

Edwina was right. It seemed heartless even for Wilson. I could hear Marcus saying, *Nothing is too heartless for Wilson.* But still, it didn't make sense.

"Well, I'll leave you alone with that stuff for a bit," said Edwina, patting my hand.

"Thanks."

Out the window, I could see a lone boy walking, his skateboard under his arm. He looked lost in thought, oblivious to his surroundings, solitary and yet also content, and I wondered if that was what it had been like here for Wilson Ravenel (Had anyone called him Will? Had "Will" used contractions?), back before his parents died and he was reincarnated as Wilson Cleary. I hoped so. When the kid was out of sight, I went back to reading, so distractedly, my mind still with the thinking boy out the window, that I almost didn't see them. Two names. In wonder, I ran a shaky finger over them. Walter and Helen Ravenel. Wilson's parents, my grandparents. And an address.

CHAPTER TEN

Willow

WHEN I WAS A child, my father was a devotee of the historical marker, those metal, hump-topped rectangular signs you find standing in fields or along roads or affixed to buildings. He was the kind of person who stops and reads what lots of others just pass by, even if it means pulling over on the highway with cars whizzing past or stopping dead on a city sidewalk when you're already late for the symphony or an IMAX film about the Galapagos. As secretly impatient as I'd gotten with this over the years, I have to admit that it is rather nifty, the way the past and the present can bump up against each other: the stop on the Underground Railroad cozying up to the sneaker store; the birthplace of the famous sculptor reborn as a windowless nightclub called Tits for Tats (!).

Equally nifty is the way knowledge can lead to more knowledge. For instance, after a quick but harrowing highway stop in Chancellorsville, Virginia, I was inspired to research Stonewall Jackson's left arm, which, according to the marker, had been amputated there on the battlefield. I found out that the arm had been given its own Christian burial, only to be stolen from its resting place by Union soldiers and spirited off to parts unknown, and this became a jumping-off point for a project on burial rituals and grave robbery through the ages, a project that gave me nightmares for weeks, but that smacked of brilliance, if I do say so myself.

With such an upbringing, it's probably not strange that I had played a game for years in which I erected imaginary historical markers along my own life's path. All right, maybe that is strange. I mean, for a while there, when I was nine or ten, I even started writing them down in a notebook, pencil drawings of painstakingly lettered, hump-topped signs announcing such events as: "WILLOW CLEARY'S FINAL BALLET RECITAL. HERE ON THIS STAGE IN JUNE OF HER TENTH YEAR, WILLOW, DRESSED AS A PANSY, DANCED HER FINAL DANCE TO "ALL IN THE GOLDEN AFTERNOON" FROM ALICE IN WONDERLAND. BECAUSE SHE WAS SO SAD ABOUT HAVING TO QUIT BALLET, SHE SLIPPED AND FELL DURING THE CHAINES TURNS, BUT HER MOTHER SAID NO ONE NOTICED." At Bethany Beach, Delaware: "WILLOW CLEARY GOES INTO THE OCEAN FOR THE FIRST TIME"; in front of the two-headed human fetus suspended in a jar at the Mutter Museum of medical oddities in Philadelphia: "WILLOW CLEARY DISGRACES HERSELF AND HER FATHER BY BURSTING INTO TEARS IN FRONT OF EVERY-ONE"; and in the hallway outside of my father's office: "WILLOW CLEARY SAYS HORRIBLE THINGS TO HER FATHER ABOUT HAVING TO QUIT CROSS-COUNTRY AND AL-MOST KILLS HIM."

Actually, I never wrote that last one down. For one thing, by the time it happened, I no longer kept the notebook. For another, to have to see it written out that way would have smashed my guilty heart to flinders.

I hadn't played the historical marker game for ages, of course, but if I still had, I would have mentally stuck a big shiny sign in the man-icured grass beneath the giant oak tree in the south field of the Web-ley School, one that read: WILLOW CLEARY, AGED SIXTEEN, HAS HER FIRST-EVER ARGUMENT WITH A BOY HER AGE—AND WINS. At least, I thought I won. Luka might have had a different take on the outcome, but even he couldn't have denied that, at the very least, I held my own.

The argument was about Dorothea Brooke, one of the central characters in *Middlemarch*. If you haven't read it, you should, but here's really all you need to know to understand our argument: Dorothea is a wealthy, beautiful young woman barely out of her teens who dreams of doing something big and world-changing, so, despite her family's horrified disapproval, she marries a much older, unhandsome, emotionally detached scholar named Edward Casaubon, whom she deeply admires, with the thought that she will help him finish his "great" work, which has something to do with religion, and send it out into the world for the benefit of all; the marriage is a failure, mostly because Casaubon isn't very interested in finishing his book or in having a wife, and after the sickly Casaubon dies, Dorothea admits to herself that she is in love with her friend, Casaubon's young, handsome cousin Will Ladislaw, who has loved her all along; and even though no one approves of this suitor, either (because Will is not rich and Dorothea is), she marries him and lives happily ever after.

I adore Dorothea. Adore! Which is how the argument got started.

It was one of those out-of-nowhere, brilliant, orange and cobalt fall afternoons, so Luka and I decided to talk about our English project outside, instead of in the library. At first, the decision appeared to have all the makings of a disaster because for a few long, agonizing seconds, I could not for the life of me figure out how to *be on the ground* without looking like an idiot. Should I sit cross-legged? Legs stretched out? Legs tucked under? Or like Luka, knees bent, elbows propped on them? My mind and heart raced. Finally, I opted for a sideways, bent-legged position that instantly mortified me because it was so *girlish,* like some nauseatingly prissy version of that statue of Hans Christian Andersen's Little Mermaid who sits on a rock, minus the partial fish tail. So I shifted to having my legs stretched out in front of me, remembering a split second too late that in fitted black pants, my storky appendages would look exactly like ebony chopsticks, but then I simply couldn't shift yet again because *nothing* could look worse than writhing around on the ground, twisting myself into shapes like a crazed origami person. I cursed my legs, along with my pathetic self-consciousness, and the afternoon might have gone to hell in a hand-basket except that as soon as we got started talking about the book, I forgot all about how I was sitting and just sat.

"So," said Luka, "what did you think of the book?"

It was one of those thrilling, exasperating, impossibly wide-open questions to which there are far, far too many responses, but I had to try to answer it. I owed as much to the book, to George Eliot, and to Luka for choosing me, so I took a deep breath and gave it a go.

"Well, for one thing, I found it interesting how Eliot is so distant one minute, and then so intimate the next, and at one point it hit me that this style really mirrored the story because there are these large, public issues at stake and then there are the characters' relationships, and the two don't stay separate at all, when you think about it. They overlap all the time. Um, another thought I had was that there was a lot of attention paid to women's looks. I admit that I haven't really come to any conclusions about what Eliot was doing with this, but there's the fact that the most beautiful woman, Rosamond Vincy, had the worst values and the plainest woman, Mary Garth, had the best, but then, of course, there's Dorothea who is definitely beautiful, but not in your typical . . ."

At about this time, I caught sight of Luka's face, which was be-mused and also twitchy around the mouth in a way that clearly meant he was trying not to laugh. Obviously, I should have died of embarrass-ment if for no other reason that, when it came to interacting with kids at school, dying of embarrassment was my fallback response, but for some reason, maybe because he was still somehow coming across as nice, I didn't. I cut off midsentence, lifted my eyebrows, and said, "Am I amusing you?"

He grinned with one side of his mouth. "When I asked what you thought of the book? I was really just asking if you liked it."

"Ohhhhh." I grinned back. "I did like it. I loved it, in fact. How about you?"

I would have supposed Luka to be too cool to truly consider a question like this, much less give a serious answer, but he tipped his disheveled-haired head to one side and appeared for all the world to contemplate. It occurred to me for the first time that there might be some lofty echelon of coolness that allowed a person to forget about cool and act interested in what he found interesting. Who knew? What I didn't know about coolness could fill a book even longer than *Middlemarch*.

Luka said, "Yeah, I liked it. It was funny, which I definitely did not expect. There were some caricatures, obviously, but a lot of the characters were down to earth and cool. Fred, Mr. Farebrother, Celia, Mary Garth. I liked how Will wasn't some perfect guy and was actually kind of directionless for most of the book. But, God, *Dorothea*." He made what I can only describe as a vomit face. I had the fleeting thought that if you could be handsome while making a vomit face, you had to be pretty handsome, but my next thought was *What?*

"*What?*" I said, narrowing my eyes at him. "You didn't like Dorothea?"

"Ugh. She was so annoying. Didn't you think she was insanely annoying?"

Let me be clear. I don't think you have to like characters in order to love them. I love a lot of characters with whom I would never want to, as my peers say, hang. Hamlet, for one. Practically every single character in *Wuthering Heights,* for another. But Dorothea Brooke? Dorothea Brooke I liked and loved and admired and cherished. She just tries so hard to be a good person. How can you not love that? I set my jaw.

"No one," I said, "could be annoyed by such a person as Dorothea Brooke. She's so pure-hearted and generous and *nice*."

Luka had the nerve to roll his eyes.

"Come on. She thinks she's better than everyone, except for Casaubon who is clearly a loser. Everyone she knows tries to talk her out of marrying the old guy, but she thinks she's smarter than all of them."

"She *is* smarter than all of them!"

"You're saying she was right to marry him?"

"Okay, no. Obviously, that was a bad decision, but she made it for the right reasons. She wanted to devote herself to something beautiful and important. And all those other people, yes, maybe they were trying to talk her into doing the right thing, but for all the wrong reasons."

"They thought he was a pompous ass, which he was."

"They made fun of the way he *blinks,* for heaven's sake. Do you really think someone shouldn't marry a person because other people don't like the way he blinks?"

Luka shook his head. "If he weren't a pompous ass, if he were a nice guy, probably they wouldn't have made fun of him like that."

This took me aback for a moment because it hadn't occurred to me before. But as soon as Luka said what he said, it seemed true, even, maybe, universally so. If you liked a person, or if you loved him, you didn't mind his physical imperfections. Someone's narrow shoulders or knobby wrists or slightly bugged eyes, for instance, might even endear him to you more. But if you disliked someone, well, it was all grist for the meanness mill. Truth be told, once I'd noticed Bec Lansing's vaguely round cheeks, her one physical glitch, I'd mentally hissed "chipmunk" at her every time I saw her, with glorious satisfaction.

"True," I conceded.

"Tell me this: Do you think Dorothea actually thought Casaubon was hot? The guy had *moles.*"

"So?"

"White moles. Two of them. On his face."

"So?"

"On his *face.* With hairs growing out of them."

I shrugged.

"Willow." Luka leaned toward me. "Hairs. Moles with hairs."

I had to laugh at this. "All right. So he wasn't hot, even to Dorothea."

It should be noted that I had never before used "hot" as a descriptor for a human being and, prior to this conversation, would have sworn I never would.

"But Dorothea was thinking of less superficial things than hotness," I said and immediately thought *Do people* say *hotness?*

Luka gave me another bemused but friendly look. "Uh, yeah. Sure they do."

"What?"

"You just asked if people say hotness, and they do."

For the love of God, I had said it out loud. How had that happened? Was it possible there was a fine line between comfortable and pathological and that, after ten minutes with this boy, I'd already crossed it? Perhaps because I had done exactly that, I decided not to worry about it. I shrugged. "Oh," I said. "Well, thanks for letting me know."

"No problem. So admit it: Dorothea thought she was above physical attraction, but she was wrong. If you're dating a person, if you're *marrying* a person, hotness matters. It's fundamental."

I looked at Luka there on this grass, with his shoulders, his white, square, straight teeth, his long black eyes, the leaf shadows on his honey-colored skin. I thought, *You're not exactly a disinterested party when it comes to that particular subject, are you?* But this time, I made damn sure I only said it inside my head.

"Fine," I said. "Yes, she made a mistake."

Luka leaned his head back, looked up at the canopy of oak leaves. "Yeah, it's almost always a mistake for a young person to be with an old person."

For the first time during our conversation, I felt a hot rush of embarrassment, which made no sense, since I had never "been" with anyone, much less a person who would remotely qualify as old. But I shoved the embarrassment aside and got back to the business of defending Dorothea.

"But that doesn't make her annoying. She made a mistake because she was idealistic and naive; that could happen to a lot of people."

"True," said Luka, still staring up at the tree, "that it could happen to a lot of people. False that it doesn't make her annoying."

"But listen," I said. "She could've run home when she realized what a louse Casaubon was, but she stuck by him. Why are you smiling like that? Standing by one's commitment is noble!"

"'Louse,'" said Luka, with a short but real laugh. "Nice word choice."

"Thank you. Now admit that I'm right."

"I was rooting for her to dump the guy, but, yeah, I guess sticking with him was noble."

"It most certainly was. And she learned from her mistakes, too. You can't say she married Will for the wrong reasons. In the end, she realized she was an ordinary person in that way: falling in love. If she was a wee bit arrogant to begin with, she found humility later, right?"

"Okay, you're right," said Luka. He looked at me, shook his head, and laughed again.

"What?"

"'Wee bit,'" he said.

He gave me a thumbs-up, and I gave him one back, without a thought to whether doing so was in keeping with thumbs-up etiquette, about which I had not the slightest idea.

Luka and I stayed under that tree for almost an hour, not making all that much progress on our paper, but, even though I had previously bemoaned the time-squandering aspect of group work, I found I didn't mind. There was no reason on earth for it to be so, but talking to Luka was the easiest thing I'd done in such a long time. These days, I was almost never relaxed, not at school, not at home, not even with Mr. Insley, around whom I was happy, yes, oh, so happy, but far too—I don't know—*exhilarated*, perhaps, to ever really relax. Somehow, the lawn beneath that oak tree felt the way my house used to feel, like breathing space, like a sanctuary so safe you forgot there was anything to be safe from. When Luka got out his cell phone to check the time, I had the wild urge to wrest the damn thing from his hand and fling it to the four winds.

"Shit, I have to go," he said. "I have swim practice in less than an hour. Totally lost track of the time."

"Oh, sorry," I said.

"Nah, it was good."

He stood up, a tall shape against the sky—the silhouette of his spiky hair looking remarkably like the Sydney Opera House—and reached out his hand to help me up. For a blank split second, I stared at it; I had never held hands with a boy my age, even in a comradely, matter-of-fact, entirely non-boy-holding-hands-with-girl way, but, before he noticed my hesitation—I hoped—I grabbed hold (it was a good hand, much larger than mine, not especially rough or smooth, not sweaty) and he helped haul me to my feet.

"Thanks," I said.

It would amaze me later, how I wasn't paralyzed with awkwardness about what to do with his hand once I was upright. In a move that I fancied almost qualified as smooth, I let go of it and, in the same motion, brushed the grass off the backs of my legs. "Are you practicing here at the school?"

"No, high school swimming doesn't start for a while. I swim year-round with a club team."

"Oh, my. Every day?"

"Twice a day, during the week. In the morning before school and again in the evening."

"Holy smokes. You never miss?"

"Not that much, but if I have a lot of homework, I usually try to grab a quick workout by myself in the school pool and skip my real practice. Coach Wheelwright, the Webley coach, gave me a key."

We started walking toward the door to the library. In the distance, I could see some girls running, the cross-country team I guessed, and felt a pang of longing. But it was hard to truly long to be somewhere else when where I was was so pleasant and normal-feeling.

"Well, that explains it," I said, nodding.

"What?"

"Your hair."

He smiled wryly and scratched his head, making his bronzy, goldy hair stand even more on end.

"Yeah, right, it's pretty rough. My mom says it's no color known to man and that the strands break off like glass, which is true."

"It reminds me of a hedgehog, except metallic."

"Wow. No one's ever called me a metallic hedgehog before," said Luka.

"I find that very hard to believe," I said.

Luka laughed. "Hey, how are you getting home? You want a ride?"

And that's when I stopped being relaxed because I remembered that I was supposed to have a quick driving lesson with Mr. Insley. Afterward, he'd do what he always did, which was to drop me a few hundred yards from my house, and I'd walk the rest of the way. I had told him I had a group meeting after school, but I hadn't told him it would last over an hour. Like Luka, I'd lost track of time. I was gripped by the sudden, worrying thought of Mr. Insley sitting in his office, fiddling with his wristwatch, waiting, but was simultaneously gripped by the idea of just forgetting the lesson and riding home with Luka. I suppose I just wanted the easiness to go on a little longer. What to do, what to do? But my dilemma only lasted a few moments because right then, the cross-country team got close enough so that I could see Bec leading the pack (of course!), her hair streaming behind her, and when she caught sight of Luka, she started waving the wave of a person on a deserted island who spots a ship and broke into a dead sprint. In a matter of seconds she was upon us, although if she saw me, she never let on.

"Lukey!" she yelled and leaped gleefully onto his back, her arms wrapped around his neck.

And, just like that, I became invisible.

"You're killing me, here. God, what do you weigh now?" said Luka, pretending to stagger. "One eighty? One ninety?"

I gave Luka a quick wave, which he didn't see because I was invisible, jogged over to the library door, and was inside before anyone noticed I'd left. Or, in the case of Bec, noticed I was ever there in the first place. For some stupid reason, I found my chest was heaving in the short, jerky way that meant I would cry if I didn't calm myself. So I stood for a little, trying to subdue my heart, breathing in the papery, dusty smell of the library with slow, careful breaths. *They don't matter, silly girl, not Bec, not even Luka, not one student at this godforsaken school matters. How could you ever have thought otherwise? Did you forget what you have, what is all yours and no one can touch?*

Of course, I hadn't forgotten. How could I? None of them mattered, none. I stood in the back of the library, drawing myself upright, easing my shoulders back, reminding myself of the truth I had so recently learned: nothing can touch you, not guilt or fear or sisters who are not sisters; no one can hurt you, not enemies or loneliness or friends who stop being friends when other people show up; you can rise above anything, anything, everything when you are in love.

And I was—oh, was I ever—in love.

WE DIDN'T HAVE THE driving lesson that day and not because Mr. Insley was upset with me for being so late. As it turned out, he had gotten trapped into a conversation with the dean about an unruly student and came striding briskly into his classroom a full two minutes after I'd gotten there. He was so charmingly out of breath and apologetic, and I was so exhausted from the encounter, or non-encounter as it were, with Bec (and, if I'm honest, still smarting from Luka's having dropped me like a hot potato) that I didn't even mind his canceling the lesson and simply taking me to the usual drop-off spot near my house. I didn't say much on the ride home, just listened to Mr. Insley make fun of Dean Fogerty ("he of the bombast, rulebook rigidity, and copious potbelly") and felt grateful to be with someone who liked me enough to make fun of his superior in my presence. Before I got out of the car, though, Mr. Insley's mood shifted to serious, and he laid a hand on my arm. Even through my coat, I could feel the jolt of electricity.

"Willow," Mr. Insley said, his eyes locking with mine, "I think—and I hope you'll agree with me—that we're ready to go further."

My heartbeat broke into a gallop, and a little tinny buzzing started in my ears that might have been fear and might have been joy.

"Oh. I. Um, well, that's fine," I managed to say. "I mean, yes, that sounds like a good idea."

"Excellent! We've stuck to parking lots and short jaunts, but I think we should take the plunge and go for a real ride."

Twin waves of relief and disappointment washed over me, and I couldn't for the life of me say which was the bigger of the two. I smiled.

"You really think I'm ready?"

Mr. Insley's prominent, light blue eyes twinkled at me, full of the spirit of adventure.

"I do! But we'll need a sizable block of time. Any chance you can get away this Saturday? Is there perhaps something you could tell your parents?"

I nodded my best sharp, saucy, can-do, WAC officer nod.

"You bet," I said.

"Good," he said, giving my arm a squeeze and leaning closer to me. "Grand. How about eleven A.M. at the park? Are you sure you're game?"

When Mr. Insley looked at me that way, so rapt, waiting with bated breath for my answer, I felt more special, more interesting than I ever had in my life. The man could have suggested anything, a balloon ride across the Pacific, a whirl on the flying trapeze, and I would have agreed to it with all of my heart.

"The gamest!" I said.

His face changed again, then, grew—I didn't just imagine it— tender, unmistakably tender.

"That's my girl," he said, softly, and as I walked down the shoulder of the road toward home, outwardly walking, but inwardly dancing, leaping, flying, these last words of his went off like fireworks, like bursting blossoms of pure light, over and over again inside my head.

Oh, I was his girl. Was I *ever*.

I DIDN'T KEEP A diary, and if I did, I would not have dared to write about the days that had passed since the first time I'd met Mr. Insley in the park, but the driving lessons, all four of them, each more bright and precious than the last, were written on my soul as surely as anything ever had been. In fact, my soul held two versions of every lesson, the long and the short. I had stored every detail and, at night when I'd go to bed, I would take the long versions out, unfurl them, one by one, and bask in every second, every word and glance. But each lesson also contained a moment or two, high points, jewel-like, utterly full, supersaturated, and when I had less time, when I was sitting at dinner, say, or in class, I would release this shorter, highlight version, let it fly across my memory like a comet.

One: My foot on the gas pedal, jerking the car forward like a racehorse out of the gate. Slamming on the brake, so that both our heads bobbed hard. Humiliation rising in my chest and then Mr. Insley's splendid laugh ringing through the darkness, making everything, every single thing in the world, all right.

Two: Right after school, pale, intermittent sunlight wafting through the car windows. Seeing Mr. Insley with new, shy, excited eyes because he is wearing aviator sunglasses and a flannel newsboy cap. After we practice driving all around the parking lot, we park and sit on the hood of his car, drinking coffee from a thermos he's brought; he gives me the cup, drinks from the thermos itself. Steam hovers over my cup like a tiny ghost, and the sun disappears behind a cloud, and I shiver, and Mr. Insley takes my scarf from my lap, winds it carefully, two times, around my neck, and I see myself in his sunglasses, and he says, "There."

Three: We practice backing up, parking, using the turn signal. When I look into the rearview mirror, I can feel him watching me, and his gaze is like something hot pressed to my cheek, the side of my neck. Sitting atop the car afterward, the hood warm through my jeans, he asks if I'm happy. I cradle my coffee in both hands, tip my face to the sky, and say, "Yes. I love driving with you," when what I really mean is "I love driving *and* you." He says, "Good. I do, too, but I meant in general." "In general, I don't know. Not ever as happy as this." He says, "If it is not overstepping to say so, sometimes, I feel that you're a trapped bird, waiting to be set free." I realize, the second he says it, that I do feel that way. I look at him, thinking *Set me free*. He smiles, reaches out, lifts a lock of my hair, and says, "And oh, what feathers. In all my thirty years, I've never seen hair like yours."

Four: We go for a longer ride, a few miles down the road and back. I'm scared, gripping the wheel hard, but also thrilled at his faith in me. When we get back to the parking lot, I get out and spin in circles, laughing with joy. Driving is awful and miraculous, and I am good at it. He catches me by the hand, and I think—oh, good God, please—he is going to pull me to him, and then he grins and gives me a hearty handshake of congratulations. "Thank you so much for teaching me, Mr. Insley," I say, and he keeps hold of my hand, touches the tip of my nose with two fingers, and says, "Please. Call me Blaine."

ON SATURDAY MORNING, EVEN though I wasn't scheduled to meet Mr. Insley until eleven, I told my mother I was doing homework with some "school friends" (Ha, an oxymoron if ever there was one!) at a nearby coffee shop at eight thirty. I told her we would eat breakfast together and then head to the library to study, and that one of them would drop me off later in the afternoon. Muddy was so happy about this, her face all aglow at the thought of my having friends at school ("Breakfasting together! How chummy!"), and so eager to accommodate me, even offering to drop me at the coffee shop, that my stomach tightened with guilt. Although I had been lying to her fairly regularly lately, this lie was especially elaborate and so felt especially wrong. But there was nothing for it; I had to get out of the house early, before my father woke up and wanted to see me because if lying to Muddy was hard, lying to my father, as he lay in bed, still slow-moving, hoarse, and creased from sleep, would've been unbearable. No, scratch that. Not unbearable. I would have borne it because I would have borne anything to buy precious hours with Mr. Insley, but the guilt would have burned like coals of fire.

I need to stop here in order to state for the record that I would have given anything to speed my father's recovery and that I cherished, with all my heart, every sign that he was getting better. When I came home from school and went to his room to find him out of bed, sitting at his writing desk or in his red velvet armchair, safely encased in the cone of light from the bronze gooseneck floor lamp, a book in his lap, I was filled with gratitude. I wanted him to be his old self, I did, I did, I did, but I had to admit that the fact of his not being quite there yet made meeting up with Mr. Insley much simpler than it would have been. Or, rather, than it would *be,* when my father got better. But I would cross that bridge when I came to it.

The coffee shop was a couple of miles away from the state park parking lot, and running it would have taken me no time at all. But for once I had the chance to meet Mr. Insley without being either sweaty or school-day disheveled, and I'd dressed with special care that morning. The secret truth is that I love clothes. I'd known my share of the home-spun variety of homeschooled kids, the ones who wear long skirts, jumpers, flannel clogs, and Guatemalan pullovers and have their un-cut hair hanging in braids, but I had never been one of them. Good gracious, no. I'd never perused a fashion magazine, not even in the grocery line or dentist's office, but whenever my family went on field trips to New York City, I paid careful attention to every woman who walked by. My father would have considered such an interest shock-ingly unintellectual, but luckily, he loathed shopping, and my mother gave me mostly free rein, so I had quite a wardrobe, at least until I'd started dumbing it down for high school in order to survive.

But Mr. Insley had called me an "old soul" more than once; I didn't have to dress like a teenager for him. We were going for a drive in the country, so I wore dark brown wool trousers, a cashmere-mohair blend sweater the color and weightlessness of cream, and a caramel-colored suede jacket. Mr. Insley brought so much to our relationship, experi-ence, wit, erudition; the least I could do was look nice.

As perfect as our times together had been, I felt in my bones that

today would be different, special, even momentous. A turning point.
With each step along the road toward the state park, this feeling deep-
ened, and as soon as I caught sight of Mr. Insley, leaning against the
driver's side door in his hat and sunglasses, and a tweed overcoat I'd
never seen before, I knew I was right. He didn't wave, just watched my
every step, until I was just a few feet away, and then he moved toward
me, took both my hands, and, oh, dear Lord in heaven, kissed me on
both cheeks, first the right, then the left.

"Willow," he said, "you look like the very incarnation of autumn."

In my addled state, I blurted out, "Uh, so do you!," which was mor-
tifying, but only briefly, because it made Mr. Insley break into one of
his glorious, heal-all laughs.

The drive was long and harrowing, all narrow, winding, shoulderless, country roads lined with trees and fields and, sometimes, ditches
that seemed deep as moats. More than once, as I hung like death to
the steering wheel, my eyes riveted on the road, I found that I'd forgotten to breathe, and all the while, Mr. Insley talked, told me how a
cousin with a green pickup truck had taught him to drive on exactly
these kinds of roads, out near his grandparents' lake house, when he
was thirteen years old. There'd been scrapes, near misses, a flood, an
encounter with the police and a bear, all driving related, everything
happening in that one summer, which was possibly the best of his life,
and his stories were fascinating, they really were, but I was focusing
too hard on the road to say more than "oh" in response to them, which
made me feel sort of vacuous, but it didn't really matter. What mattered
was Mr. Insley's trust in me, and I didn't let him down, but when we finally pulled into the parking lot of a stone tavern called the Union Jack,
I nearly cried with relief that the drive was over.

"You were marvelous, Willow!" said Mr. Insley, gleefully.

"Thank you," I said, blushing. I considered adding "Blaine" but
somehow just couldn't. As much as I had loved his having asked me
to call him by his first name, as much as I was dying to do so, I found
that, when push came to shove, I couldn't swing it. I'd tried practicing

at home, in my room, but even there, "Blaine" felt desperately clumsy in my mouth. Because Mr. Insley looked faintly pained whenever I called him "Mr. Insley," for the moment, I called him nothing at all and hoped he didn't notice.

The tavern was ancient, crowded, and cozy, with wooden beams, dark wainscoting, wide-plank floors, a fireplace, and a mind-boggling row of beer taps at the bar. Mr. Insley ordered a Guinness, and somehow, this made alarm bells go off in my head, although I didn't quite understand why. Maybe only because it meant I would have to be the one to drive home, which probably would have happened anyway.

"And another for the lady?" said the waitress, with what looked very like a wicked gleam in her eye but might not have been. She might actually have thought I was old enough!

"No, thank you," I said, with a touch of hauteur. "Just a cup of Darjeeling, if you've got it, with cream."

"Good enough," said the waitress, with a wink.

Because he wanted me to have the full English tavern experience, Mr. Insley ordered an insane amount of food: bangers and mash, Yorkshire pudding, fish and chips, toad in the hole, Welsh rarebit. I didn't have the heart to tell him that in deference to my Anglophile father, English tavern food was the single cuisine my mother had mastered, despite the fact that, being a vegetarian, she could eat almost none of it. I believed it was a testament to my parents' love for each other that bangers and mash was my mother's specialty; we'd had it just three nights ago.

I was too agitated, in a good way, to eat much, but that was all right. Just being there with Mr. Insley was like the best kind of dream. Within those dark, close, firelit walls, we were in our own world, one that existed outside of time and light-years away from the Webley School. The two of us were one with the crowd and also above it, like an old world prince and princess in disguise, experiencing the life of commoners, and loving every minute. I talked more than usual, mostly about books, since my daily life was certainly too mundane for such an occasion, and if I say so myself, I sounded the way I'd always wanted to when I talked to Mr. Insley, star-bright and wise beyond my years.

When we'd eaten all we could, and the waitress was retrieving our check, and I was feeling the first tremors of sadness that our time in that place was ending, the high point happened, shining and perfect: Mr. Insley grabbed my hand under the table, and said, "I can't help but tell you that I think you're fantastic, Willow. I hope that's all right."

Beyond words, I pressed my lips together, nodded, and held fast to his long, thin, somewhat jumpy hand (it was as though all his wonderful, feverish energy were concentrated in that one hand), wanting to memorize every nuance of it, every bone and tendon.

"You know what I'd like?" he said, leaning in until our faces were inches apart. "I would like to show you the boat I'm building."

I had not expected him to say this, probably because I hadn't known he was building a boat or even that he was the sort of person who built things. He seemed sort of not to be, actually. But as soon as his words had sunk in, I realized how romantic they were.

"Oh, I'd love that," I said.

"It's at my house. That is, it's in a shed just behind my house. The house isn't much, really, small, even a little shabby. I rented it merely for the shed, which the old owner used to store his collection of motorcycles. The shed is nearly as big as the house and just right for boat building. Will you come sometime? Soon?"

"Yes," I said. That yes felt so big, bigger than a promise.

Mr. Insley started to say something else, then dropped his eyes. When he looked at me again, there were spots of pink burning in each of his cheeks.

"I'll just say it. Lately, for weeks, when I think of sailing away in that boat, I imagine you with me, the wind tousling your magnificent hair. Isn't that silly?"

I was so moved by this that my eyes smarted with tears.

"Oh no," I said. "Not silly at all."

The spell of that tavern was so strong that, although it dimmed when we walked out into the afternoon light, it didn't disappear. We floated in its golden cloud down the walkway and all the way to the car, and it was still there when Mr. Insley came close to me, opened my hand, put the car keys into it, closed my fingers, and then, oh glory of glories, pressed his lips roughly against my knuckles, letting them linger there for one, two, three, four seconds. What ran through me, down my arm, up my neck, and across my scalp was a current of what I knew was love.

As Mr. Insley was lifting his face away, over his shoulder, I caught sight of a man. He was standing next to his own car, brazenly watching us, his black brows quizzical below the cuff of his knit cap. I couldn't see his eyes through his sunglasses, runner's glasses, the kind that wrap around, but I didn't need to see them to feel them boring into me. Us. Under that gaze, the tavern magic vanished, and, in its absence, I faltered, nervousness tightening my chest, but then, all by myself, no magic necessary, I lifted my chin and shot the man a smile of pure triumph. *Stare all you want,* I wanted to tell him, *and you'll still never understand love like this*. But he turned away before I got the chance.

This time, driving all the long, twisting road home, even as the clouds thickened and the sky got so dark I had to turn the headlights on, I wasn't scared at all.

CHAPTER ELEVEN

Taisy

I HAD THE KEY TO my father's house for six days before I used it. The practical reason for this was that, just a few steps from the circular front drive, there was a break in the cypress hedge that led straight into the backyard, so I could get from my car to the pool house without stepping foot in the main house at all. The less practical reason was that, while I am ordinarily a person who resists injecting symbolism into real-life events on the grounds that doing so is usually self-serving and always corny, I found it impossible to even think the words *the key to my father's house,* without doing exactly that. *After nearly two decades of being locked out, Taisy Cleary had the key to her father's house. In a moment she had never expected to experience and would never forget, Taisy Cleary was given the key to her father's house. Taisy Cleary grasped the key to her father's house in her hand and knew that nothing would ever be the same again.* And so forth.

The fact that Caro, not Wilson, had given me the key diluted the symbolism a bit, as did the fact that, when she gave it to me, she explained, very apologetically, that the key did not allow absolute access to the house because, while it unlocked the regular locks, it did not unlock the deadbolts, quickly adding that they only used the deadbolts at night and that Willow unlocked them as soon as she woke up in the morning. But even diluted, the symbolism persisted: possessing the key to my father's house meant so much to me that it was just sad. So, in order to avoid confronting this fact, I avoided using the damn thing altogether.

But then I was at the gourmet grocery store one afternoon, saw a lone crate of Stayman winesap apples—dull, dark red, spotty, far appleier looking than the glossy heaps of Red Delicious—and remembered Caro mentioning that she loved them, so I bought her a sackful. When I got home, I walked around to the pool house as usual, put my groceries away, and walked back to the front door bearing my lone sack of apples. I tried the door, found it was locked, swore, and stood there like a lump on a log, roiling with emotion, not the least of which was disgust for the fact that I was roiling with emotion.

You're his daughter, I told myself. *Daughters have keys to their fathers' houses all the time. They use these keys to open the doors of their fathers' houses all the time.* But of course, I never had, not in seventeen years, so I stood on that front porch, helplessly a-roil, wanting to be able to use the key without having it feel momentous. God, *why* did everything to do with Wilson have to be so fraught? I considered leaving the apples on the porch, and that's what decided it for me: the only thing worse than using your key to open your father's door and having it be momentous was to have using the key be so momentous that you couldn't even bring yourself to do it. I stuck the key in the damn keyhole and turned it.

The house was so quiet that my footfalls echoing on the marble floor were thunderous, and I almost left the bag on the hall table and walked out, but if I chickened out now, I would never forgive myself. With a growl of exasperation, I shoved my key ring in my jacket pocket, shifted the apple bag from one arm to the other, and made a beeline for the kitchen. When I got there, I found a big blue glass bowl on the marble countertop that held just two piebald bananas and that seemed to be waiting for me. I pushed the bananas to one side and filled the rest of the bowl with my apples. There I was in Wilson's house, taking liberties, and, oh *crap,* it felt good.

I was so busy with this that it wasn't until I was settling the last apple into the bowl that I saw Caro. On the kitchen table, next to a bowl of what appeared to be the same butternut soup with mushrooms, a tub of which I'd just bought for myself at the gourmet grocery, lay what first registered to my brain as some kind of wild-haired creature—an oversized very long-haired guinea pig perhaps—but which turned out to be Caro's head. It wasn't resting on her folded arms or even on one hand; her left cheek lay directly on the tabletop, her hands out of sight under the table. As soon as I figured out it was her, I thought, *Oh thank God none of her hair ended up in the soup.* Hot on the heels of that came, *Please, please, please don't let her be dead!*

As I beat my hasty way over to her, I banged my hip on the edge of the counter and hissed, "Shit!," and I guess the word or the hiss of it broke through Caro's consciousness in a way that the crackle of the paper bag and the plop of the apples into the bowl had not because she lifted her head with a start, pressed her palms to her eyes briefly, and then stared at me, blinking so blankly that I wondered if she might be drunk or worse.

Dear God, I thought, *Willow already has Wilson, with all his Wilson-ness plus a bum heart, for a father. She does not need a drunk for a mother.*

But after a few seconds, Caro's eyes began to clear and her face firmed up around the edges the way people's eyes and faces do when they wake up from a deep sleep, and Caro looked around her, down at her soup, up at me, and smiled, "Golly damn," she said. "You caught me napping."

Napping. As though everyone just settles in for a nap with their head practically inside their soup bowl.

"I'm sorry," I said, quickly. "I just found some Staymans at the grocery store and thought I'd bring them in for you. I almost left them at the door, but, you know, I had that key you gave me, I guess it was a few days ago, six days or something, and I thought . . ." I trailed off at long last and just nodded sideways at the bowl of apples.

"How thoughtful," said Caro. "Oh, I'm afraid I've startled you. You see, I've never been a very good sleeper. It's just a case of bad genes, which, thank goodness, I did not pass down to Willow. Anyway, when I can't sleep at night, I fear I'm prone to catnaps."

Cats curled up in a splash of sun. Cats didn't drop down, mid-lunch, as though struck by a thunderbolt.

"My friend Trillium calls them 'power naps,'" I said, playing along. "It's amazing how she'll just tip her head back anywhere and sleep hard for fifteen minutes and then wake up refreshed."

Caro grabbed little bunches of her hair on either side of her head and pulled them away from her face in what I assumed was the curly-haired equivalent of running your hands through your hair.

"I'm afraid I don't feel quite so refreshed after my naps. It takes me a while to get my feet back under me, I guess."

Suddenly, catching sight of the giant, antique-looking wall clock, she hit her fist on the table so hard her soup bowl rattled. "Damn!"

"What's wrong?" I asked.

"I'm supposed to be in the car right now, on my way to pick up Willow. She's taken to staying after school to work on a project with a classmate for English. Usually, she stays longer, sometimes for a few hours, but she has a big math test to study for. She asked me to pick her up in front of the school at four o'clock."

I glanced at the clock. 3:55.

"If you leave now, you should only be a few minutes late. Can you just text her and let her know you're on your way?"

Caro looked at me, startled.

"Oh, no. She doesn't have a cell phone. Wilson thinks they cause human relationships to wither on the vine. And, you know, she never needed one back when she was always at home."

Oh, brother. Cell phones? Wilson could wither a human relationship with his tone of voice alone, as I had reason to know. Oh, but poor Willow, in high school without a phone!

"Aha. Well, I'm sure she won't worry if you're a few minutes late, will she?"

Caro sighed and, with that sigh, energy seemed to rush from her body. Her eyelids drooped, her shoulders sagged, and, suddenly, she looked far less awake than she had just seconds before.

"As I mentioned, it takes me a bit of time to regroup after a nap. I know it sounds crazy," she said, with a wan smile, "but I'm not sure I should be behind a wheel. I don't suppose you have time? She said she'd be waiting right outside the school."

"Oh! Me. Well, sure. Of course. I know where Webley is. I'll go right now."

As I drove, I wondered about Caro. She'd certainly seemed energetic enough when she was banging the table and saying, "Damn!" And weariness had fallen over her so fast, like someone had flicked a switch. Had she done the flicking herself? Had she seen me and made the split-second decision that I should be the one to pick up Willow? But why? I remembered the apple cake breakfast, her slip about Wilson's boarding school. Was it possible that Caro was a case of still waters—no, not still, but rippling, eddying, hazy, meandering waters—running deep?

Because she wasn't expecting my car, I got a chance to idle at the curb for a few minutes, watching Willow when she didn't know I was watching, something I'd never done before. For one thing, I just plain didn't see her much; for another, when I did, she was all wariness, on full red alert but also disdainful, as though I were some lowly bug that just might sting. Now, watching her unobserved, I was surprised at what I saw. She sat on one of the benches that lined the sidewalk leading up to the front door of the school. All the benches were dedicated to someone, with little brass plaques saying to whom, and I happened to know that Willow's was the Dotty Pikkels bench. Allie Pham, a ballet

friend of mine who'd gone to Webley, had received her first kiss on
that bench from a lacrosse player named Stan Manley, and Allie had
written "I love you, Dotty Pikkels" all over her notebooks for an entire
semester until Stan the Man broke up with her and she scratched out
all the "loves" and turned them to "hates."

Now, Willow sat on Dotty Pikkels, twirling one end of her scarf
in her hand, her hair blazing, her coat open, and, stretched out on the
ground at her feet, leaning back on his hands, his long legs out in front
of him, was a boy. Even from a distance, I could tell he was beautiful,
part-Asian probably, great shoulders, hair standing up in jags, a smile
like an angel's. The way he sat, all that thoughtless grace, taking up
space with such fluid assurance, reminded me of Trillium, and I knew
it was good to be this kid the same way it was good to be Trillium.
I'd pictured Willow in high school as a fish out of water, pictured her
walking miserably down the crowded hallways, being left out and lost,
but here she was, all teasing, chatty volubility, shaking her finger at a
handsome boy like it was the most natural thing in the world.

As soon as she noticed me, though, she stiffened, and you could
just see it, her going from open to shut, closing her personality like
someone closing an umbrella. But I could see the fear in her eyes even
before she opened the car door.

"Is my mother okay?" she said. "Did something happen? Is she at
home?"

She clutched her backpack to her chest, and I wondered if it were
to stop herself from shaking, and for the umpteenth time since I met
her, I wanted to fold her into a deep hug.

"She's at home and fine," I said, quickly, "just a little tired. She
was taking a power nap and hadn't quite woken up from it when I
happened to see her, so she asked me to come get you. No big deal."

"You saw her? Asleep?"

Willow's dismay was palpable. How could it matter so much if I'd
found her mother sleeping?

"Well, yeah, but she woke up and we talked. She's fine."

"Where?"

"Where was she sleeping, you mean?"

Willow gave a tense nod.

"Um, I found these apples she liked at the market, so I came inside to leave them in the kitchen, and I saw her at the table."

I waited—anxiously, hopefully—for Willow to ask exactly how I'd gained entry to her house, but all she did was close her eyes, her body going limp with relief.

"Oh, she was inside," she murmured, then caught herself, and straightened. "It's just that once I found her asleep on the garden bench, which is no big deal, of course. She's an artist, and sometimes she loses track of time at night and forgets to sleep, which I think is a common thing for artists. Completely normal and understandable. But I just wouldn't want her to fall asleep outside now, when it's getting colder and everything."

"Oh. Well, if it were really cold, she probably wouldn't get comfortable enough to fall asleep anyway, right?"

Now that her fears were put to rest, all her hauteur came back. Willow gave me a blatant you-have-no-idea-what-you're-talking-about look, then shrugged and stared out of the window.

"So is that the boy you were working with?" I asked.

"Who said I was working with a boy?" said Willow, coldly, still looking out the window.

"No one. Your mother said you were staying after school to work on a project with a partner, so I guess what I meant was is that boy the *person* you were working with on your project."

"Oh. In that case, yes."

If there was a gene for smugness, she'd inherited it straight from Wilson, down to the last tiny, exasperating snippet of DNA. But I would take the high road if it killed me.

"Looks like you were setting him straight on something," I said, with a laugh.

"How do you mean?"

"You can tell," I said, "even from a distance, when two people are arguing. It's in their posture, their facial expressions, the way one of them, say, wags her finger at the other. The two of you were the spitting image of people having a friendly argument."

She shrugged. "Oh."

"And you were the spitting image of the person who was winning."

For a moment, I thought she'd smile, but she bit it back and shrugged again. She had the teenager shrug down pat, slight twitch of the shoulder, even slighter sideways jerk of the head, as though even in belittling you, she would not waste precious energy. I wanted to tell her, though, that three shrugs in as many minutes was overkill; it revealed her as the amateur she was. It was a petty thing to want, I knew, and instantly, I felt ashamed of myself. As punishment for my pettiness, I would say something that she could really sink her smug teeth into.

"Anyway, he was cute."

I tossed the sentence out there like a wounded seal, and sharklike, she couldn't resist, turning away from the window to regard me, contempt in every feature. Right then, although she looked nothing like Wilson, she looked exactly like Wilson.

"'Cute.' I'm afraid I don't know what that means. I didn't exactly grow up in a household in which we bandied about words like 'cute.'"

What sixteen-year-old girl bandied about phrases like "bandied about"? Still, ouch. But she wasn't finished.

"So I can't actually speak to Luka's cuteness or lack thereof, except to say that if Luka is actually cute or anything along such lines, I haven't noticed."

What *I* noticed is the way she inserted his name into that sentence, twice, even though I knew she couldn't possibly have wanted me to know what it was. She said it because she couldn't help herself, because she just liked saying it, because saying it made him a little bit more hers every time she did it. Probably she didn't realize any of this yet; maybe she wouldn't admit it to herself for a long time, but I knew. I'd been there.

Ben, lips pressed together at the beginning, open in the middle, tongue on the roof of my mouth at the end.

Been there? Ha. I was still there, heaven help me. I stole a glance at Willow who had spent her life so cherished, so boxed up and restrained and watched over in her pretty, tiny, high-walled world. What would happen when she let her feelings loose upon that world? I imagined them running rampant, trampling the garden, jumping the walls or burning them to the ground.

Heaven help you, too, Willow, I thought.

IN MY RUSH TO pick up Willow, I'd left my cell phone in the pool house, and when I got back, after she'd shot me a terse "thank you" and sailed through the front door while I walked around the house to the backyard, there was a message from Ben. Since I didn't have his number, I didn't know it was from Ben, but his first words were "Hey, Taisy, this is Ben," and they knocked the breath clean out of me. When I'd more or less recovered, I listened a second time. There was no way not to hear the awkwardness in his voice, but it didn't matter. He'd called.

"Hey, Taisy, this is Ben. I was hoping you might have time to talk soon. I'm headed over to my dad's to drop off some groceries and do a little work in the yard, but I'll have my phone. I'll be around later, too. Okay, thanks. Take care."

I was about to call him back, my finger was actually hovering over his number, but instead, I headed out the door. I could have driven to Ben's father's house in my sleep, which was a good thing, since, rocked by the aftershocks of hearing Ben's voice saying he wanted to talk to me, I wasn't exactly at my most focused. In fifteen minutes, I was there. The old green Ransom's Garden World pickup truck was in the driveway, but there was no sign of Ben. I stood in the yard just looking at the place. The house was small, old, and with its irregular brickwork, teeming window boxes, funny stone chimney, twisty-boughed trees, and leaded glass windows, it looked as it always had, like something out of a fairy tale.

I pressed my thumb to the brass doorbell button and listened, with closed eyes, to the familiar off-key, two-note chime. It had driven Mr. Ransom nuts, that chime, since, his less than stellar singing voice notwithstanding, he had a good ear, but, now, I was happy that he'd never had it fixed. I heard footsteps inside the house, and the door opened, and there was Ben. He wore jeans, a frayed Middlebury sweatshirt, running shoes, and a look of surprise. It wasn't elation, which I would have preferred, but since the last time I'd seen him, he had walked away from me mad, I would take it. He rocked back on his heels as though the sight of me had thrown him off balance.

"Hey," he said.

"Hey."

"I was, uh, just unloading some groceries." He hooked his thumb in the direction of the kitchen.

"I see."

"Yeah, my dad used to be a big grocery shopper, loved it. You might remember that. But once Bobbie got sick, I don't know, I guess he got out of the habit of shopping. Just wanted to stick close to home. So I started doing it for him."

"Oh no, I hope he's still cooking. He always loved that."

Ben smiled. "Yeah, he's just getting back to it. Made his special meatballs just the other day, in fact. Oh, and he's started complaining about my shopping, which seems like a good sign. I got the wrong brand of tomato paste, apparently, last time I went, so I think pretty soon, he'll fire me and get back to doing it himself."

"Good," I said. "He told me about Bobbie. Sounds like he went through the wringer. I'm so glad he's feeling more like himself."

Ben nodded, thoughtfully. "He and Bobbie were something. I mean, I could have sworn that people didn't come much more buoyant than my dad, but I think Bobbie had him beat. Together, they were—" He broke off, took a breath, and shook his head. "Sorry."

"Why?"

He gave a wry smile. "From groceries to death to true love in the first two minutes of our first conversation in seventeen years."

"Our second, actually," I said, and immediately winced. "I probably shouldn't have brought up that first conversation, should I have?"

"Yep. That one was a bust, no thanks to me. I shouldn't have walked away."

"Well, I wasn't exactly tactful, asking you out of the clear blue sky to take off in the car with me."

"I guess it took me off guard. Just a little."

"You know, I never could be tactful around you. I am around other people, I'm pretty sure. But when I was with you, it was like I knew my mind better than I do when I'm with anyone else, but I forget to hold back or edit. I just blurt out whatever I'm thinking."

When I looked up at Ben, I could see that without moving at all, he'd pulled back from me.

"And look at how I just did the very thing I was talking about," I added, lamely.

His eyes warmed ever so slightly. "Oh, yeah? I didn't notice."

"I switched to present tense halfway, through, too, didn't I?"

"Possibly," he said, with a flicker of a smile, but then he added, "Forget about it," in a way that made me think he really wanted to.

"For crying out loud," I said, "I am too awkward to live."

Ben should have laughed at this, but he didn't, and we stood there, not looking each other in the eye. I found myself staring at Ben's running shoes, which were bright orange and extremely high-tech. I remembered how Ben had always loved to run. I flashed back to his face after a high school track meet, his cheeks streaked brilliant pink in the spring air.

Finally, he said, "I'm a pretty nice guy, letting you stand out here in the cold. You want to come in?"

I glanced over his shoulder, into the house. I had been so happy there, as happy as I'd ever been anywhere. Oh, hell, happier.

"I don't know," I said. "I was always so comfortable in that house. If I got inside it again, I might start blurting crap out right and left, and scare you off forever. You think?"

Another tiny thaw. "Well, I guess that's a possibility."

Then, we lapsed into a stilted silence. Oh, this dance of back-and-forth, comfortable, uncomfortable, Ben opening the door a chink, then shutting it, was playing havoc with my nerves. I wanted to grab him by the shoulders, shake him, and say, "Just give in! Just like me, like me, like me!"

"You called me," I reminded him. "How'd you get my number?"

To my boundless relief, Ben chuckled. "I'm not sure. Wait, didn't you leave a message at the store? Or two? Or, hold on, was it four?"

"Three," I said. "I wanted to apologize for the lack of tact thing in our first conversation."

"No need for that. But thank you."

"You're welcome."

We stood, finally looking right at each other. I was drinking him in, every detail—the way his eyebrows were thick but so tidy, as though they'd been combed, the way his neck moved when he swallowed—as unobtrusively as I could, and I hoped he was doing the same to me, but I sort of doubted it. Mostly, he had the aspect of a person who wasn't sure what to say next.

Finally, I said, "So did you call to talk about anything in particular? It's okay if you didn't, of course, if you just wanted to catch up or whatever."

Ben snapped to, and his face grew serious, his eyes narrowing and turning down at the corners the way they did when he was worried. *Uh-oh,* I thought.

"Actually, there was something. It's about Willow."

I jumped at the sound of Ben saying her name; it was so strange, like two worlds colliding.

"Do you know Willow?" I asked.

"Not really. I've seen her run, though. I've done a few races since I've been back home, 5Ks, 10Ks. She's good."

"How did you know it was her?"

He gave a half grin. "The sight of Wilson cheering his head off on the sidelines was pretty hard to miss."

"Wow. Wilson? Cheering?"

"I know. Crazy."

"Very crazy."

He shifted uncomfortably from one foot to the other.

"You sure you don't want to come in?" he asked.

I glanced into the house again and felt that I would have given almost anything to be inside it, curled up at one end of the fat sofa or tucked, with my legs under me, in the leather armchair.

"Here's the thing," I said. "This house is the one place—and I've thought about this a lot, so I'm pretty sure I'm right—it's the one place where nothing bad ever happened to me. And I was nice here. It was so easy to be my nicest self in this house."

"Oh," said Ben. "Well. I'll tell my dad that. He'll like it." He didn't say *he* liked it, and I saw that his eyes had shifted back to neutral.

"So, anyway," I said, quickly, "I'd really like to keep it that way, with not one negative association, and from the look on your face, I'm pretty sure this thing to do with Willow is a thing to worry about."

"Okay, so you want to take a walk instead?" he asked.

"Sure. You need to get a jacket?"

His eyes twinkled; I know people always say that, but only black eyes truly twinkle, and Ben's eyes were truly black. He shook his head.

"What?" I asked.

"You're still the person who thinks everyone should get a jacket," he said.

This one slender, tossed-off sentence came to me like a gift. Ben remembered things about me. I could feel myself beaming. We started walking.

"You know, this may be nothing," said Ben, "I hope so, but the other day—a Saturday, I drove to this English pub to meet a friend for a beer."

A flutter went through me when he said "friend." I wanted to ask about the friend, but I'd put a moratorium on blurting stuff out, at least for the duration of this walk, and I could think of no tactful way to ask, "What was the gender of this friend? Was she pretty? And how close, on a scale of one to ten, would you say the two of you are?" Anyway, I'd noticed that, in spite of his worry, now that Ben was talking about the present—or at least the recent past—instead of *our* past, the stiffness had gone out of his voice and his shoulders. I wanted to keep it that way.

"And I pulled into the parking lot," he went on, "and got out of my car, and was just about to head inside when I saw Willow."

"You saw Willow in the parking lot of a pub? That's weird. If Wilson were up and around, well, English pubs have to be right up his nutty Anglophile alley, but Caro doesn't seem like the type. She's a vegetarian, for one thing. Do English people even eat vegetables?"

"If they do, you never hear about it, but, no, she wasn't with Caro."

"Oh."

"She was with this guy, a much older guy."

"What? Are you sure?"

Ben rubbed his forehead with his palm. "Okay, not absolutely sure. I didn't really see him because his back was mostly to me, and he was wearing a cap, but there was something about the way he moved. And his hands, they looked somehow older. Not old, just like an adult's hands. I saw his right hand really clearly when he touched her."

I came to a dead stop.

"He *touched* her? How do you mean?"

"No, sorry. All he did was lift her hand and kiss it. Nothing creepy. Except."

Frightened, I turned to face him. "Except what?"

"I can't explain it. These are all just impressions, but even though it wasn't technically creepy, it was creepy. I've tried to figure out why. Maybe it was the way he seemed so proprietary or maybe it was the age difference, or what I thought was the age difference. I just know that my first instinct was to pull him away from her."

"Why didn't you? Wait. I didn't mean to sound like you should have or anything. I just wonder what stopped you."

"Well, for one thing, it was a kiss on the hand. That's it. And for another, before I could do anything, she saw me."

"Really? What did she do?"

"She just gave me this smile, and it wasn't only self-possessed. It was—"

"Smug?"

"Queenly," said Ben. "She looked like the exact opposite of someone in trouble."

"But you're still worried?"

"She's, what, sixteen, seventeen?"

"Sixteen."

"At sixteen, you can be in trouble and not even know it."

We kept walking. Ahead I could see the side of a blue house. Mrs. Pando. She'd always come running out with cookies for the dogs, not dog treats, but actual chocolate chip cookies, and we'd take them from her and say we'd give them to them later for dessert and then we'd eat them ourselves.

"Mrs. Pando," I said and then winced. For a second, I'd forgotten to stick to the here and now. I braced myself for Ben to ignore me or to get distant, but maybe he'd forgotten, too, because he said, easily, "I wonder if she ever figured out that dogs can't eat chocolate."

"Oh, God, I hope not," I said.

"Me, too."

"Was he tall?" I asked. "The guy?"

"Not short. Taller than Willow. Probably not as tall as I am."

"Tan?"

"Not that I noticed."

"Huh. Well, I saw Willow with this kid the other day, a boy from her English class, probably about her age, which would make him old enough to drive, assuming he has parents who aren't Wilson."

"He was tall? And tan?"

"He looked tall, although he was sitting down at the time. But, yes, definitely tan. Maybe half Chinese or Korean? And beautiful."

Ben gave me an amused look.

"I know. Now who's being creepy?" I said. "No, but, really, his beauty wasn't of special interest to me. It was just an unavoidable fact."

"Did they seem to be together?"

"It's possible. They were talking in this very animated way. But they seemed more like friends who are meant to be together and somewhere deep down want to be and will be one day, but who just don't know it yet."

"You could tell all that just from seeing them talk to each other?"

"I'm a woman," I said. "We're fine-tuned that way."

"Got it."

"So could it have been him? Luka?"

"I can't swear it wasn't. Unfortunately, I never saw the blinding beauty of his face."

"Ah. That *is* unfortunate. What about the car? Was it a teenager car?"

Ben stopped walking to think. "You know what? It was. It was some kind of Japanese sedan. Older model. A Toyota, I think. Not in great shape."

"Aha. The kind of car that used to be the family car before the family got a new one and gave the old beat-up one to the teenager."

"I guess. I hope you're right. It seems like sort of an odd place for two teenagers to have a lunch date on a Saturday afternoon, but maybe."

"Remember Willow's not your typical teenager," I said. "She's been molded by the biggest Winston Churchill fan to ever wear round glasses."

Ben laughed. His face when he laughed gave Luka's, gave anyone's a run for its money. How I wanted to touch it, just tuck a finger into the divot in his lip. But we kept walking, and that's when I noticed how close we were to the tree. The Tree. It was just around the next curve in the sidewalk. The tree against which I had leaned when Ben kissed me for the first time. It had been late evening; we were walking the dogs; the streetlights were burning. We'd stopped to talk under the tree, and Ben had kissed me, and when we finished kissing—and it took a long time—we looked down and saw the dogs, sitting side by side and staring gravely up at us with their violet-shaped faces.

If I saw that tree, if I were to walk close to it, with Ben next to me, I might fall to the ground beneath it and cry; I might climb into it and refuse to come down; I might lean against its broad trunk and wait for what would probably—oh please not probably—what would *possibly* never come again. I knew I should stop, turn around, run away, but I couldn't do it. With the past, in all its lost, exquisite sweetness, hurtling toward me, I kept walking.

I was two sidewalk squares ahead of Ben before I realized he'd stopped. I turned around. Ben was looking at his watch.

"Hey, I'm sorry," he said, hurriedly, "but I really have to get back."

"Oh," I said.

"Are you okay to walk back by yourself?" he asked.

"Yeah, sure. See you later. Thanks for telling me about Willow."

"No problem." He jogged backward a few steps. "Okay, then."

He turned and slipped into a graceful lope, running shoes flashing. I stood alone on the sidewalk, watching him, trying not to watch him, until he was out of sight, and then waited another minute just to be sure he was back inside the house. Then, I walked back to my car and drove to Wilson's.

CHAPTER TWELVE

Willow

I AM FLOATING ON THE surface of a pond, weightless, air skimming my face, my hair fanning out around me. Flowers drift through my open fingers; my dress billows like a jellyfish around my legs. Boughs and flower stalks bend in from the edges of the pond, an everywhere of emerald green, and through branches, fragments of blue sky. I am so calm. Utterly, utterly light. Then, a voice begins to speak. I can't understand the words because my ears are mostly underwater, but I know the voice is Mr. Insley's. He must be sitting near the edge of the pond, but I don't see him. At first, I struggle to hear what he is saying, but the water is so pleasant, and I don't want to work at anything, so after a while, I stop trying. I hear thunder, but I'm not really scared, just a little. There is no current; I don't travel, just float. I feel something stirring under the water, something big displacing the water, swimming under me, and I think, That should be scary, but it isn't. *Mr. Insley's voice gets louder, more insistent, but I still can't understand what he's saying because the thunder gets louder, too. Almost soundlessly, Luka's head and shoulders emerge from the water's surface, and I turn to look at him. He streams silvery water; droplets shine on his eyelashes and the tops of his cheeks. He is so bright that I close my eyes and strain to hear what Mr. Insley is saying; I know it's something important. But the sound of his voice turns into a banging sound. Bang, bang, bang.*

Bang, bang, bang.

I woke up with a start. The thunder was real; rain was starting on the roof, swishing against the tiles. The slapping was real, too. My blood turned to ice water. *Oh, dear God, the back screen door!* I clutched at the deadbolt key hanging from a chain around my neck, my fingers cold against my breastbone, and then, I leaped out of bed so fast I knocked over the lamp on my nightstand, and half stumbled down the stairs, my breath a sharp in-and-out of *oh no oh no oh no*. The kitchen was a mess, dunes of flour on the countertops, sugar gritty under my feet, but, this time, no burners were on, no gas smell filled the kitchen, thank heaven for that. I ran out the door, then ran back, and closed it firmly, praying that the sound of its banging hadn't already woken up my father.

"Muddy!" I called, my voice high and urgent, a needle of sound against the blurry backdrop of rain. "Muddy, Muddy!"

The yard was so dark, but out of the corner of my eye, I caught a glimpse of something pale, far away near the pool house, and a voice came across the grass: "I have her, Willow. Over here." Eustacia. I ran as fast as I could, which was fast.

The two of them were standing under a tree, and even in the dark, I recognized the abstraction in my mother's eyes. Her wet pajamas clung to her body, making her look so frail that it pained me to see, but at least her face was tranquil.

"I can't remember where I left it," she said, looking in my direction, if not exactly at me. "But that's okay."

"Of course, it's okay," I said, quietly. "You'll find it in the morning."

Gently, I took her by the shoulders and led her to the pool-house porch, where it was dry. She sat in the rocker but didn't rock, just folded her hands in her lap and looked at them. When I turned around, I found Eustacia standing at the bottom of the porch steps. She opened her mouth to speak.

"It's not what you think," I whispered, ferociously, from the top step. "She's not crazy. Don't you dare even think it."

Eustacia regarded me, her eyes wide in her wet face and full of what looked far too much like pity but that could have been—but probably wasn't—ordinary kindness.

"Willow," she said.

"Don't!"

"Don't what?"

I stabbed my finger in her direction.

"Don't feel sorry for her. Or for any of us. Why are you even getting involved in this anyway? It's family business."

Eustacia's lips tightened.

"You know what? It's a really stupid time for the two of us to argue, but there's really no need to treat me like the enemy here. I heard her. I came outside. If you think I shouldn't have, tough shit, kid."

"Talking profanity like a common street punk," I said. "How unsurprising."

My belligerence was childish, uncalled for, unfair, but—oh, wow—it felt good. Still, deep down inside, a tiny voice was whispering the truth, that the only blameworthy person here was I. Eustacia shook her head, sighing.

"Fine. Now, don't you think we should put her back to bed? Or she could lie down here at the pool house."

"No."

"Your mother is soaked to the bone, Willow. And by the way, I don't think she's crazy. I think she's sleeping and that it would be better for her to do it in bed."

"She wouldn't like to wake up here."

"Well, then, walk her back to the house before she wakes up. How long does this usually last?"

"Sometimes a few minutes, sometimes a lot longer. She doesn't do it very often. Only when she's having a really long bad-sleep streak. Insomnia makes it happen, but that's not her fault. Some people just can't sleep as well as other people. Most of the time, though, she's absolutely fine."

I walked my mother down the porch steps, the architecture of her shoulders and back—the beams and buttresses that held my mother upright—feeling heartbreakingly breakable against my arm, and started off with her across the lawn.

"Do you want help?" asked Eustacia.

"No."

I glanced back at her. She was still standing there, looking small under the big tree, buffeted by wind, but strong and straight, her arms wrapped around herself. I wasn't warming to her or anything, but I could not deny that the woman had excellent posture.

"Thank you," I added, and I saw her nod.

ONCE MY MOTHER WAS safely under the quilts in the guest room where she'd been sleeping since my father's heart attack, and I'd cleaned up the kitchen as best I could without being too noisy, I lay flat on my back in my own bed. Tears of relief and guilt slid down my temples and into my hair. Ever since my father's surgery, it had been my job, my sacred duty, to lock the deadbolts at night, and I'd never once forgotten. Thank God I'd locked the one on my mother's studio door earlier that evening, but just because I deserved it, I imagined her in there, barefoot in her pajamas, shards of glass all around her, her mind shrouded in that strange lucid/cloudy twilit state. Imagined her turning on the glassblowing torch, the dagger of blue flame. *I'm so sorry, Muddy, so so so so sorry.*

After a long while, I stopped crying and remembered my dream, not the part about Luka, which wasn't important—of course, he *would* be swimming, the water rat—but the part about Mr. Insley. I wondered if this was what being in love would always be like, dreaming inscrutable dreams about your beloved and forgetting your duties because your head was so full of him, him, him that everything else was crowded out. I hoped not. If I could not take care of the people in this house, I was a brute, an ingrate of the first water, unforgivable.

And if Mr. Insley were that present in my mind when I was away from him, well, it was nothing compared to how he was when I was with him. He was a whirlpool, pulling me in; a high wire on which I walked with the ground so far below, everyone else tiny as ants; a narrow, twisting, breathtaking road. Intoxicating. Exhausting. Sometimes, after we'd spent time together, my muscles actually ached from my being so—I don't know—hyperawake, so tightly coiled. And nervous. Nervous in the best possible way but still nervous, waiting for his reactions, for the next thing he would say or do, wanting so much to say or do the right things back. Maybe someday, I would settle in, remember how to breathe like a normal person in his presence. I loved the way things were, but I didn't see how they could go on like this forever, and I wanted them to. I swear I wanted our love to last forever and ever and ever.

THE NEXT MORNING, I was so tired, tired in that way that makes you feel like you have a fever, like you've lost a layer of skin, like you'd vibrate like a violin string if someone touched you. Almost as soon as I got to school, someone did touch me, didn't just touch but knocked into me so hard I dropped my books, and I didn't just vibrate, I was seized by a minor inner earthquake.

"God, watch where you're going, spaz!" said Bec.

I didn't ignore her and crouch down to gather up my books, as I might have on another day. Buzzing and prickly and full of earthquake, I took two steps in Bec's direction, stood stock-still, and stared her in the eye.

"What?" she spat.

"Why?" I asked. My voice seemed to come from a cool place at the exact center of my body and was almost perfectly flat, all inquiry, not a trace of whine or accusation.

"Why, what?" she said, tossing around amused glances to her flat-ironed entourage.

"Why do you hate me?" It was the voice of someone merely interested, calm as stone.

Something happened then. I don't know why, maybe because of what I'd asked or the way I'd asked or just my—for once—failure to be afraid of her, but something altered in Bec, a wall fell down or a curtain went up or *something* so that what suddenly stared back at me was naked, her true face, her underface, stripped bare of sarcasm and scorn, and what I saw in it, raw as a scrape, was a child's kind of hurt, sorrow mixed with confusion. It didn't last. Before I could take two breaths, the old face slid down like a garage door.

"Hate you?" she said, with a sneer. "Seriously? Why would anyone bother to hate *you*?"

She and her friends walked away, laughing, and, sapped, I turned around to pick up my books, but they weren't on the floor anymore. Luka stood there, holding them.

"Nice friend you've got there," I growled at him, breaching the unspoken rule in our friendship that we did not mention Bec to each other, ever.

If he heard me, he didn't show it. He said, "Let's go. Why aren't your books in your backpack, anyway? You haven't even gone to your locker yet, have you?"

"No. I was looking over some things in the car on the way here. But just because someone's holding her books does not mean she deserves to have them knocked to the floor."

I reached out my arms to take the books from him, but he ignored me again. I'll say that for Luka, he was good at ignoring. He started walking in the direction of my locker, and then stood there, leaning against the one next to mine, handing me my books, one by one, as I sorted through what I needed for class.

"We need to work on the project, really break the whole thing down, interview by interview," he said.

Luka and I were making a film about Dorothea's marriage to Casaubon, a pseudodocumentary.

"I still think you're wrong about never showing the interviewer. No one likes a disembodied voice," I said. "Disembodied voices are sinister." I flashed back to Mr. Insley's voice in my dream. But, no, that was completely different.

"Nope, nope, nope. Not wrong. But we can talk about it later. It's sunny. How about we sit outside under the tree during lunch and work on it?"

I shut my locker door.

"We're not allowed to sit outside during lunch."

"Actually, we are," said Luka.

I thought about myself hunkered down in that hideous stairwell, gobbling, when I could have been outside on a bench during lunch period like a normal person. *But then Mr. Insley wouldn't have found you*, I reminded myself, *and where would you be now?*

"Liar," I said.

"I never lie," said Luka.

"Really," I said, skeptically. "Never?"

"Really," he said, seriously. "Never."

"Luka, if we were allowed to eat outside," I said, "why wouldn't I know that?"

We started walking.

"Uh, because you don't know a lot of things, especially about school?"

I pretended to trip him. He pretended to stumble.

"Anyway, I can't," I said. "I have other plans."

I was eating with Mr. Insley, just as I always did, but I didn't tell Luka that. I didn't care if he knew—because he probably did know—I just didn't want to talk about it with him.

"So cancel them," he said.

"Nope," I said, lightly. It may have been the first time in my life I'd said "nope." I liked it. The word popped in the air like a soap bubble.

"All right, so meet me after school under the aforementioned tree."

I was driving with Mr. Insley after school. We no longer called our meetings "lessons"; I'd graduated to just "driving."

"Can't," I said, airily. "Plans."

"Come on, Willow," he said, nudging me with his shoulder.

If I had a large sum of money, I'd bet it all that most girls at Webley would have folded like a starry-eyed house of cards at one of Luka Bailey-Song's nudges, but I was not most girls. Instead of folding, I yawned, colossally, only remembering to cover my mouth at the tail end of it.

"Oh, am I boring you?" asked Luka.

"Can you keep a secret?" I asked.

"Yeah. I never tell my friends' secrets."

"You never lie, and you never tell your friends' secrets."

"Right."

"Well, if that's true, how very honorable of you," I said. "But what if you have to lie in order to keep someone's secret? Hmmm, Mr. Honorable? What then?"

"I don't lie. But if a friend's secret is part of the truth, I just don't tell the whole truth."

"Which is different from lying."

"It is," said Luka. "Totally."

"I'm unconvinced, but no matter. The secret is that my mother is a somnambulist." I don't know why I wanted to tell him, since I had never voluntarily told a single soul, had in fact gone to some lengths to protect her by keeping it a secret, but for some peculiar reason, telling Luka did not feel like I was betraying my mother or my family or anyone.

"Wow."

"It means she's a sleepwalker."

Luka shot me a look. "I know what it means. I'm smart, remember?"

"Oh, right. Forgot. Except that she doesn't just walk; sometimes she bakes or talks. Once she got in the car and started the engine, but she woke up before she drove it."

"Shit."

"Indeed. Anyway, last night, she had a somnambulistic event out in the rain, and I had to take care of her."

I told him this so easily, the same way I'd told him about Eustacia just days before. Who knows what I would tell him next? I used to be able to predict what I would do, but those days were over. Now, I surprised myself all the time.

Luka turned to me, concerned. "She's okay?"

"Yes."

"What about you?"

This is what it is like to have a friend, I thought.

"Fine, thank you," I said. "Just tired. Hence the yawn. Here's my classroom, Luka. Thanks for helping pick up my books."

Luka said, "Listen, I have a free period at the end of the day, so Coach said it was okay if I did some laps. If you change your mind, I'll meet you in the hallway outside the pool after school."

"Okay, water rat," I said. "But I won't change my mind."

AT LUNCHTIME, MR. INSLEY was late to his classroom and I was earlier than usual, so I saw the writing on the board before he did, thick, black blaring out from the white. It had taken a lot of work to make the lines that thick: "SHE'S 16, PERV." It took up the entire board. At first, I couldn't understand what it meant, and even when I did, I didn't realize right away that I was the "she," and then, just as Mr. Insley walked into his classroom with his lunch bag, I realized it. Under his breath, Mr. Insley said, "What the bloody hell?," before he noticed me standing there and demanded, "How long has this been here? Has anyone else seen it?"

His tone was as harsh as if I had written the words myself. Tears spilled out of my eyes. I was so tired.

"I'm sorry," I said, with a ragged little sob. "I'm really sorry."

Mr. Insley's face softened. He took two steps toward me, then spun around and shut the door. In an instant, his arms encircled me, pulled me in. My face was against his shirt. I didn't fall apart, as I had in the stairwell, just went ragdoll-limp, my arms dangling at my sides, leaked tears, and let myself be held.

"You smell like limes," I said, finally.

He didn't let go, just loosened his grasp, and looked down at me.

"It's all right, you know," he said. "I got thrown off for a moment, but it's nothing, just stupid, jealous, callow teenaged vandals. They don't matter. How could they?"

"It scared me," I said.

I pulled back. Out of the corner of my eye, I could still see the writing. The word *perv* made my stomach clench. Could there be any truth in it? Was anything here perverted?

"What are you thinking?" asked Mr. Insley.

His face was so sensitive, his brow wrinkled with concern.

"That I trust you," I said. "That being in your arms makes me feel safe."

He leaned toward me, closed his eyes, and breathed in.

"You smell like roses," he said.

I almost corrected him. Jasmine. My shampoo was jasmine scented. But how could that matter? Telling someone that they smelled like roses, even if they didn't, quite, was the antithesis of perverted.

"What are you thinking?" he asked again, and the tender pain in his voice was lovely to hear, but awful at the same time. He was looking at me like I was a small, broken thing, an injured bird maybe. I had to put a stop to it.

I straightened and gave him a smile. *Stiff upper lip, Willow,* I thought, firmly.

"I am thinking we should erase the bloody board and have lunch. I'm starving."

The clouds in his eyes lifted. He swiped my chin with his thumb. "That's my girl!"

Halfway through his sandwich—adorably, Mr. Insley still ate the food of his childhood, bologna sandwiches with mustard, peanut butter and jelly on white—Mr. Insley abruptly interrupted his story about how he'd found an error in one of his graduate school professor's books on the Pre-Raphaelites and had been honor bound to point it out, and said, "It's what most of the world would think, you know. That you are too young for me."

My heart fluttered. Carefully, I swallowed my mouthful of moussaka.

"I suppose so," I said, slowly. "I hadn't really thought about it much." This was true. I'd thought mostly about how people might think it unseemly for a student to be in love with her teacher. I hadn't really considered the age difference.

"Knightley was sixteen years older than Emma, you know," I said. I almost brought up Dorothea and Casaubon, but since their marriage was a disaster and since Casaubon, being close to fifty, actually qualified as old in a way that Knightley and Mr. Insley most certainly did not, I decided against it.

" 'Tis true!" said Mr. Insley.

"And anyway," I said, "we haven't—. I mean to say, we aren't really—" My face went hot.

Mr. Insley reached across the desk and wound a lock of my hair around his finger. "Aren't we, though?" he whispered. "I know it's been mostly unspoken, but, Willow, aren't we?"

Oh, my heavens, he was so still and quiet, but when he said that, I felt like everything started racing. The room around me blurred. It was just like being dropped into the seat of a moving roller coaster. That I had never actually ridden a roller coaster was irrelevant. I gasped.

"I-I hope so," I whispered back.

How limpid his pale blue eyes were, how fragile the skin beneath them.

"I guess you are very young, but I feel as though our souls are the same age, as though you were much older than your peers. If anything, your soul is older than mine. Do you know what I mean?"

I nodded, feverishly, although I didn't really agree. When I was with other people my own age, I didn't feel older, precisely; sometimes, I felt much younger, like a clumsy child. Mainly, I just felt different. And when I was with Mr. Insley, he never felt *old* to me—perish the thought!—but I felt very young indeed.

Then something happened. A fleeting, tiny event that penetrated the marrow of my bones, rearranged the atoms in my body, ripped, at least momentarily, the fabric of my own personal universe. Yes, I am exaggerating for effect, but only a little. It was tremendous.

Mr. Insley whispered, his voice huskier than I'd ever imagined it could get, "I think about you constantly."

Slowly, slowly, he lifted his hand, his forefinger outstretched and, slowly, slowly, moved it across the foot and a half that separated the two of us, and with this finger, he touched my lower lip, tugging it downward ever so slightly, and then sliding his finger onto the inner part of it, the damp part. *He is touching my mouth,* I thought, *he is opening my mouth with his finger,* and just as the thought darted across my brain, the bell rang, ending lunch period, and I jumped backward, like I'd been stung by a wasp.

"Good-bye," I said, quickly, standing and hastily gathering up my things, and then I added, "Thank you."

The man had kissed my hand for four seconds, held me in his arms for longer than that, but this touch, this brief touch, his finger on my mouth, well, it was something different altogether.

"Good-bye, dear girl," he said.

I rushed down the hall, my stomach in knots of what I knew was happiness, just of a kind I had never experienced before, the kind that feels like running down the side of a steep and stony hill. *I am so happy,* I thought, *just gloriously happy.*

So I don't know why, when school ended and I stepped out into the

November afternoon, instead of walking in the direction of the woods, where there was a shortcut to the gas station at which I usually met Mr. Insley for our driving sessions, I followed the brick walkway that led to the thrillingly named Brilliant Natatorium ("Brilliant," after the family who'd paid to have it built, according to Luka; "Natatorium," a fancy word for pool, according to the *Oxford English Dictionary*). The door was unlocked. As soon as I stepped from the silent hallway into the actual pool area, a swell of swampy, chemical-scented air enveloped me. I remembered how, back when I used to take swim lessons at an old indoor pool, I'd hated that transition, like walking from the sunlit world into a hot, moist, dark underground cave (I had always looked up, half expecting to see bats hanging from the ceiling), but now it felt soothing. It was brighter in here than in that other pool, for one thing, light beaming in from the bank of windows at one end of the room. The pool entrance didn't lead to the deck, but to a raised spectator section, cement bleachers from which you could look down at the swimmers, so I went to the bottom row, the one closest to the pool, and sat.

Luka was swimming butterfly, and even though I'd heard the name of the stroke often enough before, until I sat there watching him, I'd never thought about the lightness it implied. For all the strength rippling through his shoulders and arms, how silken his movements were, how clean and nearly silent. His swimming loped, oscillated, moved in crests and troughs, like in physics. Oh, my friend Luka. He was a sound wave. He was a seal. He was as supple and as rhythmic as music.

I watched and felt reverent. I wanted him to swim on and on, but because he would eventually stop and the magic would end, I left while he was still swimming and went out into the hallway to wait for him. I knew that he would walk out soon in sneakers and jeans, with his hair wet, and be his everyday, same old self, but he wouldn't be the same to me. I wondered what it would be like to do something so well, to carry *that* around in your body like a secret, every day, all the time, when you were sitting at your desk or walking down the hallway.

Listen to me: I had visited the Grand Canyon at sunset and the

Eiffel Tower at night, had been to the Metropolitan Museum of Art *six times,* and I swear to you that there may be things in this world more beautiful than Luka Bailey-Song moving through the water, but I had never seen a single one.

THAT NIGHT, EVEN THOUGH I had spent the entire day exhausted, I couldn't sleep. So much had happened since the night before, and my mind was hopping and restless, like a bird ready to peck the day to pieces and lift every tiny bit to the light. But I didn't want to give into that, to obsess and churn and analyze. I wished hard that I didn't have to be alone with it all, but my mother, God bless her, was sound asleep, and my father was, too. I remembered how when I was little and woke up in the night, I would slip out of my room and lie down on the floor outside their bedroom door. Some nights, I would hear them talking, their voices nothing more than a hum, and others, I would listen to my father snore softly. Just being near them was so reassuring. But I was sixteen. Even I wasn't weird enough to camp outside my parents' door at the age of sixteen, so instead, I decided to spy on Eustacia.

She was still awake, baking cookies, brownish ones, possibly molasses, in the pool house's tiny oven. I caught their buttery fragrance even through the closed window. The television was on. We had one at the main house, too, but used it only to watch DVDs: documentaries, science and nature programs (*Planet Earth* was my personal favorite), Leonard Bernstein's *Young People's Concerts.* But this was a bona fide show, some kind of British thing, from what I could tell. The characters wore World War II—era clothing, and there was an older man with a serious face who might have been a police detective and a young red-haired woman in a brown uniform. I stood at the window and watched the show through the glass, and even though I couldn't hear a word and had next to no idea as to what the plot might be, there was something comforting about watching the people move around their green, old-fashioned, countryside world. The hats were comforting. Ditto the sensible shoes. The cars, those funny, cumbersome, humpbacked cars were somehow the most comforting part of all.

I'd like to use the excuse that my guard was down, that the events of the day had left me vulnerable, but the truth is I was lulled, seduced by the idiot box like so many others have been, and, like so many others, I paid a price.

What happened is that I forgot myself and leaned against the window, which let out a silence-shattering, bone-rattling creak. The window creaked, Eustacia jerked her face in my direction, and I froze, trying to wish myself invisible. It must not have worked because Eustacia came stalking toward the window, the cookie spatula raised like a weapon, and peered into the darkness. Suddenly, her face broke into a smile, and she waved, and the next thing I knew, she was on the porch of the pool house, singing out, "Willow! I'm so glad you came!"

Ugh. I had a desperate split second to decide what was worse: having her know I was spying or letting her believe that I would ever desire to be in her company. With a sinking heart, I opted for the latter. Sort of. Although I managed—rather deftly, I thought—to avoid actually saying that I wanted to spend time with her.

"I couldn't sleep, and everyone else was asleep, so I thought I'd just walk over. And, well, it's late. So I decided to look in to make sure you were awake."

All true. Only my faintly conciliatory tone was a lie.

"Oh, gosh, I'm a night owl," she said, with a dismissive wave. "I'll be up for hours more. Why don't you come in and try these cookies? They're molasses."

Heaven help me, I felt a tiny pulse of pleasure at having guessed correctly the variety of cookie. When you have been caught in a humiliating position, you take your triumphs where you can, but my humiliation was destined only to deepen. Within minutes, I found myself seated at the infamous white tile-top table, a cookie in hand, discussing television—what Wilson called "the dry rot fungi of the American soul"—of all things, with Eustacia, of all people. The show she was watching turned out to be a BBC (right again!) detective series (and again!) set during World War II (and again!).

"I'm not much for television shows," she claimed (of *course*), "but I adore *Foyle's War* with all my heart. I actually brought my own boxed sets with me. Oh, Foyle, those steady eyes, that calm voice. When Foyle is on the job, all's right with the world. I love characters like that."

"I never watch television," I said, stiffly, "but I can imagine that such a character would be very reassuring."

Eustacia leaned her head a little to the side and smiled, a friendly, slightly puzzled smile like one might give an okapi at the zoo, a smile that said, *I am inclined to like you, even if I'm not sure whether you are a giraffe or a zebra.* If I were being honest, I would have to say that, while I am not a particular fan of the dimple, a somewhat nice one flashed in her left cheek when she did so. Even so, it was maddening how often, when I tried to put her off or freeze her out, she simply appeared not to notice. Either her smiles were some subtle form of mockery or she was woefully oblivious to social cues. That she could be so presumptuous, so overstepping as to actually *like* me, well, it was too annoying a possibility to consider.

But given what happened next, I was forced to consider it. Damn it all.

The show came to what I had to admit was a satisfying end, with the bad guys caught and Foyle as unflappable, and, yes, as reassuring, as anyone could ever be, and it was lovely, except that, with Foyle and the rest gone, Eustacia and I were alone, with a post-television silence that she would surely, before long, want to fill with conversation, because she was just that type. I sat there, toying with a cookie, and hoping against hope that she would not bring up the subject of my mother's somnambulism, thinking, with all my strength, the words *Don't bring up Muddy, don't bring up Muddy, don't bring up Muddy,* so that when she said, nervously, the dimple appearing and vanishing in her nervous cheek, "There's something I've been wanting to talk to you about," my heart dropped like a shot goose.

"Oh?" I said, icily. For a girl who had spent most of her life in the presence of people she liked, when it came to the cold, aloof tone of voice, I seemed to be a natural, if I do say so myself.

To my dismay, she walked over and sat in the chair opposite mine at the white tile-top table. The overhead light falling on her hair made it so shiny, it was irritating. You needed sunglasses just to look at the woman. And, as she sat there, considering how she would word whatever over-stepping thing she had to say to me about my mother, the dimple flashed on and off, on and off, like a hazard light. *Outrageous presumptuousness ahead* warned the dimple. I steeled myself accordingly.

"Okay," she said, "there's probably no way to say this that isn't wildly awkward, and you may well have other people in your life that you can talk to about this sort of thing, and if you do, wonderful, but just in case you don't, I wanted to say—"

She stopped for breath.

I lifted my eyebrows, as cool as a cucumber—gosh, I was devastatingly good at that—waiting.

She laughed and shook her head.

"Well, that was a melodramatic, if rambling, opening, wasn't it?" she said.

Under completely, radically other circumstances, if we were two complete strangers, maybe, who had bumped into each other on a street corner, I could see how her manner might be disarming.

She slapped the table with her two hands.

"All right. Here it is: it's a totally natural thing to be your age and to meet someone you're attracted to and who's attracted to you. I mean, young love can be a beautiful thing. A lucky, lucky, beautiful thing."

I allowed myself a moment of relief that she wasn't going to talk about Muddy's somnambulism, and then I popped open the floodgates and let the outrage fill my soul. *Young love*, indeed! I stared at her with as blistering a gaze as I could muster, which was very, very blistering. But she went on. She *went on*! And as she did, with each word that tumbled from her lips, my blood got hotter and hotter until, by the time she finally shut up, it was out and out boiling.

"But it can also be confusing or overwhelming," she said, "and you might have questions or just things you want to talk over with someone, a sympathetic, unjudgmental listener, someone who has been in your shoes, and I just want you to know that I'm here."

I gathered myself, trying to keep my voice calm, but I'm afraid it trembled anyway.

"In my shoes," I said, with my hands balled into fists and my teeth clenched so hard my molars ached. "My? Shoes?"

Eustacia's dimple vanished. "Okay, maybe this was a bad idea," she said.

I rose slowly from my seat at that stupid, godforsaken table, that relic of a dingy and bygone era, and said, "What could you possibly know about my shoes? I am capable of feelings that you wouldn't know the first thing about."

She didn't blanch or quail or stammer out an apology. Instead, she gave me the okapi smile! My God, the woman must be mad.

"I know it seems that way, that no one in the history of humankind has ever experienced what you're experiencing," she said, "and I guess no one has, quite. Everyone's first love is unique. But there really is common ground."

"What . . ." My voice was truly quaking now, with rage. "What common ground could we possibly have? If I belong to someone—and I'm not saying I do—it's heart and soul. Like Jane belongs to Rochester! Nobly. Completely."

Eustacia's lashy eyes went soft in a way that made no sense, and she was nodding her head, understandingly. Oh, that nod, that condescending nod. It made me snap.

"You don't know anything!" I spat. "For you, at my age, it was just sex! It was sordid. That's why my father got so disgusted with you and made you leave!"

Eustacia went stiff as a board, and her eyes flared like torches. Her voice, though, damn her, was steady as that British detective's.

"You know all about me, do you?" she said.

"Yes! Some stupid boy got you pregnant and dumped you, and my father wouldn't stand for it, and he threw you out! You and your entire sordid family!"

Silence. A red-hot, pulsing silence. It beat like a bass drum in that little room.

When she spoke next, I saw that I was not the only one with a gift for the icy tone. "Is that what he told you?"

I faltered. I wanted to lie, but why should I dissemble like a common criminal? I wasn't the one who had done something disgraceful. Also, I couldn't have Eustacia go around thinking that my father had considered her story worthy of telling.

"No," I said, tossing my head. "Not in so many words. But that's immaterial. I know. I've known for a long time."

"Sit down, Willow," she said, every syllable an icicle, jabbing.

I sat. I shouldn't have. I don't know why I did. But my body lowered itself into the chair.

"I did not get pregnant," said Eustacia. "But I did have sex with the person I loved. Once. And only after."

I didn't care to hear her lies, not one whit, but maybe she had cast a spell over me like the witch she was because the next thing I said was, "After—what?"

Her dark eyes were full of fiery anger, so distilled and so perfectly contained that if I hadn't known better, I might have mistaken it for calm.

"After I married him," she said.

CHAPTER THIRTEEN

Taisy

I DIDN'T GIVE HER THE whole story because I didn't give her the whole why. Despite telling her more than I'd ever told anyone, lighting truth after truth after truth like candles, in the end, I left certain ones standing in the dark, unlit. Don't get me wrong, I didn't hold back much, despite her stubborn jaw and glowering stare. And I did give her the real, overarching why, my most precious thing, which was that Ben Ransom and I were the Dog Star, the brightest, surest light, the one that found me every time I turned my eyes to the sky. You could navigate your life by a light like that. Could? You'd be crazy not to.

No, what I didn't give her was the rest of the why, the nitty-gritty, why-then, why-so-sudden why. Why didn't we wait? Why did we decide, on a rainy late September evening, to get secretly married a week later, two days after my eighteenth birthday, at a Clerk of the Peace in Georgetown, Delaware? This why wasn't precious or pure or so big you could fit an entire life inside of it, like the other one. It was small. It had a name. Two names, really. Three, if you counted Willow, and while she wasn't even in the world yet, she counted all the same. So there it was, the other why: Wilson, Caro, and Willow.

It was Ben who discovered them. He was on the first field trip of his senior year: a Cezanne exhibition at the Philadelphia Museum of Art with his French class. His assignment was to find a painting and write an essay in French, analyzing it, so instead of taking a group tour, the students were free to roam around with friends or alone so that, when inspiration struck, they could park themselves in front of a painting to take notes. Which was a good thing because it meant that when Ben came upon my father and his paramour paramouring on a bench in front of *The Bathers,* he was only with two other guys and so did not have to bear witness to an entire tour group of teenagers gawking at my father's public display of adultery.

Not that any of them knew my father. They didn't even know me, since when Ben came to live with his dad (for no other reason than that he liked his dad and wanted to get in a few good years with him before he went off to college), he didn't transfer, but kept going to his Quaker school in Pennsylvania. Still, if you have to come upon your girlfriend's father canoodling with his jailbait-looking (Caro was twenty-two), immensely pregnant gal pal in front of a gargantuan painting of naked French people, it's better not to have an audience.

Later that night, after Ben told me and I was telling Marcus, Marcus cut into my tearful, scattered, raw-throated exposition by saying, "Oh, shit, were they *making out*? God, don't tell me that. Because you know what? That's nauseating. Dad is, like, *old*. And *Dad.*"

"Not exactly making out," I said, with a sob. "Worse."

Marcus's eyes widened. "Worse? Wait. They weren't having sex, were they? Oh, Jesus, they were, weren't they? Some kind of old guy, pregnant lady, clothes-mostly-on, public sex? How the hell did Ben not rip his own eyes right out of his head after seeing a thing like that?"

"Not sex," I said, bursting into fresh tears. "Worse."

"Worse than public sex in front of a French impressionist painting in a major American museum?" asked Marcus. "Holy shit. What? Cannibalism? Were they, like, eating human brains straight out of the skull because otherwise . . ."

"Stop it," I said, covering my face. "He was whispering to her and running his hand back and forth over her giant belly, and smiling, and *crying*!" I wailed.

Marcus went still. "Crying? Dad was crying?"

I nodded with mute misery.

"Hold on," said Marcus. "Is Ben sure?"

"He said there were tears pouring down his cheeks. It was serious crying. And he was smiling at the same time."

"Maniacally? Like he was deranged?"

My answer came out as a whisper. "Happily. Like he was happy."

But even if I had told Willow this why, I don't know if I could really have explained it. The cause and effect was there: because I found out my father had a pregnant much younger girlfriend who made him happy enough to weep with joyful abandon in a public place, when he had, to my knowledge, previously never wept for any reason anywhere ever, thus ensuring, with every tear and belly stroke, the end of our family as we knew it, I decided, the very next night, to ask Ben to marry me in a week, as soon as I turned eighteen, which was exactly one month after he had turned eighteen.

But as for the reasons for the cause and effect? Blurry. Complicated. I wasn't—and I've thought about this a lot—acting out of some childish revenge impulse. I wasn't punishing Wilson. I wasn't doing it to send him a message or to get a reaction or even to get his attention; I really, truly wasn't. My wanting to marry Ben right then and there, in high school, when even I had to admit it didn't make much logical sense, had not much to do with Wilson at all. Maybe I wanted to create my own family, since my other one was combusting. Maybe I wanted something solid to hold on to or something that was irrevocably mine. Maybe I wanted to show myself that I wasn't damaged by Wilson's betrayal, that I still believed in love. I think what I mostly felt was that I wanted balance: to counter Wilson's sneaky, traitorous act with one that was beautiful and brave and lasting.

But I didn't say any of this to Willow. In my head, I could hear

Marcus prodding me, chiding me: *Tell her. Tell her that not you but dear old Muddy was the one whose boyfriend got her knocked up. Tell her that Wilson was a liar and cheat. Tell her she was a redheaded bastard, born before Wilson and Mom's divorce was even close to final. It's your chance. You don't owe any of them anything. God, don't be a sap, Taisy.*

But I could not do it. Wouldn't do it. Not for love or money or revenge or even because it might have done Willow some good. Because it really might have. She was so sure that her father was a paragon, more god than human, and who knew better than I the perils of worshipping Wilson Cleary? And the girl had been raised to think that her family was better than everything, finer than the outside world, that the only way to live righteously was to keep walls between herself and this world or to look down on it from a great height, and that was no good either, was it? But it didn't matter. Maybe Willow would figure it out on her own, do the math, put together the timeline. I half hoped she would. But she wouldn't hear it from me. I could not sit there and look into that child's face and tell her that Wilson, that her family, all of them were just exactly as human as everyone else.

So I told her about how I had sat with Ben on his tiny front porch at dusk, holding his hand, watching the paw-soft rain fall on the grass, and asked him to marry me, and how afterward, he had sat very, very still, not saying anything, as I made my pitch: we would keep it a secret, live in our separate houses until graduation, and then go to the same college and wait until it felt right and then tell everyone and have a real wedding, or not; it didn't matter. I was going on and on, telling him how we would know we belonged to each other, how it wouldn't change anything, how it would change everything, when he said, "Yes."

"Yes? Really? You want to?"

He looked at me with his clear black eyes and said, "If you want to, I want to."

"No," I said, disappointed. "I don't want you to do it just to make me happy."

"Well, that sounds to me like a good enough reason to do anything, but that's not what I meant."

"Okay. So what did you mean?"

He brought his brows together, thinking. I loved it that he was a person who liked to puzzle things out. I loved watching it.

"It's weird," he said, finally. "The way it makes so much sense to me that I don't know how to explain it. It's just—if you want something, I want to give it to you. Or more like, if you want something from me, that something is the thing I want to give you. Because you want it. They're two sides of the same coin." He shook his head, frustrated.

I smiled into the rainy yard. *I will marry this person and have him near me forever.* I kissed him, and he kissed me back, distractedly, because he was still thinking. He pulled away.

"Look, how about this," he said, excitedly. "Reverse it. If you want to give me something, it's something I want. Automatically. By definition. Because it's you."

I kissed the underside of his wrist and pondered.

"I get it," I said, smiling at him.

"Ha! You do? Well, since you're the only one who would, I'd better marry you."

"You'd better snap me up quick," I agreed.

The morning I turned eighteen, we made excuses to our parents and schools and went to get our marriage license. We drove (Ben drove; Wilson's rule was that Marcus and I couldn't drive until after we turned eighteen, making me the only kid I knew who had a marriage license before I had a driver's license) to a Clerk of the Peace in the next county so that we didn't have to worry about running into someone we knew. We got there an hour before the office opened and were back at school before lunch. Twenty-four hours later, on Friday, October 4, having waited for the requisite period of time and done all manner of lying and fancy footwork with our parents and schools, we were back in the clerk's office.

It was eighty-five degrees outside, so I wore a sleeveless white eyelet sundress and sandals. Ben had given me a bouquet of purple freesia, and when we walked into the office, the clerk, a woman named Ada Wayne, closed her eyes and said, "Oh, those flowers smell like a happy future to me," and I hugged her. The ceremony was a blur after that, except for Ben, who came through my senses more and more sharply, until he was the most vivid, most tangible, plainly *there* thing I'd ever seen or heard or touched, and he stayed that way for the rest of the day and night, the first night we'd ever spend together.

Our parents weren't expecting us home until the next morning (more fancy footwork), so we drove to the beach. Since it was past Labor Day, there were no lifeguards, but the ocean was full of people. Ben went in, but the water was too cold for me, so I stood on the sand and watched him, bouncing on my toes with joy and at the same time full of awestruck solemnity, thinking, *This is how it will always be: all these people, parents and children, old couples and teenagers, land, sky, and water, wind, grit, weather, and a taste on my tongue, going on and on, and always, in the midst of everything, shining out from the rest, my person, the one who can pick me out, know me, find my face in crowds, hear my voice over other voices, who will look at the ocean and say that speck is my speck—for year and years and years.*

I told Willow that. I also told her that we spent the night in a hotel we could just barely afford, with an old-fashioned elevator, buttery sheets, chocolates on our pillows, and a view of the ocean. I had already told her that we'd had sex once, after we were married, although that isn't technically accurate, even though we did have just the one night together. But I didn't give her details. God, no. Can you imagine?

I didn't tell her about the first time, how new we felt to each other, how the easy comradeship, the months and months of dating fell off like a husk and left us so unfamiliar, elemental, so thin-skinned that I was right on the edge of (but never tipping over into) scared. His mouth burned wherever it touched me, and I forgot to be smart, funny, nice; I forgot everything about myself. And then, the second time, all of it came back. Every tiny piece of history, the dancing gourds, the dogs watching us kiss, every math problem, study session, meal, walk, inside joke, every daily act of friendship and offhanded, ordinary kindness was right there with us, and, maybe that sounds crazy, but all I know is I had never before been so generous or felt so blessed, and in the seventeen years to follow, I never would again.

That last bit, the generous and blessed part, I did tell Willow because I needed her to understand that being with Ben mattered. *You don't have to defend yourself to her,* I could hear Marcus say, *Who cares what she thinks?* But I did have to, and I did care. Having lies about me and Ben out there, alive in the world, had felt wrong to me for seventeen years. I couldn't change Wilson's view of us, but maybe I could change Willow's, and even if I couldn't, just trying had to be the right thing: countering a lie with the beautiful truth.

I don't know if she bought it, but I think she did, at least a little. Her eyes stayed angry, but the rest of her betrayed her. She leaned closer, her jaw and hands loosened, her lips relaxed, and when I paused, steeling myself to tell the rest, she said, "So you got married. But you're not married now, are you? How's that?," which struck me as a mean way of saying, "I want to know what happened next."

Wilson is what happened, the way he always did.

He caught us. The fact that we were fully clothed and not doing anything but kissing—okay, lying down kissing on the living room sofa in the dark, but still—didn't make a bit of difference.

We weren't in the habit of hanging out—much less making out— at my house, mostly because of Wilson, but on this night, we thought we had the house to ourselves, at least for a few hours. We were wrong.

You have to understand that there was no morality in Wilson's seemingly moral outrage, not one scrap. Even before I knew about his rampant philandering (because I found out later, from my mother and Marcus, that Caro was not the first), I knew that he didn't think much about right and wrong, at least not Right and Wrong, capitalized and absolute.

No, what passed for a value system for Wilson was plain old snobbery. Cheating was wrong because only stupid people had to cheat. Beating people up was wrong because if you couldn't win with your wits alone, you were stupid. The vast majority of wrong things were wrong simply because to do them lumped you in with the lowbrow and the tasteless, the great unwashed. Gambling, stealing, doing drugs, driving drunk: unsavory crimes committed by unsavory types, people who wore bill caps, drove cheap cars in which they smoked with their children in the backseat, ate fried food out of bags, and overplucked their eyebrows, who watched television shows with laugh tracks, and had not gone to graduate school.

For Wilson, pregnant, unmarried girls—or teenaged girls who had sex and were thus in danger of becoming pregnant, unmarried girls—were in the same category as people who went to vo-tech schools or had careers in retail. That his daughter would deliberately place herself in such company made her stupid, and, in Wilson's moral (amoral) universe, being stupid was the most unforgivable sin of all.

When he caught us, he yelled something at me along those lines. He didn't call me names, since only stupid people had to resort to name-calling, but he said my behavior was idiotic, a disgrace, an embarrassment, that of a common tramp ("whorish" came later, right before Marcus, my mom, and I left for North Carolina). I'm not sure if it was "tramp" or "idiotic" that caused Ben to snap, but suddenly he was leaping up and standing between me and Wilson, which put him maybe three feet from my father, and even though Ben didn't do so much as raise his hand, Wilson—and this is critical—flinched. He stepped back, two steps, and as soon as he did that, showed fear, there, in front of witnesses, I understood that he would hate Ben, and possibly me, too, for the rest of his days.

"Don't talk to Taisy like that," Ben said. "She doesn't deserve it."

Wilson puffed up like a bullfrog.

"You!" he bellowed. "You have evidently decided she 'deserves' to be the fallow field for your wild oats. How manly of you. I am sure you

make your father proud. And when she is a high school dropout dan-
dling a bastard child on her knee, will she have deserved that as well?"

I held my breath, waiting for Ben to slap Wilson down with his
own ugly words—*wild oats, bastard child*—and I think he was just
about to, when he turned his head and looked at me. I should have
given him the thumbs-up; I should have blurted out the words myself.
Marcus and I had decided to tell our mother about Caro, so all of it
would come to light soon enough anyway. What I should not have
done, should not even have thought of doing, was protect Wilson. But
that's just what I did. I gave the slightest shake of my head and whispered, "Don't," and after a beat, Ben nodded. Oh, if only I'd let him
say it! If he'd said that, screamed at Wilson, called him a hypocrite
and a cheat, told how he'd seen him at the museum with his own eyes,
maybe he would not have said what he said next, what he said *instead,*
and maybe our lives—Ben's and mine—would have turned out so differently.

He began like this: "Dr. Cleary, how could you know nothing
about your daughter? You've lived with her all these years. You're her
father, for God's sake, and you don't have a clue who she is."

His dark gaze was translucent, unwavering. His composure took
my breath away. Ben had always harbored reserves of quietude, but he
could lose it like anyone else when he was pushed. Now, his serenity
gave him a kind of magnificence, while at the very same time, it made
my heart sink because I knew—and I knew that Wilson knew—that
Ben's composure shamed my father more surely than those two stumbling, flinching steps backward ever had. Rudyard Kipling was one of
Wilson's heroes. I'd been hearing it all my life: "If you can keep your
head, when all about you are losing theirs . . ." Temper was for toddlers;
yelling was for drunks and street punks. If Wilson had a book of life
rules, "Composure wins every time" would be right there at the top.

He turned ten shades of red. A vein bulged in his forehead. He
looked at me, and said, in the ugliest, most venomous voice imaginable, "I know exactly who you are."

"She's my wife." My husband's voice was like water falling through a shaft of sun.

God, it was as though some epic battle of good versus evil were being enacted in that living room. Wilson so red and bloated and old and cruel, Ben so pale and straight and noble and young.

But in the end, Wilson won.

At this point in the telling, Willow forgot herself, hit the tile-top table with the flat of her hand and yelped, "What? How?"

I rubbed my eyes.

"He made us annul the marriage," I said, drearily.

"He did? On what grounds?"

Was that indignation I heard in her voice? Was it possible that Willow, a chip off the old Wilson block if ever there was one, was on my side? But no sooner had I thought this than the ice queen came back. Ice queen with a generous dollop of nasty.

"I mean, I thought you could only annul marriages when they weren't consummated, which yours obviously was," she said, her tone making my and Ben's single night of conjugal bliss sound like a visit to a brothel.

Oh, that girl.

I cleared my throat. "'The Court shall enter a decree of annulment of a marriage entered into under any of the following circumstances,'" I quoted, and then said, "One party being unable or unwilling to consummate the marriage was just one of them. I think there were six others."

"Oh," said Willow.

"'One or both parties entered into the marriage under duress exercised by the other party' is the one Wilson wanted me to use."

"He wanted you to say you were forced?"

"Yes, by Ben. I wouldn't do it. Finally, I agreed to 'One or both parties entered into the marriage as a jest or dare.'"

Just saying it made me want to die of shame.

"Oh," said Willow. "Gosh."

We sat in silence, both of us running our forefingers down the little grouted channels between the tiles on the table.

"But wait," said Willow, looking up at me.

"What?"

"Why would you agree to anything? You were eighteen, right? Eighteen means you were an adult, so how could Wilson *make* you get an annulment?"

A question to break your heart. A sinkhole of question that could swallow you body and soul.

"I wanted to keep the peace," I said, and yes, there was a shrill note of pleading in my voice. "And I didn't think it would be the end. I thought the annulment would be a formality, and that we'd stay together, and just get married again, later, when we were older. I tried to make Ben understand that."

"But you didn't," said Willow the Ice Queen. "You didn't get married again and you didn't make Ben understand."

I shook my head. "No! He was so angry at me. I didn't think he'd react that way. As soon as I told him what I had agreed to, what I had been *made* to agree to, he shut me out, stopped answering his door, stopped answering my calls. It was wrenching."

I swiped at my eyes.

"But you know, I think I could have won him back, gotten him to understand, eventually, but—" I broke off.

"But what?"

Willow's face, between the two heavy curtains of bright hair, was pale and all eyes. She looked so heartbreakingly young.

Carefully, I said, "But then, in the space of a week, my family combusted. My mother left Wilson and took me and Marcus to live in North Carolina. All that week, I tried everything I could think of to reach Ben, but I never could. And then we were gone, and, for a year, even after we were both in college, I wrote him letters, but he didn't answer any of them."

Willow said, crisply, with a toss of her head, "Well, did you really expect him to?"

"Yes," I said, simply.

"Hmpf," she sniffed. Then, she got up from the table and walked to the door.

"I have to go," she said, with her back to me.

"Willow, I did the wrong thing. Obviously. I've regretted it so bitterly for so many years. But I was not much older than you are now, and it was *Wilson*."

If anyone could understand the power that those last three words contained, it was surely Willow, and suddenly, I wanted her understanding so much it hurt. I had betrayed the person I loved most in all the world, smashed my own heart and all my hopes to smithereens because Wilson had told me to, and, heaven help me, I wanted there to be one person on the face of the earth who understood why I'd done it.

"You know what it's like to be Wilson's daughter, and you also know—I'm sure you know—what it's like to be in love. If you'd been in my place," I said, "what would you have done?"

She turned around, and I could see the struggle on her face: True Love versus Wilson. But I'd been there, hadn't I? I knew what she would choose.

"You want to know what I think?" she asked.

I nodded.

"I think," she said, savagely, "that if you didn't love Ben enough to stay married to him no matter what, then you didn't love him enough, period. So maybe you were right to leave."

I fell back, stunned. She spun on her heel, tore open the door, and walked out, but in two seconds, she was back.

"I take that back. You weren't right. You were a fool."

She slammed the door so hard, it shook the windows in their frames.

THE NEXT MORNING, AS soon as the sky made its first, almost imperceptible, shift from black to blackish gray, I called Ben.

"Taisy," he said, and his fuzzy, just-woken-up voice saying my name sent a streak of heat through my body.

"I know. I'm relentless," I said.

"Hey, I wouldn't say that," he said, with a husky laugh. The laugh gave me courage.

"No, I mean that's my plan, to be relentless."

"Your plan."

"To hound you. I'm a good hounder. I'll dog you, as well, if necessary. Why do all those stalker verbs have to do with dogs? Other animals hunt better than dogs, right?"

"Well, there's badger. You could badger me."

"Badgers are sissies."

"They're vicious, when provoked. Plus, they have these special jaws so that they can bite something and hold on forever," said my fact-loving Ben.

"Badgers have short, little legs and stripes. Stripes! How could they be vicious?"

"Tigers have stripes."

"And long legs. Which settles it: I'll tiger you, if necessary. I have a lot of tigering tricks up my sleeve."

A quiet fell during which I strained to hear him breathe. When he finally spoke, his voice was serious and gentle. "So what is it you're tigering me relentlessly for?"

The kindness in his voice pierced me. It was the tone of someone who is about to burst your bubble but really, really doesn't want to.

All of you, I wanted to tell him. *Body, soul, every day of the rest of your life.*

"A second chance," I said.

"At what?"

"Us," I said, impatiently. "What else?"

"Taisy, listen."

"It's okay," I said. "You don't have to say anything right now."

"I need to," he said.

"Really? Can you just not?" My eyes filled with tears.

"I'm sorry, but I have to tell you this. I can't go back."

"So we won't. We'll start fresh, right here."

"I can't get back together with you," he said. "I just can't."

I set the phone on the table in front of me, shut my eyes, and breathed long breaths. After a few seconds, I picked the phone back up. "So that's it? We'll just walk back out of each other's lives forever? You're that mad at me?"

"No, I—" Ben hesitated and I knew right then—in the space of that pause—that he couldn't do it. He could not tell me to go away for good. Hope unfurled inside me.

"What about this?" I said, quickly. "What if I relentlessly tiger you to be my friend? We were always friends, right? Even when we were in love, we were friends, too."

"Yes."

"Yes, we were friends? Or yes, I can relentlessly tiger you to be my friend?"

He laughed. I could hear him saying the word before he said it: "Both."

"All right, then you've got yourself a deal. Now, can I tell you my second reason for calling?"

"At five thirty A.M.," he reminded me.

"Right."

"Your first reason being to tell me that you're relentless?"

"Yes."

"Just for the record, I would have believed you at seven o'clock A.M. just as much. Seriously. Seven thirty even."

"So noted. But my second reason for calling was to ask you to go on a drive with me."

"So you finally got your driver's license."

"Is that a yes?"

"Where are we going?"

"If I tell you that, you might not agree to come. In fact, you almost definitely would not."

"Way to sell it, tiger," he said.

ACCORDING TO ROBO HEPBURN, it would take two and a half hours to get to Wilson's childhood home. I'd considered not telling Ben where we were going, at least until we got there, but practically as soon as he sat down in the passenger seat, he said, "This trip is Wilson-related, right?"

"Hold on a second."

I started the car and my tires squealed as we flew out of the driveway. Not until we were headed down the road, did I say, "Yes, it's Wilson-related."

"You took off like a cannonball, didn't you? And now you're going, what?" He leaned toward me to check the speedometer, the side of his head nearly brushing my cheek. I touched the spot on my face he had almost touched. "Twelve miles over the speed limit?"

"I did and I am."

"Banking on the fact that I won't want to jump out of a moving vehicle, huh?" The corners of his mouth curled up. "Smart move."

"Thank you."

In as few words and with as much nonchalance as possible, I told Ben about the book and about how I was chasing down Wilson's invisible childhood. I hoped I sounded like a sassy, hard-boiled reporter from a 1940s comedy and not like a daughter desperate for her father's approval. Apart from smiling at "the life story of a mind, if you will" rendered in my best Wilson voice, the long "i" in "mind" stretched out like melted Stilton, Ben stayed quiet, looking out the windshield, his profile unreadable.

Once I had finished, he didn't ask me any questions about Wilson. He said, "Tell me about being a ghostwriter." So I told him about Trillium, my first ghostee, how magical it felt, falling into someone else's psyche. I told him about my secret weapon: the right question.

"The first time I discovered it, I was writing Trillium's story, and I was stuck."

"You mean you didn't know what part to tell next?"

"Sort of. But it was more like I was stuck outside of her personality, like I'd been in and gotten locked out and needed to find the right rock, the one with the key under it, so I could get back. I didn't panic. She panicked enough for both of us, but I just waited for the rock to show itself, and then it did. I called her in the dead of night and said, 'I just need to know: What was the first gift you were given that you truly believed you couldn't live without?' and after a tiny, breath-sized pause, she said, 'My Trixie Belden books, five of them from a lady whose house my mother cleaned. I was nine.' And I pictured Trixie, girl sleuth, blond and curly-haired and irrepressible, with her gang of cute friends, her Westchester County farmhouse, her funny brothers and sparkly-eyed parents, and . . . click!"

Ben wasn't looking out the window anymore. As I told him this, he looked at me, nodding, his face sharp with attention. He'd always liked anything about how minds work. And sure enough, he said, "That's really cool. You always did have an interesting brain." It was better than if he'd called me beautiful.

"Okay, how about if I try it out on you," I said, challengingly.

He shrugged. "Sure. Why not?"

"Let me think." I peered at him through narrowed eyes. He peered back.

"Got it," I said. "Are you ready?"

"Shoot."

"Why did you break off your engagement?"

Ben tipped his head back and laughed.

"What?" I said.

"Trillium gets the best gift question, and I get this?"

"I don't choose the question," I explained, serenely. "The question chooses me."

"Uh-huh."

I waited.

Finally, Ben said, "She kept expecting me to use plant metaphors in conversation."

"What?"

"She was one of those women who have a highly romanticized view of botanists."

"There are women like that?"

Ben's eyes were twinkling like the entire Milky Way. "Oh, yeah. Are you kidding me? The plant thing makes a certain kind of woman crazy."

"So—what? She expected you to say things like 'Your eyes are the color of a baobab tree. Your lips are the color of a pokeberry'?"

"Pokeberries are black. And poisonous," Ben pointed out.

"Well, it's a good thing you broke up with her then, isn't it?"

Ben shook his head, his smile filling the car. It occurred to me that I could actually do this friendship thing. It wasn't my first choice, but if friendship meant riding next to Ben, bantering back and forth, making him smile, I could do it. For a while anyway.

"That's not the real reason, is it?" I said.

"No. Well, that was annoying, but the real reason, I guess, is that, when Bobbie got sick, I had to come home, and there was nothing really keeping her there because she travels for work, but she wouldn't leave."

"She wouldn't leave Wisconsin for you?"

"Nope."

"I mean, no offense to Wisconsin, but it isn't exactly Paris, is it?"

"It is not. She wouldn't leave, and I wouldn't beg her to—it didn't really occur to me at the time, to be honest—but also, I wouldn't stay. Or promise to come back. And I think that tells you something. If you can leave so easily, maybe it means you should."

And after he said this, I heard Willow's voice from last night inside

my head: *If you didn't love Ben enough to stay married to him no matter
what, then you didn't love him enough, period.*

"Can I tell you something that Willow said to me last night, after
I told her the story of us, back when we were eighteen?"

I heard Ben breathe in. "You told her about that? I didn't realize
you guys had heart-to-hearts."

"It's a recent development," I said. "Can I tell you what she said?"

"I—guess?"

I told him. When I glanced at him, he was staring out the windshield again, his cheeks reddening.

"Well," he said. "This conversation has taken an unexpected turn."

"It must be my interesting brain at work again."

He didn't smile.

"Here's the thing, though. She was right," I said, quietly. "I would
never have admitted that before, not up until last night. I blamed
Wilson. I blamed my mother for making us move away. I blamed
myself, for a thousand things, but never for not loving you enough. It's
true, though. I loved you so much. I'm pretty sure I loved you enough
to jump in front of a train for you, but not enough to tell my father to
go to hell. And I am so sorry for that."

He looked at me and scrubbed at his hair with his fingers, thoughtfully.

"It means a lot that you said that to me," he said. "Thanks."

I nodded and then added, "I'm much better at telling him to go to
hell now. Just, you know, for the record."

A ghost of a grin. "So noted," he said.

WILSON'S CHILDHOOD HOME WAS a brick Cape Cod with two
peaked dormer windows, a screen door, and a front stoop. It was
perched at the top of a gently sloped front yard, was neither large
nor tiny, shabby nor fine, a plain, sturdy, ordinary house in a plain,
sturdy, ordinary neighborhood. There was an orange pumpkin on
the stoop and, hanging on the front door, a decorative fall wreath

that Wilson would have loathed with every bone in his body.

"It's so—ordinary," I said. "So middle-class American."

"Yeah, no wonder Wilson tried to erase it from his permanent record," said Ben. "I'm amazed he didn't have the place bulldozed."

I bristled. "Well, there's also the fact that both his parents were killed while they lived in that house."

Ben's face hardened a little. I groaned.

"I'm defending him," I said, wearily.

"I shouldn't have said anything."

I gave his arm a tug. "No! You should say what you want to me. And of course, you're right. Wilson would rather have been raised anywhere, a Bangladeshi slum, the heart of the Amazon rain forest, *anywhere* but in that perfectly pleasant house."

Ben didn't answer.

I said, "Slavish devotion is a hard habit to break. But I swear I'm working on it."

"Okay," said Ben, but he didn't look convinced.

"I *am*," I said. "You don't get it. How could you? Your dad is the best man I know."

"Well, I can't argue with that, but . . ."

"You grew up with that dad and a great mom *and* a great stepfather, all of whom thought you were the sun and moon. I spent my life trying to get my father to think there was one thing special about me, and you were adored without lifting a finger. Good grief, listen to me. No, don't. Shut up, Taisy, you jealous brat. Ugh."

"Not ugh," said Ben.

"I don't really mean the part about lifting a finger. You were thoughtful and smart and hardworking and loving. God, you were Super Son. I just mean—oh, shut *up*, Taisy, you big, fat whiner."

"Hey, you're definitely not big. Or fat. And I see your point about me and my dad versus you and yours."

"That's not my real point. My real point is that I'm trying to change, to get free of him."

"Maybe," Ben said, "but look where we are. I want what you're saying to be true as much as you do, but what about this project? What about your being here because Wilson called you? The only reason we're together now is because of that phone call."

"Would you really describe us as together?" I said, perking up.

"Taisy."

"You're right; we're only together because Wilson called me. But does that matter? I mean, not to be a jerk, but you didn't exactly call me, either. Ever. In seventeen years."

"No, I didn't." I waited for him to explain why or to tell me about all the times he'd wanted to over the years, but he didn't say anything else. His silence stung, but I plunged ahead.

"But listen, today? What we're doing? It's not about Wilson. It's for me. I can't explain why, exactly, but I need to understand how he became the man he turned out to be."

Ben said, slowly, "Maybe he was just born that way, Taize. Some people are."

I nodded. "Trust me. I have seriously considered that he might be a sociopath. I've taken a lot of comfort in that possibility, actually. Marcus thinks he is. But you should see that man with Willow. He loves her. So what went so wrong that he had to turn into an old man before he figured out how to love someone?"

"You've got me there."

"Would you really describe me as having got you?"

Ben smiled and shook his head at me.

"As I friend, I meant," I said.

"You're relentless," he said.

"Thank you," I said.

THERE WAS ONLY ONE funeral home in town, Philpott's, a grand, Georgian affair with white pillars and a circular drive.

"Now, this is the kind of place Wilson wishes he'd been raised in," I said. "Minus the dead bodies. Or not."

"To the funeral home born," said Ben.

I wanted to find out where my grandparents were buried. I'd brought two bouquets of orange dahlias to place on their graves.

A man named Robert Philpott took us into his somber high-ceilinged, oak-paneled office, where we sat in somber black chairs. Even the desktop computer was black; I wondered if they'd had it specially made. The only bright thing in the place was Robert Philpott's hair, which was so riotously red it seemed to shed light, like a bonfire. It struck me as a good idea, that hair; I imagined it would make even the recently bereaved feel a little happier.

"We've computerized all our records," said Robert Philpott, in a low, velvety voice, his manicured fingers hitting the computer keys almost soundlessly, as if hush had become second nature to him. "Walter Wilson Ravenel, January 1979. Helen Kittle Ravenel, 1999."

I stared at Robert Philpott, blankly.

"Wait, that can't be right. They died in an accident on the same day. It must have been around 1958."

Robert Philpott's velvety voice got a little less velvety. "I'm quite sure that our records are correct. We treat the deceased with the utmost care, their records included."

"But this means that they were alive during my lifetime," I said.

For some reason, the thought made me shiver. Ben slipped his arm around the back of my chair. I remembered the office at Banfield Academy, Edwina Cook's fancy nails clicking away at the keys, calling up surprises from Wilson's past. It was so strange, all these hard drives out there, harboring facts about my father's life, facts he'd sawed off like dead wood and thrown away.

"Is there maybe another way you could check?" Ben asked. "Do you have the original records?"

Robert Philpott's face went cold under his fiery hair.

"We kept them, naturally, but in a separate storage facility to which I do not have immediate access. But I can check the obituaries. My mother clips them from the paper and keeps them."

"How nice of her," I said.

"Our work is human work, Ms. Cleary," said Robert Philpott, softening. "We remind ourselves as often as we can that the deceased aren't just names. They had lives just as we do."

"That's lovely," I said because it was.

"Excuse me; I will get my assistant to locate the right album."

He disappeared out the heavy oak door, which resealed itself behind him as soundlessly as an envelope.

"You okay?" asked Ben.

"Who lies about their parents' tragic deaths?"

"There must be a reason for it," he said. "I mean, I can't imagine what it is, but there must be."

"Thanks," I told him.

Robert Philpott made his silent return, bearing a thick leather photo album.

"Jacob is still locating your grandfather's obituary, but here is Helen Ravenel's."

She had died after a brief illness fourteen years ago. Even Willow was alive fourteen years ago. I wondered if Helen Kittle Ravenel knew, as she went about her daily life in her brick Cape Cod, that she had three grandchildren, one of them not three hours away.

The obituary was a blur; I would need to make a copy of it to take with me and read later. But one sentence jumped out: "Helen Ravenel is survived by a son and a daughter, Barbara Ravenel Volkman, of Philadelphia, son-in-law George Volkman, and their three children, Walter, Samuel, and Thomas."

Correction: Helen had six grandchildren.

And Wilson had a sister.

CHAPTER FOURTEEN

Willow

ON THE DAY WE showed our *Middlemarch* video to the class, even Luka was nervous. I could tell by the way he kept adjusting the knot of his tie. We had agreed to dress up, and I'll tell you that Luka walking down the halls in a coat and tie was the Webley equivalent of a victory parade. People, male and female alike, applauded, wolf whistled, cat-called, pretended to swoon, reached out to touch him and then acted like their fingers were burned.

"God," I growled at him under my breath, "it's like you're Henry V and you just won the damn Battle of Agincourt when all you did was put on a blue jacket."

"Come on, Cleary," he said, with a grin. "Don't you think I look even a little dapper?"

"I think you look dapper," I said, coolly. "I don't think you just beat the stuffing out of the entire French army."

" 'We few, we happy few, we band of brothers,' " he intoned, pumping his fist in the air.

If Luka thought he could impress me by quoting Shakespeare, well, he was right, the infuriating boy. I sniffed and rolled my eyes.

"You look great, by the way," he said, giving me one of his walking-down-the-hall nudges. I had eschewed my usual high school student disguise in favor of an emerald-green knit dress, black tights, and black ankle boots. My legs looked like pipe cleaners, but the color was unquestionably good on me.

I said, "Thank you. I can tell our peers agree with you, given all the wolf whistles my appearance is eliciting."

Luka tucked in his lips and pretended to put his pinkies in his mouth.

"Don't bother," I said. "Not all of us need our egos stroked by such obvious and pedestrian public displays."

When we got to class, I was nervous, too. I know because I caught myself fidgeting with my hair, what my father called my "tell." I used to do it only when I played chess or took a test. In recent months, I did it maddeningly often, particularly in the presence of Mr. Insley. Luka and I were nervous not because we didn't think our project was good. It's that we thought it was tremendous, brilliant even, and we really wanted everyone to agree.

The evening before, in the same study room in the public library where we'd shot the video, we had sat side by side and watched it. It was the first time I'd seen it since Luka had done the editing, and afterward, what can only be called euphoria abounded. We high-fived each other. We clapped our water bottles together. Luka had even engaged me in a victory dance, a kind of jitterbug pas de deux that was happily short-lived but made me laugh until I was out of breath.

The film was composed of interviews, characters talking against a backdrop, although since Luka had seen the light at last regarding the disembodied interviewer's voice, you never actually heard the questions; they were merely (brilliantly!) implied in the answers. We stuck mostly to using dialogue from the novel itself, with tweaks here and there, although, at times, we took the poetic license of putting the novel's narrative voice into the mouths of the characters. Luka and I played all the characters, he the males, I the females. We didn't wear costumes, just black shirts, and we put signs around our necks with the name of whomever we were portraying: Dorothea's uncle, her sister, the strapping Sir James Chettam, the busybody Mrs. Cadwallader, Casaubon, Dorothea's true love Will Ladislaw, Dorothea herself. Luka was wonderful, a really good actor even though he said he liked all the other parts of the project better.

"I want to make movies," he'd told me. "My parents want me to be a brain surgeon. Literally. But they'll get over it."

Luka told me that I was wonderful in the film, too. Actually, what he said was, "You're, like, made for this. Check out your face, which first of all, looks incredible, but also see how you totally turn into each character just by making the smallest adjustments? So cool."

And if you'll forgive the immodesty, it *was* cool. I watched myself in a state of wonderment, if you want to know the truth. I hadn't known I was doing all those things. For instance, when I was Mrs. Cadwallader, I hadn't decided to let a smile play around the edges of my lips, to raise my eyebrows, to turn my voice razor edged; I'd just *been* Mrs. Cadwallader as she said the line, "It's true what Sir James says, Casaubon has no good red blood in his body. Somebody put a drop under a magnifying glass, and it was all semicolons and parentheses. Oh, he dreams of footnotes, and they run away with all his brains."

"See?" Luka had said. "You're even good at being that old bat, which is interesting. I mean, of course you were good at Dorothea, since you basically *are* Dorothea. But how the hell did you pull off Mrs. Cadwallader? Amazing."

"What do you mean I *am* Dorothea?" I asked. "Because I believe I recall your describing her as—what was it—'insanely annoying'?"

Luka smiled. "Well, I've revised my position since then. But she's, you know, this beautiful misfit, kind of misguided in some ways, okay, many ways, a ton of ways, but always well-meaning. And she can seem kind of, uh, distant, but she also has this effect on people."

He dropped his eyes. It was a rare thing to see Luka shy. Even though I would not have unheard what he'd said for all the tea in China, even as I was cradling "beautiful" in the palm of my brain like a jewel, I also could not bear his embarrassment. I had to end it.

"The effect of causing people to make vomit faces? Is that the effect to which you refer?" And then, for good measure, I made one. It took some effort. If I had ever made a vomit face before, when I wasn't actually vomiting, I could not recall it.

"Ha!" said Luka, with a laugh. "You are shockingly good at that. Look at you, Cleary, full of hidden talents."

"That's the effect you meant, correct?"

Luka's face went river-rock seamless the way it did when he was giving something his full attention. Most people, when they are concentrating, bunch up, wrinkle, but Luka smoothed. Smooth forehead, smooth arched cheekbones, smooth, smooth jawline. I was hard-pressed not to reach out and run a finger down that face; I imagined it would feel like glass, but warm.

"Nah. I meant that she makes the people around her want to be better, like you do."

I closed my eyes briefly, absorbing this, giving that sentence its full due because here was a historical marker moment if ever I'd had one: LUKA BAILEY-SONG PAYS WILLOW CLEARY THE COMPLIMENT OF A LIFETIME.

"Oh," I managed to say. "Well, thanks."

For a fleeting instant I considered trying for cool-headed irony or casual insouciance, but my joyful smile would not be conquered; I may as well have been trying to stop a speeding train. I sat there, stared at my face-as-Mrs. Cadwallader's-face frozen on the computer screen, and grinned like a damned fool—or a blessed one. Out of the corner of my eye, I saw Luka steal a glance at me. A flash of white, a dip of his head. Oh, we were ridiculous! Behaving as though unrestrained happiness were a crime against humanity.

"No problem," said Luka, quickly. "Hey, you want to watch the film again?"

It was even better the second time.

But it is one thing to sit in a tiny room and watch a film you made with just the person with whom you made it and another altogether to watch it on a big screen in a darkened classroom with twenty other people, one whose approval you value so much it makes your stomach burn. But once the film got rolling, I sat riveted. This time, for the first time, I watched it as a regular viewer, not as the person who made it, paying less attention to all the tiny pieces and more to the story we were telling. It was the story of Dorothea's growth, her transformation from ambitious idealist who held herself above her fellow human beings, to an ordinary happy woman, and we used the narrative arc of her romantic life to demonstrate this. It wasn't a story that wrapped itself up with a bow in the end, not entirely. Yes, Dorothea found true love with Will ("We are bound to each other by a love stronger than any impulses which could have marred it"), but she also resigned herself to a life of helping her husband ("I like nothing better, since wrongs existed, than that my husband should struggle against them, and that I should give him wifely help") instead of being a hero in her own right.

The funny parts came mostly at the beginning, with all the characters weighing in on Dorothea's engagement and marriage to the old, ugly Casaubon. ("Good God, it is horrible! He is no better than a mummy!" "He has one foot in the grave!" "Look at his legs!"), and the film got more serious as it went on. The only thing Luka was better at than the comedic parts was being Will Ladislaw. When he said, with shadowed eyes, a rasp in his voice, and sudden hollows in his cheeks, "I never had a *preference* for her, any more than I have a preference for breathing. No other woman exists by the side of her," I think it's fair to say that the classroom engaged in a collective swoon.

The clapping started before the lights went back on. There were whistles, a war whoop. We were a hit! In the midst of the clamor, Luka and I turned to each other and gravely fist-bumped (a first for yours truly), and then both of us, at the same time, forgot the rule against unrestrained happiness and smiled.

"Ready?" asked Luka.

"Ready," I said, and we stood up and walked to the front of the room to give our presentation. That's when I saw Mr. Insley's face and gasped as though I'd been struck. To say there was no joy in his expression would be the understatement of the century. His face, that face I had studied with every ounce of my attention, the face I had cherished from its wide brow to its prominent blue eyes to its narrow chin, was a white-lipped mask of rage. And I swear that it wasn't until that second, in a flashbulb pop of understanding, that I considered how our film might look to him.

The older, scholarly first husband of whom no one approved. The naive young girl desperate to please him. Phrases fizzed through my mind: "white moles," "beautiful lips kissing holy skulls," "I think when a girl is so young as Miss Brooke is, her friends ought to interfere a little to hinder her doing anything foolish." It was all I could do not to cry out, "But it's got nothing to do with us! It all started with my and Luka's argument about Dorothea and grew from there!" And there was also—I am sorry to say it—a small part of me that felt just plain irritated with him. Here I was, at long last, after months of being scorned and reviled and ignored, standing tall and triumphant, my ears ringing with the approval of my peers, and he was the only one in the room—well, except for Bec—who wasn't cheering me on.

As I was standing there, jostled by conflicting emotions, Luka reached out and put a steadying hand on my shoulder.

"Willow," he whispered. "Are you ready?"

And, just like that, I was.

But before we could start, just as we were clearing our throats and straightening our notecards, Mr. Insley said, in an ice-pick voice, "Unfortunately, your film ran over the allotted time limit, so we will not be able to hear your presentation today. I will attempt to squeeze it into a future class, but I certainly can't promise. Please retake your seats."

The classroom went dead quiet, and I felt tears fill my eyes. Luka looked so mad, he almost shimmered with it, and he was opening his mouth to say something to Mr. Insley, when a voice came gliding across the room from the direction of the door: "Oh, it would be a terrible shame, Mr. Insley, to leave such a gorgeous project unfinished. I believe I've never seen a student film nearly so accomplished. And there are ten minutes left in the class."

Janine Shay, one hand on her hip, her lipsticked smile curving like a scimitar. Until she spoke, I hadn't realized she was there. Mr. Insley must not have realized it, either, because his eyes nearly popped from his head. Later, when I remembered his face, I would feel compassion for him having been shown up by an intruder in his classroom, his personal kingdom, but right then, all I felt was relief.

"Wouldn't you agree, class?" asked Ms. Shay.

Nods. One low-key war whoop. We did the presentation.

On the way out, tremulously, I attempted to smile at Mr. Insley, my beloved, but he stared down at the papers on his desk as though he were trying to set them on fire with his eyes.

"I'll see you at lunch," I said, softly, so that only he could hear. A muscle in his cheek twitched. Otherwise, nothing. Panic began to roar in my ears, but I beat it back with the certainty that he loved me. He loved me, and I would explain everything. Right then, I realized—with guilt and rue—that, in the past week or so, I had been thinking less about Mr. Insley when I was away from him, maybe because I was getting used to the idea of him, maybe because I had been so busy. But all it took was the prospect of losing him for my love to rise up and seize me by the throat. Now that I stopped to consider, I saw it was usually in my moments of deepest anxiety regarding our relationship that I loved him the most. Odd, but then love was odd, wasn't it?

At lunch, his classroom was empty as a tomb.

As I was walking away from it, I spotted Luka, his jacket off and slung over his arm, his lunch bag in his hand.

"Luka!"

We ate outside, under our tree. Careless of the cold, as always, Luka threw his jacket to the ground and sat in the gray, autumnal weather in his shirtsleeves. I tucked my knees under my chin and fiddled with my food. We discussed our success, of course, but I found that my heart wasn't quite in it.

"Good thing Ms. Shay showed up," said Luka. "Now, Zany Blainey won't be able to give us a shit grade just to punish us."

I flushed. "Oh, I don't think he'd do that," I said, hastily. "All we did was go over the time limit, right?"

"We didn't. We hit the limit exactly. But so what if we'd gone over? Max Bolton's violin piece inspired by the Rosamond character went on for ten minutes longer than ours, and Insley ate it up, even though he obviously doesn't know crap about music."

"Why would you say that?"

"Because for starters, seventy-five percent of that piece was ripped straight out of Mozart's 'Violin Concerto Number Five.'"

"You know this how?"

"Dude, my mom's Chinese. I've been playing violin since I was four years old."

"Hmpf. Stereotyping, I see."

Luka smiled. "Hey, I'm allowed. And anyway, did you see Insley making that big show of keeping time, doing a little conductor act with his pencil? But he was totally off rhythm. It was painful."

Full disclosure: I had noticed this. I'd winced at first, inadvertently, but ultimately found it quite endearing.

"I suppose," I said, vaguely.

Luka threw a pretzel nugget at me.

"Hey, what's wrong? We're amazing filmmakers. We rule the world. Remember?" he said. Luka was the sort who had so many different kinds of smiles that it was tempting to categorize them. Now, he was smiling his "prompt" smile, a small, private, head-pitched-slightly-forward affair the purpose of which was to get me to smile back. I tried to oblige.

"I suppose I'm just sad that it's over," I said, and as soon as I did, I realized I meant it. Did I ever! The Mr. Insley worries were only part of my sadness.

"Working on that project was the most stimulating experience of my entire school career."

Luka shook his head.

"Okay, (a) you should avoid using the word 'stimulating' in all conversations; and (b) you meant to say 'working on that project *with you, Luka,* was the most stimulating experience of my school career.' "

"Hmm. Before you strain a muscle patting yourself on the back, consider that I've been in school for less than a single semester."

"Hey, I knew when you said 'school career' you really meant 'life,' " said Luka. "I could tell."

"You could tell no such thing," I said.

"I can read you like a book, Cleary, a book with extremely long, very confusing sentences."

At the sight of his merry face looking at me, sadness fell again. At that moment, the bell ending lunch sounded, and as we gathered our things, the world before me blurred. Tears, real tears, not just of the eye-tingling variety, but the kind that wet your cheeks. In front of Luka. I could have kicked myself. But this felt, for all the world, like the end of something.

"Hey, stop that!" said Luka, alarmed. He left his belongings in a heap on the ground and came over to me and tugged a hank of my hair. "We make an awesome team, right?"

I nodded, not trusting myself to speak, lest I burst into sobs.

"So here's the thing: the project's over, but we aren't. Okay?"

It was as though a skylight I hadn't even noticed was there opened, letting in a brand-new kind of light, and that light fell right on Luka. Because I'd been living and breathing *Middlemarch,* and because I was a hopeless nerd, a line from the book leaped to my mind: "Each looked at the other as if they had been two flowers which had opened then and there." Oh, I felt breathless, newly bloomed, and so confused. *You love*

Mr. Insley, I thought, and of course, I did, but then, God help me, not in a baffled rush, but carefully, deliberately, I put my arms around the person who stood before me and gathered him in. His white cotton button-down shirt was thin, so that his back was there, under my hands, and the strange, startled thought I had was, *Oh, he's just a boy.* Luka the great, the popular, the larger than life, became, under my palms, life sized. In all my sixteen years, I had never felt so suffused with tenderness. It was unbearable.

Then the skylight closed. And I let go. Let go? I practically pushed him away.

"We're going to be late," I said, stiffly, not looking at him.

Luka stood there for a second, not saying anything. I don't know if he was looking at me or not; I could not lift my chin to find out.

"You're right," he said. "See you later."

We went our separate ways. After a few steps, I broke into a run.

When I got to my locker, there was a note in it from Mr. Insley. He must have pushed it through the vents in the door. He hadn't signed it, but I would have recognized his handwriting anywhere: *I am sorry to have missed lunch. Fate intervened. Can you come to me after school?* Oh, he wasn't angry with me anymore! I pressed the note between my two palms, in an attitude of prayer, and let the relief—that everything was the way it used to be before the film, before Luka had felt so terribly fragile and precious in my arms—wash me clean.

In my last class of the day, I opened my notebook to find this in black marker on what had been the next blank page: 16 + 30 = RAPE. I didn't know what it meant exactly, but just knowing inexactly was enough to make every muscle in my body clench. I was on the verge of tearing it out and ripping it to shreds, but then I thought, *I will show it to Mr. Insley and he will talk it away.*

As it turned out, I didn't show it to him immediately, as I'd planned, because the minute I walked through his door, he shut it behind me and took me in his arms so fast that I fell back against the door with a *thunk*. Even as I gladly let myself be swept up, I hoped fervently that no one walking by had heard.

"Darling," he whispered. "I thought this damned day would never end."

Mr. Insley's face was so close that I could feel his breath on my lips. In a single motion, he pressed his cheek against mine and slid a hand roughly up the side of my neck into my hair. I gasped, audibly. It was just so new and so *ardent*. Even his opening my mouth with his finger had not been quite like this.

"Tell me you missed me," he whispered, his lips flicking moistly against my ear.

"I missed you," I whispered back. Even though I had just seen him a few hours ago, I had missed him, the version of him that loved me and that I loved, not the one whose entire being was contorted with anger.

He leaned a few inches away and took my face between his thin hands. I was sure he was going to kiss me, and I wanted desperately for him to do it, but he just stood, caressing my face, looking into my eyes, until I was blushing so deeply, I knew my cheeks had to be hot to the touch. *He has done this before*, was my sudden thought, and the idea did not repulse me as I knew it should have. No, heaven help me, I relished it because what it really meant was that he was a man. He had lived in the world, known other women, maybe even many others, and still, it was me whom he wanted. For the first time since I'd met him, I felt a heady rush of power.

In time, he let go of me, except for my hand, and led me to his desk. We sat down on it, shoulder to shoulder.

"May I tell you something?" I asked him.

"Anything."

"Remember that day when there was writing on the board?" It was an idiotic way to put it, since when was there not writing on the board? But I knew he would know what I meant.

"Yes."

"I got another, um, message."

He made a disgusted face. "Those sad, twisted little animals," he said. "I got one, too."

"Different from the last one? Um, a kind of addition problem?" I didn't want to say the words or show him the notebook.

"Yes."

"What does it mean?" I asked.

"For us? Nothing. It has not a thing to do with us. How could it? But, technically, generally, it refers to a law, one that says a physical relationship between a person thirty or over and one between the ages of sixteen and eighteen cannot legally be considered consensual. It assumes that the sixteen-year-old is not mentally or emotionally mature enough to make decisions on her own and is therefore automatically being tricked, violated, taken advantage of by the older party."

I sat in silence, considering this. What we had just done, there against the door, had certainly been physical, but I hadn't felt violated. I'd felt like my blood had been turned, magically, in an instant, to hot maple syrup.

"No," I agreed. "That has nothing do with us."

"I won't lie to you, though," said Mr. Insley. And stopped.

"What?"

"No, I can't tell you," he said, shutting his eyes. "Forgive me for bringing it up."

"Please," I said.

His eyes met mine. If powder blue eyes can be said to smolder, his were.

"I have imagined you in my bed," he said. "Your milky shoulders against my sheets, your glorious hair spread across my pillow."

My mouth went dry.

"Have you imagined the same?" he asked.

I shook my head.

"Ah. Does the idea repel you?" His voice was so gentle.

I shook my head again.

"Does it frighten you?" He leaned very, very close, awaiting my answer, eagerly.

"I don't know."

"I can live with that," he said, nodding. "Darling Willow, you must know that I would never push you, not the smallest nudge."

"I know," I said. "But thank you for saying so."

"Come to my house this weekend," he said, squeezing my hand so hard it hurt.

And, oh God, what a stupid roller-coaster of a girl I was because, yes, I had just been turning to molten sugar in his embrace, and yes, when my being in his bed was just a wistful, floating desire of his, I was, as my peers said, into it, sort of, anyway. Now, though, post-embrace, my head clear once again, by which I mean again full of my usual confusion, and with the prospect of going to Mr. Insley's house wherein the aforementioned bed no doubt abided being no longer a dream but an actual invitation, I floundered. Stop. Let me clarify that. I didn't flip around, uncertain; I lay flat on the bottom of the ocean, staring blankly up with my two eyes, and did not want to go. What I wanted was to run seven miles, or sit and talk to my father about who was more admirable, Winston Churchill or Theodore Roosevelt, or make something amazing, like a film or something, with a good friend.

But there was Mr. Insley, asking me to come the way he did everything: passionately, every piece of him leaping into animation.

"I don't think I should," I said, more weakly than I meant to.

"Should? No, most certainly you should not; you should go to school, do homework, joke with your peers, go to the mall. But what does 'should' have to do with someone like you? You are above 'should,' my girl."

"It's just—my father hasn't been well, and I know it's not something he would want me to do."

Mr. Insley laid a hand on my hair.

"My dear Willow, your father knows better than anyone that you are not a typical young woman. He's groomed you to be singular, extraordinary, a dove among pigeons. I think we would like each other, your father and I; I think—at the risk of sounding arrogant—I am exactly the kind of man he's been preparing you for."

Had my father been preparing me for any kind of man? The idea took me off guard. Maybe. He was practical, after all; he knew I would marry someone someday. I guess. But it was not something we had discussed. I thought about Taisy and Ben, how he had forced their annulment at eighteen. But I was not Taisy, and Ben was not Mr. Insley.

"I haven't thought about that much," I said, "but I think he would say I was too young right now."

As soon as I'd said it, I realized my mistake. Age was the last thing I should have mentioned. I braced myself, awaiting Mr. Insley's whitelipped rage, but it did not surface. He sat very still for a few seconds, and then gave me a smile.

"I am sorry to be presumptuous, but is it possible that you underestimate him?"

Certainly, this was the first time I had been accused of *that*.

"What do you mean?"

"I guess I am asking: Do you think your father would want you to *date*?"

He said the word like he was spitting out a piece of rancid meat. And to be honest, I could imagine my father saying it in just the same way.

"Go to dances in the gym?" Mr. Insley went on. "Would he want you to sit in movie theaters eating greasy, yellow popcorn or go to basketball games in a Webley red sweatshirt? Do you think he—Wilson Cleary—would want you to be the girlfriend of a teenaged boy?"

To this last question, probably to all of them but definitely to the last, there was one, resounding answer: No.

"Come to see me, Willow," said Mr. Insley, cupping my face in his hand. "We were made for this."

I gripped the edge of the desk. The muscles in my chest were so tight. This wise, ardent man had saved me from the ugly stairwell, from the cafeteria, from hallways full of people who hated me. He had taught me how to drive. When he was near, I felt shining and iconic, like I wasn't so much myself, Willow in her boots and parka, as I was a girl in a book—Dorothea or Catherine Earnshaw—or a woman in a painting.

"You are spun out of moonlight, Willow," he whispered. "You are poetry."

There, for one flashing second, unbidden, was Luka, throwing a pretzel at me under the oak tree. I blinked him away. Mr. Insley's face, full of passion, was inches from mine.

If you say no, you will lose him.

"Yes," I told him, "I'll come."

CHAPTER FIFTEEN

Taisy

I CALLED BEN AND ASKED him to have dinner with me. To be precise, I called and asked if I could cook him dinner at his house. One friend cooking dinner for another.

After a few beats, he said, "Sure. Why not?," and his nonchalance only broke my heart a little.

"We've demonstrated that we can talk while on the move," I said. "Walking, riding in cars. I thought why not see if we can have a conversation while sitting?"

"I feel like the polite thing to say would be, 'No, I'll cook,'" he said, "but, uh, over the years, my cooking skills haven't evolved at the same rate as, say, my fashion sense."

"Oh. Wow."

"Hey, my fashion sense isn't that bad. It's just not that fashionable."

"You prefer a classic look."

"Thank you."

"And I'm even pretty sure that those khaki pants you wore the other day were not the same ones you had in high school."

"Are you kidding?" he scoffed. "I threw those out months ago."

"So about the cooking. I did offer to cook, but I also invited myself over to your house. Obviously, these two things cancel each other out, which means for you to offer to cook would be overkill, politeness-wise."

"That's a relief. But I might be able to score some dessert from my dad. He's back in the kitchen with a vengeance."

"Perfect." When I said the word, I tried to make my tone voluminous enough to cover the dessert, Ben's dad, Ben's dad being back in the kitchen, and Ben himself, who most certainly was.

THAT DAY, I GOT a letter. Caro left it on the pool-house porch, with a note that said, "Hi, Taisy. This came for you. Love, Caro." Oh, but the mystery that was Caro never stopped deepening! I hadn't even known that she knew my nickname. Marcus and my mom had possibly called me that during the visit-from-hell on Willow's first birthday, but Caro had surely never heard it since, and here she was getting even the spelling right. And then there was that "Love."

The letter was a mystery, too. Hardly anyone knew I was here, and Trillium, my mom, and Marcus either called or texted me every day. I'd had my mail sent to my mom's, but she would've told me if she were forwarding something here. Besides, the sender had addressed the letter to "Eustacia." Exactly three people in the world called me that, and one of them apparently didn't anymore. The envelope had a typed label, no return address, and was so light it might have been empty.

It wasn't, alas. Inside, was a note that said: "Dear Eustacia—You should ask your sister Willow how things are going at school. It's not my place to tell you what's going on, but I'm not talking about her grades. Sincerely, A Friend." It sent a shudder up my spine. The message wasn't made up of letters cut from magazines—it was just a print-out, Helvetica type—but it felt as ominous as if it had been. I wondered if it had to do with Luka; I hoped not. The two of them had looked so happy and at ease out in front of the school that day. Still he was both a high school kid and ridiculously good-looking, which could be—but wasn't always—a recipe for trouble. Or could the trouble have to do with girls? High school girls made fascist dictators look like dewy-eyed cocker spaniels; everyone knew that. And then I remembered the man Ben had seen Willow with, the one who had impressed him as both older and a creep. Willow didn't seem to go much of anywhere apart from school, unless you counted the occasional stop at an English pub with creepy old men. Could the man have something to do with school; could the note have something to do with that man? My head fizzed with possibilities, all of them awful.

When I went out to buy cooking supplies for dinner at Ben's, I made a split-second decision and a quick stop: I bought Willow a cell phone and added it to my plan, an act of audacious overstepping that would enrage Wilson, if he found out about it. And there was a chance he might. My relationship with Willow was improving, mainly in that it now seemed almost to *be* a relationship, but it was still shifting and slippery and subject to pitfalls, particularly if you considered that the last time we'd really spoken, she'd called me a fool. So there was a decent possibility that she would take the phone straight to Wilson, but I was willing to risk it.

That evening, before I drove to Ben's, I walked across the yard and went in through the back door of the main house. Key ownership notwithstanding, I still felt anything but at home in Wilson's house, so I had hoped to find Caro and ask her permission to chat with Willow. But Caro was nowhere in sight. The downstairs seemed to be empty, in fact, so after a few humiliating false starts—foot on step, foot off step, turn around, turn back—I made my way up the stairs, only to face a hallway lined with four doors, all shut. Because I'd visited him there, I knew the one on the end was Wilson's room. I scanned the others for clues, but they were all bare. No playful WILLOW'S ROOM— KEEP OUT sign to aid me. No white message board, doodled over with flowers or song quotes. No girlish scarf tied around the doorknob. As

I stood there, on the edge of losing my nerve, the door at the end of the hallway opened and there stood Wilson.

"Eustacia!" he said, startled. His eyes fairly boggled at the sight of me, but quickly, he collected himself, tightening the belt of his dressing gown with a firm tug. "Was there some matter you wanted to discuss with me? I am busy at the moment, but I would be happy to send for you at a more convenient time."

"Uh, actually, no," I said. "I came to see Willow."

Wilson was so surprised by this, he began to sputter, and the sputter became a full-blown cough. When the spasm had passed, he said, "Did you send word that you were coming?"

I laughed. I couldn't help it. It was a good thing Wilson's house was gated and set so far back from the main road because God help the Girl Scout who showed up unannounced selling cookies. "By what? Errand boy? Carrier pigeon?"

Behind me, a door opened. I turned around, and there was Willow, her light brown eyes wide open and round as quarters. Evidently the wonder of my showing up unexpectedly would never cease.

"Taisy?" she said.

"Hi, Willow," I said. "I was hoping for a quick chat with you."

"Oh!" she said. She glanced at her father. "Daddy, are you all right? I heard you coughing."

Wilson waved off her concern. "Right as rain, child," he said, heartily, and then with a grand "Carry on then!" went back into his room and shut the door.

Willow turned her attention back to me, and, now that I had a head-on view of her, I noticed how tired she looked, tired and maybe also unhappy, her usually sharp eyes listless, her queenly bearing all gone to wilt.

"Hey," I said, quietly. "Do you have a minute?"

She nodded, then opened the door to her room, and stepped back to let me enter. "Please come in."

Willow's room was lovely, like something out of a magazine, but, like her door, it was eerily devoid of anything suggesting a sixteen-year-old lived in it. Of course, I wouldn't have expected lava lamps or boy band posters. But there was no bulletin board tacked with photos; no stack of magazines on the bedside table; no bin of makeup supplies; no landline phone; no coat stand decked with scarves, hats, and hoodies; not an iPod dock or CD player in sight.

The walls were cool gray with a hint of violet, and nearly all of one of them was taken up with a bookshelf full of hardcovers, the spines perfectly aligned. On the wall opposite the bed hung a long glass sculpture that looked, sort of, like overlapping, translucent scallop shells in shades of blue and purple, and from the center of the ceiling dangled a chandelier of what looked, sort of, like an upside down bouquet of calla lilies caught in a rain shower. Both were unmistakably Caro creations and unmistakably ravishing. In one corner of the room, near the big window, was a dark rose armchair covered in velvet. Willow gestured to it and said, "Would you like to sit down?"

I sat. She turned her desk chair around and sat, too, so that she was more or less facing me.

"I have something for you," I said. "I thought it might come in handy, now that you're going to school and everything."

"Oh?" she said, vaguely. "Well, that was nice of you."

Maybe I'd caught her off guard by coming to her room or maybe the trouble at school to which the letter had referred was getting to her, but she seemed more open, less imperious than I'd ever seen her.

I held out the tidy white box with the phone in it, and she didn't recoil at the sight, but simply reached out and took it.

"It's a phone," she said, quietly, and then, like she was trying out the phrase, she added, "A smartphone."

"Open it up," I suggested.

As she did this, I could see the sheer niftiness of the packaging working its magic on her. The phone was a slip of silver and shone like a rectangle of moonlight as she turned it over in her hands. Oh, the persuasiveness of exquisitely designed inanimate objects! She pushed the button and the screen lit up like Times Square.

She sat still, staring down at it, and I braced myself for her to thrust it back at me or to toss a disparaging remark ("Cell phones are causing human relationships to wither on the vine, Eustacia, don't you know that?"), but instead, she lifted her chin and said, wonderingly, "Is it hard to learn how to use?"

"Easy as pie," I told her. "And I have an account at the online store I can give you the password for, in case you want to order any extra apps."

"Oh," she said, confusion crossing her face. "Apps."

"Why don't you read the instructions and then ask me if you have any questions? I'm no techie, but together, we can probably figure out whatever it is."

She hesitated, then gave the phone another quick glance, and nodded.

"Also. I, uh, put my number in the contacts, in case you ever need it," I told her, trying to sound casual. "You can call any time, if you find yourself in need of a ride or, well, anything at all. And if you never have a reason to call or would prefer not to, no worries there. I just thought . . ." I trailed off.

"Okay," she said, gravely. "Thank you."

Her thank-you was followed by a tiny, glimmering smile. It disappeared almost as soon as it arrived, but it left me feeling closer to Willow, as though my gift and her smile had worked to clear a small circle of space in which we could sit and be normal with each other. If there was ever a time to ask her how things were going at school, I suppose it would have been then, but the circle felt fragile as frost, like a breath could make it disappear. So I said, "Well, good, then," and put my hands on the arms of the chair.

But before I quite got to my feet, Willow said, her face pinking, the words tumbling out, "Eustacia, I'm sorry I said that the other night, about you and Ben. In the pool house."

I froze, crouched in midrise, then dropped back into the chair.

"It's okay," I said. "You don't need to apologize."

She shook her head. "No, I do. You see, I don't really know any-thing about love. Not nearly enough to have any business judging someone else." She mustered a weary, flat-eyed smile. "In fact, I'm rather muddled on the subject. Like, hopelessly maybe."

I smiled back. "You know what, though? You were right about me and Ben. I didn't love him enough back then to deserve to keep him. I never understood that until you said it. And I apologized to him the very next day."

"Really? Did he forgive you?"

"I think he might have. But there's a big gap between forgiving someone and giving them another chance."

Willow considered this. "I guess he would have to believe that this time you would love him enough." Then, as if catching herself, she added, "Um, right?"

"Right. He would. And I would."

"You would?"

"Actually, I already do. But that doesn't mean I can convince him. In fact, I'm beginning to think I never will. We're friends, though, and that's something."

"I bet you can," she said. Not a trace of guile or animosity. Nothing in her face or tone suggested, for instance, that I would let my sordid, slutty wiles do the convincing. Her lack of meanness and disapproval was positively scaring me. Whatever had taken the wind out of her sails had done so with a vengeance. There was also the possibility that she was just starting to like me, and maybe that was true, too, but there was no trace of the white goddess, the upright, scorching-eyed Willow who had always been. Something had happened.

"Thanks," I said.

Willow touched the button to bring the phone's screen flaring to life again. I considered leaving, but I got the sense she wanted to say something else to me. Finally, without looking up, her finger flitting over the touch screen, in a low voice, she said, "Did you ever say no to him?"

"Ben?"

"Yes. Besides the, um, annulment, I mean. Did you ever tell him no when he asked you to do something that you didn't want to do?"

Worry slid cold fingers down my neck.

"Sure," I said. "Usually, though, when we were deciding something, we talked about it. If one of us just truly didn't want to do it, we'd let it drop."

She nodded, still not looking at me. Then: "Was there ever someone in your life to whom you just could not say no?"

Oh, God. I kept my voice calm. "Wilson."

She didn't leap to defend him, just nodded again, still not looking up.

"What about you?" I asked her, as carefully as I could.

I thought she might tell me. The light from the chandelier cast a greenish glow across her pensive face, and for a second, she was otherworldly, mermaidlike, and so fragile. When her eyes met mine, though, she looked like any teenager who realizes she's said too much.

"Nope," she said, shrugging. "Not really."

AFTER BEN AND I carried in shopping bag after shopping bag (and one large red cooler) of dinner supplies—not only food (in various stages of preparedness) but also flowers, a vase, candles, candleholders, matches, wine, trivets, olive oil, spices measured out into Ziploc bags, oven mitts, paper towels, parchment paper, placemats, cloth napkins, salt and pepper shakers, and two green bottles of bubbly water—I stood in his kitchen unloading them, while Roo and Pidwit wove around the bags, sniffing ecstatically, their stubby tails tick-tocking. Ben watched me with the twinkle in his eyes getting increasingly twinklier, then dropped his head back and laughed a laugh that was like Mardi Gras and the Fourth of July rolled into one.

"I overdid it, you're thinking?" I said, grinning. "Four giant bags and a cooler full of I'm-desperate-to-impress-my-friend-Ben? Is that it?"

"More like four giant bags and a cooler full of my-friend-Ben-is-so-lame-he-probably-doesn't-even-have-napkins," he said. He reached inside one of the bags and pulled out the saltshaker. "Or salt. Salt? Now, that's just insulting."

"Hey, I knew you were renting. I thought you might not have all the dinner accoutrements."

"Yeah, but you're living in a pool house, right?"

"A very well-stocked pool house. I'm sure it was Caro's doing. Wilson isn't exactly the kind of guy who would say, 'Taisy's coming. Better make sure she's got some silver trivets and linen napkins on hand!' "

"Huh. So I was thinking you invited yourself to cook here because you didn't have what you needed at the pool house." He looked at me, questioningly. "But that's not why, I take it."

I lifted the salmon papoosed in white paper out of the cooler, and instantly, the dogs stopped their excited perambulations around the shopping bags, stood stock-still, and lifted avid faces to gaze at the fish.

"Aha, I see we have some Alaskan sockeye fans in the house," I said.

Ben kept looking at me and, slowly, raised his eyebrows, twin black parabolas. I sighed. "I know what you're thinking," I said, "and you're right."

His eyebrows, unappeased, continued to wait.

"Maybe I thought it would be uncomfortable for you?" I ventured. "Being in Wilson's house, even if it isn't his house-house?"

"Maybe," he said, neutrally.

"Your face is going to stick that way, you know. How would it be, to walk around every day with that knowing look? I don't think that'll win you many friends, Ben."

Silence. I sagged. "I'm sorry. I've been tiptoeing around the guy my entire life. Even when he was hundreds of miles away, I tiptoed. But next time, I promise, pinky-swear, cross my heart and hope to die, that I'll invite you to the pool house. Wilson be damned. Okay?"

His brows came in for a landing. "Okay."

"You're not mad?"

"How could I be mad at someone who brings me trivets?"

OVER BEN'S PROTESTS, I ate dinner with Pidwit curled up on my lap and Roo sitting on my feet.

"You'll spoil them," said Ben.

I looked down at Pidwit, tucked neatly between my lap and the underside of the table, his sleeping face perfectly serene, not even the wings of his eyelashes fluttering. "I don't know," I said, skeptically. "He seems awfully comfortable." I narrowed my eyes at Ben. "Almost like he's done this before."

Ben laughed. "Before—or every day. Pid is what you'd call a classic lapdog, but I usually don't let him inflict himself on guests."

"Inflict? Are you kidding? It's an honor to have him here."

"Some people would call it uncivilized. Or unhygienic."

"Oh, but just *look* at that face!"

Ben grinned. "Yeah, that's pretty much how all arguments about not giving in to Pid's every whim end, especially the ones I have with myself."

While we ate, Ben talked some more about leaving Wisconsin, a topic that was quickly becoming one of my personal favorites.

"I just wasn't cut out for teaching," he said. "I wasn't terrible at it. I'm pretty sure I taught the kids what they were supposed to learn, and most of them seemed to like me well enough."

"I bet they loved you."

Ben shook his head. "I doubt it. Kids know. They know when someone's heart isn't in it, and I just didn't like being in front of a classroom that much. It felt unnatural, having mostly one-sided conversations with forty strangers all at the same time. We were discouraged from really knowing them or spending time with them outside of class, and even if we hadn't been, I never wanted to be *that* professor."

"The sad, desperate one who hangs out in student bars and is always dropping the names of cool bands into conversations? No, I don't see you as that guy."

"But teaching is a good job, and there are people who are born to it, and if you have one of them, you never forget it. I could have kept doing it, but you know what I missed?"

"Your old friend Taisy?"

Ben smiled. "The wonder. I mean, you were the kind of student I was. Remember how you'd learn something or read something, and it would just blow your mind, and you couldn't stop talking about it? Actually, you and I had a lot of those conversations."

"Gregor Mendel," I said. "For at least two weeks, you and I were crazy in love with Gregor and his pea plants."

"Darwin and his finches, too. And leafcutter ants. And Emily Dickinson."

"And *The Sound and the Fury,* even though it was really hard. Oh, and remember when we found out that light acts like a particle *and* a wave?"

"Yeah," said Ben, "I'm still not over that one."

"Me, either."

"Anyway, there just wasn't any wonder in teaching, for me. Sometimes, in doing research there was, although not enough, but never in the classroom, which seemed not really fair to any of us."

"How about what you're doing now? Studying gardening, working with plants. Is there wonder in that?"

"There is, actually." Ben shrugged, sheepishly. "Hey, I know a lot of people do jobs their whole lives that they don't find fascinating. Wonder is a luxury. But I wanted it, and not just in my job, but in—" He trailed off, his cheeks turning red.

Inside me, hope grew wings and soared. Ben lifted his wineglass and drank, not looking at me.

"I know," I said. "Relationships."

"What about you?" he said. "Is there wonder in your job?"

"Ben."

Our eyes met. "Sorry," he said, "I didn't mean to turn the conversation in the direction of—" He broke off again and rubbed his forehead with his palm.

"Love?" I said. "But that's my favorite direction. And do you think maybe you did mean to? Subconsciously?"

Ben smiled, reluctantly. "It's my subconscious, so I can't say for sure. But I don't think so."

I shrugged. "If we're going to be friends, we'll have to talk about the past seventeen years eventually, right?"

"I guess."

"And occasionally, we'll have to allude, in passing, to our prior relationships, won't we?"

"I guess."

"All right, so—everyone I was ever involved with after you was nice, well, except the guy in college who cheated on me for two straight years. The rest were nice, funny, smart." My voice got softer of its own accord. "But I never looked at one of them and thought, 'How in the world was such a person as you ever invented? This exact combination of things—eyes, hands, sense of humor, the face you make when you're figuring out a physics problem, the sound of your voice—how can it even exist? And by what grace have you ended up sitting here talking to me?'"

Ben's single dimple flared in his cheek. "You did physics problems with all your boyfriends?"

I shook my head and smiled back at him. "No."

Pidwit stirred in my lap and looked up at me with his tiny, sleepy, flower face. "What do you think the long-term effects are of living every single day in the presence of this much adorableness?" I said. "Have they studied that?"

"Adorable, loyal, trusting, *and* funny." Ben gave a slightly weary chuckle and then added drily, "When your dogs take your breath away more often than the person you're supposed to marry, it's probably time to reassess."

Definitely.

"Okay, well, I see what you mean, but it has to be said that, when it comes to dogs, these two are exceptionally wondrous."

Ben didn't laugh, just sat there regarding me with such plain, wide-open appreciation that, if it hadn't meant disturbing Pidwit— not to mention the candles, flowers, serving dishes, and Ben—I might have leaned across the table and kissed him right then. He blew out a sigh that was half groan and dropped his napkin onto the table.

"Yeah, well, it's true that once you've had wonder, it's hard to get used to not having it," he said.

"It's not hard," I said, firmly. "It's impossible."

AFTER DINNER, WE ENDED up sitting in front of the fire, which, alas, wasn't as romantic as it sounds, since I was in a chair, and Ben was on the couch, and the kitchen lights were on. With Roo and Pidwit curled up—two spoonfuls of Yorkie—on their round bed near the hearth, I told Ben about the anonymous letter.

"Do you think you should go talk to someone at the school?" he asked.

"You know, she's just starting to trust me," I said. "Not long ago, she thought I was the slut sister from hell, here to steal her father's heart and wreck her life, but now she's confiding in me. Sort of. And probably only out of sheer desperation because she doesn't have any female friends and doesn't want her parents to worry about her or think she's not perfect. But still, she's reaching out, and I don't want her to retreat."

"I can understand that," said Ben. "But what if—"

I held up my hand to interrupt him.

"I know. Which is why, I'd go tell someone and risk her hating me forever in a heartbeat, if I thought it would help. I can see that she's working through something, but she's not there yet. This girl has never trusted anyone, as far as I can tell, except Wilson and Caro. And if I jump in too soon, she might never trust anyone else ever again."

"Well, that would be bad," agreed Ben.

"It would be disastrous. No one should have a universe made up of just herself and two other people."

"Especially when one of those people is Wilson," said Ben.

I waited for my knee-jerk reaction to defend Wilson, but it never came.

"It's his fault, you know," I said. "Whatever bad thing is happening at school. He's kept that girl so isolated and protected that she hasn't acquired the normal instincts for danger. It's like those animals that evolve on islands with no predators."

"And then the rats show up."

"Exactly!"

Even in my worried state, I could not help but notice Ben in the firelight, how the shadows swept into all the little dips and hollows of his face.

"What do you think happened to Wilson?" I asked Ben. "How does a person never learn to love properly?"

Ben contemplated this, his eyes full of concentration and firelight.

"You're writing a book about him," he said, finally. "You said that whenever you get stuck, you think of the right question to ask the person. What would you ask Wilson?"

"Ha. He'd never answer."

"Still."

"Okay. How about: Why did you lie about your parents' dying in a car accident? Or: Why did you change your name? Or: Why did you despise your first two kids?"

Ben said, "Who did you ever headlong, all-out love without having to try?"

"My mom," I said quickly. "Trillium. Marcus. You."

Ben smiled. "Thank you, but I wasn't actually asking you."

"I know," I said. Suddenly, I could not bear to be so far away from him. And he missed me; I was sure of it. Even if he wouldn't admit it to himself, all that talk of wonder meant he missed me. "Can I come over and sit beside you for a second?"

Ben narrowed his eyes at me, suspiciously.

"Come on," I said. "I need to ask you something."

"Okay."

I left two feet of space between us. I reached across the gap and traced an arc from his temple to where his cheekbone peaked below his eye. He breathed in, sharply. "What's this bone?" I asked. "The one around your eye."

"I'm better with plants," he said, "but I think it might be the zygomatic bone."

"I missed your zygomatic bone so awfully much," I told him. "Both of them."

He circled my wrist with his fingers, barely touching it, and for a few seconds, there we were: the fire crackling and flickering, my fingers on his face, his around my wrist. Just us, like we'd been slipped into a pocket. Then, Ben opened his hand and let go, lightly, like he was releasing a firefly but still he let go, and sat back against the couch cushions, and I moved my hand away and did the same.

"I'm sorry," I said, with a rueful smile at the fire. "Tigering."

"You want to hear something crazy?" said Ben.

"Yes," I said.

"When we got married, I thought it would last."

I shut my eyes.

"Seriously," he went on. "And 'thought' is the wrong word. I knew like I knew, I don't know, that three was a prime number or that my dad was my dad. I was confused about other things, but on that point, I was rock solid. And then, you know what?"

"It ended," I said. "I ended it."

"Right," he said. "It still ranks as the worst thing that ever happened to me." His voice held no trace of meanness. He was stating facts.

I turned to face him. The outline of his profile was lovely but remote, like a coastline you see from an airplane.

"I did a terrible thing to you, and I have paid for it bitterly, not that that matters," I said.

"That's not what I wanted," he said, and then lifted the corner of his mouth. "Okay, I wanted it at first, for two years, maybe three. Maybe three and a half. But after that, I hoped you were happy."

"You did?"

He sat, thinking. "No. Not exactly."

"Oh."

"I mean, I did stop hoping you were unhappy, and I wasn't mad at you, but I put it away."

"What?"

"All of it. The good and the bad. Us. I boxed it up and moved on, and I promised myself that I would never get it all back out. It was the only way I could get through it."

"And never includes now?"

"It has to."

I knew what I'd seen in his face just moments ago when I touched him and he touched me back, and it was so hard not to say, *You want me. You do!* But I was afraid he'd end everything right there. Besides, if you have to tell someone that he wants you, maybe it means he doesn't want you enough. I looked at him and said, "I guess I can understand that."

"Thank you," he said, sincerely.

I held out my hand, trying to tell myself that it wasn't just so he would touch me again. "Friends?"

Pull me against you, I begged him, silently. *Bury your face in my hair.*

Ben took my hand in his and gave it a firm shake. "Friends."

CHAPTER SIXTEEN

Willow

To PUT IT BLUNTLY, Mr. Insley's house was not what I'd expected, a two-story brick-front snaggletooth jutting up out of a flat yard in an otherwise tidy neighborhood, not picturesque enough to qualify as ramshackle, no bushes or flowers to soften the crumbling edges. A metal mailbox tilted drunkenly at the end of the short driveway. A cracked, empty terra-cotta planter squatted on the front stoop, and a blanched NO SOLICITING sign hung next to the door. Surrounding the backyard, but visible from the road, was a low chain-link fence. A chain-link fence! At a private residence! I had not known such a thing existed.

When Mr. Insley opened the front door, I fear he saw the look of dismay on my face because he said, wryly, "Welcome to my humble, but very humble, abode." He took my hand and walked me down the worn green carpet runner that led through the house to the kitchen, saying, "I find I'm mostly indifferent to my surroundings, a side effect of living too much inside my head, I suppose. It's only when others come over, which isn't often, that I realize how austere my living quarters are. Besides, it's a rental."

While *austere* was not perhaps the word I would have chosen, since it suggested to me simplicity and spareness, and Mr. Insley's house, what I caught a glimpse of, seemed more like dingy and cluttered, I did admire him for not caring.

"Honestly, I don't care that much about my own room, either," I told him. "It's just a place to sleep and do homework."

It was true. I had never felt especially attached to the room; I'd surely never considered it an extension of my personality. It was fairly austere, now that I thought about it. That it happened to be also quite lovely was all my mother's doing. The room was planted in the middle of rather a lot of grandeur, but that was more accident than anything else. My father had told me that when he bought the house, he'd simply snapped up the first one that came along that had a place for my mother's studio; the fact of its fanciness was purely incidental. Still, I didn't mention the grandeur to Mr. Insley.

I thought perhaps we were stopping in the kitchen, which was bright compared to the rest of the house, but, instead, Mr. Insley opened the back door and we went out onto a small wooden deck. To my relief, the yard was nicer than the house. There was a black metal mesh table and chairs on the deck, some blue ceramic pots of yellow mums, and out in the yard, two more chairs, a low wooden bench, and a copper fire pit full of new logs. Most of the yard was taken up by the shed he had told me about, which wasn't so much a building as a sort of arched, metal tunnel, like a very rickety covered bridge, open at both ends. Inside the shed, it was dark, but I could see the outlines of what I knew must be the boat Mr. Insley was building.

"This is nice," I said.

Mr. Insley's face in the watery sunlight was lean and fair, his eyes the same color as the sky. His hair looked smooth, like he had just brushed it, and I liked the idea of his getting ready for me to arrive. Then, a cloud covered the sun, and I shivered. I wore running clothes, black tights, and a fitted red Gore-Tex jacket, exceedingly unromantic clothing, but I hadn't had the energy to come up with a pretext for being dropped off near Mr. Insley's neighborhood. I wasn't even sure where I would have had someone drop me, since, apart from a gas station and a supermarket, there didn't seem to be much around his neighborhood except more neighborhoods. Mr. Insley lived just five miles from my house, but right at the place where both the country and the city gave way to suburb.

"Are you cold, my dear? Let me light the fire, and then, I'll get you something to put on."

It seemed that we would be staying outside for now, which was a relief to me, despite the chilly air. It seemed also that Mr. Insley was not, at least immediately, going to reprise the rush of physical passion that had thrown me so off balance, literally and figuratively, the last time I'd seen him, and this was also a relief. Still, while he was inside the house, I had the mad impulse to just run away, but how would I face him Monday morning? Of course, the deeper question was: If all I wanted to do was run away, then why had I come in the first place? But I put that one aside to think about later.

When Mr. Insley came out with a loaded tea tray and a hefty brown sweater, I thought, *Maybe this is going to be okay.* Yes, I was completely inexperienced, but I had to think that a rose-sprigged tea set and a plate of petits fours were incompatible with unfettered lust. I pulled the sweater over my head. Even through my layers of running wear, it itched.

We sat in the chairs near the fire, with the tea tray on the wooden bench before us. Mr. Insley talked about his hero Dante Gabriel Rossetti and Rossetti's muse, a woman named Elizabeth Siddal, which led to a general contemplation of muses and of how being the inspiration for great art was just as important as making great art yourself. I was just so glad to hear him talk the way he had in the old days, the days before he put his finger in my mouth (I had begun to view this as a dividing point, like the birth of Christ: BF and AF) that I didn't pay that much attention to what he was saying. In the moments when I tuned in, I found myself vaguely disagreeing with him, but I didn't care enough to argue, and I didn't want to rock the boat, especially when it was drifting upon such flat and translucent waters. We sipped our tea; I smiled; Mr. Insley looked dashing and fiery-eyed, as he always did when he discussed the Pre-Raphaelites; and from time to time, he got up to poke the fire in the fire pit. It was so easy to love him right then, to feel dazzled and proud to be with him and only a little nervous.

But the mood of the day shifted before I even realized it, and those petits fours—white with tiny rosebuds like the tea set—turned out to be not so innocuous after all. Mr. Insley had been being so careful, circling me so tentatively, that I was lulled into relaxing and failed to notice when the circles began to get smaller.

Then, he broke off in the middle of a sentence having something to do with Elizabeth Siddal's long, white, inspiring neck, and said, in an alarmingly low and husky voice, "Willow, my girl, you haven't tried a petit four." Before I could say that I didn't want one (I loathed fondant, although I would not have told him that for all the world), he had picked one up, bitten it in half, and then, licking his upper lip, stretched his hand out in the direction of my face. At first, I thought he merely wanted me to see the inside of the petit four, and then as his hand went lower, I thought perhaps he wanted me to smell it, and I thought, *Oh, I hope it doesn't have marzipan. I loathe the smell of marzipan,* and all this happened so fast that before I knew it, he had pressed the cake to my lips.

He was feeding me. Feeding me! Like a mother might feed a child, except the look in his eyes was not maternal. Not at all. Automatically, I opened my mouth. And after I had closed my lips around the thing, Mr. Insley rested his finger against them for one second, two, three, rising from his seat, moving to kneel in front of my chair, his finger on my mouth like it was stapled there, and then his face got close, closer, and he moved the finger away, and was kissing me. His mouth wasn't rough. It was as soft as a butterfly, covering mine with flutters and tiny tugs, and it wasn't scary. But maybe it was the suddenness or because I was worried about what to do with the lump of cake on my tongue (Chew—unobtrusively? Swallow—whole?), but I found I was too distracted to like it, and this made me sad. It was my first kiss, and I wasn't even paying attention.

Which is maybe why, when he finished and pulled his face back, I gulped the petit four, leaned forward, and kissed him again. This time, I made sure to concentrate. This kiss lasted longer and became more complex, our mouths slightly open, clinging and unclinging, his tongue flicking around a bit. What interested me is how isolated an event it was, involving only our two mouths. There had been times in the past, mostly when we were driving, when I'd feel his eyes on me, and his mere gaze was enough to make the hairs on my neck stand on end. But now, this kiss felt dreamlike, a pleasant grappling between two sets of lips, two tongues, four rows of teeth. Mr. Insley might have been anyone. The rest of my body might have been anywhere.

When we finished, Mr. Insley smiled at me and said, "Now, you have to come look at my boat."

As we were walking to the shed, I noticed that the grass under our feet was mostly green, but there were some places where it was dead and brown, not patches, though, as you'd expect, but lines and curves. Oh, I was an odd bird! I'd just had my first kiss—my first two, but I had decided to only count the second—and was walking hand in hand with my beloved, and I was noticing dead grass.

"What are you looking at, my love?" asked Mr. Insley.

"The grass," I blurted out. "It seems to be dead in places."

My psyche writhed with mortification.

Mr. Insley gave me a sidelong, quizzical glance and then looked at the grass.

"You're right. Looks like weed killer gone amok, but I never use the stuff. A couple of my neighbors have complained about the state of my yard; perhaps this is retribution. Ah, the obsessions of the bourgeoisie!"

I did not mention the team of gardeners who showed up at my house every two weeks.

I am not really a boat person, and this boat was not really a boat,

more of a ribbed wooden husk propped up on sawhorses, but Mr. Insley's pride in it was touching. His eyes grew misty; he ran a hand along
its side, fondly. The shed was really quite horrible, cobwebby with
some messily stacked firewood, a lawnmower that was evidently sel-
dom used since it was wreathed in ratty webs, and a can of gasoline.
Nearer to the boat, there were some tools lying around, along with a
couple large containers of wood varnish, but even so, the boat seemed
to not have been worked on in some time. There were cobwebs strung
across it, dead leaves scattered around inside it, and what had every
appearance of being a nest tucked into what was perhaps the stern, unless it was the bow.

Suddenly, it struck me that the boat had the distinct look of a project that would never, ever come to fruition, and here was poor Mr. Insley, loving it so dearly. I looked at him, with his doting expression, his
tweed overcoat and old brown wingtips and felt that, at the center of
Mr. Insley's life, there was a great empty space. No one should live that
way. Pity swelled my heart. Impulsively, I hugged him, the first embrace between us I had ever initiated. He said, "Oh!," and hugged back.

"Isn't it marvelous?" he said.

"Yes," I lied. "Very."

We stood, arms around each other, staring at the boat.

"When it's finished," he said, gleefully, "you and I will sail away,
and the wind will send that hair of yours streaming!"

That's when I heard what sounded like a cough or a laugh coming
from just outside the fence at the other end of the shed, followed by a
crackle of leaves and twigs, what could have been the sound of someone running away, someone who had been standing there. Watching
us. Mr. Insley rushed over to the fence, but there was no one in sight.

"Damned neighborhood kids," he said, returning with a reassuring smile. "Nothing to worry about."

"Of course not," I said, but my hands were shaking. I pulled the
long sleeves of the sweater down over them so Mr. Insley wouldn't see.

He wrapped me in his arms and then let go.

"This damn sweater," he said, with a mischievous grin. "I can't even feel that you're there."

And, in one quick motion, he took it by the bottom hem and pulled it over my head and off.

"That's better," he said.

He wrapped me in his arms again and then, again, let go. He patted my lower back.

"What's this?" he asked.

My cell phone, zipped into the back pocket of my running jacket. I took it out.

"I thought you didn't have a phone," he said, his smile turning slightly wooden.

"Oh, I didn't," I said, hurriedly. "It's new. I brought it with me so that I could ask you for your number."

His face relaxed.

"Ah. And you must give me yours."

I swallowed hard. The only numbers I had were Taisy's, my home number, and Luka's, which I got when we were doing the project. I wasn't even sure why I had stored Luka's number, except that it was the only other cell-phone number I had in my possession. But no one but Taisy had mine. For some reason, I didn't want to give it to Mr. Insley, but there he was, taking out his phone. I gave him the number, and he called my phone from his, which evidently meant that his number was now on mine, imprinted, maybe irrevocably. It was strange how I felt more bound to him by this than I had by the kiss, which seemed to dissolve into the ether as soon as it ended. I understood very little about such things, but I imagined our relationship riding radio waves, bouncing off towers. I imagined satellites spreading the fact of us through the blackness of space and all over the earth. Wearily, I wondered if there were a way to undo it, an app to erase it all.

"I should go home now," I said.

His arms went around me again.

"All right," he said, smiling. "I'll drive you home on one condition."

"Oh. What's that?"

"That you promise to come again, soon. Come in the evening, and I will make you dinner."

"Well, that might be hard."

He squeezed me tighter, smiled wider.

"Oh, well, then I'm afraid you'll have to stay," he teased. He lifted my chin with his fingers. "Now, promise."

Neither fear nor lust nor joy coursed through me. Instead, unaccountably, I thought about the unfinished boat, the NO SOLICITING sign, the dark house with its threadbare floor runner. The wingtips. The fence. For God's sake, the *fence*. I rested my hand against his cheek.

"I promise."

I HAD HIM DROP me off a mile from my house, and I ran home, fast, to remind myself that I was I and that all of it was mine, legs, arms, rib cage, streaming hair. I pulled the sweet fall air into my chest and let it scrub my face clean.

Before I could open the front door of my house, Taisy did, which is how I knew, right away, that something was terribly wrong. I froze, clamped a hand over my mouth. Taisy touched my shoulder.

"Hey," she said. "Don't look like that. It's okay."

"Did he die?" I asked, bleakly.

Her eyes widened. "No! No, no, no, no, no, of course not. He had some chest pains, and your mom thought it best to call an ambulance, but it's probably nothing. She's at the hospital with him."

Then, heaven help me, I burst into tears, long, clawing sobs that burned my chest.

"It's all my fault! I should have been here," I almost shrieked. "I should have been here."

Taisy led me into the house and sat me down on the living room sofa, keeping her arms around me. I could not help it: I leaned my face against her sweater and cried my heart out.

"Hey, hey," Taisy said, soothingly. "None of this is your fault. How could it be?"

"I-I lost focus. Like with the door, when Muddy went out into the rain. I let things distract me."

"Oh, Willow, honey," she said. "You've been bombarded with so much change in the past few months. You're handling it beautifully, beyond what anyone could expect."

I shook my head. "No, you don't know!" I wailed. "You don't know how I have let him down."

"You have to stop that," said Taisy. "You are a sixteen-year-old. You're supposed to focus on your own life. And you're supposed to make mistakes. Don't you know that?"

"No one is ever supposed to make mistakes," I said, gasping.

"Now, I'm sorry," she said, firmly, "but that is just wrong."

I didn't really believe her, but being held felt so nice. Taisy and I sat like that for a long time, so long that, outside, the sun set; darkness filled the windows. I may even have slept a little. When the phone rang, I sprang up and ran for the kitchen. It was Muddy.

"It's fine, darling girl," she told me. "It wasn't another heart attack, just some inflammation around his heart that sometimes happens after surgery. He's taking medicine and will come home tomorrow."

I dropped into a kitchen chair, relief pouring through me. I gave Taisy the thumbs-up. She smiled, and I smiled back, and weirdly, this wasn't weird at all.

After Taisy had gone back to the pool house, I went up to my room, sat on my bed, and felt steady, more like I was home, truly home, all of me right here, than I had in a long time. Then, I took out my phone, and quickly, before I could stop myself or analyze why, I called Luka.

"Hello?" he said.

"This is Willow," I said. "You are the official recipient of my first cell-phone call."

"Well, well, well," he said. "Welcome to the twenty-first century, Cleary. How does it feel?"

There was a laugh in his voice. Satellites and cell-phone towers catapulted that voice across the sky, bouncing it from star to star to star. Luka's voice—and mine, answering.

"Wonderful," I said.

CHAPTER SEVENTEEN

Taisy

I DON'T KNOW WHETHER IT was because I'd seen the extraordinarily ordinary house she'd grown up in or because I expected someone Wilson had rejected to seem more, well, *rejected* (and, yes, I know how ironic that is, coming from me), but, whatever the reason, Wilson's sister, Barbara, was a shock. A chic shock. A long, black licorice whip of a woman with cat's-eye glasses, blood-red lips, and a steel-gray, mathematically precise bob. Even her house was intimidating, a Society Hill row house, early-eighteenth-century Georgian on the outside, midcentury Modern on the inside, with that indefinable something that even people who don't have any of their own recognize as style. The kind of place that makes you glad you wore mascara and the Trillium boots and even gladder that you brought a friend, especially one who flung open his (pretty black) eyes and bit his knuckle in faux terror as soon as Barbara turned her back to lead us into the house.

As soon as she got us inside, she turned and said, severely, one elegant finger elegantly raised, "I have not been waiting for this moment. I want to be clear on that point. I stopped giving a damn about Wilson over fifty years ago. But since this moment has arrived anyway, I am extremely happy to see you," and she encased me in a genial, if angular, hug.

"Thank you," I said, "for letting me come."

I had contacted her through her website "B. Ravenel Volkman Interior Architecture," a stark, black-and-white, bare-bones page with just an e-mail address and a phone number, an insider sort of website, one for a business that doesn't sell itself because it assumes you are already sold. I e-mailed, briefly describing who I was and asking if I might meet with her, and she'd sent back one word—"Fine"—a date and time, and her home address.

Now, she said, "First I feed you; then we talk, but only if you agree not to put anything I say into a book."

I must have looked taken aback because she said, "I looked you up, naturally. I know you're a not-so-ghostly ghostwriter. If you are doing a book on Wilson, I cannot in conscience be part of it. Are you?"

"No," I said.

Ben gave me a sharp look, but I wasn't lying. For some time now, I had been toying with the idea of telling Wilson he would be better off with another writer, but right then, sitting in his sister's house, I decided for sure.

"He hired me to write one, but I realize now that I can't write the book he wants me to write. Frankly, all I've done is research the parts of his life he's expressly ordered me to steer clear of."

"Why?" Her face was spare and hard and scary-wonderful, like Georgia O'Keeffe's or Martha Graham's. There was nothing to do in the face of such a face but tell the unvarnished truth.

"We've been more or less estranged since I was eighteen, and, even before that, we were never close. Nothing even close to close. I want to understand what made him the man he is."

"For your own benefit?" Her eyes were fiery. "Or his?"

"Mine."

She smiled. "All right, then."

She fed us espresso in tiny black cups and lemon ricotta cookies on square black plates. And when she had drained her cup, she began to talk. She was a mesmerizing speaker, her facial features full of fine-tuned eloquence, her right hand moving like a dancer at the end of her wrist, the rest of her still and taut.

"My father was an accountant who wished he were a mathematician. He loved numbers; they were the only thing for which he had any affection, as far as I could detect. He wasn't a kind man. Now, I see that his bitter disappointment in himself and his life warped him. He was smart enough, but not brilliant, and he hated that. When I was a child, though, I just thought he was plain mean. Because he was mean, especially to Wilson."

Barbara shook her head and shrugged, with such languid grace that it looked like a piece of choreography. "Some fathers like that would have seen their second chance in a child like Wilson. They would have basked in reflected genius and trumpeted the boy's every achievement to the world. I know this isn't a good way to parent, but it would have been better than what my father did to Wilson."

"He undermined him?" I asked.

"At every turn. He mocked his achievements, reveled in his failures, although there weren't many of those. And I'm talking about from as far back as I can remember."

"That's rotten," said Ben.

"Yes," said Barbara. "That's just the word for what it was."

"What about your mother?" I asked.

"My mother was the sort who kept her mouth shut. I think she was cowed by my father. I certainly was. A lot of people were."

"Wilson, too?" I asked, trying to imagine Wilson being cowed by anything.

"No, I don't think so. Although it was impossible to say what was going on inside Wilson's head. Maybe he was hurt; maybe he secretly wanted my father's approval. The older I get, the more I see this as likely. On the outside, though, he seemed to despise my parents, roundly."

"Always?" I asked.

"Possibly," said Barbara drily. "I'm four years younger and only caught on to it when I was six or thereabouts, but even then Wilson had the air of someone who was capable of despising precociously."

At this, Ben's lips twitched into a wry smile.

"Ah," said Barbara to Ben. "I take it you know him."

"Knew," said Ben. "I'm pretty sure he despised me, too."

Barbara shrugged. "What can you do? What can anyone do with a person like that?"

"What did you do?" I asked.

"I adored him," said Barbara.

"Oh," I said, startled. "So did I."

She gave me a sharp look. "I got over it, with effort. How about you?"

"I'm working on it," I said. "Getting close, I think."

"Excellent," she said. "Possibly it was just a way of protecting himself against my father, but Wilson's problem seemed to be that he was so smart that he thought smart was everything, which is terribly wrong, of course."

"Did he have friends?" I asked.

"He didn't do well with other kids, although no one bullied him. We didn't talk much about bullying back then, not like people do now, even though it happened all the time. But Wilson was too big for his age, maybe, and too un-invested for the bullies to truly take an interest. It's hard to hurt someone who doesn't give a damn about you. At the time, I couldn't tell for sure, but, when I look back, I see that he was lonely, lonely without realizing it, which might be the worst kind of loneliness of all."

"He had you, though," I said.

"He did, such as it was. A long time ago, when my first grandchild was a toddler, I began to hear my son and his wife use this term 'parallel play,' and I realized that's what Wilson and I did, even though he didn't play in the traditional sense. He read or wrote in his notebook or performed scientific experiments, while, nearby, I colored or played with jacks or Tinkertoys or dolls. Later, I mostly drew. I loved to draw. He would let me be near, but he never asked to see my pictures. He only looked at them when I showed them to him. And then—"

She broke off and her fingers curled into a soft near fist, as if she were holding something tiny and breakable.

"What?" I asked.

"He changed, got colder, angrier, even more distant. I believe he hated us. He was gone or in his room almost all the time. It was the summer before he started eighth grade."

"Why?" I asked. "What happened?"

Sorrow filled her face, and she seemed about to explain, but she just popped open her fingers in a single-handed, shoulderless shrug.

"He went through a rough patch I suppose you could say. In any case, that year, he applied to boarding school. Did it all himself, researched schools, picked one, filled out all the paperwork, interviewed with a local alumnus, applied for financial assistance, got my parents to agree to it all, packed his things. He even wanted to take the train, but, for some reason, my parents insisted on driving him. I went along. We didn't stay for more than an hour, didn't attend the parent reception or go on the tour. It was clear that Wilson couldn't wait for us to leave. I sobbed all the way home in the car."

"You were, what? Ten? That must have been awful."

She smiled. "Tragic. I would never have admitted it to myself, but I think I knew he was gone for good."

Carefully, I said, "I visited the school and looked up his records. I saw that he changed his name before eleventh grade. And stopped listing a home address."

"Oh, yes. That's when he emancipated himself. At an honor student function, he met a member of the school's board of directors, a man named Cleary. He was rich. He didn't adopt Wilson, was more a benefactor, like something out of Dickens. I guess Wilson changed his last name in order to honor him because he was never actually a member of the man's family. I don't even know how much time they spent together. But apparently, as difficult as he was, Wilson could charm people when he needed to."

"He still does," I said.

"I don't doubt it," said Barbara. "The school gave him a stipend on top of his full scholarship and enrolled him in work-study. It had to have taken some finagling, as well as some string-pulling on the part of Cleary, who was a very fancy attorney, but, at sixteen, Wilson was able to demonstrate enough financial independence to get legally free of my parents. And that was it."

"It?" said Ben. "You mean, he never came home after that?"

"Never. Not one time."

"Really? Your parents agreed to that, even your mother? She didn't fight him on it? She didn't try to get him back?" he asked.

There was my Ben, full of the bewilderment of one who's been adored by at least two, sometimes three, sometimes *four* parents his entire life. But I got it. Or, if I didn't quite get it, I wasn't stunned. I knew how easily some people could let go of their children.

"You know, I think my mother admired him for it, at first," said Barbara, "took it as a sign of his independence. I'm sure my father was jealous because he was jealous of everything Wilson did, but he was also probably glad to be rid of him. However, no one can ever quite know what's going on inside other people's hearts, especially when they're closed-off people like my parents were, and I never talked to them about it, not directly. But, no, they didn't fight for him. When my father died, it was the first time I ever saw my mother cry about Wilson, and it was mostly out of anger. She wondered what kind of person would fail to show up at his father's funeral. He didn't so much as send a note."

"What about you?" I asked. "Did you fight for him?"

"I wrote him letters, sent him drawings I'd made, and when I was older, over the years, I tried to get in touch with him now and then. Never in person—I'd grown too proud for that—but I wrote him at the university, called him a few times. The one time I persuaded him to speak with me—I was twenty-one, about to get married, and I suppose I felt a surge of family feeling or something—he told me to let the past go. So I did. He erased me, and I erased him back."

"Why do you think he did it?" I asked.

Her eyes flashed scorn, and for a moment, I could see a trace of Wilson.

"Well, that much seems obvious. We didn't fit into his story," she said.

"Yes, but why not make you a footnote, a two-sentence paragraph?" I said. "I've thought about this, and I still cannot figure out why he had to erase you. He told my mother that your parents had died in a car accident when he was at boarding school. He never even mentioned a sister. Why?"

Her dancing hand dropped to her lap and she sat, thinking. Then, slowly, she said, "The boy he had been, up until he was twelve and grew hateful, would not have gone so far, I don't think. He would have left and stayed away. He might never have spoken to my father again, but he would not have cut us off like a diseased limb."

"Did someone—hurt him?" I asked.

Barbara said, gravely, "Abuse, you mean. Physical or sexual. No. Nothing like that. But he was damaged all the same."

Again, I knew that she was holding something back. I waited, but she didn't say anything more. Presumably, she had been harboring this piece of Wilson's story, which was also her story, for decades. Who was I to try to wrench it from her now?

"Still," she said, hotly, "people have wretched things happen in childhood and they grow up. They grow past them. Nothing can justify the way Wilson, the adult Wilson, behaved toward a sister who did nothing, God help her, but love him."

She glanced at her wristwatch, a plain, heavy face on a wide black strap.

"I fear I must leave in a few minutes to meet my husband for dinner. He's just getting out of a meeting, now."

"Your husband?" I said. For some reason, despite the fact of her three children, the thought of her being married startled me.

She smiled, luminously, and it was as though every edge she had softened. Whatever had warped Wilson into a failure at loving his fellow man hadn't warped Barbara. "My sweet George," she said. "Forty-five years."

Then, she looked straight at me and said, teasingly, wrinkling her sculptural nose, "I triumphed, you see. One can be dumped by the great and terrible Wilson and still live a happy life."

"That's my plan, too," I said. I glanced at Ben, who gave me an encouraging grin and a thumbs-up.

Just before we left, I asked to go to the bathroom, mostly so that I could see more of Barbara's marvelous house. Luckily, the powder room was at the back of the house, which meant that, on my way to it, I got to walk through a study, and the dining room, and the butler's pantry, and the kitchen. The place was perfection, every inch. It was on my way back through the dining room that I noticed: first, the wall hanging—wild and delicately spiny, like a cluster of sea urchins made of glass—and second, the chandelier over the table—hundreds of minute iridescent blue and silver glass droplets pouring like rain from a circle of steel. As I was staring up at it, the lights in its center came on, making me gasp. Barbara stood there, by the switch.

"Yes," she said. "It's one of hers."

I nodded toward the piece on the wall. "That one, too."

She nodded.

Barbara lifted her hands. "I guess I am not as good at erasing people as I would have had you believe."

"You've been keeping up with him," I said.

She flicked her hand, impatiently. "I have no interest in his career, his accomplishments." She gave me a tender look. "I've been keeping up with you. His family. I just—I thought someone should, someone from Wilson's side."

"My writing. You said you looked me up. Did you mean yesterday?"

"Yesterday and a long time ago, too. I've looked you up over and over. Does that make you feel infringed upon? That I was out there all along, keeping up with you as best I could?"

"No," I said. "How could it? It makes me feel watched over."

She leaned against the wall and briefly touched her finger to the nosepiece of her glasses. I swear I saw tears in her eyes.

"I've wanted to know his family. I couldn't help it. But I never thought I would."

The clean blue rain-light from Caro's chandelier fell over the room, over the table, walls, floor, over me and Barbara, my aunt.

"There are more of us," I told her. "I'm just the beginning."

AFTERWARD, I INVITED BEN for coffee in the pool house, mostly because I wanted to drink coffee with Ben in the pool house, but partly because I wanted to show myself, Ben, Wilson, the whole world, that I could. Because he'd driven us to visit Barbara, we were in his car, and the fact of Ben's car in Wilson's driveway gave me a small, petty thrill of satisfaction. We were halfway across the dark yard, leaves and stalks crunching under our boot soles, stars glittering, when I said, "She doesn't look like him at all, does she?"

"No," said Ben. "But she looks like you."

"She does? I always thought I looked like my mom."

"Your face does, but you have Barbara's hands, and her neck, and the way her head, you know, moves around on her neck."

I stopped in my tracks and spun to face him. Since he'd only been walking a foot or so behind me, he almost crashed into me. Ben was right there, so close. I could see his breath, the thimble-shaped shadow above his upper lip. To steady myself, I tried to remember what that was called, that indentation. I stood thinking for so long that Ben said, "Hey, Taisy, you okay?"

"Her *hands* look like mine?" I said. "See, you're just flattering me now. Shamelessly."

"Come on, you're saying you don't see it?"

I pulled off my gloves, stuffed them into my pockets, and held my hands out in front of me. They were long and pale in the dark, ghost hands.

"Her hands are like ballerinas," I said.

"Like yours."

"No, I don't mean they are like the hands of a ballerina. I mean they are like ballerinas themselves."

"I know."

"So delicate and supple. And they dance. Pirouettes. Arabesques."

"Like yours," Ben said again.

I stared wonderingly down at them. "Really? You mean it? If that's true, how have I never noticed?"

"Because they're yours." He shrugged. "I noticed."

We stood there, so close to each other, with the stars hanging right over our heads, looking down at my two hands like they were rare, precious objects, the kind of things Caro might make out of glass, and that's when I knew, all at once, without a trace of doubt, that Ben loved me. Ben loved me in exactly the same no-holds-barred, body-and-soul, cliff-diving way I loved him. It was a pure and simple certainty.

"Philtrum," I said, looking up at him.

"What?"

Briefly, I touched the dent between his nose and upper lip. "I see your philtrum in my dreams. Along with your zygomatic bone. Not to mention your zygomatic arch."

"You're the first person who ever *has* mentioned my zygomatic arch." His voice was light, but I'd felt him shiver at my touch. I put my hands in my pockets. After I'd said what I needed to say, there would be no end of touching, but for now, I wanted the moment to be as direct and pared down as possible.

"Listen to me," I said. "Willow was right when she said that I didn't love you enough, back when we were eighteen. But I would love you enough, now. I swear I would."

Ben's face was completely still.

"No," I said, shaking my head. "I wouldn't just love you enough. I'd be relentless. I'd be so over the top, like those storms that pummel the coast with a hundred-fifty-mile-an-hour winds and three feet of rain."

Ben smiled but only with the corners of his eyes. "You'd be a love hurricane is what you're saying?"

"Yes, and even if you don't let me, I'll love you like that anyway because I just can't help it, and a hurricane without a coast, flailing around out there by itself, well, it's just sad."

Ben didn't take me in his arms or laugh for joy. Instead, he looked at me, not adoringly or angrily, but like he was trying to figure me out. Even in the darkness I recognized it: it was his physics face.

"You would really want to do that again?" he asked, finally. "Be Ben and Taisy? After all this time?"

"I never stopped," I said. "Even when there was no Ben, I was Ben and Taisy."

For a long time, Ben was silent. Then, he said, "But I did stop."

"What?" I shook my head in disbelief.

"I told you," he said. "I boxed it all up and left it behind."

"No. You might have told yourself that, but it's not left behind. It's right here." I took hold of his coat sleeves and tugged. "Right here. Ben and Taisy. Don't tell me you don't feel the same way."

He pulled away from my grasp and took a step back.

"That whole first year, every time I got a letter from you, I put it in a box, unopened, and when I went to college, I left that box in my dad's basement."

"You never read my letters?" I felt sick.

"And then when I went to college, I made my roommate get the mail and throw away anything you sent before he even got back to the room."

"God. You were that cruel?"

"Cruel?" Ben bit out the word. "Do you have any idea what it cost me? To not read those letters?"

"How could you not read them? You were ruthless."

His eyes went big and angry. "I was *broken*," he almost shouted. "I never believed in anyone the way I believed in you. And you threw me away."

"But I didn't! I always loved you. I was broken, too. If you'd read my letters, you would have known that."

"You left. That's what matters. You signed a paper saying that our marriage was a *joke,* and you left. It doesn't matter if you loved me while you did it. Maybe it even makes it worse."

I didn't think this was right, but I wasn't sure. What I knew is that he loved me, now.

"You love me," I said.

"Don't."

"However you felt about me before now, you love me. Right this second."

His jaw tightened in a way that I knew meant he was furious. He said, "Remember when you said that I hadn't exactly called you, ever, in seventeen years?"

"Yes."

"I never would have. If you hadn't shown up, I would have lived the rest of my life without ever seeing you again. That's what I wanted."

"Now you're just being mean."

"It's true. And I should have shut this down the day I saw you sitting on the bench in the nursery with my dad."

I stood, reeling. But eventually, I gathered my wits about me. I thought about what Ben had said.

"But you didn't," I told him. He turned his face away.

"But you didn't," I repeated. "Why not? Did you ever ask yourself that?"

"Stop."

"If you'd really put it all away, why did you care so much about never seeing me again?"

"Stop."

"Tell me you don't love me."

Ben glared at me.

"I did awful things," I said. "I was a coward who did not deserve you. But I deserve you now. And you're the one who's a coward."

"I'm leaving."

I don't know what would have happened next; maybe he would have left; maybe we would have stood there fighting for hours and then he would have left, but what did happen was a voice, high and scared, flying in from the direction of the house: "Taisy! Taisy! Taisy!"

"Oh, no," I whispered. "She never calls me that."

I took off hard across the yard, with Ben right behind me.

Willow was standing there in sweatpants and a T-shirt, no coat, hair like a wildfire around her frightened face.

"Honey, what is it?"

"I promise I was paying attention," she cried. "It wasn't even late! I was doing homework in my room. I never lock the doors this early."

I put my arms around her.

"Shh," I said. "Nothing is your fault. What happened?"

"She was reading on the sofa, but she must have fallen asleep. She would have told me if she had to go someplace. She wouldn't have just left!"

"She left?"

"Her car's gone. Please don't call 911. Please. I don't know what they'll do. She can only have been gone a few minutes! Just find her!"

"Willow, listen to me," I said. "You stay here in case she comes back. I'll go with Ben in my car."

I turned. He was already nodding and walking backward, in the direction of the driveway.

"Ben?" said Willow. She saw him, then, and said, "I'm sorry."

"Don't be silly," I said. "Stay here!"

Once we were in the car, I filled Ben in, as much as I could, about Caro's sleepwalking.

"She's asleep, but she can operate a car," he said. "That's amazing. Scary, but amazing."

"I've been reading up on parasomnia," I said. "It's rare but not that rare. Most people grow out of it, I think. Anyway, it's fascinating how the brain works. Parasomniacs have been known to cook, drive, even have conversations, all while they're asleep."

"You know, I'd forgotten this until now, but I had a housemate in college whose younger brother was a sleepeater. Apparently, once he ate a whole package of bacon, uncooked. He visited a couple of times, and when he was awake, he was a really normal guy, not especially deep or troubled or anything."

"A whole package," I said, with a shudder. "Yeesh."

We talked like we hadn't practically been screaming at each other just a few minutes before. But our fight was still there, hovering, and I'm not sure how long we could have gone on ignoring it, but it didn't take long to find Caro. Her car was about a mile down the road, pulled over on the shoulder with the engine off.

"Wow," said Ben, as we pulled up behind her. "She even turned on the hazard lights."

Ben waited in my car, ready to drive it back to Wilson's if everything was all right. When I got to Caro's car, I could see her sitting with her hands resting lightly on the steering wheel. She looked up when I opened the passenger door but not at me. I had read that it was better to wake sleepwalkers with a loud noise instead of shaking them, so I said her name loudly. Nothing happened until the fifth time. She jumped in her seat, and then I watched her eyes uncloud, recognition dawning.

"Taisy," she said, confused.

"Hey there, Caro. Everything is all right."

She rubbed her temples, straightened, and looked around her.

"Oh, no." Her big eyes filled with tears.

"It's okay. You're half a mile from home. How about we head back there now?"

"No one got hurt?" she asked.

"No one at all. Everyone is fine. Look at you, you're even wearing your seat belt."

"So I am."

"Come on, let's go home, shall we? Willow will be so happy to see you."

Caro winced as though she'd been stung, and I instantly regretted bringing up Willow.

"My poor girl," said Caro.

"Listen," I said. "Why don't we switch places, and I'll drive us home?"

I got out, walked around to her door, and opened it. Slowly, she got out, and when she was standing, she looked so lost and frail and shivering that I hugged her, and, with unexpected strength, she hugged back. Over her shoulder, I waved to Ben, and he nodded and drove away.

Before I started the car, she said, "Wait. Can I ask you something?"

"Sure."

Her face wasn't frightened anymore, just dreadfully tired. "Taisy, would you ever consider staying?"

I stared at her. "You mean permanently?"

"I don't mean in our house," she said, quickly. "Just—nearby." She sighed. "I know you have a life. And I know I have no right, that I am the last person who has the right to ask you for anything."

"I wouldn't say that, not anymore." I smiled, ruefully. "But Marcus would."

"And he would be right. I just thought that maybe it hadn't occurred to you, the idea of staying here, and that if—and only if, God, of course!—you thought it might make you happy, we would be so glad."

"Why?" I asked.

Caro gave me a gentle, baffled look, as though my question were slightly crazy.

"Because you make all of us better, of course. Especially Willow. And the longer you are here, the more I can't imagine you ever leaving, and not because you rescue me from my ridiculous nocturnal ramblings, either."

"No?"

She smiled. "Well, that's nice, of course. But mostly it's because you are what's been missing. You wake us all up, you expand our world, especially Willow's. And I know that those are selfish reasons."

I suppose they were selfish, and, honestly, I felt guilty about not feeling more resentful. Or resentful at all. Marcus would hate that, but, for better or worse, I wasn't Marcus. It wasn't just that I liked being needed; it's that I liked being needed by Caro and Willow. I was even beginning to suspect that I needed them, too.

I said, "I'm not sure that Willow needs me, but she does need more people in her life. She needs a bigger world."

"She needs you *and* more people."

I didn't say anything for a long time.

"I can't promise to stay," I said. "And I want you to know that if I did, it would not be for Wilson. To be blunt, I'm finished with trying to make him love me. I don't need that anymore. I don't think I even want it, especially."

This last statement was a bit of a stretch, but the rest felt true. I waited for her to fly to his defense, or to reassure me that, deep down, my father cared deeply about me, but she just gave me a tired smile and said, "Good." I absorbed this and found it didn't hurt much.

"You should also know," I went on, "that if I became part of Willow's family, it wouldn't stop with me."

"What do you mean?" asked Caro.

Our eyes met and held.

"I mean—what if we were to crack this thing wide open?" I said. "Invite everyone in."

Radiance broke through her exhaustion. "Oh, Taisy, that is exactly what I was hoping we would do."

When we got back to the house, my car was parked in the circle. Ben's was gone.

CHAPTER EIGHTEEN

Willow

EVER SINCE THAT FIRST trip to Mr. Insley's house, I had been checking in with myself several times a day, monitoring how much I loved him, like a nurse checking the vital signs of a patient, and what I found was that the patient was still alive but fading a little more each day, presenting with an increasingly thready pulse, labored breathing, and—oh, this simile is just too morbid! Here it was: I loved him the way you love someone you've once loved desperately, and to whom you will be forever grateful for saving you from death by loneliness and for making you feel pretty and smart when you most needed it, and who has a sad, dark house, a dissertation that will never be finished, and a boat that will never see the water. In short, I did not want to sail away with him (a good thing, considering the boat), and I did not want to kiss him anymore ever, but I did want him to be happy, three things I realized I needed to tell him before our relationship went any further. Scratch that. Three things I needed to tell him in order to stop our relationship dead in its tracks. For good. It would be nice to stay on congenial terms with him, too, of course, and even nicer to get the A in English that I rightfully deserved.

I had already tried twice that week. On Monday, I'd stayed after class to ask if we could talk at lunch, and mischievously, he'd said, "No, our next conversation will be at my house over dinner or not at all!," and when I went to his room at lunchtime, sure enough, he wasn't there. On Tuesday, he handed back a paper to me with "A word, after class" written at the top, a form of communication he had used before, so I'd stayed, and, as soon as everyone was gone, Luka shooting me a quick backward glance as he walked out, Mr. Insley said, sorrowfully, "Willow, I fear our lunches must come to an end, at least for a while," words that, not long before, would have slammed down on me like a heel and ground my soul to dust. Now, I felt a rush of light-headed relief that I tried my darnedest to hide.

"Why?" I asked, gravely.

From the inside pocket of his jacket, he slid a folded piece of notebook paper stained with what looked like yellow paint, unfolded it, slowly, and held it open for me to see. I AM WATCHING YOU, it said, in thick black lettering.

"At lunch yesterday, as I was eating in the teachers' lounge, I found it inside my sandwich. I bit into it, actually."

Mustard. I was struck by the desire to laugh, but then worry quenched it.

"Did anyone see it?" I asked.

"No," he said, with a touch of coldness, as though my question were insulting.

"I'm sorry," I said, reflexively. "Of course not."

"But I'm afraid this might mean that our anonymous prude is not a student after all. Or that we have more than one prude on our trail."

"What? Why?"

"My lunch languishes, poor thing, all day in the teachers' lounge refrigerator, an old, only semi-clean appliance to which the student body has no access."

"Oh," I said, somewhat blankly. Oddly, even though I had seen the other messages and been disturbed by the language of them, I had somehow never fully absorbed that they were the handiwork of a true-blue, individual person, which was stupid of me. Maybe out of sheer denial or because the world of high school was so new and big and baffling to me, I'd instead attributed the messages to a vast, faceless culture of adolescent meanness. Now, it hit me that whoever had sent the notes was real and had possibly not merely seen me with Mr. Insley and thrown out blind, if unsavory, innuendos, but had maybe truly been watching us. And the idea of that person's being an adult chilled me to the bone.

"Who?" I asked, even though I mostly did not want to know. "Who would do that?"

Mr. Insley shrugged. "As I think I've indicated, just as you feel yourself to be an entirely different species from your peers, so am I not cut from the same dull cloth—intellectually and in myriad other ways—as many of my so-called colleagues. They are small and narrow people, and, frankly, they resent me. So it could have been any of them, but if I had to guess, I would say the insufferable Ms. Janine Shay."

Ms. Shay? Even though I could imagine that she disapproved of Mr. Insley and could even imagine that she'd been keeping an eye on the two of us, I simply could not picture her balancing on a chair to write those colossal black letters on the whiteboard or stuffing a note into a sandwich.

Mr. Insley regarded me with mournful blue eyes. "Alas, my Willow, it feels more and more as though we are each other's only ballast in a provincial and narrow-minded sea. And, oh how I will miss our lunches!"

"But maybe we could have just one more?" I said, with a sinking heart and a glance at the clock. "I was hoping to talk about something with you. It's quite important, and there's no time now. I have to get to class."

"Can't be done," he said, wistfully. "Someone may be watching us even now."

Startled, I darted a glance at the doorway. Because it was almost time for the next class, the crowds in the hallway were thinning. People were flying noisily by, but no one was stopping. No face leered around the doorjamb.

He tapped me on the chin and gave me a playful grin, one eyebrow raised. "No, I'm afraid you have no choice but to come to my house for dinner. There's nothing else to be done!"

"But I don't see how I can," I said.

I noticed that the smile stayed on his mouth but disappeared from the rest of his face. "I'm sure you'll think of something."

That night, I thought about writing him a letter, but, somehow, I could not bear the possibility of its existing, lingering—a concrete fact—in the world after our relationship had ended.

So the next day, when Mr. Insley handed back my graded *The Portrait of a Lady* quiz (which, incidentally, I aced), and I saw written at the top: "Tomorrow at 6:00, Chez B.I.," I stared at the words for a long moment, and then, with a sigh of resignation, folded the paper in two. I nodded to Mr. Insley on the way out the door and threw the quiz into the first hallway trashcan I found.

Now, in my room, I tied my shoes, stood up, and surveyed myself in the mirror. Unlike the day of the drive in the country, I was in full teenager regalia: ponytail; skinny, dark jeans; a cropped, fitted striped sweater with a long tank top underneath; and—heaven help me— sneakers of a variety called Chuck Taylor that I'd purchased during a shopping trip with Muddy the evening before. I'd planned on the red version, but, at the eleventh hour, my heart failed me, and I bought dark blue, low tops, not high. Even so, I hardly recognized myself. The whole kit and kaboodle screamed, as it was meant to, *I am a callow sixteen-year-old, practically a babe in arms, and much too young for a thirty-year-old man in battered wingtips and raveled tweed.* I can't say I hated the way I looked, which took me off guard. As I left my room, there was even a new, youthful spring in my step; I damned near skipped.

My father was in his room, where he'd been spending more time lately, recovering from the attack of pericarditis, and as luck would have it, my mother was attending a meeting of the local Artists Guild, so I left without telling a soul where I was going, a first for me. Muddy's meeting included dinner and would take several hours, by which time I planned to be safely home and free as a sneaker-shod bird. I had expected to have a full-blown case of the butterflies, but I was cool as a cucumber as I zipped my cell phone into the pocket of my parka, slipped out the door, and ran lightly down my long driveway to the street, where the cab I'd called (another first!) was waiting.

I hit a weak moment when Mr. Insley opened his wretched front door. His smile was so guileless and hopeful, and he didn't throw himself upon me and wrestle me into an embrace, but merely leaned over and planted a comradely kiss on my cheek.

"Darling girl, how lovely you look!" he said.

I stepped inside. His house looked better this time, still dim, but less cluttered and with lighted candles set here and there. I could see firelight doing a golden dance on the living room walls, and the house smelled golden as well, like apples and cloves and cinnamon. Mr. Insley started to help me off with my coat, but I remembered the cell phone in my pocket and suddenly felt that I did not want it too far out of my reach. I gave an ostentatious shiver.

"I'll keep it on for a while, if you don't mind. I'm one of those people who takes a ridiculously long time to warm up."

He smiled. "It comes from being so slender," he said. "We will do our best to fatten you up tonight, but first, let me give you some mulled cider. Nothing warms in quite the same way."

"That must be what smells good," I said.

"Smells and is," he said, ladling some into a cut glass mug. For a single man with a moth-eaten carpet runner, Mr. Insley had some very nice crockery.

"What a pretty glass," I remarked.

"It was my grandmother's," he said. I wondered if he meant the grandmother who owned the lake house in New Jersey, but the possibility of her being dead and passing down her glassware made me so

sad that I couldn't even ask. How Mr. Insley had cherished his summers at that house! I understood right then that this was going to be
harder than I thought. Sitting in your room, planning how you would
break it off—cleanly, surgically—with a person was a very different
thing from his standing before you, with his carefully ironed shirt, his
childhood stories, the special drink he'd made, his pretty glass mugs
from his possibly dead and beloved grandmother. It could break your
heart: people becoming, in the blink of an eye, so dreadfully human.

Which is maybe why, when Mr. Insley came up behind me and
tugged my hair band off, releasing my ponytail, I only laughed, and
maybe also why we got through all of dinner without my having
broached the subject of the breakup. We ate at a wooden table set up at
one end of the living room, which was warm from the fire, too warm,
really. I took off my parka and slipped it onto the back of my chair.

Mr. Insley brought the soup first. It was delicious, butternut with
mushrooms, and it took a moment for me to realize that it was the same
soup my mother always got from the gourmet grocery. As it would turn
out, I would recognize all the dishes as having come from the same
store, while Mr. Insley rambled on about how he'd made them himself,
even to the hand-ground spices. Perhaps because I was already softened up by the grandmother mugs, I wasn't put off by these lies. I was
touched.

It wasn't until I took the first sip of my cider, which had been too hot
for me to drink when he'd handed it to me (I loathe drinks that scald
my mouth), that I felt the first tremor of alarm because even though
the cider had cooled to lukewarm, it burned going down my throat. At
home, I had been allowed to have wine at fancy dinners (little more
than a splash, barely one swallow's worth) since I was eleven, so I recognized the burn. Not wine, but definitely alcohol. My English teacher,
serving me liquor. For a mad instant, I considered propping my foot
on the table to show him my sneaker, but instead, I set the glass down
several inches from my plate and avoided it like the plague.

During dinner, Mr. Insley talked about Rossetti again, about the women who had modeled for his paintings, like Alexa Wilding and Elizabeth Siddal, ethereal beauties who had inspired him and some of the other painters of his set, as well. He got so excited about the topic that midway through his arugula salad, he set down his fork.

"Wouldn't you like to see them?" he asked, his eyes like blue flames. "Won't you come look?"

"The muses, you mean?"

"Yes!"

I didn't even know what he meant, but his bubble was so big and shimmery that I couldn't stand to burst it. I should have said no. I really should have.

"Um, okay," I said.

Before I knew it, he had me by the hand, tugging me with childlike excitement, up the stairs, where I most assuredly did not want to go. Upstairs meant bedrooms; bedrooms meant beds, one of which he had imagined me in, me and my milky shoulders. It had been part of my plan to not, under any circumstances go upstairs, but short of tearing my hand from his and running away, I could do nothing but grimly go.

The room he led me into, though, harbored no beds whatsoever, and I nearly melted with relief. It was his office. One wall was lined with shelves, which were, in turn, lined with books, and in the center of the room was a dark wood table, more a kitchen table than a desk, piled with books, notebooks, a silvery laptop that looked new, a big printer that looked old. He flipped the wall switch, and light flooded the room. My eyes went straight to the books, but Mr. Insley turned me around to behold a wall plastered with pictures, some of them prints, like you'd get at an art museum, some of them looking suspiciously like pages of books. I recognized a few of them in a vague way and understood that they must be Pre-Raphaelite paintings, although I hadn't known to call them that before now. I stood there, letting it all sink in: picture upon picture of pale-faced, big-eyed women with clouds of coppery hair. Unthinkingly, I reached up and took hold of a hank of my own.

Mr. Insley was pointing to different pictures, excitedly naming the artist, the painting, the muse, but I was hardly listening because I'd caught sight of one low on the wall that made my heart stop: a woman floating on a pond, surrounded by flowers, a tumult of green on every side, her hands open, her face to the sky. My very own dream. I wasn't stupid enough to think I'd had a premonition of this moment, but somehow all Mr. Insley's talk of the Pre-Raphaelites way back when must have jarred the painting loose inside my mind—a full-color memory I hadn't even known I possessed—and set it adrift in my dreams. I handed over a few marveling seconds to the mysteries of the subconscious, before I drew closer to the picture and crouched before it.

"Ah," said Mr. Insley. "That one's Lizzie Siddal. Isn't she ravishing?"

Ravishing?

"She looks—dead," I said.

Mr. Insley chuckled. "Well, it is a depiction of Ophelia, although I reckon she's supposed to be alive in it. She wasn't actually dead until her skirts dragged her under, 'down to muddy death.' Remember?"

"Still, look how she's staring so blankly. Look at her mouth. She looks dead."

"You have a point," he said, leaning closer to the picture. "And no wonder, since Lizzie nearly died herself while it was being painted."

"Really?"

"Well, she got quite sick, anyway. Millais painted the setting on the banks of the Hogs Mill River in Surrey, but when it came time to render the figure, he had Lizzie lie for hours, completely dressed, in a bathtub full of water. Since it was winter, he used lamps to heat the water, and, at one point, he was so intent on his work that he let the lamps go out. She got chilled and consequently, fell ill."

Even though I was almost positive that getting chilled did not make people sick, viruses and bacteria did, I didn't mention this, since it was beside the point. The point was that the painter believed the cold would make her sick and at the very least knew it would make her wretchedly uncomfortable, and still he didn't take more care about the lamps. As if in commiseration with Lizzie, a chill ran over my scalp.

"That's abominable," I said, vehemently.

"Willow," said Mr. Insley, with dismay. "Do you think so?"

"Yes. Horrible."

"But I always found it wonderful, to be so caught up with your artistic process, so thoroughly in the grip of your muse that you forget everything else. And Lizzie, to lie in the cold water, maybe for hours, to sacrifice herself that way . . . You don't find it wonderful?"

Slowly, like a snake uncoiling, I rose and turned to face him.

"I don't want to do this anymore," I said.

His eyes snapped open wide. "No? Well, by all means let's go back down and finish dinner."

I shook my head. "I don't love you, Mr. Insley," I said, flatly. "It's what I came to say."

The muscles in his cheeks slackened with shock.

"But you're mine. I'm yours."

"No," I said. "I'm sixteen. I wasn't made for you." It was an odd thing to say, but it seemed to me to be perfectly accurate.

His jaw tightened; the skin on his face also tightened, which made him look older, bonier, spinsterish. A few minutes ago, I might have felt pained for him, trying to be so manly and looking like this, but I had moved to a cool, firm place beyond compassion.

"Willow, what have I done to deserve this?"

"It's not what you've done. It's who you are."

He made a disgusted face. "Who I am? Dear God, don't tell me you're saying what we have together isn't *right*? Have they crawled inside your head?"

"No one has crawled inside my head. *I* am saying that we're not right. I don't exactly mean morally, although, who can tell? Maybe that's part of it. But there's just a basic wrongness about us. We don't fit."

"Into the provincial world, you mean? Oh, Willow, I am so disappointed in you."

These words had always comprised the worst thing anyone could say to me. On the rare occasions my father had done so, they had cut me to my marrowbones. Now, from Mr. Insley, the words were a tiny pinch, an annoyance like a mosquito bite or a burr in my sock.

"We don't fit—together or into the world," I said.

"No? Let me show you something," he said, reaching his hand toward me.

I didn't take it, but when he dropped it and walked to the window at the far end of the room, I followed. He switched off the overhead light and pointed down at the backyard.

"Go on," he said, "look." He stepped back so that I could.

It was dark but cloudless, a crystalline evening, and there was enough moonlight and streetlight for me to see it: dead grass—grass killed—in the shape of a number. 16.

"Oh!" I said, with a gasp.

"You're right that we don't fit into the world," Mr. Insley murmured from inches, centimeters behind me, his face nearly nestled in my hair. "*That* is the world, a sad, black-souled, benighted, jealous person dragging weed killer into my yard in order to threaten what he doesn't understand. That will always be the world."

He lifted my hair and dropped a dry, feathery kiss onto the place where my neck met my shoulder.

"I'll do my damnedest to protect you from that world, I swear it. And together, we'll turn away from it and make our own."

As soon as he said that, a possibility came charging out of the darkness to hit me, head-on. I stiffened.

"Did you say protect me?" I asked.

He kissed me again, this time higher up on my neck.

"Yes," he whispered. "Cling to me, darling, delicate, moonlit girl. I'll gather you in. I'll keep you safe."

My mind wanted to race, but I forced it to slow down, to be methodical; it was important. *The whiteboard message; the one in my notebook to which he had supposedly gotten a twin I never saw; the message in his sandwich.*

Cling to me.

Every time, after every anonymous message, I had done exactly that. Even that last time, when I was staunchly resolved to run away from him forever, I ran toward instead. And here I was. I'd been duped, played.

The word came out of me like a breath, "You."

"Yes," he said, hoarsely. "I."

I shut my eyes, briefly, then turned around and forced a smile. "You know, I think it's time—"

For me to go home, to get away, to get as far away from you as I can. But suddenly, I was scared, scared that he might not let me leave, that if I ran, he might chase me. I could not bear to be chased, grabbed.

"I think it's time we went down and finished dinner," I said, through my smile. And then, because I saw his face fall, possibly because he was thinking of the bed in the room just down the hall (God, I hoped not!), I gritted my soul, if not my teeth, and added, "By the fire. It's so cozy down there."

Thank goodness, his expression turned fond, and he winked and said, "As you wish, my lady."

As we walked out into the hallway, my heart was racing so hard that I couldn't think. I needed to calm down, devise a plan, so I said, "But first, may I?," and gestured toward the hallway bathroom.

"But of course," he said, gallantly, with a small bow. "I'll be downstairs."

Once inside the cramped room, I sat on the edge of the tub, my head in my hands. I could hear things, Mr. Insley walking around, singing something, banging dishes, and because I had turned into a raw nerve, the slightest noises making me flinch, I reached over and switched on the overhead fan. It was one of the old sort that sounds like a helicopter about to take off, except louder, noisome white noise if I'd ever heard it, but once I'd gotten over being startled out of my skin, I found that the fan did the trick. I could hear nothing outside of that bathroom.

For the first minute or so, all I did was curse myself for leaving my parka, with the cell phone in it, on the back of my chair downstairs, since I could, right that instant, have been calling the cab company, the number of which I'd plugged into my phone, and hiring my getaway car. I tried to remember if there'd been a phone in Mr. Insley's office, but I didn't think so, and the only number I had off the top of my head was my home number, which even in these dire straits, I was loath to use. *Quit your useless whining,* I told myself, sternly, *and your childish panicking, and for God's sake, think!*

I thought and, after a long time, here is what I came up with, my not-so-grand plan: I would feign illness, stomach cramps, possible food poisoning, or—better still—appendicitis. *Left side,* I reminded myself, *left, left, left.* I considered insisting to Mr. Insley that I needed an ambulance—now, there was a getaway car for you!—but decided against it. What would I possibly say to Muddy when she had to come to the hospital to pick me up? So—not bad enough for 911 but bad enough so that he would have to take me home right away. *Put on a show,* I told myself. *After all, Willow, acting is something you can actually do. Remember the film you made with Luka!*

Luka. Luka. *Luka.*

Oh, gosh. Just holding his name, those two shining syllables, in my mind was enough to carve a hole in the ghastly moment. I could look out of the hole and see a place beyond, sunlit and green. *You will get through this,* the name told me. I closed my eyes and saw him. Luka, swimming. Luka, nudging me with his shoulder, as we walked down the hallway. Luka, telling me how I made people want to be better. Luka, eating lunch with me under our tree. If you're lucky, your moment of truth happens on a mountaintop or on the windswept moors or even in a well-appointed drawing room with someone playing the pianoforte in the background, but mine plodded up a dingy staircase and down a dim hallway to find me in this cramped, roaring, godforsaken bathroom, and thank heaven it did. I sat there, hunkered down on the edge of the bathtub, flabbergasted at how blind I had been. Distracted by Mr. Insley, I had missed the whole point of these past three months.

It was like reading a book and only noticing the punctuation. It was like trekking all the way to the North Pole only to fail to see the aurora borealis rippling the sky because you are too busy staring at a patch of dingy snow.

"Luka," I whispered, "I have been a fool. But I promise I will do better just as soon as I get myself out of this godforsaken house."

I practiced pained faces in the mirror. I gasped and pressed my palm to the lower left side of my abdomen. I doubled over. I knew that I was staying a ridiculously long time in the bathroom and wondered that Mr. Insley hadn't come up to knock on the door. But I told myself that the long stay would only bolster my claim of illness. I straightened, gave myself a thumbs-up in the mirror, then opened the door, and was instantly thrown back by the thick smell of smoke. Had something gone wrong with the fireplace?

And then: *whoosh, whoosh,* and a reverberating banging, as though someone were backstage at a play, making thunder sounds with a piece of sheet metal. What fresh hell was this? I glimpsed an orange glow coming from Mr. Insley's office and stumbled down the hall and through the room to the window that looked out on the backyard. Good God, the yard *was* fresh hell! I watched, frozen with a kind of eerie, detached fascination. Flames carpeted the grass around the boat shed, and the shed itself was a tunnel of fire, smoke pouring out of it. It swayed like a ship on a stormy sea, and then there was a terrific *boom,* and, before my eyes, the structure, makeshift and flimsy to begin with, pitched sideways and collapsed. Sparks fountained crazily, metal and burning pieces of debris flew across the grass toward the house. *The house!* The house I was standing in. In an instant, my fascination turned to horror, and I tore out of the room and down the stairs.

"Mr. Insley!" I half shouted, half sobbed. "Get out, get out of the house!" But he was nowhere to be seen.

I dashed into the living room, where the fireplace fire was smoldering lazily. Outside the back window, I could see the seething yard.

"Mr. Insley!" I screamed again. I snatched my parka from the back of the chair and was about to run out the front door, when the thought struck me that maybe he was in the backyard. I hadn't seen him from the window, but maybe he was trying to put out the fire and needed help. Maybe he was hurt out there. I ran through the kitchen, and with my heart pounding, stepped outside. Heat, stinging smoke, a rushing sound, and a profusion of orange light met me. I peered into the yard and didn't see Mr. Insley anywhere, but I called his name once, before I noticed that the deck on which I was standing had caught fire at one end. With tears running down my face, I ran back through the house and pitched myself wildly out the open front door.

The front yard was amazingly quiet and cold. A siren started up, its faraway whine spiraling in the crisp air, and I saw a few of Mr. Insley's neighbors start to come out of their houses. I stood for a moment on the edge of his yard, unsure of where to run, when I spotted him on the other side of the road, standing under a streetlamp. *He just ran, he didn't even come pound on the bathroom door or try to get me out,* I thought, fleetingly, and just as I thought it, he saw me. Our eyes met, and I waited for him to run over to me, but instead, he started mouthing *Go, go,* and making low, discreet shooing motions with his hands. *He doesn't want anyone to know I was here,* I thought, and because I wanted it probably even less than he did, I started running away as fast as I could run, which, as I believe I've mentioned, was fast.

I got well clear of his neighborhood and had gone maybe a half mile more when the fire trucks came rumbling and wailing toward me, and without thinking, I jumped off the shoulder of the road into the shallow ditch next to it and lay there, my eyes squeezed shut, my hands clamped over my ears, until they'd passed. Then, I was crying, hard gusting sobs each of which stuck in my chest before it hit the air. I couldn't have stopped if I tried, but I didn't try, just waited for the sobbing to be done with me. It took a long time, and afterward, I ached from head to toe.

I sat up, took out my phone, and called Taisy.

"Hello? Willow?"

I didn't even say hi, just, "Can you come get me? Please?"

"Of course, I can! But are you okay?"

"I don't know. Yes."

"Okay, sweetheart, just tell me where you are."

I looked frantically around me: trees and road, no signs. When I tried to recall even Mr. Insley's street name, my mind went blank, and I had thrown away the paper with his address on it as soon as I'd gotten to his house because I couldn't stand to have it on my person a second longer. I shut my eyes, trying to remember what it had said.

"Oh, God!" I cried. "I don't know!"

"That's all right. Listen to me. Are you listening?"

I nodded before I realized she couldn't see me. "Yes."

"Are you in a safe place?"

For the first time, I realized I wasn't. A ditch next to a dark street, cars whizzing by every couple of minutes. But I turned and looked into the slice of woods farther back from the road. The looming trees could have been scary, but maybe because I'd recently been terrified out of my wits, they weren't. They looked ordinary and calm. I stood up and walked into them and leaned against the biggest trunk.

"Willow?"

"Yes," I answered. "I'm safe here."

"Good. Now, just stay right where you are, and be sure to leave your phone on; I can use it to find you."

I had no idea what this meant, but I said, "Okay," and then, "But, Taisy?"

"Yes, honey?"

"Do you have to hang up? I know you'll be driving, but could you just stay on the line and maybe say something to me now and then?"

There was a pause. "I need to hang up for just a second to figure out where you are, but I'll call you back soon and then I'll stay on the line."

Which is just what she did. While she drove, she put the phone on speaker, a thing I hadn't even known was possible, and told me a funny story about her friend Trillium. I didn't really follow it, just held on to her voice until she reached me, which didn't take very long.

After she pulled over, got out, and hugged me, she held my face in her hands and gave me an anxious, searching look that made my eyes well up yet again, and then we got in the car, and before she started the engine, she said, "Just tell me whether you're hurt or not. You don't have to tell me anything else."

But I did. I started at the beginning and told her everything.

CHAPTER NINETEEN

Taisy

Because I figured that escaping an inferno and a complete creep in the same night would make anyone hungry, on the way home, I stopped at Café Verdi, the pizza place that had been a family (minus Wilson) favorite when I was growing up. At the sight of Willow's face as she surveyed the array of pies on the marble counter, I asked, "Have you had pizza before?"

"Yes," she said, quickly, never taking her eyes off that counter. "Three times. At both cross-country end-of-season dinners and once in Italy, but that one had potatoes on it and no sauce. The first two times, I only ate the plain cheese pieces, but I'm wondering, if maybe, tonight, well . . ." She swallowed hard.

"We'll take a large half sausage, half pepperoni," I told the man behind the counter. I turned to Willow. "Do you want some fries? They have really good fries."

She pressed her palms together. "Well, I'm not really allowed to eat them. With good reason of course."

Of course. It had driven me crazy as a kid, how Wilson would dig into a plate of bangers and mash or pork pie without a second thought but called "pure poison" all foods he considered middle-class American. The only thing he reviled more than french fries was tuna casserole. I watched inner conflict play across Willow's face.

"But I think I would like to try some," she said, at last.

Then, we took our food and had a slumber party in the pool house. When she wasn't inhaling fries, Willow talked, and even though I was roiling with disgust at the pretentious, manipulative, low-life bastard that was Mr. Insley, I tried to save the name-calling for later and simply listen. I knew that sooner or later we would have to face the tough question of whether she needed to tell the story to Caro and the even tougher one of whether she needed to tell the school about the creep teacher—and apparent statutory rapist wannabe—in its employ, but not that night. She told me about how the anonymous messages had served to drive her closer to Mr. Insley and about her theory that he had planted them himself, which did seem like something a guy like that would do.

"But do you really think he would set his own yard on fire?" I asked her.

"Well, I know that sounds outlandish, but he must have," she said. "If he did all the rest, and I think he did, he must have done that, too."

"I read a book once," I said, "where a guy set a fire so that he could save his girlfriend from it and be a hero. Except—"

"Yes, I know," she intoned, rolling her eyes. "Except that Mr. Insley ran out of there like a scared bunny rabbit. But I suppose it was just another piece of the plot to make me fear the big bad world and run to him for refuge. You know, I had just told him I wanted to end our relationship. Maybe he decided it was time to take extreme measures."

"Maybe so," I said, but I wasn't so sure, partly because I believed he was too much of a scared bunny rabbit to risk being caught at his house with an underaged girl, no matter how old a soul she seemed to be, and partly because I knew something Willow didn't know, something that made her theory that Mr. Insley had done it all a bit shaky.

She found so much relief in believing that no one else was involved that I almost didn't show her the note that had come for me in the mail, but I just couldn't keep it from her. She read it, then slowly raised her eyes and stared into space, thinking.

"I'm having trouble seeing how this fits," she admitted, finally.

"I am, too," I told her. "When I got it, I wondered a couple of things: why it had been sent to me and not your parents, and why the person didn't come right out and tell me what the trouble was."

Willow read aloud, "'It's not my place to tell you what's going on . . .' That's rather nice, isn't it? As though someone wants to help but doesn't want to get me in trouble. She or he wants to leave me the choice of telling or not."

"Which could be why the person sent it to me and not to your parents. I might seem like someone less likely to force you to tell or to go straight to the school."

She caught my eye and smiled, shyly. "Neither of which you did, to my everlasting gratitude."

I smiled back. "The note is why I bought you the cell phone, though. So it really did help."

Willow looked thoughtfully down at the note. "Whoever wrote it wanted there to be someone watching over me, maybe. You know, Mr. Insley tried to blame Ms. Shay, the school guidance counselor, for putting the note in his sandwich. I still think he did that himself—or just wrote a note and smeared it with yellow mustard—because I really can't imagine Ms. Shay doing such a thing. She's got these silly reading glasses, but she's really quite dignified. This letter seems more like a thing she would do. Perhaps she suspected something untoward was happening with Mr. Insley and me, but since she wasn't sure, she just sent the letter to you? If she had asked me directly, I would not have admitted it, and maybe she knew that. I haven't told her about you, though."

"You didn't have to tell anyone," I said, drily. "People just know.

This is a pretty small pond, and Wilson is a pretty big fish. Nearly every time I go out, I run into people who say they heard I was back in town. Sometimes, I'm not even sure who they are."

Willow knit her brows. "It just seems much more likely that one person did everything. But this letter . . ."

"Look, let's not worry about it now," I said.

"Maybe now that it's over, it doesn't even matter," said Willow, hopefully.

I couldn't imagine that the world would let us leave it at that, but I didn't say so. I said, "These fries are delicious."

"These fries are heaven and nirvana and the Holy Grail rolled into one," said Willow, with what sounded exactly like a giggle.

Later, after we'd watched an episode of *Foyle's War,* Willow remarked, "Now, there's a television show that my father might actually like," and then she blushed and dipped her head, and added, "Sorry."

"For what?" I asked.

"I feel strange talking to you about my father," she said, quietly. "Our father."

"Yes," I agreed. "He's in danger of becoming the elephant in the room, isn't he?"

She smiled. "He might like that actually. The elephant is an animal he admires."

I sat for a moment, thinking of—marveling at—how the story of my trip here had, at some point, stopped being just, or even mostly, the story of me and Wilson and started being a lot of other stories: of me and Caro, me and Ben, me and Willow.

"Look," I said, "Wilson is a different father to you than he was to me and Marcus, and frankly, I think it's high time I stopped resenting it and high time I set aside the question of why. So how about this: we, you and I, accept that fact and then forget about it. When he comes up in conversation, which he will, or when we are both with him, which will happen, I won't attack him and you won't defend him."

After a while, she nodded, and then said, "Okay, and what about also this: we forgive him."

My smart sister, with her big, earnest eyes.

"I think maybe that's what I was trying to say," I told her. "But what do you have to forgive him for?" I shook my head. "Sorry, you don't have to answer that."

"No, it's all right," she said, thoughtfully. "I'm beginning to see that he made some mistakes while raising me. Inside my head, until recently, I never let him be a person who could make mistakes, which just isn't fair, when you think about it. Anyway, I know he wanted to protect me, but he shouldn't have kept me away from people so much."

Her eyes were suddenly sad. "Especially you," she said. "He led me to believe that you weren't a good person, and he shouldn't have because you are."

"I'm glad you think so," I said.

She sighed and leaned back against the sofa cushions. "I love my parents, but I see that in their different ways, they don't really quite live in the world, not the world-world. And I want to."

"Good," I said. "I was worried that you might not, after all that's happened."

"With Mr. Insley, you mean." She turned to me, and said, "Do you want to know something? I really never want to see Mr. Insley again, but even tonight, I couldn't hate him because he just kept being a round character instead of a flat one. You know, like in literature? When people are round characters, your heart just keeps aching for them even when you don't want it to. Which can be confusing." She laughed. "But good, too, I think."

"I think so, too."

"Taisy?" said Willow, suddenly. "I hope you'll stay in—"

She broke off, with an odd look.

"In touch?" I asked.

She hesitated, and then said, her cheeks glowing pink, "I was going to say that, but while I was saying it, I realized that what I really meant was to leave the 'in touch' off. I know that's silly because you'll have to go home sometime."

This moment, I thought, *imprint it, keep it, keep it, keep it.* How had this girl turned out, after all, to be so easy to love?

"We'll see about that," I said. "But along those lines, I have an idea I want to run by you."

And for the rest of the night, we plotted.

THE NEXT AFTERNOON, AFTER requesting, through Caro, and receiving permission to speak with Wilson, I started off alone. He sat in his armchair, looking for all the world like a king holding court, red robe and all, and even though he did not invite me to sit down, I pulled his desk chair closer to him and sat.

"I can't write your book, Wilson," I said.

"I am afraid I do not understand," he said, frostily.

"It's simple enough," I said. "I can't write it, and moreover, I don't want to write it. I'd be happy to give you the names of some other very reputable ghostwriters, if you like."

"You do not want to?" he asked, with a touch of acid in his voice. "But I requested that you write it. You cannot simply quit."

"I can, and I am."

Wilson threw his head back and laughed a scorching and—for a sick man—hearty laugh.

"I'm glad you're amused," I said.

"Ah, but the joke, as they say, is on you, Eustacia."

Just days ago, a remark like this would have sent my hackles up. Now, I merely looked at him.

"You see, I had no intention of publishing such a book anyway," he said. He tapped his fingers on the arms of his chair, slowly, like an evil mastermind in a movie, although he probably had never seen a movie like that.

It was on the tip of my tongue to say that I was quite sure no one else had any intention of publishing it, either, since Wilson wasn't exactly Winston Churchill or Justin Bieber or even James Watson, not even close, but I held off. For one thing, Wilson was so arrogant as to be basically insult-proof, and for another, Willow was down the hall in her room, waiting for me to call her in for the most important part of the conversation. More than anything else, though, I was tired of reacting to Wilson Cleary. At long, long last. So I just sat, silent and impassive as a cat.

"Which brings us to the question of why I really asked you to come here," said Wilson, with a gleam in his eye.

"I wasn't going to ask," I said.

"Of course, you were," said Wilson.

"I won't say I'm not a little curious, but the truth is that your reasons don't matter."

Wilson glared at me. "Oh, but they do."

"No, they really don't."

"Stop being childish."

"Look, it's true that I came because you called and asked me to, but now, what I'm doing here, my *reasons* for having this experience, none of that has anything to do with why you asked me to come."

"I do not understand."

"And that doesn't matter, either." It was a statement of fact without a drop of anger.

"Eustacia," said Wilson, in his kingliest manner, "this is no time for you to take some tiresome stand. I have certain things to say to you, things that, whether you are adult enough to admit it or not, will interest you very much."

Talking to Wilson was like standing at the end of a football field trying to have a conversation with an entire marching band. I hummed a little of "And the Saints Go Marching In."

"Excuse me?" said Wilson.

I sighed. "Never mind."

He cleared his throat and began. "After my heart attack and sub-sequent surgery, I came to understand, for the first time, that I will not always be here. I do not plan to make my exit for some time, but I do see that it is inevitable. Once I understood this, other revelations followed."

He paused. I waited. I scratched my elbow because it really did itch.

"I realized," he went on, "that I have made some regrettable mis-takes in my life. One in particular."

Another grand pause. Oh my, I recognized this moment. It was the one I'd spent years waiting for, dreaming about. My heart should have been pounding; my breath should have been bated. My father was about to admit that he was wrong to cut me out of his life. But look at me: I felt like I was watching a movie—and not one that would change my life. *Get on with it,* I thought, *just spit it out.* But because it was clear that he would not continue until I said something, I said, "I see."

He announced his transgression thusly: "I have raised Willow as though I would be here forever."

Willow. Willow. Of course, Willow. This was all about Willow.

I had not come so far that this didn't hurt. It wouldn't kill me or maim me. It might not even leave scars, but it hurt.

"In many ways, of course, I have done right by her. She has a su-perior education," said Wilson. "She is not silly or gossipy or anorexic."

I had to suppress a smile. Leave it to Wilson to put silliness on par with anorexia.

"She is not obsessed with video games or social networks, makeup or television. She gives not a whit for boy bands or for boys at all."

I kept silent.

"And she is altogether lovely." The affection in his voice was un-mistakable.

"She is," I agreed.

He went on as though he hadn't heard. Probably, he hadn't.

"But when I considered how she would be without me one day, forced to negotiate the outside world alone, I realized that she might be at a disadvantage, that she might lack the tools to deal with surroundings and people decidedly less rarefied than those to which she is accustomed."

Pause. "Oh," I said.

"Of course, I know that she has a mother."

Another suppressed smile. *Oh, Wilson.*

"A loving and, in ways, brilliant mother, but Caro has some of the vagaries of the artistic personality and is not, herself, particularly schooled in the ways of the culture at large. So in order to aid my daughter in surviving the world outside this house, first, I sent her to school, and then . . ." Enormous pause, drum roll pause. "I called you."

"School I get," I said. "But why me?"

I saw a flash of irritation in Wilson's eyes, probably at my low-key response after all his buildup, but there was nothing to be done about that.

"Despite your unpromising youth," he said, "you have turned out rather well. You do not know it, but I have been keeping tabs on you. Your performance in college was excellent; you have no criminal record, not so much as a driving violation; and you are not an addict of any kind. You are physically active and well groomed."

There was no earthly way to contain my smile, at this; it was all I could do not to hoot with semihysterical laughter, but Wilson didn't seem to notice.

"While I believe you made a critical error in not attending graduate school—in not getting so much as a master's degree—you have managed to craft a lucrative and largely respectable career for yourself, and, very wisely, you have remained unmarried, so there is no man in your life to complicate matters."

"Okay, but surely you have other people in your life, former colleagues, friends who fit the bill, have advanced degrees, *and* no troubled history with you. So why me?"

Wilson shrugged. "I knew you would say yes."

Of all the things he'd said, this was the zinger, the one that knocked the laughter right out of me. Because it was true: I had always, even when it broke my own heart, said yes to Wilson.

He went on to propose a plan that involved my living in his pool house for roughly the next two years and devoting myself to educating Willow in the ways of the world.

"I assume your job is portable, but if not, I am prepared to compensate you for its loss and any other you might incur. Along with living rent-free, an annual stipend is certainly a good possibility."

"You're trying to *buy* me?"

He emitted an extravagant sigh. "That is an ugly and melodramatic way to describe it, Eustacia. I am willing to do what is necessary to secure you as a—what do they call it?—life coach. For Willow, until she goes to college. I am even happy to draw up a formal contract, if you like, making the terms of your employment clear."

When I didn't answer, he added, "I am prepared to include health insurance."

"No."

His face began to turn red. "No?"

"No."

"Have you no sense of family obligation? Have you spent your life so jealous of a child that you would refuse to help her?"

Wilson, talking to me about family obligation. Oh, for the love of God.

"I care about Willow," I told him, evenly. "I will be part of her life in some capacity from here on out, depending on what she wants and what I want. But our relationship will be ours, mine and Willow's, and we will conduct it on our own terms, as sisters."

This last word took me by surprise because it was still so new and delicate, like a fern that was just beginning to uncurl. I hadn't meant to unveil such a precious thing in the presence of Wilson.

"Sisters!" he scoffed.

"And now, if you've finished," I said, "Willow and I have something to tell you."

WILLOW WAS AMAZING WITH Wilson, although even that seems not quite fair to say because she so clearly wasn't manipulating him or handling him. Her honesty shone in every word and gesture. They were just two people being in an authentic, long-standing, years-deep father/daughter relationship, and, from where I stood, that was perhaps the most amazing thing of all. She told him our plan, which was to have a full-blown, all-inclusive, turkey-cranberry-sauce-friends-and-relations Thanksgiving dinner.

She rooted herself firmly, more like a redwood than a willow, and said, "We aren't asking your permission, exactly, because we know you won't give it. But I would like it so much if you would not fight this, Daddy, because I want it more than I have ever wanted anything. More than that fancy telescope when I was seven, more than a tree house when I was eight."

"Tree houses are dangerous. I could not have you falling," said Wilson.

"Yes, I know. But a dinner with family and friends isn't dangerous. We have spent so long being just the three of us, and I have loved it. But you opened us up when you invited Taisy, which was a brilliant move and exactly what we needed, and it is not something you can set in motion and then cut off." She smiled. "Think of Newton."

"You are turning science into metaphor for your own purposes," he scolded.

She grinned. "I'm a kid. I'm supposed to be irresponsible. A family set in motion stays in motion, and this one is expanding."

"Whom do you want in it?" he asked, with a groan.

"Everyone."

He looked at me. "Your mother."

"Of course," I said. "And Marcus."

"Not Marcus," said Wilson.

"Daddy," said Willow, gently. "You're forgetting that he's my brother."

"You wanted him to come, too," I said, "when you called and invited me. Remember?"

"Only because I knew he would not," said Wilson. "It was a gesture of goodwill."

An empty one, I thought, *meant to manipulate me.* But I kept quiet.

"I don't know if he'll come this time," I said, "but I think he will."

"He is impertinent and a drunkard," said Wilson.

"He hasn't had a drink since his first year of college," I told him. "As for his being impertinent or not, well, I can't make any promises."

Wilson opened his mouth to speak, his face pinking up.

"It doesn't matter," said Willow. The girl was plain steely. "He is my brother, and I want him. Brothers and sisters should know each other. They should be in each other's lives, even if it's difficult. Taisy says families are messy, but it's a kind of mess I want."

She and I exchanged a glance. I had told her about Barbara, not the whole story of the estrangement, of course, since I didn't actually know it and it was not my story to tell anyway, but I'd told Willow that they had lost touch a long time ago.

"Just like you and I did," she had said. "We have to invite her."

"There's a lot of history there," I'd told her. "Maybe we should save it for another time. And, anyway, if Wilson knows she's coming, he might refuse to be part of it."

"Then, we'll have to do our best to avoid telling him," she'd said, coolly.

Now, she said, "I need this. I've already spoken to Muddy, and I think she needs it, too. I know it might be unpleasant for you, and I'm sorry. But please don't fight it."

Wilson looked from me to Willow. "You are banding together against me." There was a tinge of wonder to his voice.

"Not against you," I told him. "This isn't about defying you."

"No?" said Wilson, skeptically.

"No," said Willow, staunchly. "We're just banding together to make something happen, something good."

Wilson ran his hands down the lapels of his royal red robe. "I do not give this farcical dinner my blessing," he said, "and I want nothing to do with the planning of it. Do not consult me about so much as the menu, although I would advise strongly against casseroles. But I will not fight you."

"Thank you."

Willow and I said it at exactly the same time.

CHAPTER TWENTY

Willow

BACK IN MY HOMESCHOOLING group days, there had been a parent leader named Mrs. Feeley (I am not making that name up) who disdained the words *tell* and *show* and *give* like they were ants at a picnic. Everything under the sun was *share*. We shared—or were encouraged to share—stories, advice, moments, answers, essays, photos, gluten-free-sugar-free cookies, thoughts, feelings, jokes (as in, "I see that smile, Willow; perhaps you'd care to share the joke with the rest of us"), and elaborate doodles we did when we were supposed to be sharing silent fellowship. At the time, her insistence on the word made me want to pelt her with spitballs or cardboard-flavored cookies and shout, "Share *this*, why don't you? And *this*, and *this*, and *this*!"

But after I'd told Taisy the story of my relationship with Mr. Insley, I was forced to revise my position on the word *share*. Because right afterward, the very second I'd finished telling, that's just how it felt, not like I'd handed it over to her, but as though we'd said, "One, two, three," and hoisted the whole sorry tale—and not just the tale but the series of events itself, all those weeks—onto both sets of our shoulders so that—poof!—it wasn't just mine; it was ours. And, oh, did that make a difference! Before I left for school the morning after the fire, Taisy had hugged me and whispered in my ear: "The Cleary sisters are here, so never fear!" And I never did.

Still, every day he failed to show up felt like a gift. He wasn't there that first day, which was Friday, and he wasn't there the following Monday. By Tuesday, the rumor mill was in full churn, and I'm afraid that I heedlessly set aside my newfound compassion for the human condition in general, and for Mr. Insley's humanity in particular, and reveled in every word, true or not.

Word was Zany Blainey had taken leave because someone had tried to burn his house down. Word was that a girl at a neighboring school whose uncle's brother-in-law's sister was a fire investigator said that Mr. Insley had confessed to doing it himself. Word was he got frustrated with some stupid boat he was building, doused it with wood varnish, and set it on fire. Word was he was drunk at the time. Word was he was so dumb he thought that because the boat was inside a steel shed, the fire would just burn itself out. Word was the entire yard went up like a pile of dry straw. Word was he took such crappy care of his lawn that it basically *was* a pile of dry straw. Word was he was a renter. Word was his landlord was livid. Word was Mr. Insley was at the very least going to have to pay a big, old fine. Word was Webley was getting calls from irate parents about a firebug teaching their kids. Word was the board of directors had come down on that asshole like a ton of bricks. Word was no way was the pyromaniacal piece of shit coming back.

There was no word, not a one, about Willow Cleary having been there the night of the fire, for which I was giddily grateful. Still, a little, nagging voice in my head kept saying that I was a fool if I thought I could put it all behind me quite so easily, especially since another little, nagging voice kept saying that Mr. Insley's conduct had been, at best, unbecoming a teacher and, at worst, well, I wasn't even sure (Dastardly? Dangerous? Right on the edge of illegal?) and that it was my duty to do whatever I could to stop him from behaving in such a manner toward someone else. In short, the nagging voice said, it was my duty to *tell*. But I didn't want to! Not just yet anyway. I wanted to enjoy these golden, carefree, Insley-free days, which I was sure would end at any moment. So that's what I told myself: the day I walked into English and found him there was the day I would tackle the issue of whether and who and just exactly how much to tell.

Meanwhile, I hung out—as my peers say—with Luka, not only at lunch, which we persisted in eating under our tree even on the coldest days, but also in the hallways before school and between classes. We walked each other to each other's lockers. We sat together in English because the substitute didn't know we had assigned seats. After school, we strolled, shoulder to shoulder, down the path that led to the natatorium where Luka had swim practice, and before I ran off to catch my ride home, we said, "See you tomorrow."

It was fun and chummy and just as it had always been, except for the moments when I was seized with the urge to blurt out, *If you needed me to, I would carry you on my back across the frozen tundra;* or *You are the funniest and the smartest and the kindest and, good God, look at your teeth!;* or *I could talk to you forever;* or *You are more beautiful than Queen Nefertiti, and, if I could, I would build a pyramid in your honor with my bare hands and every block of it would be another piece of how much I love you.*

Because I did. I loved him. I loved Luka Bailey-Song. Not the idea of him, not the attention he gave me, not the way he had rescued me from loneliness, not the way he made me feel special, even though just having a conversation with him made me feel like the Hope Diamond and a white tiger and Einstein's theory of relativity rolled into one. I just loved him, the him of him. I wanted him to be happy. I wanted him never to be sad. I wanted him to live forever. I wanted to kiss the exact center of his chest and the crook of his arm and his closed eyelids and his mouth.

And, oh, I wanted him to love me back and had no idea how to make this happen. I wondered if there were a standard method out there that I didn't know about (since I knew nothing about anything), a social protocol, something I could learn. If only I could have sent him an invitation: "You are cordially invited to be in love with Willow Cleary. RSVP as soon as is humanly possible. No gifts."

Instead, one lunch period, when we were sitting under our tree, I said, "I think you should take me to a swim meet."

Luka gave me an arch look. He was a master of the arch look, particularly the arch look with overtones of waggishness. "You do, huh? Why?"

I shrugged. "I've never been to one."

"You've never been to a NASCAR race, either."

"You don't know that."

Luka grinned. "Uh, yeah, I do. So do you want to go to one of those, too?"

"I don't know what they are," I said.

"Does that matter? I mean, if never having gone before is enough reason for you to want to go, then why pick a swim meet—correction, *my* swim meet—specifically?"

If I could take one thing only to a deserted island, it would be you.

I rolled my eyes. "What's your point?"

"My point is that you want to go to my swim meet because it's mine."

"Ha. Circular reasoning much?"

"Nope, you're not getting off the hook." He narrowed his eyes at me. "Say it: you want to go because you want to go someplace with me, specifically, in order to, specifically, see me, specifically, swim."

I would carry you in my arms across a burning desert. Just ask.

"I have seen you swim," I said.

"You want to go because you want to go someplace with me, specifically, in order to, specifically, see me, specifically, swim *again*."

"Well, again and faster. Presumably, in a race you'll swim faster. That's the idea, right?"

"Say it."

Be brave, Willow, brave, brave, brave.

"Fine." *Brave, brave, brave, brave.* "I want to go with you because you're specifically you, and when I watched you swim that time, you were specifically beautiful, and also because I want to see you swim fast. Very fast." I paused. "Oh and win. Winning isn't necessary, of course, but it would be good."

For a second, all Luka did was look at me with the nicest eyes.

"You thought I was beautiful?"

"I'm not saying it again," I said.

He smiled the kind of smile that is the reason for wars and poetry.

"How about this?" he said. "My next swim meet is right after Thanksgiving. I'll take you to it, if you take me to Fall Fling next weekend."

Inside, I was running in circles, waving my arms, and singing the "Hallelujah Chorus" at the top of my lungs.

"Fall Fling is a dance," I said. "I've never danced before. Unless you count ballet, but most people wouldn't, would they?"

"Nope."

"I feared as much. And even that was years ago."

"But even if you had danced before," said Luka, "it wouldn't matter. You know why?"

"Why?"

He winked. "Because you haven't really danced until you've danced with me."

I laughed. "Fine."

Right then, the lunch bell sounded, and I was only amazed that every bell within a hundred-mile radius of us hadn't started ringing its pretty little heart out in celebration. We got our things together, stood up, and started walking.

"Next weekend right before Thanksgiving break," said Luka, "I'll pick you up at six, and we'll meet people over at my house for food and pictures. Oh, and invite your parents. That's what happens: parents come, they say a lot of corny stuff, they get all teary eyed at how grown up we look, they make us pose in all kinds of stupid ways, and they take pictures."

I didn't even bother trying to imagine my father saying corny stuff on such an occasion, much less getting teary eyed. I knew he'd never come, but I pushed the thought of him from my head.

"It sounds like fun," I said.

Luka smiled down at me. "Thanks for inviting me."

"You're welcome."

And then, without slowing down or missing a step, Luka put his arm around my shoulders, squeezed me closer, and kissed the side of my head.

MY MOTHER IS JUST different from the rest of us. When she isn't tortured by sleeplessness, she spends most of her days in a state of graceful semi-oblivion, breathing a finer air than everyone else, and seeking out beauty, the kind she can turn into art, the way some missiles seek heat. But every now and then, she startles the heck out of me by taking a sudden and giddy interest in the things of this world. Volkswagen Beetles. Monopoly. Whoopie pies. High-heeled shoes. The amazing career trajectory of J. K. Rowling (whose books, having been written in the twentieth and twenty-first centuries, were off-limits to me).

Now, it was the Webley School Fall Fling. When I told Muddy, with no small amount of trepidation, that a boy had asked me to a dance, her face lit up and she squealed (squealed!), "Yay! This is going to be such fun!" That evening, she made a surreptitious run to the drugstore and purchased three teen fashion magazines, and then led me, finger to her lips, to the pool house, where she, Taisy, and I fell on them like ravening wolves. She experimented with hairstyles, tugging and pinning and spraying goops and unguents at my head while I did my homework. She made an appointment for me to get a "mani/pedi," a term I'd only recently learned from an overheard bathroom conversation at school and that I would've sworn I'd go to my grave without ever hearing fall from my mother's lips. She took me and Taisy on a dress-shopping excursion, not to our local mall but to the gargantuan one almost an hour away, a trip so long and involved—and, yes, wonderful—that we ended up staying until the place closed.

We were all so caught up, riding the glorious wave of her excitement and our own, that we managed, up until the day before the dance, to avoid the subject of telling my father. When Taisy, finally, reluctantly, broached it, Muddy immediately volunteered, and I was tempted to let her, especially since her very presence had always worked a kind of soothing magic on him, but at the eleventh hour, even as she was beginning to mount the stairs, guilt ambushed me, and I trotted up them ahead of her as fast as I could trot.

When I got to his room, he was sitting at his desk, tapping away at his computer, ruddy faced, nearly hearty, so much like his old self, that, for a second or two, I forgot my dire mission and just rejoiced in the sight of him. He still spent much of the day in his room, coming down mostly just for meals and never leaving the house, but now it was because he was working on a project. He had always disliked talking about his work while it was still in progress (although he was extremely generous in expounding upon it once it was finished), but from the few, over-his-shoulder sneak peeks I'd managed to steal, I was almost positive he was writing the book he'd hired Taisy to write, a kind of travelogue of his intellectual journey.

I stood there in the doorway for a moment, just watching him, before I cleared my throat to announce my arrival.

He heralded me with a swivel of his chair in my direction and a booming "Willow, my girl! Enter, enter!" I took a few steps toward him, halted, and pulled myself straight as a sentry.

"Daddy, if it's all right with you, I won't waste time with preliminary small talk. I think this situation calls for plunging in straightaway."

He waved his hand in the air. "By all means, plunge!"

I gave a brisk nod and said, "Here it is: tomorrow evening, I am attending a school dance with a fellow student, a young man named Luka Bailey-Song."

Everything I knew about my father had led me to expect that, at hearing this, he would begin to flush and would then proceed to grow redder and redder as the conversation continued, but to my amazement, the opposite happened: his cheeks got a shade lighter—they could even have been said to *pale*—and, while I couldn't be sure, I thought his eyes went misty. *Oh, God, what have I done,* I thought. I waited for the other shoe to drop, for him to clutch his heart, fall from his chair. But he didn't. He said, quietly, "My dear girl, you might be hurt. You know so little of the ways of the world."

At this tenderness, my own eyes misted over. "I know more than I used to," I said, with a smile, "but it's true that I am still rather wet behind the ears. However, I may not know the world, but I know this boy. He is my true friend."

I did not add that he was my only friend or that I was hopelessly— no, *hopefully*—and eternally in love with him.

"A high school dance?" scoffed my father. "Surely, you are above such nonsense."

Two months ago, this sort of argument would have worked wonders on me, but since then, I had made a list of mistakes as long as my arm, longer; except for everything to do with Luka and academics, my entire high school career had been one long, mainly unfunny comedy of errors. A girl who had kissed her English teacher not once but twice and in the yard of his house to boot, a house that would nearly burn down with her inside it, was surely not above a high school dance.

"Daddy, you sent me to high school to experience high school. Dances are part of that."

"Boys your age have terrible judgment and lack empathy. It is not their fault, necessarily; their frontal lobes are still developing and are connected to the rest of their brains by the flimsiest of circuitry."

"Luka plays the violin and gets up at four thirty every morning to swim. He is possibly the best student in our grade, and he's kind and good and funny, and, when no one else would even speak to me, he chose me as his English project partner." I smiled. "Which should be evidence enough of his good judgment."

"Hmpf," said my father. Then, he said, "Is this how it is to be now, Willow? You tell me what you will do rather than ask me?" He didn't sound angry. He sounded sad.

I'd actually been compiling a mental list of things I was planning to tell him I would do: get a driver's license, read literature written after 1900, beginning with *Harry Potter and the Sorcerer's Stone*, and watch every *Foyle's War* episode in existence, for starters. But I decided I'd save those things for another time.

"Only when I am certain I'm making the right choice," I said, with a sigh, "which I daresay won't happen very often. I think my frontal lobes have quite a long way to go themselves."

My father laughed. It was a brief laugh, possibly also slightly forced, but a laugh nonetheless. It occurred to me that perhaps I wasn't the only one here learning how to adapt. I walked over to him and kissed his cheek.

"Even so," he said. "You must promise that, if the need arises, you will trust your lobes over his."

"I solemnly swear from the bottom of my heart and of my entire cerebral cortex," I said, holding up my right hand, "that my lobes get the final word."

My father tapped me lightly on the forehead. "That's my girl!" he said, and in a flash, there—in my father's room!—was Mr. Insley's voice inside my head, saying the same words. *Go away,* I told his ghost, *I could never be your girl. I hate you,* and, unfair or not, for that moment anyway, from the bottom of my everything, I meant it.

I DREW THE LINE at the grand staircase entrance. I would not, for love or money, descend our curved staircase while Luka waited in the foyer below, eyes agog, mouth agape, even though my mother and Taisy avowed that it was such a "classic" moment as to be practically mandatory.

"I would find it unbearably awkward, horrifically melodramatic," I told them. "And so would Luka."

"I know!" Taisy yelped. "That's part of what makes it classic!"

But I stood firm, and they gave up after minimal hounding, probably because I submitted to the rest: hair, dress, nails, shoes, jewelry, makeup, the crash courses on popular music and how to pin a boutonniere (both taught by Taisy, of course), and a pool house viewing of a film called *Pretty in Pink* during which popcorn, pizza, and fancy grapefruit soda (my first soda experience!) flowed like milk and honey. Wait, scratch "submitted." Submitted implies, perhaps, reluctance on my part, and certainly does not reflect the utter abandon with which I threw myself into all these preparations. And as I looked in the mirror, when it had all come to fruition, when I was a finished product, I liked what I saw. Liked? I was *dazzled*.

Taisy had been right about the dress, which was above the knee, thin-strapped, sequined, slightly flapper-esque, and *silver* of all colors. On our mall excursion, when I'd seen the dress on the hanger at the store, my hand had gone right to it, as though yanked by an irresistible force, but I knew it was useless to hope. Someone as paper-white as I could surely never wear such a color, just as someone so stork-legged could surely never wear such a length, but Taisy had dismissed these misgivings with a toss of her head.

"Nonsense!" she said. "Your skin has warm undertones; you have distance-runner legs, which are lovely; and with that magnificent auburn hair, you can pull off almost anything. Try it on!"

They'd oohed, they'd ahhed; it was, as my peers say, awesome. For the rest of the shopping trip, they had plotted my ensemble like generals.

"Berry-stained lips and nails," said Taisy to Muddy. "Don't you think?"

"And silver peep-toes!" said Muddy to Taisy. "Oh, and it will be chilly outside, and, oh my goodness, I have the loveliest royal blue velvet evening coat that will hit just below the hem of the dress!"

"Wonderful! Oh, wait, and I have a tiny, jeweled evening bag, a wristlet just big enough for a cell phone and lipstick that will be perfect," said Taisy. (I had told Muddy about the phone a few days before, and she had given it her blessing.)

"Perfect!" sang Muddy.

When they had come upon the sparkly dragonfly hair clip in the fancy department store, their faces glowed with a light that was out and out celestial.

"We'll just pull back a small section in front, don't you think? And leave the rest wild?" Taisy asked Muddy.

"Brilliant!" said Muddy. "Oh, and I'll do a bit of the ringlet thing I tried the other day. Remember the ringlet thing, Willow?"

I did.

And, by and by, all of what they had foreordained came to pass. As I stood before the full-length mirror in my bedroom, with Muddy and Taisy all smiles in the background, hands clasped in hope that I would like what I saw, I felt a great surge of love for the world, the girl in the mirror included. Not just because she looked pretty—dewy faced and lashy eyed and fiery haired—but because she looked so avidly, unabashedly joyful. Her entire person glowed with a joy so bright, it almost outsparkled her dress. It was impossible not to root for a girl like that.

"How do you feel?" asked my mother.

"Like tinsel!" I told her.

While I stood firm in eschewing the staircase entrance, I deferred to them in the matter of who would answer the door when Luka arrived.

"Let your mom get it," instructed Taisy. "And you come walking in from the living room. I'll be standing by with your coat and bag and the boutonniere and the camera. We'll follow the two of you to Luka's house for the picture-taking extravaganza, of course, but we need to be sure to get some front door shots."

And these things, too, came to pass. All went as planned, except that in the minutes before Luka was due to arrive, I was suddenly seized by a tremendous fit of nervousness. I sat on the living room sofa, jittery as a jumping bean. My knees bobbed, my heart skittered, and Taisy had to remind me three times not to touch my face with my restless hands. When the doorbell rang, it was all I could do not to run out of the room and hide in the kitchen pantry. But I stayed put and the rest went like clockwork. Taisy manned her station; Muddy walked to the door. I heard her open it; I heard my mother say, "Hello, you must be Luka," and then, there in my house where I lived every day, was Luka's voice.

"Hi, Mrs. Cleary," he said. "It's nice to meet you."

Unexpectedly, he sounded nervous, too, which made me feel just a tiny bit steadier. Breathing almost like a normal person, I stood and walked out of the living room, and when I stepped from the rug to the marble floor, at that very first tap of my shoe, Luka turned around. His jaw did not drop; he was neither agape nor agog. He simply looked happier to see me than anyone ever had in my life, and, when he smiled, the drunkenly spinning world righted itself and everything, everything was fine.

"Hey, look at you," he said, admiringly.

I laughed. "I've done nothing but look at me for hours. I'd rather look at you."

He held his arms out to the sides so that I could better inspect him. I made a twirling motion with my finger and, dutifully, he turned in a circle. He wore a gray suit, a white shirt, and a silvery tie (we had conferred on this point, since Muddy had sworn that all would fall to wrack and ruin if we did not match). In one hand, he held a nosegay of red rosebuds.

"Your hair," I said, squinting up at it, "has been subdued. I mean, somewhat."

He raked his fingers through it. "Turns out there's this stuff called conditioner."

"You are very debonair," I pronounced. I looked at Taisy and Muddy and added, "Isn't he?"

"Yes," they said in unison.

"Do I look like I just won the Battle of Agincourt?" he asked.

"Yes," they said again. They could have had no idea what he meant, of course, but it didn't matter. Luka could have said, "Is it okay if I take ownership of this house and everything in it?," could have said it in *Greek,* and those two good women—agog and agape as anyone ever was— would have said, breathlessly, "Yes."

"Much cleaner and less bloodstained," I said. "Although that could all change when I pin on your boutonniere."

He laughed and held out the roses. "Here."

"For me?" I asked. I meant the roses and his hand holding them and the arm attached to the hand and every part of him thereafter, in- cluding the smile he was giving me right then, focused and private, like a secret handshake, like a quick kiss on the side of my head.

"Who else would they be for?" he said.

PERHAPS BECAUSE I HAD spent days under the spell of *Pretty in Pink,* which had made quite an impression on me, since it was not only my first teenage-romance movie but my first movie of any kind ever, I had secretly been wishing for the Fall Fling to be one, long, drawn-out love scene. Which would have been a certain kind of wonderful, although maybe not the kind for which I was actually, when push came to shove, ready. Instead, what the dance gave us was another kind altogether, a kind of wonderful I'd been pining for without knowing I pined, and it was this: *fun.* Oh my goodness, that dance was fun! Fun like I'd never had because it was *group* fun, noisy, crowded, jostling, feeling-the- bass-in-your chest fun. The closest I'd ever come to group fun was be- ing on the cross-country team, but this was even better.

For the first half hour or so, I kept an eye out for Bec, and then, I decided just to seize the bull by the horns and ask Luka if he thought she was coming.

"Nope. She's got this new boyfriend, a freshman at Penn that she met at some party. She's visiting him."

"A boyfriend. So she's not madly in love with you?" I said it lightly, but the truth was that I was dying to know.

Luka looked surprised and laughed. "Uh, no."

"Are you sure?"

"Well, I know it's hard to believe," he said, "because I'm obviously so lovable, but I'm sure. We've been friends since kindergarten. In ninth grade, we dated for, like, a month, mainly because everyone was always saying we should, but it was just too weird."

"Oh," I said. "So you're friends."

Luka's face got serious. "We're friends the way people are friends who have known each other forever. But I don't like everything she does. When I think she's being a jerk, I tell her."

Suddenly, none of it mattered, and the fact that we were dressed to the nines, standing in the middle of a dance, talking about *Bec* struck me as a colossal mistake.

"This is a dance, isn't it?" I demanded. "So why aren't we dancing?"

He grinned. "We are," he said, grabbing my hand, and the next thing I knew, we were.

And maybe because Bec wasn't there to enforce her decree that no one was allowed to like me, or maybe because Luka had issued some decree of his own, although it seemed more likely that his sheer Lukaness had just won out in the end, people were nice to me. They included me. Without ado or apologies, girls who had never met my eyes in the hallway once in all the weeks I'd been at Webley danced next to me on the dance floor, elbow to elbow, hip to hip, all grins, like it was the most natural thing in the world. We threw our hands in the air. We shimmied under the spinning lights. Between dances, we chattered about shoes and lipstick and hair. For the first time in so long, I was in

a crowd of people and felt neither like a naive child nor like an old lady;
I felt sixteen going on seventeen, just exactly.

The boys were part of the dancing group, too, with Luka right in
the center, jacket off, tie loose, hair increasingly unsubdued, mostly
because other people kept messing it up. I didn't blame them; my fingers itched to touch it, too. Sometimes, I wouldn't see Luka for a stretch
of time, which was surprisingly fine, and then he'd catch my eye across
the room or appear with a bottle of water for me or a funny remark in
my ear, and that was even better.

At the end of the night, he held out his hand, and we slow danced,
my fingers entwined on the back of his neck, and I don't know if we were
supposed to or not, since the rules of slow-dancing were, naturally,
a mystery to me, but we talked the whole time. Maybe this wasn't exactly movie-romantic, but even as Luka told me that my dress made me
look like the Chrysler building in the best possible way and I answered
by stepping on his foot on purpose and as we whispered about how the
new ninth-grade math teacher and the boys' soccer coach had just been
caught making out in the broom closet, part of me was hyperaware of
Luka's lips, how close they were to me, and also of his hands pressing
against the small of my back, and of the smell of his neck, and of his
overall, general, monumental, overarching, heart-stopping *luster,* and
what I thought was, *I want it to always be this way, even if he falls in love
with me back, and dear God please let him, but even if he does, I don't want to
leave anything behind. I want it to be both things at once. True friendship and
true love at the very same time.* I wondered if such a thing even existed.
If it didn't, I would tell Luka that we had to invent it.

We were invited to an after-dance party at a girl named Caitlin's
house, but Luka asked me if I wanted to go have bacon pancakes at an
all-night diner instead, an invitation that came as an enormous relief
to me, since my only high school party point of reference was the one
in *Pretty in Pink* during which people behaved insultingly and danced
in their underwear.

"I bet you'd like the diner. It's the kind of place where everyone tells you their names. And we could talk," he said. "Not that this wasn't fun, but I miss talking to you."

I cocked my head. "You miss talking to me or you want pancakes?"

He grinned. "Did I mention they were bacon pancakes?"

I waited.

"Talking. The pancakes are secondary," he said. "So what do you think?"

"Well, I think it depends," I said.

"Depends, huh? On what."

"On whether the bacon is inside the batter or on top."

He leaned in and gently tugged one of my curls until it was straight. "Which one will make you say yes?"

"On top. And in between, if the pancakes are stacked."

He let the curl go. It bounced like a spring.

"Then that's where it is."

THE PANCAKES WERE CRUNCHY, spongy, sweet, salty, syrupy heaven, but talking to Luka was better. Under the bright lights of the diner, I told him how close Taisy and I had gotten, and he told me that his older brother, Jackson, had started college that year and that he missed him so much more than he'd expected to. He told me how it felt to swim, and I told him how it felt to run. I told him about my mother's glass art and my father's heart attack and how it had changed him and all of us in so many ways. He told me that his parents watched all his swim meets and were great about them, but they were hard on him about everything else—school, behavior, violin, thank-you notes (how many guys wrote thank-you notes?)—but that he could never manage to totally resent them because they were also really funny. Then, with my fork, I carefully crumbled the bits of bacon that were left on my plate and told Luka how I felt when he chose me to be his English project partner.

"Like someone had thrown me a lifeline, and I am not exaggerating, and you probably didn't have the first idea of what it meant to me," I said.

I glanced up from my plate to see Luka looking down at his, with an expression of embarrassment on his face. "It meant something to me, too, you know," he said.

I shook my head. "You don't have to say that. I don't mean I'm not grateful because I am, terribly, but for you, picking me was a casual act of generosity. I know it was. I do realize that you didn't exactly get nothing in return because, after all, I am pretty smart."

I raised my eyebrows, awaiting affirmation.

"Really smart," said Luka.

"Thank you. But so are you. You didn't need me. You could've pulled off something amazing with anyone. You were being nice because you knew no one else would pick me. For you it was a small act of kindness; for me, well, it changed my life. Right there and then, in that moment. And I've wanted to thank you."

Luka made a face. "Ugh. Okay. Enough with that. Look, whatever it meant or didn't mean to me then, it means something now. A lot. It's weird to think that back then, we didn't know each other at all."

"We know each other now, right?"

"Now? Now, you're like my favorite person in the world that I'm not related to."

"Really?"

He pretended to ponder my question. "Well, Mrs. Westlake, the lunch lady is pretty great. I mean she tells me I'm a sight for sore eyes every single time I go through the line, and you never say that, but—" I kicked him under the table, and he said, "Yes, really."

And, at this, all unexpectedly, sadness struck me like an arrow. My mouth crumpled. Tears stung my eyes. I tipped my head back, blinked, and fanned my face with my napkin.

"Willow?"

"Makeup," I said. "It's waterproof supposedly, but you never know."

"Hey," said Luka, softly. "Look at me." He put his thumb on my chin and, slowly, I lowered it until I was looking at him. Worried, he scrutinized my face, and I let him. I didn't care about my mascara. I didn't try to hide how sad I felt. What was the point?

"Okay, I want to think you're crying because you're happy," he said, "but I gotta tell you, it doesn't really look that way."

"I'm just wondering—" My voice broke. In about thirty seconds, if something didn't change, I would be crying my ridiculous, miserable eyes out right there in that diner, in front of Bubba the waiter and Josie the head fry cook and heaven knew who else. "I'm sorry. Can we talk about this someplace other than here?"

Luka handed me his keys. "Sure, definitely. You go get in the car. I'll pay and be out in a second."

It was a grim, grim three minutes. I sat in the dark car, shivering, fighting tears and despair, fearing, to the marrow of my bones, that I was about to ruin everything. Because I had to tell him about Mr. Insley. I'd been a fool to think I didn't have to. He was Luka, and I loved him, and I told him everything important. To just let myself go on being his favorite nonrelative without telling him would be like stealing money from his wallet, making fun of him behind his back. It would be treason. When he got in the car, he started the engine, turned on my seat warmer, and said, "Please tell me what's wrong."

"You're so nice to turn on my seat warmer," I said, starting to cry again.

"Willow. Just say it."

I pulled the velvet coat tighter around me and leaned away from him, my shoulder pressed against the car door. "I'm wondering if there's anything I could tell you that would make you stop liking me."

"No."

I shook my head. "How do you know?"

"Because the only things that could make me stop liking you are things you would never do."

"You don't know that."

"Yeah, I do. Would you kick a puppy? Would you rob an old lady at gunpoint?"

I couldn't help smiling, but then I said, "It's bad, Luka."

Then, that blessed boy reached over, took my hand, and pulled me closer, until our faces were no more than a foot apart. He put his other hand around my shoulders. He smelled like coconut conditioner and maple syrup.

"It's not bad enough," he said. "I promise."

I looked out the windshield at the lit-up diner, the parking lot full of cars. "Can we go someplace else?"

"Anywhere you want."

"Just someplace without anyone else in it."

And so my secret, fleeting, pre-dance fantasy of parking on a lonely side street with the boy of my dreams came true, except that instead of kissing him under the moon, I told him the story of the worst, most idiotic, most shameful thing I had ever done. I started at the beginning, with the day I raised my hand in class for the first time and didn't stop until the night Taisy picked me up, my hair smelling like smoke, from the clutch of trees by the side of that awful, name-less road. I included every anonymous message and my theory that Mr. Insley had sent them. I included the driving lesson. I included both kisses. I spared Luka—and myself and Mr. Insley—nothing. I asked Luka not to say anything until I was finished, a promise he kept until we got to the part wherein Mr. Insley ran out of his house with-out me and then shooed me away like a stray cat. At this, Luka said, in a low, angry voice, "Fucking coward."

When I finished telling, Luka said, "I'm really sorry, Willow."

"You? Why would you ever be sorry?"

He pushed a hand through his hair in frustration. "I don't know. There were rumors. Bec and her friends." He let his hand flop into his lap. "I saw the way he looked at you. I should have just asked you about it. I'm sorry. Listen—"

"Shh," I said. "Stop."

"But if I'd talked to you, maybe you wouldn't have gone there the night of the fire."

I shook my head. "No. No more apologizing, and no more talk about what you did or didn't do because you did the very best thing."

"No, I didn't."

"You were friends with me. I had been so lonely, lonely like I can't even describe."

"He saw that," said Luka. "He used it. None of this is your fault. He's an adult. The way you grew up, you were practically Amish."

"Well, I wouldn't go that far."

"Okay, but you didn't know anything about creepers like him, and he knew it." He added, viciously, "I hate him."

"No," I said, quietly. "Well, it's okay to hate him, but don't think I was just an innocent victim. I made choices. Yes, I was lonely and lost, but I was also flattered. He seemed so sophisticated. He told me I was smarter and better than anyone else my age." I paused, thinking. "You know, more than anything, it was the words he used that made it so hard for me to say no to him. One time, he told me I was spun out of moonlight. That sounds corny now, but when he said it, I felt like a character in a book." I shut my eyes. "Oh God, I was an idiot."

"Don't say that," said Luka.

"Honestly, in those last days, more than anything, I just did what he wanted because I felt sorry for him. Which is just stupid."

"You didn't do what he wanted in the end, though. You told him it was over, even before the fire. And I know that scumbag didn't make it easy. You should feel proud of yourself that you got away from him."

I drew closer to Luka.

"You know what?" I said. "You helped me so much. Being with you, that's what made me see him differently. Talking in the hallways. Making the film. It all felt so normal and happy and not scary. Not like a novel. Better."

Luka gave me a wan smile. "Better than *Middlemarch*?"

"Better than anything. Do you still like me?"

My hand was lying on my leg. Luka looked down at it and then held it. "Yes. Do you still like me?"

I leaned over and kissed the high, curved dune of his cheek. I didn't want to tell him that I loved him in the same night I had told him about Mr. Insley. But I loved him more than ever.

"Yes," I said, "yes, yes, yes."

ON THE WAY BACK to my house, I invited him to Thanksgiving dinner.

"I realize you probably won't be able to come because you'll have your own dinner, but I wish you could."

"What time do you eat?"

"People are coming in from out of town, so late. Six."

"We eat at two, so that we have time to get a second wind and eat again," said Luka. "So I could just come to your house for round two."

"Isn't that, um, quite a lot of food?"

"Nah, not that much more than usual. Hey, you want to come to mine? Jackson'll be home."

"Will he be home for a few days?" I asked. "I would love to, but I should help my mom and Taisy get ready. My father is not altogether enthusiastic about this family dinner, to put it mildly. He may be a bit of a stumbling block."

"I get it," said Luka, "but, yeah, Jacks'll be home all weekend and then again at Christmas. Don't worry. You'll meet him."

"Okay. So come as soon as you can. You can meet *my* brother and my aunt and my uncle and my dad's ex-wife and—oh wow." I groaned.

Luka glanced over at me. "Meet them at the same time you do? Is that okay?"

"Very, very okay."

"You want the moral support, huh?"

I squeezed his hand. "I want *you*."

"Good," he said, looking straight out the windshield. "I want you, too."

WHEN WE GOT TO my front porch, I said, "Thank you for going to the dance with me. I loved it. I loved the diner, too."

Luka put his arms around me.

"I think you have a crush on Bubba," he said. "Not that I blame you."

"Bubba is a prince among men. He told Josie to put my bacon exactly where I wanted it."

"But *I* told Bubba."

"Which is why I have a crush on you, too. Obviously."

Luka leaned his forehead against mine. "Thank you for wearing this dress."

"Thank you for using conditioner. Coconut is my favorite."

"Thank you for skipping the party with me. You are *my* favorite."

I hugged him harder. "Thank you for listening to my story."

"Thank you for trusting me with it."

I felt so held. I felt so peaceful. I took this tiny, glowing, breathing space of time, this threshold between his saying the last thing he'd said and my lifting my face to kiss him, and I cherished it and thanked it, and then I lifted my face, and there was Luka. Luka's mouth and his chest against mine and his hands in my hair and on my neck and mine on his back, and, all the while, his mouth, his mouth, his mouth. I'd never been so *with* someone; I'd never been so with myself, right inside my own skin. I was nerve endings and a melting core. We kissed until we were breathless, and then we held on to each other for a while more, his chin resting on the top of my head, not saying anything.

"I wish—" I stopped.

He dropped his head so that his cheek was against mine.

"What do you wish?" he whispered.

"I wish that was my first kiss." I shouldn't have said it. How could I have said that? How could I have brought up my real first kiss at a time like this? And, God, Luka must have had hundreds of other kisses, which just didn't matter at all. "Oh, Luka, I'm sorry I said that."

But when Luka pulled back so he could look at me, he was smiling.

"Hey, it is your first kiss. Remember? It's like the dancing. You haven't really been kissed until you've been kissed by me."

I pressed my lips to the side of his neck and whispered in his ear, "And you haven't really been kissed until you've been kissed by me."

He whispered, "Believe me, I know."

And then that precious, precious boy of mine kissed me again.

CHAPTER TWENTY-ONE

Taisy

ON THE EVE OF Thanksgiving, when I picked up my mother at the airport, she took one look at me and said, "Oh my sweet child, you've decided to stay, haven't you?"

"What?" I said.

"I told Grampa Pete you were going to."

"You did?"

She started walking at her usual fast clip, her wheeled suitcase gliding along behind her.

"He thinks you should wait until spring to put your house on the market, and I have to agree. We've had so much rain this fall, and no house shows well in the rain."

"Oh," I said.

"Although I did run into a young couple at the coffee shop who are thinking of upsizing."

"You did?"

"I got their number, should you want it."

I tried to take the handle of the bag from her, but she marched on.

"Mom."

"You know what they say about a bird in the hand," she said, cheerfully, "although it may be wiser to wait and see what a Realtor has to say."

"Mom."

"Of course, Marcus said there was no way in hell you'd stay up here, this close to Wilson, but that's just more of his projecting his own state of mind onto you, like always. Not that he isn't right most of the time. I always thought that was a twin thing, your being of the same mind about so many things, without so much as conferring. I read the most fascinating article about twins the other day—"

I stopped in my tracks. *"Mom!"*

She turned around, puzzled.

"What's wrong?" she asked. "Did you forget something back at the gate?"

"Listen to you!" I said, throwing up my free hand. "You can't just step off an airplane, declare I'm selling my house, and then sail right on to other things like it's all settled. What made you even say I was staying? I haven't said a word to you about the possibility of relocating."

My mother gave me a startled stare. "Are you saying you're not?"

I groaned. "Just answer the question, please."

She shrugged. "Well, I thought so from how you sounded during our phone conversations and our texts. You had the—what do I mean?—*syntax* of a person who'd made up her mind. And then when I saw you, radiant and pink-cheeked like I swear you haven't been in forever, I knew. Is it Ben or Willow?"

"What?" I asked, bewildered.

"Oh, come on, Taisy," she said, impatiently. "Keep up. You'd never be so *incandescent* on Wilson's account. And from what you've been saying about your—finally!—evolving relationship with him, I'm guessing you wouldn't stay on his account either. So is it Ben or Willow?"

"You just zero in, don't you?" I said. "You're like one of those drone bombers."

"Well?" said my mother.

Sometimes, it's best just to give in. "Both," I said. "Sort of."

This time, it was my mother who stopped in her tracks. She put her arms around me and squeezed, before she pulled back and gave me a piercing look. "Only sort of? Sort of Ben or sort of Willow?"

My eyes got damp. "Willow and I got off to a rocky start, but I expected that. What I didn't expect is that I'd keep discovering more about her to love."

My mother squeezed me again. "That's wonderful, sweetheart. I hoped the two of you would find each other one day."

"If it weren't for Wilson, we might not have," I said. "Which is—weird."

"All the same, it's wonderful. And what about Ben?"

"I love him."

"Well, when did you ever not love him?"

"I know," I said. "But I love him better than I did before. Fiercer. More fiercely, I guess I mean."

"You did your best. Wilson was just always like a force of nature in your life. Well, until now."

"Now, I'm the force of nature," I said, with a smile. "I told Ben I loved him like a hurricane."

"He loves you back?"

"Yes," I said. "He isn't quite ready to know it yet, though."

"But you know he does? You're sure?"

"Yes."

She made an impatient click with her tongue. "Well, what is he waiting for? You've already spent seventeen years apart."

"He said that after what I did to him, he boxed up what we'd had and put it away and promised himself he'd never go back."

"Oh," she said. "Well, I suppose he thought he was doing what he had to do."

"Mom, he didn't even read my letters. Not one of all the dozens I sent him."

"Hmmm," she said, frowning. "Now that may have been self-protection overkill. So he promised himself he'd never go back to you, and he's holding himself to that? Seventeen years later?"

"We had a fight," I said, sadly. "A big one."

"I see."

"We haven't spoken since, but last night, I sent him a text inviting him and his dad to come today to help with Thanksgiving and then come back tomorrow for dinner. I told him it wouldn't have to mean we're back together. It could mean whatever he wanted it to."

"That's awfully accommodating of you," said my mother, crisply.

I knew it was just worry that was making her snippy, but her tone bothered me, anyway.

"I'm not being a pushover, Mom," I said.

She softened. "I'm sorry," she said. "I just want you to be happy."

"I want to be happy. I want him back. I'll do whatever it takes."

"You're a force of nature, are you?" She smiled.

"Hurricane Taisy," I said.

"Well . . ." Her smile broadened.

"Well, what?"

"Well, then that boy had better board up his windows," she said.

I KNEW THAT HE would either come early on or he wouldn't come at all. Mad or not, he wouldn't keep me waiting or toy with me, not because he was in love with me, but because he wouldn't have treated anyone like that. It just wasn't in his nature. I'd told him two o'clock. Between two and two fifteen, I dropped an entire carton of milk on the floor (luckily, it bounced) and cut my thumb with a paring knife, so that I had blood running down my arm when the doorbell rang and could not answer it.

My mother gave me a significant look. "Shall I?"

"Yes, please."

Just as they had the day in Ransom's Garden World, the dogs appeared first, Roo bounding with his tongue out and tiny Pidwit elegant as a high-stepping pony. With the sort of squeal I would not have thought my sister capable of, Willow scrambled around after them, to their boundless delight. Next came Mr. Ransom, and then Ben, bearing a flower arrangement that covered almost his entire face. When he set it down on the kitchen table, our eyes met and he gave me a sheepish smile and a shrug that could have meant *I love you with all my heart and soul* but also could have meant a lot of other things, like *If the pilgrims and Indians could cook dinner together, so can two old friends.*

"Hey," he said, lowering his brows. "Are you okay?"

"I think so," I said, "now that Roo and Pidwit are here."

"No, I meant—" He gestured to my hand.

"Oh, right," I said. "Hey, what could be more romantic than greeting you with a giant wad of blood-soaked gauze?"

He gave me his northern lights smile. "I can't think of single thing," he said.

ALL TOLD, THERE WERE seven of us—Mom, Caro, Ben, Mr. Ransom, Willow, Luka, and I—nine if you counted Pidwit and Roo, which of course we did. We baked pies, pie after pie. Pumpkin, apple, pumpkin chiffon, caramel apple, apple crumb, pecan, chocolate chess, and a pear and cranberry tart. My mother and Caro worked on the crusts, with Caro expertly cutting out leaf shapes and lattices, freehand. Mr. Ransom made the fillings. Ben cored and peeled and sliced, and once I'd stopped bleeding, I helped him. Everyone talked around the two of us; the kitchen was full of noise, but Ben and I were quiet, a stillness at the center of things. Any other time, our lack of conversation might have worried me, but, somehow, it felt natural, like, after all the strife and emotion, we'd agreed to take a breather. It was good just to have him there, to watch his hands peel apples.

Willow didn't even bother trying to tear herself away from the dogs, cooing and baby-talking to beat the band, her dignity and reserve gone completely up in smoke at the sight of their black noses. She and Luka played with them, inside and out in the garden. When Caro and I looked out the back window, we saw them on one of the benches: Willow sitting, talking; Luka lying on his back with his head on her lap; and the dogs curled up, Roo on Luka's chest, Pidwit on his stomach.

"Nice," I said.

"Beautiful," said Caro.

That morning, before anyone had arrived, Caro had said, "Just enjoy yourselves; leave Wilson to me," and now and then, during the pie-making, she would disappear upstairs, with food and drink. At some point, I wandered out into the yard and called Marcus.

"You should've come today. It's nice, and Wilson is holed up in his room like a hibernating bear; it's like he's not even here."

"Yeah, well, don't push it, buddy. I may not come at all," Marcus growled.

I wasn't worried. He'd ended the conversation in which I'd invited him the very same way, and then, an hour later, I'd gotten a call from the best hotel in town notifying me that Marcus Cleary was reserving—and footing the bill for—a small block of rooms for himself and my out-of-town guests, and they wondered if I had any special requests. It wasn't lost on me that it was the same hotel we'd stayed at during the god-awful post-Christmas trip all those years ago. That was my Marcus: generous and sardonic, *I've-got-your-back-Taize* and *No-human-being-should-have-to-sleep-under-Wilson-Cleary's-roof* all in a single gesture.

"Ben's here," I told him.

"Well, march him upstairs to say hi to Wilson already. That should be enough to blow up that bum ticker, and then we'll really have something to be thankful for."

"Way to have the holiday spirit, mister," I said.

"Good job about Ben, by the way. I'm just going to pretend to myself that he was your secret motive for going up there all along. It makes me like you more."

"The Ben thing is still kind of up in the air, but you like me plenty. Have I mentioned how grateful I am that you're coming?"

"Don't get too grateful; I still might not."

"Okay," I said. "See you tomorrow, Mako."

"See you tomorrow, Taize."

AT FOUR O'CLOCK, THE doorbell rang. Willow ran to answer it, Pidwit in her arms. I heard the creak of the door, I heard Willow say, "Hello, may I help you?" and then, glory of glories, I heard a voice sing out, "Look at that *face*! And *you*! So tall and lithe, but I guess you'd have to be with a name like Willow. Oh, and your *hair*! It's like a choir of angels, sweetheart." I dropped my paring knife and ran for the foyer, and there she was, all fur coat and updo and luminosity to rival the sun's.

"Trill!"

"Darling!"

An extravagance of hugs.

"But I thought you couldn't come? What about the Hawaiian get-away with what's his name?"

"I lied!" she said, jubilantly. "I dumped what's his name a week ago. I just wanted to surprise you."

"I am now officially in a state of bliss," I told her.

When she saw Ben, she said, "Well, hello, handsome! Same red, windburned lips. Same fisherman's sweater and corduroy trousers."

Without so much as a confused look or a glance at his jeans and long-sleeved gray T-shirt, Ben grinned and said, "Hey, Trillium. Nice to meet you."

When everyone had gone to the hotel or, in the case of Luka and Mr. Ransom, home, and it was just Ben, Willow, Caro, and I cleaning up, Willow came to Ben, a dog in the crook of each arm, and said, "I don't want to put you on the spot, but could I be so bold as to ask if your dogs could please spend the night here? We would love to host them, and you'll be here early tomorrow to help cook anyway, and you did bring that small container of food so I can feed them, and they could sleep in my room." As if in cahoots with her, the dogs gazed at her rapt face, adoringly. "Or, if you think they wouldn't like to stay all night, could they just be here with me while you go hang out with Taisy in the pool house? It would be so extraordinarily wonderful, but I will understand if you'd rather not."

Ben looked from Willow, to the dogs, to me, to Caro, and back to Willow. "Uh, they'd be fine here, but are you sure? Sometimes, in the middle of the night, they dig pretend holes to sleep in, and they're very—thorough diggers. It can go on for quite a while."

The expression on Willow's face suggested that she had been waiting her entire life to be awakened by the pretend thorough digging of Pidwit and Roo. "Did you hear that, you tiny, wittle sweethearts?" she baby-talked to them. "You're staying, you're staying! It's my second sleepover!"

"Thank you," said Caro to Ben and she put her slender arms around him and hugged him.

On the way over to the pool house, Ben said, "Man, you should've shown up that first day with a couple of puppies. Willow would've been putty in your hands."

I sniffed and said, " 'While you go hang out with Taisy in the pool house,' indeed."

"What?" said Ben.

"I believe we just witnessed a conspiracy in action."

"To get the dogs to spend the night, you mean?"

"That and to make it so that you didn't have to go home tonight and so that we could be alone."

Ben said, "Caro and Willow? They'd do that?"

I felt myself blushing, but I kept my tone matter-of-fact. "Willow is in love and thinks everyone else should be, too. Although she may have just been an unwitting pawn in Caro's plot because Caro is a plotter from way back, a shaper of other people's destinies. I wouldn't be at all surprised to find out that she was the one who first suggested that Wilson invite me here."

"Really? She seems sort of distracted."

"She's the puppeteer. We are the puppets. Luckily, she's a nice puppeteer with only her puppets' best interests at heart."

Slowly, Ben said, "And she thinks it would be in our best interest for me to spend the night with you in the pool house."

"Okay, that sounds creepy. I think she thought we would have things to talk about, and I think she thought it would be nice if we had plenty of time to do it."

"What do you think?"

"I think we should talk and maybe have a glass of wine and then watch the *Planet Earth* with the weird, deep sea creatures. Have you seen that one?"

Ben laughed. "Not recently. But if there's a Dumbo octopus, you've got yourself a deal."

ON THE PORCH, BEN grabbed my hand, and I spun around to face him.

"You knew I would come," he said. "Didn't you?"

"Yes. I wasn't positive it would be today, but I knew you would."

"How?"

Carefully, as though my life depended on doing it right, I ran my finger along his zygomatic arch. "Remember those fights we'd have back in high school?"

"We had some pretty good ones."

"Well, most of the time, I'd be flying around, screeching and stomping, while you stayed annoyingly calm."

"I wouldn't say *annoyingly* calm. I'd just say calm."

"You'd be wrong. But anyway, there were a few times you got really mad, and I'm talking about eyes-blazing-like-bonfires-voice-booming mad, the way you were the other night in this garden, and do you know what all those times had in common?"

I waited while Ben puzzled this out. It was a lovely thing to watch: his eyes alive with thinking and then all at once lit with understanding.

"Okay," he said, abruptly, "let's go inside."

"Say it. Say what made you really and truly mad."

"I really want to see that Dumbo octopus."

I waited. Ben picked up my hand, pressed his mouth to my palm, and said, "What made me really and truly mad was when I knew you were right."

I took his face between my hands, and our kiss was not a trip down memory lane. We weren't Ben and Taisy, sixteen years old and leaning against that tree in his neighborhood. The kiss wasn't at all, not one thing, like coming home. It was new. Unprecedented. Groundbreaking, and I didn't care just then exactly what ground we were breaking. I didn't need to know what our being together meant, where we were headed. Conversation could wait. The Dumbo octopus could wait. I had been aching for seventeen years to get my hands on this man. We hardly made it through the door before I was unbuttoning his shirt.

But because I was who I was, I couldn't quite give way without clearing a few things up, and this was crazy because all I wanted was for it never to end: the muscles of his bare back shifting like continents under my hands, his mouth in a slow slide down the exact center of my body, every nerve ending raw and singing, especially the ones in the places he hadn't touched yet, anticipation edging out everything else, lapping like a tide at my ability to think, to speak, pulling language and logic out to sea, until there were only two words left, and, instead of letting them go, at the last second, I caught them. I said them: "Ben, wait."

In an instant, he stopped and rested his cheek against my hipbone, his breath stammering against my skin. When it slowed enough, he said, "Are you okay?"

I slid my fingers into his hair. "I just need to say something."

I waited for him to pull away, but he didn't. He pressed his mouth once into the hollow beneath my hip and then, never taking his hands off me, he moved up to lay his head on the pillow next to mine.

"Tell me," he said.

"I just realized that I need you to know what this means to me."

"Taisy." He kissed my shoulder and my neck, and then propped his head up on his elbow so that his face was all I could see, a Ben-sky. "Let me tell you what I think it means, first."

"Okay, but— "

He kissed the corner of my mouth. "If we do this, it will mean that you won't be able to leave me. Not just that it would break your heart, but that you will not be able to do it."

"That's right," I said, awed at his prescience, although I guess I shouldn't have been. When it came to reading my mind, Ben had always been a close second to my mother and Marcus.

"I know it's right, not because I can read your mind," he said, "but because that's what it means to me."

Tears filled my eyes. "But I lied about us, and I ended our marriage, and I left you."

"And I gave up on you, pushed even memories of you away. I never read your letters, and you were right when you told me that was cruel. All that was my version of lying and leaving."

I saw it then, how guilt had no place in this bed or our lives. If we wanted to step from this moment into our future, to wake up every morning in wonder, we both had to let it go. Could it possibly be that easy? I looked up at Ben, who was here with me after so many years. His eyes alone loved me the way no one else ever had; they made me want to give him everything he could ever want. Yes, I thought it could be just exactly that easy.

"There's no other way to do this except to stop being mad at ourselves and at each other for all the mistakes we made," I said. "Once and for all."

"I will if you will."

I rolled over, lay on top of my true love Ben, and kissed him. "I just did," I said.

WILSON'S DINING ROOM TABLE was as long and shiny as a lap pool, but even it wasn't big enough to accommodate what my brother had labeled, "The Cleary Family Thanksgiving Dinner to End All Cleary Family Thanksgiving Dinners, If We're Lucky," so Ben and his dad carried the kitchen table into the dining room and stuck it at the end of the big one. By the time Caro and Trillium covered both with gold tablecloths, set them with the china, crystal, and silver, and spaced the candles and centerpieces just so, you could hardly tell where one table ended and the other began. As I stood surveying the glittering room, Trillium came up and put her arm around me.

"Looks like a family dinner to me," she said.

"Am I crazy to do this?" I asked.

"You're *you* to do this," she said, kissing my cheek. "It'll be good. Have faith."

At five o'clock, Marcus arrived, with his hair newly cut and wearing a pumpkin-colored checked shirt under a brown jacket. Before I took him in to see everyone, I pulled him aside. "You look great," I told him. "Like something out of a magazine. Thanks."

"Don't thank me. I look great effortlessly. Is everyone here?"

"Not yet, and I'm sure Wilson will descend upon us at the last minute, so he can make an entrance." I hugged him. "Willow is so nervous to meet you. Be nice, okay? She's your sister, you know."

"I have too many sisters already," grumbled Marcus, but not before I saw something flicker across his face. He fiddled with his jacket cuffs, a sure sign. Marvel of marvels, Marcus was nervous, too.

When I took him into the kitchen and everyone greeted him, Ben shaking his hand, Trillium planting a kiss squarely on his mouth, the way she always did, Willow was nowhere to be found.

"She and Luka slipped out into the garden," whispered Caro in my ear. "She needs a moment to gather herself, I think. But she'll be back."

In a few minutes, there she was, skirting around the room, shy as a fawn, stealing glances at Marcus when she thought no one was looking. Once, she came up behind me and whispered, "He looks like you. Your hair and your eyebrows and your smiles."

"Everyone says that," I said, and because she sounded a touch forlorn, I added, "I think he looks a little like you, too."

"Truly?"

I had said it before I realized it was true, but now I could see it. "The way you're both so tall and lean. And you have narrower faces than I do."

The two of them were so skittery that I never found a moment when they were close enough to each other for me to introduce them, and then, while I was filling water glasses, Luka said, "Come look," and he led me into the kitchen, and there they were, my brother and sister, standing where the kitchen table used to be, talking. They still looked painfully shy; Willow had her hands clasped behind her back, like a schoolgirl in a movie, and Marcus was messing with his cuffs, but it was a start.

At 5:20, Barbara called to say they were stuck in traffic and would be late and to start without them. At 5:45, we began putting the food on the table. At six, every glass was filled, every candle was lit, Vince Guaraldi's "A Charlie Brown Christmas" swirled quietly in the air like snowflakes, and Wilson was nowhere to be seen.

"He'll be here," said Willow. "He promised me, and he never breaks his promises."

Now that I thought about it, I realized he had never broken a promise to me, either, if only because he had never, as far back as I could remember, made one. But I didn't say this to Willow.

At 6:15, we had all made our way into the dining room and were milling around, drinks in hand, admiring the food, when Wilson appeared in the entranceway. He was glowing with health and as immaculately turned out as ever. In fact, he was wearing an actual ascot, which I knew would make Marcus nearly delirious with mean-spirited joy. A hush fell on the room, not a reverent one, although Wilson possibly thought so, but the kind that is made up of collective unease about what to do next. Even Willow seemed to freeze, and it occurred to me that not a single person in that room, not even the ones in his immediate family—his immediate *second* family, that is—was unreservedly glad to see him.

Then, Luka, God bless him, left Willow's side, walked across the room with his long legs to Wilson, held out his hand, and said, "Hi, Dr. Cleary, I'm Willow's friend Luka Bailey-Song."

For a shaky moment, Wilson merely looked at him, and my heart went out to Willow, who had her hands clasped under her chin, as though she were praying, and then Wilson shook Luka's hand and said, gruffly, "Well, you're a tall one, aren't you?"

"And still growing." Luka's smile would have disarmed a grizzly bear, but Wilson stayed granite-faced.

Some of the others, including Ben, started stirring, setting down their glasses, moving vaguely in the direction of Wilson, but before the stirrings could develop into a full-fledged receiving line, Caro glided, with luminous grace, over to Wilson's side, took his hand, and said, "Shall we ask everyone to sit, darling? The dinner is all ready." Wilson's face softened for an instant as he looked at Caro, before he gave a leisurely, kingly lift of his shoulder and said, "As you wish, Caro."

We sat. Even though I wasn't a believer in place cards, when we'd found out that Barbara and her husband, George, would be late, we had created a seating arrangement that mixed the two empty seats in with the rest, in the hopes of making them less conspicuous. But I took care to keep Ben next to me, both so that I could put my hand on his leg under the table and because I'd seen the flash of naked hatred in

Wilson's eyes when he'd first caught sight of him and wanted to guard him against the attack I knew was coming.

Wilson took his time lashing out. I had forgotten that about him, how when it came to anger, he could be patient, choose his moment. He sat stony as an Easter Island moai at the head of the table, not touching his food, only his eyes moving as he watched us all. Somehow, to my gratitude, everyone made conversation and ate as though there weren't a glowering silence at the center of the dinner party. When we were well into eating, when Luka, in fact, was on to his second helping, Wilson tapped his knife against his water glass, waited for the chatter to subside, and said, with gusto and a sneer, "Thank you for your attention. At all but the most informal dinner party, it is customary for the host to rise before the meal commences, say a few words of welcome, and to thank his guests for coming. I have not done so, and I fear you must think me remiss. Therefore, in the interest of preserving my reputation as an observer of niceties, I want to state that I am not the host of this event."

As if someone had disputed this assertion, he nodded, convivially, and said, "Oh, yes! It's quite true!"

Willow's face across the table had gone deathly pale, her lips trembling. *Damn you, Wilson!*

He went on. "Despite the fact that this is my house, and I sit here at the head of my table, I invited none of you. I would not, in point of fact, have chosen to dine with a single person in this room, apart from my wife and daughter, Willow."

He slung his straight razor gaze in my direction. "If anyone is shirking her duty, it must be Eustacia, since I believe it was she who put together this rather unlikely guest list."

As soon as he had started to speak, Ben had grabbed my hand under the table, but while I was always grateful to touch him, I found I didn't need the moral support.

"I did," I said, simply.

And then, clear as a bell, Willow: "So did I."

And Caro, very quietly, "And I."

I saw Marcus lift his head and look sharply from one to the other, with frank admiration, but Wilson gave no sign that he'd heard them. His eyes stayed on me.

"You gave us leave to do as we liked," I told him. "Have you forgotten?"

"I humored Willow in her wish to have a family gathering. But clearly, that is not what this is."

"Oh, but it is," I said. "It can't shock you that my definition of family is broader than yours, Wilson, since yours is so narrow as to exclude two of your biological offspring."

"Let us not pretend anymore," he said, "that there was any point to this farcical evening beyond creating a situation that you hoped would—what?—embarrass me, put me in my place?"

"Because it's all about you, Wilson," said Marcus.

"No, Daddy!" said Willow. "We never meant to do that!"

Wilson smiled at her. "Not you, dearest."

"None of us! I wanted this! I wanted everyone who is here to be here."

Ignoring her, Wilson turned his attention back to me. "Tell me about that person next to you . . ." He flicked his fingers in the direction of Ben without looking at him. "He is in your life in what capacity?"

"A permanent one," said Ben.

Only now did Wilson's face begin to redden and with alarming speed. It was like a time-lapse film of a ripening strawberry. Slowly, he rose from his chair.

"Then, Eustacia, you are no longer invited to be part of my daughter's life."

Willow leaped to her feet. "Yes, she is! I invite her!" She looked pleadingly at me. "Not that you need an invitation."

"I know, honey," I said. "Don't worry."

"She's my sister," said Willow, vehemently, to Wilson. "She is *supposed* to be in my life."

At this unpropitious—or depending on your point of view, supremely propitious—moment, the doorbell rang. Caro threw me a stricken look, and I started to get up, when Willow said, "No, I'll get it," and flew out of the room. We all sat staring after her, Wilson included, as though we were spellbound. While I'd been talking to Wilson, I'd felt calm, but now my heart was pounding. I heard voices and the click of the coat closet door, before Willow, with a determined face, ushered in Barbara and her husband, George. There was no way to miss Wilson, standing in full emperor mode at the head of the immense table, and when Barbara saw him, in an instant, she froze, and, in the next instant, she thawed, every feature of her face, her entire chicly angular presence, lapsing into softness.

"Oh, Wilson," she said, tenderly. "Oh, I would know you anywhere."

Caro had assured me that the doctors had proclaimed Wilson's heart to be fit as a fiddle, but for a second, he grew so pale that my own seemed to stop beating. Wilson did not *go* pale; it wasn't what he did. For a few, terrifying seconds, he seemed to waver, as though the very atoms of his body were shaking loose from one another, but it must have just been my imagination because without sitting or even leaning on the table with his hand, he suddenly grew solid again. He didn't yell, but neither did he melt. He said, evenly, "You must leave, Barbara, and never come again. You don't belong here."

Willow cried out, "But she does! She's my aunt. Daddy, she's your sister!"

"I don't have a sister," said Wilson.

At this Barbara's face crumpled, and she pressed one of her lovely hands to her mouth. George put his arms around her.

"I don't know you. Get out of here," said Wilson, flinging his hand toward the door. "Out."

Barbara began to weep, her rich voice turning raw and ragged. "No one really believed you did it on purpose. You loved Archie."

"What?" gasped Wilson.

At this, Caro sprang up. "Don't!" she said, went to Wilson's side, and in the same protective gesture George had just made, put her arms around him.

"You were a child, Wilson. You were blameless."

Everything in the room seemed to go into slow motion. People exchanged glances; pressed napkins to their mouths; looked at Wilson; looked at anything but Wilson. As I watched, Wilson moved his head from side to side, a repeated, mechanical no.

"You loved him!" said Barbara, opening her hands toward her brother. "That's the important thing. God, all of this, this *rupture* was so unnecessary, such a waste. You were a child, and you loved Archie. Even our bastard of a father understood that, deep down."

"How dare you mention this, here, in my house," Wilson said, gasping. "Get out."

"We're going upstairs," said Caro to her husband, pulling out his chair so that he could step away from the table. He did, and with Caro's hands clasped around his upper arm, they began to walk past Barbara and George.

Barbara stepped close to Wilson and took a few long, steadying breaths. "Wait," she said. "Please."

"No," said Caro. "Not now."

But, incredibly, Wilson stopped walking and waited. Barbara wiped her eyes and said, sadly and with great kindness, "It's time to let it all go, Wilson. Long past time for both of us to let the pain go. How I've missed you." She leaned in until her face was just inches from her brother's.

"It's time," she said again, and then: "Our father was a brute. What he put you through was unforgivable. You didn't kill Archie, Wilson. He just died. *I know you didn't mean for him to die.*"

AFTER WILSON AND CARO disappeared upstairs; after Barbara had hugged me and Willow and she and George had silently left; after Willow and I bustled about serving pie to our remaining guests, who, with mindboggling good sportsmanship, ate it and talked of anything but Barbara and her shattering pronouncements; after I had kissed all but Marcus good-bye, and they'd gone back to their houses or hotel rooms; just as Willow, Marcus, and I were finishing cleaning up the kitchen, Caro came down and said, "Your father would like to speak with you. Ten minutes from now. In the living room."

Marcus was washing; I was drying, and over the sound of running water, he leaned close to me and said, "He can't just come down and tell us who he murdered. He has to hold court. 'Ten minutes.' 'In the living room.' Do you think I need to put my jacket back on?"

I smiled. "Maybe. But at least he's telling us himself instead of sending an emissary." I gave him a sharp poke in the chest. "Behave. For Willow's sake."

"When did I ever not behave?"

When we got to the living room, filing solemnly in, Wilson was already there, and it was true that ensconced in the big velvet armchair with his red satin dressing gown, and Caro by his side, standing sentry, he was at his most royal. It was all I could do not to drop a curtsy. But then I noticed his face, which looked different somehow, more open than I had ever seen it and very, very, tired, exhaustion—or maybe emotion—tugging at the skin around his mouth, making it tremble. Vulnerable. Wilson looked vulnerable, and even though part of me had probably been waiting my whole life to see him this way, I found it painful. *Sneer,* I thought, *scowl, be imperious and scornful.*

And right away, the moment we were properly assembled, as if he'd read my thoughts, he drew himself as upright as anyone could possibly sit without actually standing, and he nodded to each of us in turn, as kingly as you please. And then he commenced.

"As Rudyard Kipling put it: 'Never look backward or you'll fall down the stairs.' And it has been my hope never to have to. I had a childhood. Like Kipling's it was not particularly happy. Like Kipling, I rose above it and became my own man. But because of what happened today—"

Willow gave a guilty start and opened her mouth to speak, but Wilson stopped her with the most gentle of smiles. "I am not here to recriminate, child. You must not worry.

"Because of the melodrama that unfolded this evening," he continued, "I am compelled to look backward, if only to offer clarification. I do not need sympathy or understanding. Why would I?" *There* was the scoff. "But I want, as they say, to set the record straight and perhaps to set my daughter Willow's mind at ease."

Marcus's lips tightened at this, and I knew he was hating Wilson for only worrying about Willow's mind, not mine, but, truly, I found I did not care. I just wanted him to tell the damn story.

"I was not a popular boy, nor did I want to be. My peers regarded me with disdain as stupid people disdain anything that is beyond the reach of their understanding. My father loathed me. I am merely being honest when I say that my intellect was immeasurably superior to his, and he hotly resented that. Frankly, the man was eaten up with jealousy, and consequently demeaned me at every opportunity. Or tried to demean me. I did not give a whit for his opinion, and my own mind was the greatest solace and the best company I could wish for."

He paused, and I couldn't help myself. I said, "And your sister? What about Barbara?"

Wilson shot me a look of annoyance, then shrugged and said, "She was years younger than I, a baby really. She did not figure into my life in any meaningful way."

I remembered Barbara, with her parallel play and her drawings and her sisterly adoration, and my heart ached for the little girl she'd been.

"However, I was still a human child, and some part of me, in spite of itself, craved companionship, which brings me . . ." Wilson took a breath. "To Archie, my dog."

Oh for the love of god, a dog! I knew that if I looked anywhere in Marcus's direction that we would both burst out laughing, so I stared steadily at Wilson, and there it was again, that tremble in the loose skin around his mouth, and suddenly, the idea of a dog, Wilson's dog, wasn't funny anymore. Wilson cleared his throat.

"Someone abandoned him in our neighborhood when he was too young to be taken from his mother, and I was the one who found him. My father let me keep him, mostly because Barbara begged that I be allowed to do so, and I bottle-fed him until he could eat solid food. He was a tiny dog, no more than five pounds, a mixed breed, but probably mostly Chihuahua. He was black and white, with great triangular ears."

At this bit of description, my throat got tight, and there was Ben's voice in my head, *Who did you ever headlong, all-out love without having to try?* That was turning out to be the right question after all.

"Because he was so small, Archie was more likely than most dogs to come to harm, so I applied my intelligence to keeping him alive and well. At nine, I rigged springs to all the doors in the house to keep them from slamming on Archie. Because Archie's throat was so narrow, I threw away his collar and fashioned a harness out of an old leather chamois and some buckles I bought at a shoe repair store. I tethered a plastic owl to a fencepost in the backyard to scare away hawks. And I researched foods that were dangerous to dogs."

Wilson paused again, and Caro leaned over and kissed the top of his head. He found her hand where it lay on the back of his chair and pressed it, briefly.

"I managed to talk my mother into keeping grapes and raisins out of the house. However, my father drew the line at chocolate. He loved dark chocolate long before it was fashionable and kept bars of baking chocolate stacked in the spice cabinet. So in the seventh grade, I came up with a plan to make Archie immune to chocolate."

Again, he cleared his throat.

"I fed him chocolate chips, first just one every three days and gradually increasing them, keeping careful track of the number of ounces and of the dog's reaction to the chocolate in a journal I kept locked in my desk drawer. It was a good idea, but I do not think it would have worked. Without going into too much detail, chocolate contains methylxanthines, stimulants to which dogs are far more sensitive than people. These stimulants inhibit the activity of an enzyme that breaks down something called cyclic adenosine monophosphate, which regulates metabolism. High doses in dogs can result in seizures, irregular heart rhythms, and even death."

At the word *death,* Willow pressed her hands to her mouth. I wanted to put my arm around her, but she was sitting too far away.

"But I was not to learn whether or not my plan had merit because I made a mistake."

Caro slid her hand from the chair back to Wilson's shoulder, and he took it and held on. I saw that Caro, soundlessly, had begun to cry.

"I came home to find the nearly full, five-pound bag of chocolate chips ripped apart on the floor of my room. Every last chip was gone."

"Oh, Daddy," said Willow, starting to cry. I wondered if she were thinking, as I was—it was impossible not to—about Pidwit and Roo.

Wilson didn't look at her, just stared straight ahead. "If Archie had not been so small, the chocolate would have made him sick, but it would not have caused his heart to stop. I found him stretched out under my father's recliner, dead."

Wilson bent his head, just slightly. "I was a remarkably disciplined young man, but I was a child, and children make mistakes. I simply forgot to put the bag away. I blamed myself very harshly."

He looked up, this time at Willow. "I was heartsick and full of shame, which is why I took Archie, placed him in a box, buried him under a tree in the backyard, and told my parents that someone had taken him. I told them I left him alone in the fenced-in yard for a few minutes, and when I came out, the gate to the yard was shut, but Archie was gone. I told them someone had to have stolen him."

Willow's shoulders quaked with sobs. "You didn't mean to," she said, raggedly.

Wilson shook his head. "No, I did not. But I should not have lied. I should have faced up to what I had done, but I was not used to making mistakes. I hated to make them. I suppose lying was my way of trying to erase my error. In any case, I did not expect what happened next to happen. Barbara told everyone, all the families in the neighborhood, that someone had stolen Archie. As I have said, I was not a popular boy, but Archie was a popular dog. He was so tiny, you see, and people like tiny things. Also, he would wear a coat in cold weather, and when I walked him, the neighborhood kids would be drawn to him like iron filings to a magnet."

The note of pride in Wilson's voice was heartbreaking.

"So the whole neighborhood became involved, putting up flyers with Archie's picture all over town. Children brought them to school and passed them around. There was even a small article in the local paper, with an old photo of me holding Archie."

"So there was no turning back," said Marcus.

Wilson didn't snap back at him. He said, "No. It was like a top gone spinning out of control, so that even if I had wanted to confess to someone what had really happened, I could not have. I never would have, I'm sure of that. But then, a week or so after Archie died, we had a torrential rainstorm, and unbeknownst to me, the spot where Archie was buried caved in a bit because the earth was so saturated. While I was at school one day, my father saw the spot, and I do not know if he was just curious or if he guessed what had happened, but he dug, and he found the box with Archie, and he knew I had lied."

Wilson's face hardened. "He left the box on the kitchen counter for me to find when I got home. The box with my dead dog inside."

"That's horrible," I said. "Vicious."

"Indeed," agreed Wilson. He was the very picture of scorn now, sneer in place, all mournfulness gone. "And because my father was a jealous, pathetic little man, he made it his project to shame me publicly. He had me go door-to-door in our neighborhood, standing behind me while I confessed what I had done."

"Oh no!" cried Willow.

"My father would plant me in front of the door, reach over and ring the doorbell, and then he would step slightly to the side." Wilson smiled a terrible, bitter smile. "Not to the back, you see, because that would not allow him a full view of my face. He wanted to watch."

"God," I breathed.

"The first few times, I avoided looking at him. I recited my story of deceit and contrition, while the people I was speaking to squirmed uncomfortably or, in some cases, got angry and cursed at me. I had many a door slammed in my face. But eventually, we came to the house of a neighbor who had shown me kindness in the past, who had a particular fondness for Archie, and I found I could not meet the sympathy in her eyes, so my gaze slid away, and landed on my father."

Wilson laughed, harshly. "I have never seen such avidness, such naked enjoyment. He was eating it up, savoring every second of my humiliation. Oh, what fun he was having. And I understood, as I never had before, that the man hated me as he hated nothing else on earth. I knew that, as long as he had power over me, he would use it to try to destroy me."

Wilson made a disgusted sound. "That sounds melodramatic, like something out of a bad play, but it happens also to be true. In addition, when I next went to school, my father came and had me stand before the entire student body at our morning assembly and confess. Later, there was even another article in the paper about the local boy who killed his dog and lied."

No wonder, I thought. *No wonder Wilson cut himself off from that monster and that town. But poor Barbara.*

"Naturally, I went from being merely unpopular to universally reviled."

"But you did it out of love!" said Willow.

Wilson gave an ironic smile. "A fact everyone found easy to overlook. Children hissed *puppy killer* when they passed me in the hallway. Once, someone chalked the words onto the sidewalk in front of my house."

"Barbara didn't overlook it, though," I said. "She knew."

Wilson softened, just the tiniest bit. "I suppose she did. She never blamed me openly, anyway. So I left as soon as I could, and I put that place and those people behind me. Very successfully, I might add. I rose above the gray twilight of my childhood. I emerged unscathed. I triumphed."

He really thought that. He thought he'd emerged unscathed. Wilson, with his bad heart and his two estranged children and his precious second daughter whom he'd practically put in a cage in order to keep safe. It knocked the wind out of me, that he thought he'd triumphed.

"I think that's enough for tonight," said Caro, firmly. "It's been a long day."

She stood as Wilson got to his feet, and then she pulled him into an embrace, and he allowed it, right there in front of all of us. I saw Marcus look away.

After they left, Marcus said, "Yeah, his dad was a monster, but it doesn't excuse him for all those years of coming up short and cutting people off and being a shitty father."

"Marcus," I said, with a worried glance at Willow.

"It's all right," said Willow, blandly. She looked exhausted, hollow around the cheeks and eyes.

We sat in silence, until Caro came back. She sat down next to Willow and took her in her arms, and Willow nestled against her. "Now you know," she said, looking at me and Marcus.

I said, "Yes, we know. And my heart breaks for the kid Wilson was. Marcus was right, though. This thing that happened to Wilson was bad and his father was a rotten guy, but it doesn't explain away who he became. It's just not enough. You don't fail to love your family because of something that happened so long ago."

"But maybe it never ended for him," said Willow, pulling away from her mother, "because he never told anyone. If you never share the worst thing you've ever done with a single person, if you just carry it all by yourself, maybe it comes between you and everyone you meet, even if it's years later."

Willow's eyes found mine, and I understood that she was thinking of Mr. Insley.

"I don't know," said Marcus, "if I buy that. People get over worse things all the time. Wars. Beatings."

"I don't know either, for sure," said Caro. "But I do know that he told me this the day he learned I was pregnant with Willow, and after that he was closer to me. And when she was born, he let himself love her. He has always loved her so much, not perfectly, of course, but so very much."

"Not us, though," I said. I hated sounding so petty, especially when I didn't even feel very angry, but tonight was a night for truth telling. "I can believe that telling you that story allowed Wilson to love Willow, and I'm glad for her sake, but we were still here. We were eighteen years old. He could've loved us, and even Marcus might have let him, but he didn't even try."

"His loss," said Marcus. He was being flippant, and although he'd said it hundreds of times before, I understood that it was true. We were Wilson's loss, his great, great loss, bigger than the death of Archie, and he would probably die without ever feeling the enormity of what he had missed.

"He brought you here, though," said Willow, my clear-eyed little sister. "He let me have the chance to love you and you the chance to love me. Maybe he did that for us on purpose, to make old wrongs right."

It was on the tip of my tongue to tell her that his inviting me here had all been for her. I'd been the hired help, the life coach. But it came to me that there was just the smallest sliver of a possibility that Willow was right, that Wilson's heart was more complicated than I knew, more complicated than he knew himself. Probably not, but I decided not to shoot the possibility down. I would let it hang there, that almost-nonexistent possibility, thin as a new moon. It wasn't hope, thank God. I'd had enough of that. It would never be bright enough to light my way, but I could leave it there. I could let it be.

CHAPTER TWENTY-TWO

Willow

The boy on the block is nervous and the color of honey.
Not nervous but so ready he vibrates with readiness, ready in his
*   arms, ready in his back, ready in his jaw.*
The boy on the block is the color of honey and ready.
He folds fast, clenched chest to thighs, hands holding on, holding
*   on, holding on.*
The boy on the block is still with the stillness of soon, of verge, of
*   any-second.*
And, now, oh, now, the boy is all burst, and is, and yes.
He is stretched and flying, more air-like than the air.
He gives himself over to water, and the water receives him.
He is one long, winged pulse that beats out a song about wings
*   and water and onward and fast.*
The boy in the water is breathless.
No, I am the one who is breathless.
I love the boy on the block, in the air, in the water.
I am the one who is nervous, clenched, winged, who is the block in his
*   hands, the air he slices, the water that gives itself over to him.*
I am the one who receives him.
I am breathless, breathless, and I want to do it again.

It turns out that there is a lot of time at a swim meet when the swimmer you came to watch isn't swimming, so I wrote this poem on my smartphone. That's right: I, Willow Cleary, wrote a *poem* about my *boyfriend* on my *smartphone* at my *boyfriend's swim meet*. Almost too much history making for a single historical marker, even an imaginary one! It didn't start out as a poem. I was just fiddling, writing down thoughts, but soon, the words started to lace up and tighten like a corset, so that what I ended up with, even though it didn't have rhyme or meter like most poems I'd read, struck me as positively poem shaped. I realized it wasn't brilliant, which, since I don't fancy myself a poet, was just fine. I also realized, only after I'd finished, that it could be seen as having a little live wire of sexual desire running through it, which wasn't so very shocking to me since so did I, whenever Luka was nearby. But, honest to goodness, I wasn't thinking about that when I wrote it. I was thinking instead about how shatteringly nerve-racking it is to watch someone you love be all alone out there in front of a crowd of people doing something hard. Luka's mother, who sat with me during the second half of the meet, once she had finished her stint as a volunteer timer, agreed.

"I swim with him. It cracks my husband up," she said, laughing. "Just watch at his next race."

And she did swim: a sort of chicken pecking move for breaststroke, a rolling shoulders dance for freestyle, a reverse rolling shoulders dance for backstroke, and, oh gosh, every stroke of butterfly took her clean out of her seat. When Luka won, which he did *twice*, his elegant mother fist-pumped the air and hooted.

It was two days after what Taisy called our doozy of a Thanksgiving. When I had walked Luka to his car that night, I'd handed him a container full of leftover pie and said, wearily, "You must think we're all crazy," and he laughed and said, "No more than most families. Okay, maybe a little." And then he kissed me and leaned his forehead against mine and said, "I'm glad I was there if you're glad I was there," to which

I could only say, "I thank my stars for you, Luka Bailey-Song," and that made him laugh again.

Because Luka had had to arrive at the pool at the crack of dawn, Taisy had driven me to the meet, which was nearly two hours away in New Jersey, but Luka was to drive me home. His mother and I waited for him outside of the locker room, and when he emerged in his sweatshirt, a giant pack slung over one shoulder, his damp hair in full hedgehog, I wanted to slow time down just to watch him walk toward me and toward me and toward me.

"Has he warned you about his car?" said his mother.

"I think I rode in it already, to the dance."

Luka and his mother exchanged amused glances.

"That was my husband's car. Luka's car is a health hazard, a science experiment, a graveyard for banana peels. It's like the Amazon rain forest; anything could be in there."

"She won't even ride in it," Luka told me, grinning. "No one will. But I bet you're game, aren't you, Cleary?"

"Are we talking about bugs and mice?" I said, gravely. "Because I draw the line at vermin."

"No vermin, I swear," said Luka.

His mother raised her eyebrows at me. "If not, it's only a matter of time."

In the car, I told Luka a nutshell version of the Archie story and of my twisted, black-souled grandfather, and of how my father had left it all—and his little sister—behind. As soon as I finished, Luka said, "That must have been hard to hear. Are you all right?"

"Oh, Luka," I said with a flutter in my voice, and I leaned over to kiss his cheek.

"What was that for?" he asked.

"I tell you a grim and sordid tale, and you don't express shock or ask so much as a single question. You only want to know if I'm all right, as though that were the first thought you had." I remembered something.

"You know, Taisy did the same thing when she picked me up from the side of the road after the fire. There I was in the dark on an unknown street, reeking of smoke and covered with dirt and leaves from the ridiculous ditch I'd just been lying in, after having called her from clean out of the blue, and all she said was, 'Just tell me whether you're hurt or not. You don't have to say anything else.' What kind of person does that?"

Luka shrugged. "Sorry. Not to take anything away from Taisy—or me—but I don't really see the big deal."

"See? You're so nice you don't even know you're so nice."

Luka dipped his head the way he did when he was embarrassed, and said, "Okay, so anyway, if you want to talk more about it, that's cool."

"I don't really, not right now. I'd rather talk about your swimming."

At this, Luka relaxed, visibly. He shot me a sly look and said, "You like the swimming thing, don't you? We don't get a lot of that, not like football players. Girls who are turned on by swimmers are a rare breed. It's the goggles, isn't it?"

I laughed.

"This is good to know," said Luka, thoughtfully, nodding. "A little something to keep in my back pocket."

I sniffed. "What I was going to say is that I found it nearly unbearable to watch you."

"Ha! Liar. You think I'm beautiful when I swim, remember?"

"When I watched you swim in the natatorium by yourself, I thought you were beautiful," I corrected him. "When I watched you swim today, I thought you looked as alone and vulnerable as a lost baby seal on an ice floe."

"Great," said Luka. "I'm so glad I invited you."

"Seriously, doesn't it make you dreadfully nervous?"

Luka smiled. "Well, I don't know about *dreadfully,* but sure. Pretty much as soon as I'm in the water, I forget about it, but I'm definitely jittery behind the block."

I picked up his hand. "It was all I could do not to jump in and hold on to you while you swam, just to keep you company."

"Next time, you should," he said. "I mean, there'd be a little more drag than usual with you on my back, but I wouldn't mind."

Joy welled up in me and it must have shown on my face because Luka said, "What?"

"My two new favorite words," I told him.

" 'More drag'?"

" 'Next time.' "

LUKA HAD A TREE HOUSE.

We were talking about the favorite places we'd had as children. Mine were the little white tent that used to be in my room and my kitchen table. Luka's was the pool (any pool, apparently), his kitchen table, and his tree house.

"Why didn't you ever tell me that you had a tree house?" I demanded.

"Why didn't you ever tell me that you had a little white tent?" he said.

"Really, though. I have pined for a tree house since I was eight. My father thought they were too dangerous."

"My dad, Jackson, and I built it in the woods behind our house. I think I was eight, too. Jacks and I went out the other day, just to see if it was still there, and it was. I figured it would be. My dad's an engineer. He can get a little carried away with stuff like that."

I clutched Luka's arm. "Luka, can we go there? Right now?"

"Really?"

"Please, please, please!"

"Just to clarify: it's not fancy. It's not like one of those hobbit house things up in the trees with a chimney and window boxes. 'Tree house' might have been an overstatement, actually. It's more of a fort."

"Is it in a tree? And can you go inside it?"

"Well, yeah."

"Can we go? Oh, gosh, when I was little, I always imagined I'd go to a friend's house one day, and there would be a tree house, and we'd play in it, but then I never had a friend. Until you."

"Pulling out all the stops, huh? Isn't it kind of cold for a shivery person like you?"

"No."

"Is this just a ploy to get me alone?"

"I always want to be alone with you; it doesn't have to be in a special place."

"Good answer."

"I just want to *be* in a *tree house*. That's all I want."

"Whatever makes you happy," said Luka, and he didn't say it the way you say something that people just say; he said it like he was thinking about the words, as though he really, truly meant them.

WHEN WE GOT TO Luka's house, I said, "I want to meet Jackson; I honestly do. But can we please go straight to the tree house, first? It will be dusk soon, and I want to see the view."

"You're funny," said Luka, kissing me on the forehead. "A tree house: who would have guessed? Listen, though, there's an old blanket in the back of the car; let me just get it so you won't freeze."

"*No!*" I said, opening my car door. "Let's just *go*."

But as we were walking toward the backyard, the sun disappeared behind a cloud, and I shivered.

"I'm getting the blanket," said Luka.

"I'll get it," I said, grinning at him. "I'm faster! And I want to see that tree house."

I dashed to the car and opened the trunk. In one corner of it was a wool blanket in black watch plaid.

"Willow," said Luka, running up behind me. "Wait."

"I found it," I said.

I yanked the blanket, but it was stuck on something that was lying underneath it.

"Willow," said Luka, again, from a few feet away.

I detached the blanket and slung it over my arm. I saw that the object it had been covering was a big plastic container with a black sprayer hooked to it and a handle on top of it. The blanket had been caught on the handle. I was about to reach up to shut the trunk, when I noticed the label on the container: "Roundup Weed and Grass Killer."

Grass killer. *Grass* killer. My breath caught in my chest. *It's probably nothing,* I told myself. *It's probably for something else altogether.* But when I turned and saw Luka's face, I knew it wasn't nothing. He took a step toward me, the boy I loved, but I leaned backward and pulled the blanket to my chest.

"You?" I said.

There was panic in his eyes, the eyes I loved. A crumbling started inside me, the first, loose, tumbling stones before a landslide.

"No!" He ran his hand that I loved through the hair that I loved. I felt as though I were watching everything about him and every move he made for the very last time. "I mean, it's not what you think."

He started to say something else, but I lifted my hand to make him stop. I found I couldn't make my breathing be normal. "Luka, did you put the '16' in Mr. Insley's lawn?"

He didn't even need to answer. Guilt marked his face like a stain. But he did answer, the boy who never lied, "Yes."

The rocks tumbled and tumbled, gathering speed.

"Oh, no," I said, hugging the blanket to me. "Oh, no. It was all you."

Luka reached out and held me gently by the shoulders. "No."

"The night of the dance? When I told you the story, you didn't say a word. You let me go on and on about who might have sent all those messages."

"I was going to tell you," he said, bending in so that his face was level with mine. "I swear. I just couldn't figure out how to tell you without—" He broke off.

"What you don't say doesn't count as lying, is that it? That's your rule, right?"

"I was going to tell you. That's the truth."

"You were trying to scare me? You?" I pulled his hands roughly from my shoulders and started to cry. "For what? Fun? To taunt me?

Make me ashamed? Well, you did scare me, and what's more you could have killed me in that fire!"

"No way. I didn't set the fire."

I felt untethered, teetering, as though a hole were opening up before me and I might fall in. "Don't tell me that. You killed his grass! You had been to his yard, not ten feet from that boat shed. God, you were there spying on us, too, the first time I was at his house, weren't you?"

"I never knew you went to his house." Luka touched my cheek with his hand, but I twisted my head away. "Willow, I would never do anything to hurt you. I love you."

I flinched and squeezed my eyes shut. "You're telling me that *now*?"

"Listen to me. Please. None of what I did was meant for you. I never sent a message to *you*."

"The one on the whiteboard? And in my notebook? All those times you walked me to my locker, God, did you memorize the combination?"

"No, no, can you just let me explain?"

I stared at him.

"I put the message on the whiteboard, but I thought he would see it, not you. I thought he'd erase it before you got there. I never wanted to scare *you*, just Insley. Look, I've been thinking about it, and you must have been right: he saw how you reacted to that message, so he left the other ones. Your notebook, the one that was supposedly in his sandwich. I did leave a few others, but ones only he saw and never told you about, mostly before the one on the whiteboard. In his coat pocket, under the windshield wiper of his car. But whenever he thought he was losing you, he made one up. It's totally the kind of thing he'd do."

I was barely listening to him because my mind was racing through all that had happened, putting piece after ugly piece together, and even though he was standing right there, Luka seemed very far away.

"It was because of the papers, wasn't it? That's how you knew," I said.

"I don't know what you're talking about."

"He left me messages on the papers he handed back. There was one reminding me about my first visit to his house and another one telling me what time to come for the second, the night of the fire." My voice came out so flat, like a machine's voice. "You sit right behind me. That's how you saw."

"I promise you I never saw anything like that. Willow, I wouldn't lie to you."

Anger filled me. "What? All you've done is lie to me!"

Luka's eyes were wet, turning his eyelashes to black spikes, which only made me angrier. He had no business being so beautiful. "Here's what I did: I put the note on the whiteboard; I sent Insley a few other messages that you never knew about; I killed his grass; and—I sent the letter to Taisy."

"I want to go home, now."

His words came out in a rush, faster and faster. "That last thing, the letter, that's the only part of what I did that had to do with you. It was the day of our presentation, and I don't know if you saw Insley's face, but it was furious. He looked like he hated us, and I was worried about you, so I wrote the letter that day, looked up your address in the online directory, and mailed it from school. Every other message was only meant for him. Because he's a bastard, and I knew it, and I wanted to protect you. But those are the only things I did."

"How did you know he was a bastard if you weren't spying on us?"

Luka hesitated. "I saw how he looked at you, and—in other ways, I just knew. But I wasn't spying on you."

I felt so cold, but I didn't want to shiver in front of Luka, so I held myself still. When I finally spoke, my voice was cold, too. "So you are telling me that you did all those things, but you know nothing about that fire?"

And there it was again, the flash of panic in Luka's eyes. My heart cracked. *Oh, Luka, you are lost. You are gone from me forever.*

"Don't ask me that," he said. "Please."

"That's what I thought," I said.

He made a harsh, frustrated sound, but his voice was pleading. "It's

not what you think. I would never risk hurting you. Even if I thought
Insley was alone in his house, I would never set a fire, ever."

"Why couldn't you have just left me alone? You've broken my heart."

"Don't say that. I love you."

"Can you do something for me?"

"Anything you want."

"Go inside and don't come out until I'm gone."

"At least let me take you home."

"I'm calling Taisy. Please just go."

For a moment, all he did was look at me. "I'm sorry," he said and
ran toward the house. I waited until I heard the front door slam before I called Taisy. After I talked to her, I noticed I was still holding the
blanket, and because I couldn't stop shaking, I put it around me and I
waited for her to come.

AFTER I TOLD TAISY the whole story, between bouts of sobbing my
heart out, she sat for a long time, just holding me on the pool house
sofa, my head tucked under her chin. When I stopped shaking, she
lifted my head and said, "Let me just ask you something."

I nodded.

"Before this happened, would you have ever said Luka was a liar?"

"No. He told me that he never lied and never told his friends' secrets."

"And you believed him?"

"Yes, and not just because he said it, but because of everything else
I knew about him. I would have said that he was honest and true to the
core, which is why this hurts so much."

"Okay, will you do something?"

"Yes."

"Will you assume for the moment that Luka is telling the truth?"

"But he can't be."

"Yes, but just assume that he is, as a kind of experiment. Assume he is who you thought he was, honest and true. Because you want to know what I find curious?"

"What?"

"That he admitted to some of the things and not others. If he did it all, why admit to the note on the whiteboard but not the one in your notebook or the one in the sandwich? And why tell you about messages he sent that you never even found out about?"

"Oh," I said, blankly. "I guess that is odd."

I sat, turning over everything that had passed between me and Luka and everything that had happened with Mr. Insley. Finally, I said, "That letter to you—remember how we thought it sounded kind of nice?"

"I do. It really didn't seem like it was from someone who wanted to scare you."

Oh, how I wanted to believe in Luka, to dive headfirst into hope, but I knew that the climbing back out afterward would be wretched, brutal.

"Taisy, you don't know. You didn't see his face when I asked him directly about the fire. You didn't hear how he *could not tell me* that he didn't know anything about it. He simply couldn't do it."

"I know. Why, though?"

"That much was obvious: because he couldn't do it without lying."

I heard myself say the words. I recognized them as true: it had been obvious. For a moment, I fell into total confusion, then my head shot up; my eyes met Taisy's.

"That doesn't make any sense, does it?" I said, softly. "If he's a liar, he could have just lied."

"So assume he was telling the truth, about all of it. What are we missing? What could make all of this make sense?"

"I need to think," I said.

"And I told your mother I would help her with something in the house. Why don't you stay here for a while?"

I nodded. After she left, I stretched out on the sofa and closed my eyes. I began at the beginning, with my first day of school, and tried to remember everything I could, every word, every glance from Mr. Insley, from Luka, from everyone. I felt as though I were staring into cloudy water, trying to see what was under it. Shadows. Slender, moving objects that might have been fish, glinting silver, then darting away. I couldn't remember everything, of course. I felt that more had happened to me since September than in all my life before that, but, finally, finally, I remembered enough. The water went clear, and I opened my eyes, and fumbled in my bag for my cell phone.

"Let him answer," I said to the empty room. "Please let him answer."

"Willow?" he said, and his voice in my ear was the best sound I had ever heard.

"I love you, too," I told him. "I love you so much. Will you please forgive me?"

"I'm sorry I didn't tell you before. I couldn't figure out how."

"How to tell just your story, you mean? Just the part that was yours to tell? Because I might have asked you questions you couldn't answer, which is exactly what I did."

Luka didn't say anything for one second, two, three, and then he said, "I would never hurt you or try to scare you."

"You are such a good friend, Luka. You are honest, loyal, and true."

Luka brushed this aside with a quick, "I try," and then said, "I love you. I want to see you. Can I come over?"

"Actually, I was wondering if you would take me someplace?"

"Anywhere."

BEC ANSWERED THE DOOR. Even in the dim porch light, her beauty took my breath away. It was daunting, beauty like that. Her eyelashes alone were enough to make me want to turn tail and run, but I held my ground.

"Hi," I said, too loudly. I swallowed. "I'm sorry to show up here, unannounced, but I wanted to talk to you. Can I?"

I half expected her to slam the door in my face, but she only glanced over her shoulder. The inside of the house was full of light; I could hear voices and laughing.

"We sort of have company," she said, "My aunt and uncle and cousins from Massachusetts."

"Oh, well, we can talk another time."

"No," she said, quickly. "I just meant is it okay if we talk out here?"

"Of course," I said.

We stared shyly at each other.

"You know, don't you?" she said.

I wasn't sure what part of it she meant, but because I knew everything, or thought I did, I said, "I think so," and then added, "but Luka didn't tell me. He dropped me off here, but I wouldn't let him talk to me about it in the car, and he wouldn't have, anyway."

"Yeah, I know. He lives by the Luka code."

"Right. So he likewise didn't tell you about me and Mr. Insley, but you figured it out, didn't you?"

Her smile flickered. "I couldn't call him 'Blaine' either."

"Oh, God," I said, with a shudder. "Not even inside my head."

"I had just turned sixteen. I was a virgin, which of course, he really liked. And then I slept with him, so—I wasn't one anymore." Her gazelle eyes were bottomlessly sad.

"I could have done that, too. There were moments when I thought I wanted to. But something stopped me."

"Luka?"

"He was part of it. There were other things, like he never listened to me. He talked and talked, but he never listened. And I never felt at ease around him. I don't know. I just came to realize that it all felt wrong."

"It was wrong. The guy's a creeper, going after his students."

There was more to it than this, I knew. As I had told Luka, I'd made choices, but the fact remained that Mr. Insley was indeed a creeper, going after his students.

"He really is," I said.

She smiled a smile so full of regret that it was out of place. Her face was too young to smile that way. "I only figured that out recently, though. Luka tried to tell me. He didn't know what was going on until right at the end, but he kind of begged me to break it off. I wish I'd listened, instead of getting mad at him. But I was stupid enough to think I was in love. So Insley's the one who ended it. He said he had to because I was his student. I was crushed. But I could live with it because it was like a tragic love story."

"Star-crossed," I said, "in a narrow-minded world."

"Yep. Except that then, I saw him going after you."

"I'm sorry."

"So it wasn't because he was my teacher. He just got tired of me. It's why I was so mean to you."

"Please. It doesn't matter now."

Bec's eyes brimmed with tears. "No, it does. I spied on you. And worse." Her voice broke. She pressed the back of her hand to her mouth for a few seconds. "I swear I didn't mean for it to happen the way it did."

"I thought not."

"I'm not a firebug. I don't even like to light candles, but I'd lit some that day because it was my mom's birthday. The matches were still in my pocket. And there was all that varnish and that damn, piece of shit boat that he said he wanted to sail away with me in, to see my dark hair streaming in the wind. I lost my head, but I swear to God I only meant to burn the boat up."

"You didn't imagine that the shed would fall."

"No! I guess I should have thought of that. I couldn't believe it when I heard he took the blame for it."

"He probably didn't want anyone looking into the matter too closely. They might find out I was there. Some of his neighbors might have seen me when I came out of the house."

"And maybe he suspected that I did it," said Bec. "If they somehow traced it to me, then everyone would know that he's a disgusting predator who screws his students. Or tries to. But remember that part of the rumor that said he was so dumb that he thought, because the boat was in the shed, the fire would just burn itself out? I spread that part. Because that's what I was dumb enough to think, as much as I was thinking at all that night. I wasn't trying to hurt anyone. Not even him. I only came there to spy on you two, which was bad enough. And I'm in therapy, now. I know I'll never do anything like that again."

"I believe you," I said, and then, suddenly, I was hugging her, and she was hugging back. I had my arms around Bec Lansing, my enemy, my comrade in trouble and truth, and it felt right and good. It felt like justice.

"I wish I could do something for you," she said, wiping her eyes.

"Maybe we can do something for each other," I said.

"Okay," she said, just a little warily. "What are you thinking?"

"Will you go talk to Ms. Shay with me? Not to tell her anything about the fire, of course. But just about Mr. Insley. Because he needs to be stopped."

"The thing is that he didn't really do anything wrong, technically. He was twenty-nine with me, and, let me tell you, he had that law down pat. And with you—"

"We only kissed. I can't think that's a crime. But maybe at the very least, we can make sure that something goes into his record that would make it hard for him to teach kids anymore."

"He might deny it all," said Bec.

"I suppose he might, but I think Ms. Shay will believe us."

"And I have some, uh, proof, I guess you'd call it. Evidence. Notes he wrote me, stuff like that. I almost threw them away, but I decided not to. I'd kind of hate to drag it all out, but I will, if we need it."

"Good."

Bec nodded. "Okay. I'm in. Let's nail the bastard to the wall."

"I'm afraid it will mean we'd have to tell our parents, though."

"Which will, without question, suck. But I've been kind of thinking about telling them anyway."

We were back to staring shyly at each other. Oh, the two of us.
Caught together in that gossamer porch-light moment, Bec and I were
so honest I hurt for us. We were bruised in the same places, but we were
also flowery and hopeful eyed, as though everything we'd said to each
other had pared us down to the little girls that lay inside us still, just
under the surface.

"I should let you get back to your guests," I said.

"Do you need a ride home?"

"No, I'll call Luka. He's probably parked fifty yards from your
house."

She smiled. "No doubt."

I turned and started down her front walk.

"You know, I bet he didn't even build that boat," she called after me.

I smiled into the crisp, winter-smelling dark. "He doesn't seem
like the boat-building type," I called back. "I bet the damn boat came
with the house."

And behind me, on the porch, Bec laughed.

EPILOGUE

Taisy

He ASKED ME THIS time because he said it was his turn. On his father's front porch on New Year's Eve, but it was snowing instead of raining, so the yard was luminous and full of whispering.

"I know I should have asked you during a hurricane, with a hundred-fifty-mile-an-hour winds," said Ben, "but I didn't want to wait."

"I know we should do it in October, when we met, and I should carry a gourd," I said. "But I don't want to wait, either."

We did it in June, when hurricane season technically begins, but one didn't hit. Mr. Ransom made my bouquet, peonies with one sprig of purple freesia at its heart in honor of our eighteen-year-old selves, who had made mistakes but had the right idea to begin with.

We did it in the garden of our new house, which was close to Willow's and to my old house and to Mr. Ransom's but was in a new neighborhood altogether. Our garden was beautiful because I had the best gardener in town.

I was twelve weeks pregnant, a source of joy so piercingly sweet, so holy that we didn't consider for a second keeping it a secret. We told everyone the day we found out. Trillium shouted, "Glory Hallelujah!," and Willow said, "Oh, Taisy, can this please mean that you'll wear an Empire waist wedding dress just exactly like Elizabeth Bennet must have worn?"

During the reception, she came up to me, my maid of honor, looking like a flower with her narrow celadon green gown and bloom of auburn hair. Her handsome boyfriend was at her side. He carried Pidwit. She carried Roo.

"*This* is why those books always end with a wedding," she declared. "Not because marriage is the foundation of society or because marriage is the only practical happy ending for a woman."

"Wait," I said. "Is that new English teacher having you read Marxist and feminist literary theory? In the eleventh grade?"

Willow smiled sheepishly. "No, I've just been doing it on my own for a while, dabbling, if you will. Those theorists try their damnedest to wring the romance out of Austen and Eliot, but do you know what? The romance is still there."

Luka grinned, shook his head, and said, " 'Dabbling, if you will.' " She elbowed him, and he kissed the side of her head.

"So why *do* the books end that way?" I asked her.

"Because of this." The sweep of Willow's arm took in the entire garden. "Because everyone is here!"

Everyone was.

And everyone was at their best, even Wilson, although even at his best, he was still Wilson.

He did not walk me down the aisle. I did not ask him to. My mother and Marcus did, one on either side of me.

At the reception, Wilson did not end up in a fatherly conversation with Marcus, although I did see him talking to Barbara's oldest grandchild, who had just finished his freshman year at Brown in neuroscience. At one point, Wilson boomed, "Good man!," and clapped him on the shoulder.

I spent the evening dancing with my husband, and Wilson did not cut in, which was fine by me. Willow spent the evening dancing with Luka, and Wilson did not cut in there, either, which was even finer.

Trillium spent the evening dancing with Mr. Ransom.

"I think your dad's in love with Trillium," I told Ben.

"Who isn't?" said Ben. "I think Trillium's in love with my dad."

"Who isn't?" I said.

Marcus spent the evening dancing with everyone, especially Ben's mom, who cut a rug in her electric wheelchair like nobody's business. When he wasn't dancing, he talked to Caro, and I'm almost positive he wasn't even hitting on her.

Of course, everyone was there. I could not have had it any other way, and neither could Ben.

When you say those wedding vows at eighteen, you are committing yourselves—with all that you are and all that you have—to only each other because you are young and wreathed in glory and take up all the space there is.

When you say them at thirty-five, you are signing on for something wider: a whole garden full of people to love and to cherish, in sickness and in health, in wheelchairs and sleepwalking and heart attacks, in arrogance and graciousness, stubbornness and forgiveness, stumbling and wisdom, in meanness and in kindness that falls like snow and shines brighter than the Dog Star.

To love and to cherish, yes. Like a tiger. A hurricane. A family. Relentlessly.

ACKNOWLEDGMENTS

I am so grateful to the following people:

Jennifer Carlson, wonder-agent, guardian angel, cherished friend;

Jennifer Brehl, my editor, whose honesty and laser-beam brilliance make my writing so much better;

the incredible William Morrow team, especially Liate Stehlik, Tavia Kowalchuk, Kelly O'Connor, Rebecca Lucash, Ashley Marudas, and the ever-dazzling Sharyn Rosenblum;

Kristina de los Santos, Susan Davis, Dan Fertel, and Annie Pilson, for their generous early reading and steadfast faith in my books;

the Fiction Writers Co-Op, writers who cheer each other on, lift each other up, and from whom I have learned so very much;

my family of friends and fellow swim parents;

Finny and Huxley, who are not exactly people but who are true friends all the same, and who abide with me (on my lap, at my feet) during those long, long hours of writing;

my parents, who are far away and also always with me;

Charles and Annabel, my own precious ones, who make me fiercely glad to be living this life and no other;

and David Teague, the smartest man I know, who talks me down and through and sometimes into, and whom I love relentlessly.